NOVA'S QUEST FOR THE ENCHANTED CHALICE

"Nova's Quest is the best thing I've read since Harry Potter!"

☆☆☆☆☆

"Incredible! I absolutely devoured this novel."

☆☆☆☆☆

"Two fantasy worlds in one—simply epic! I can't wait for the sequel."

☆☆☆☆☆

NOVA'S QUEST FOR THE ENCHANTED CHALICE

☆

M.J. IRVING

This is a work of fiction. Names, characters, places and incidents are either the product of the author's imagination or, if real, used fictitiously. All statements, activities, stunts, descriptions, information and material of any other kind contained herein are included for entertainment purposes only and should not be relied on for accuracy or replicated as they may result in injury.

Text by M.J. Irving

Edited by Lauren Donovan @ The Book Foundry

Cover design by Cherie Chapman @ Chapman & Wilder

Cover illustration by Derek Payne
Map illustration by Sally Taylor @ Artist Partners
Typeset by Phillip Gessert

The right of Marsha Irving to be identified as author of this work has been asserted by her in accordance with the Copyright, Designs and Patents Act 1988

All rights reserved. No part of this book may be reproduced, transmitted or stored in an information retrieval system in any form or by any means, graphic, electronic or mechanical, including photocopying, taping and recording, without prior written permission from the publisher.

British Library Cataloguing in Publication Data:

a catalogue record for this book is available from the British Library

Published by M.J. Irving

Distributed by Amazon KDP & IngramSpark

ISBN 978-1-8382661-0-3

www.mjirving.com

*For those who have helped me believe.
For those who have believed in me.
But, most importantly, for those who have done both.*

DACAAN
HAPPENSTANCE
Kootenay Lake
• The Penetentiary
CASTLEGAR
SANCA
Sanca Creek
The Highlands
The Church
ROSSLAND DISTRICT
Duck Lake
The School
CRESTON DISTRICT
Founders Cove
Kismet
Hope River
Fortuity Forest
Providence
Serendipity School of Magic
Emerald Sea
Glass Mountain
Commencement Cove

PROLOGUE

Dreams, the kinds made with your eyes wide open, could be dangerous things. To dream is to think, to create, and to live outside of the ordinary. This has a certain type of power to it. Dreams could lead people to question, to explore, and to change. A person with a dream is like a bow being strung with a feather: powerful to the marksman, but lethal to others.

There is a certain kind of magic in dreaming. Dreams are inspired by thoughts that come from the dark recesses of the mind. They drift into one's head like a feather softly floating in the air, and can impregnate the mind with more dreams, leaving less room for the ordinary thoughts that inhabit it like great, solid stones.

Like a star, only one dream can rule its part of the universe and the bodies within, propagating its thoughts, spreading its beliefs. But sometimes dreams collide and like stars they combust, shattering worlds and everything in them.

In Dacaan, magic had been banished, as had been dreams—the ones that left your eyes wide open, that is. It had been this way for many, many years. Dreams were now gone, and the curated, ordinary world sustained. But there was also power in ordinary, since ordinary was just a dream ingrained.

Alex often dreamed with his eyes wide open; he was taught to fight it, but he couldn't help it. As he grew older, those dreams became more frequent, more vivid, more real. Alex had never dreamed with his eyes shut; he fell into darkness in his sleep. That was about to change. Everything was about to change.

CHAPTER

1

"BUT WHY CAN'T we know the stars?" he asked.

Alexander Kerr had been listening to his father's disconnected tales for many years but had never understood why he could not know the stars. He knew he couldn't ask anyone else but his father these sorts of questions, so he pressed him as hard as he could.

Jacob, Alex's father, looked at him with a moment of clarity. His eyes darted around the smooth lines and freckles on Alex's face, searching for something and making Alex feel uncomfortable. Jacob more often than not looked confused. His face was usually clouded, like he was a vacant shell with no inhabitant. Jacob had not always been this way. When Alex was young, too young to remember, his father and his mother had contracted a dreaded, life-threatening virus and were taken to the infirmary. His mother was never to be seen again, and his father returned to raise him but suffered the result of the virus: amnesia. Alex, however, felt lucky, as most who went to the infirmary never returned.

"We can know the stars if we try, but not here and not now," replied Alex's father knowingly, but with a troubling look of withdrawal. This look usually preceded his retreat from the world, the steps he took into his shell.

He removed his hand that had been stroking the side of Alex's face, sat up straighter, and looked away from Alex and out the windows at the luminescent subjects they had been discussing, which were twinkling proudly in the night sky.

"What do you mean we try, Father?" pleaded Alex, wanting to know more. But he knew it was too late for tonight, his father was already leaving him. His father was folding into himself and would lock away the key for hours, or perhaps days; it was always hard to know how long the darkness might last.

Alex swung his legs over the side of the bed. He was wearing a flannel pajama set with white and blue stripes, which were warm enough for the short walk between his bedroom and his father's. He tucked his feet into the soft fleece insides of his slippers, picked up the bedside candle, and paused for a short moment to look out the bedroom window again into the starry night sky.

The heavy drape that hung to the floor was swaying in the wind. Alex moved around his father and pulled shut the window that was slightly ajar. Even in the summer their log cabin was very cozy when sealed up but could get extremely cold in no time at all. Alex didn't mind the cold, but he felt safer with the window closed at night when the lightless hours set in.

Alex began to pull the drapes across and was grabbed suddenly and quite firmly by the arm.

"Look, it's the sign."

Frightened at the unusual reawakening of his father, Alex first looked down at his arm where his father's strong hand had grabbed it. He was often in awe at his father's strength but knew Jacob would never hurt him.

He then noticed his father's other hand pointing out the window.

Alex looked up at the night sky, more closely this time. Sparkling, dancing lights flickered and shimmered against the deepest navy background. A small sliver of moon cast a reflection on the lake, where it rippled in the water below the tall Rocky Mountains that towered behind it. He was always impressed by the beauty of the skies, but tonight something was different, something was brighter.

Stepping forward, Alex pushed the drape aside again and could see out the right-hand side of the window where his father had been pointing that a brighter light than any of the others shone fervently. It looked like a ball of yellow fire, like a star that had been thrown toward Dacaan with a tail streaming beautifully like feathers on a bird behind it. Because of its tail, it appeared to be moving, but after a few minutes it was obvious that it sat motionless in the sky. It was a comet, the first Alex had ever seen, and his jaw dropped in disbelief.

For years, Alex's father had referred to the coming of the comet in his stories, a phoenix of the sky with its long tail. Alex had thought it was something his father had made up since he was always creating wonderful, imaginary things. Alex once asked his teacher what a phoenix was, and he was told there was no such thing. That day he had been given after-school detention for no apparent reason and was told to write 'I will not make things up, I will obey' on the chalkboard one hundred times before he was allowed to go home. He subsequently missed his bus and had to walk for over an hour along the long mountain path in twilight, alone and frightened. He had vowed to himself that he would never disobey again.

Alex did, however, love hearing his father's stories, because they excited him and made him think of different worlds and their stars. He kept his words, ideas, and thoughts about these worlds between himself and his father, and he was happy that way. They were safe in their small bubble made of spruce logs, and his thoughts were safe in his mind as long as they didn't dare to come out.

As the comet hung above the wispy clouds and mountaintops, on display for all the world to see, Alex wondered if he should send a Nexus message to let Cassia, Ariadne, and Niall know. Cassia was Alex's best friend; she also lived in the Creston District, just five minutes down Sanca River from him. Ariadne and Niall were his other closest friends. The four of them had grown up together, went to school together, knew almost everything about each other, and had a group chat called 'The Clan' on the Dacaan's communication channel 'The Nexus' that they communicated through daily.

Alex reached into his pocket to pick up his communicator but quickly dropped the idea to send a message to The Clan as he saw the time on his communicator face. It was past curfew and Nexus time, so he could do no such thing. The only thing on The Nexus to see after ten at night were old episodes of the Champions, unless there was an alert from the capital. Alex hoped that his friends had noticed the comet, and he was excited to talk with them about it tomorrow. He was sure, however, that the Regime would explain it on tomorrow's bulletin and all of Dacaan would know in any case.

After standing there for longer than he'd initially

anticipated, Alex pulled the drapes shut. He turned around, but his father was gone.

"Father?" he said, not too loudly, but loud enough for his father to hear from anywhere in the small cabin. His father rarely answered when he called, however.

Alex walked swiftly out of the room and rushed down the hallway to his father's bedroom. He wasn't there.

"Father," he yelled again, this time a little more loudly as he opened the doors to the closet, shower room, and study that sat along the narrow hallway. Nothing.

Alex made his way to the main living room and kitchen, but his father was nowhere to be seen. The front door was still locked. Alex kept the key so that his father wouldn't go out in the night, a trick his Aunt Matilda had taught him many years ago before she left for Castlegar. Alex had, however, once or twice forgotten to lock the front door in the night and would realize in the morning when he had to go search for his father, who was usually walking along the stony river path that led to Kootenay Lake at the edge of their property. It would always give him a scare; he was never sure if his father would one day decide to walk out into the lake, and Alex knew he couldn't swim.

At least he knew his father was somewhere in the house that night, but where? Alex walked into the kitchen and saw that the light to the utility room was on. He usually locked this room as well, but the door was open. He walked forward, hesitantly. This room always made a cold shiver run down his spine and the hair on the back of his arms stand firmly at attention. Alex tapped his slipper forward first before moving the rest of himself across the lip of the door. He had to find his father, this was all that mattered, so he moved further into the room. At first, everything seemed in its rightful place: washing machine, dryer, deep freezer, cat food, food storage containers, and shelves with towels and sheets. But then Alex saw that the door on the floor leading to the cellar was also open.

"Father?" Alex quietly cried once again. He was nervous; he had to go down there as who knows what his father might get up to, it was so dark and dusty down there. But he had to muster the courage first. He stood silently for a minute, listening to hear if his father might out of courtesy provide a reply. He heard what he thought was shuffling. Again, fear pulsed through his veins, making him stop still in his tracks.

It was a moment before he had courage again to move one, then both, slipper-covered feet down the stairs. He was sure something would grab his feet and take him away, but he tried to fight that thought. The darkness had never been his friend.

Once downstairs, he was immediately relieved. His father was sitting in an old, wooden rocking chair. He was rocking back and forth but seemed fine. Alex looked around at all the boxes and old things that lived their own lives down there. Things he had long ago decided to retreat from, more because of the location of their existence than because of their existence themselves. His father had kept these things down here; they were old and from times before the Regime, which could get them in a lot of trouble if ever found.

He saw his father was holding a small box on his lap as he rocked back and forth. As was normal, his father was looking away, despondent, but as Alex came within arm's length, his eyes lit up.

"This is yours, Nova," Alex's father muttered as he looked up toward Alex's eyes and held the box up to him. Jacob rarely said names these days, and when he did, he rarely got them right.

"Thank you," Alex said, and a small smile that made the side of his mouth twitch upwards exposed itself.

Alex was slightly relieved at finding his father, although he did wish it weren't in the cellar. He did, however, feel a blanket of warmth rush over him at the sight of his father sitting there, rocking in the chair, and having referred to him by a name. The last time he used a name was two years ago when Alex fell down the stairs on the patio outside, and it was more of an exclamation given the racket, but he came rushing over and held him like a father should. Alex always remembered that and felt safe that his father would be there to protect him with his big, strong arms, regardless of where his mind might be wandering at the time. Nova was a name that he often called Alex for some reason, and Alex secretly liked it, thinking of it as a sort of nickname shared only between the two of them.

Alex walked so that he was about a few feet away from his father and sat crossed-legged on an old, empty crate. He wanted to make sure his father was in front of him this time so there were no disappearing acts again. Taking the box with him, he blew the dust off the top before placing it squarely on a level set of empty glasses in front of him.

He brushed his hand over the top of the box. It was cool to the touch; having been in the cellar for countless years, that wasn't surprising. The box was made of solid wood and had gold hinges and a keyhole. He tried to open it, but it was locked firmly shut. He again looked over the surface and noticed there were several engravings that looked like stars on the top corners. On the front was a horse with what looked like a horn coming from its forehead, and across from the horse sat an eagle. In the middle of them was a plaque, but Alex couldn't read what it said because years' worth of dust was embedded in the engraving. He took an old piece of cloth that he saw in a box next to him and with force scrubbed the hard dirt from the plaque, tossing the cloth back in the pile when he was done.

It was hard to see the revealed message because the light from the utility room barely made it down the stairs and only cast shadows across the top of the box. Some light from the moon shone through a window behind his father. He walked over toward the light and held the box in just the right angle so that the letters were revealed.

Nova.

Alex thought at first that he must be tired, and he rubbed his eyes, but the letters didn't change. Startled as Mr. Gray, their cat, meowed at the top of the stairs, Alex threw the box, and it landed with a thud on the floor.

"Nova, it's time," exclaimed his father, looking clearly and smilingly into his eyes.

❖

The bus stopped just in front of the cedar tree where Alex waited every day. He got onto what looked much more like a yellow submarine than a bus and walked down the rows past a lot of tired-looking faces to sit down in his usual seat six rows from the back. Alex liked the drive down the winding mountain road with its switchbacks that navigated them past many babbling brooks and fierce rivers that rushed forcefully down the mountain into Kootenay Lake.

Alex much preferred the bus to school when Cassia, Ariadne, and Niall were all also there. Luckily, today was a good day and The Clan were all onboard, so Cassia let him past and he headed for his usual seat by the window looking out over the lake. The others had been playing a short but intense game of tic-tac-toe in the condensation on the window next to his seat, but Cassia was already gloating about her win as he approached.

"Maybe next time, Niall," she crowed, winking as Alex sat down.

"Hi Alex, how are you this morning?" asked Ariadne with a smile. Ariadne was the quietest in the group, but she was the politest. She was the group mother, always prepared to share her sandwich at lunch or help them with their homework.

"Morning, Aria, I'm good thanks. Perhaps a little tired," Alex replied, realizing he was speaking through a yawn. It had certainly been a late night for him, and an unusual one.

"What were you up to last night, then? Go on, tell us!" said Cassia, who always liked hearing when others were breaking rules so that she didn't feel she was the only rebellious one. Cassia was fiercely competitive and rebellious, but she had learned how to mute her true nature in front of the teachers at Creston Elementary School and in front of the patrol.

Alex hesitated for a second too long, thinking about his father, the comet, and the box, allowing Cassia enough time to raise an eyebrow.

"Did you see it?" Alex responded quickly to overcome his delayed response, but it made him sound even more suspicious.

"See what?" asked Niall quizzically. Niall and Alex had spent a lot of time together. Niall was one of the most popular boys in school and was widely known for his sporting capabilities. He was captain of the soccer team and was expected to get chosen in the Championships on Friday to go to Castlegar. Alex tried not to think about the Championships.

Alex was careful here; he couldn't outright mention the comet. Surely no one knew the term comet since they didn't study it at school, and he had learned it from his father. He knew the risks of speaking about it, even if it was only to his trusted circle of friends. He could put them at risk, too.

"The night sky before bed, the stars shone so bright, I could barely sleep . . ." Alex made an attempt to allude to the comet without overexposing himself.

There was silence before an eruption of laughter from his friends around him and from the seat in front, who had heard the conversation.

"Oh, here he is, Alex and his stars again," laughed Cassia unforgivingly.

The laughter flared up again.

"Shhh . . ." attempted Alex, "you'll get us all in trouble."

"Silence back there, you sound like a cage full of monkeys" shouted Mrs. Winklebottom. The harsh-spoken bus driver looked small behind the big steering wheel.

A shy, mousey-haired girl named Phoebe in the seat diagonally in front looked at Alex as he shook his head in frustration. He could tell from her expression that she had not only just heard the comments but she'd seen it, she'd seen the comet.

"Come on then, is everyone ready for the Championships on Friday?" asked Ariadne in an attempt to bring the discussion back around to some sort of normality, and to take the attention from Alex and his stars.

"I'm ready for the Championships," Niall said, half standing with both hands up, looking around the bus with pride. A round of applause ensued, and Mrs. Winklebottom glared in the rearview mirror, allowing this one to pass.

"I'm practicing my song tonight if anyone wants to come listen," boasted Cassia to piggyback on Niall's fame as she linked arms with him across the aisle, making Niall blush.

"I made every single one in the family cry last night in my rehearsal," she once again gloated, directing her voice at Emilia, who was much less proud of herself but who was Cassia's biggest rival, as she had the unassuming voice of an angel.

Alex sat there trying to get the attention of Phoebe. If she looked at him again the way she did before, he would know she had also seen the comet.

"What about you, Alex?" asked Cassia.

The question caught Alex off guard, but he quickly recovered.

"I'm showcasing my illusion act," replied Alex. He was

proud of his act but also somewhat disillusioned in it already; he doubted it would be a winner.

"Well, I've been practicing my tumbling routine for months now, so I am ready to show it in the Championships and be done with it. My whole body aches," said Ariadne to herself. She was a skilled gymnast, but she was a year younger than the others and had less pressure on her to become a Champion and make a new life in Castlegar.

All upper-year students had their first big opportunity to apply for the Championships that Friday. The point was to showcase their skills and practice, but rarely did children win who weren't in their final year.

Two years ago, however, a short girl with long, brown hair named Eliza Berry had been the first contestant from Creston to become a Champion a year younger than the official age. She played the flute, and her hollow notes that seemed to sing like the song of a loon lamenting had made the audience cry. She became a Champion at ten years old and only came back once a year like all other children for her annual celebratory parade through the village and to have a meal with her personal patrol at her family home. Cassia had told Alex that the Berrys had spent months preparing for the meal and had even served a selection of seafood that they had imported from the coast for the event. They were so proud of their daughter, and their sad but triumphant faces were shown waving her goodbye that day after she finished her stay with them and got back in the coach to return to the capital.

Talk on the bus continued, but Alex focused on looking out the window. He dreaded this week's Championship and hated the idea of his friends being taken to

Castlegar if they won, never to be seen again—apart from the once a year celebration. What was worse was to be left. Only two children were usually taken in each draft, so it was impossible to think that all four friends in The Clan would make it to Castlegar. Alex was almost certain that his illusion act wouldn't make the cut, and he would be left behind. He was, of course, fine with that; he had almost purposefully made his act undesirable because he didn't want to be picked. But what would he do in Creston without Ariadne, Niall, and Cassia by his side? His friends were most certainly some of the most talented prospects in Creston and would be chosen; it was just a case of when. If not this year, then next.

Alex, most importantly, knew that he couldn't leave his father. Who would take care of him? He had heard stories of those suffering from amnesia who were left by their children and taken to the infirmary, never to be seen again. He couldn't allow this to happen; he loved his father too much, and it was his responsibility to ensure they remained safe and together.

As Alex sat there, lost in his thoughts, thinking about how his world was almost destined to change on Friday, he saw it. First a flutter out the corner of his eye, and then a yellow beak. At first he thought it was a part of the yellow school bus, but he saw it clearly when he turned his head around. Larger than life, flying beside the bus, and staring at him was the biggest eagle he had ever seen. It must have been five times his length and ten times as heavy. Its feathered wings swooped effortlessly, allowing it to soar as quickly as the bus drove along the side of the mountain. Its beady eye was looking straight at him, he was sure of it.

Startled, Alex looked around the bus. But all the other children carried on their conversations. How could they miss this? How could they not see? It was then that he again noticed the little mouse-like girl looking straight at him.

'You can see it, can't you?' mouthed Alex at her, and she quickly turned in her seat as if she'd seen a ghost.

❖

Later that day, Alex saw Phoebe near the Hall of Sciences at school. He presumed she was about to head into her next class, so he shouted her name and ran toward her. Initially, she looked back smiling before seeing who it was, but then she pulled her bag closer to her chest and put her head down, darting toward the door. Alex got there just before she had a chance to escape.

"Phoebe, I was trying to find you after the bus ride. That discussion... I know you heard me, and I know that you know," said Alex.

Phoebe's angular, mousey nose twitched. She looked up at him, into his sky-blue eyes and dark-brown hair with its recognizable white streak that ran through the front of it. Alex was one of the most handsome boys at Creston Elementary, some girls would say. Phoebe quickly bowed her head down to the floor again. Her cheeks went red, and she looked around with a frightened look on her face and tried to walk away again.

Alex was afraid that he had frightened Phoebe by blocking her entrance to class. He looked up at the clock.

"Class starts in three minutes. Please, can we talk for

two?" He grabbed her hands and pulled her toward a small, wooden bench next to the door.

"I did hear what you said on the bus," started Phoebe. She was nervous, and her hands had gone clammy, so she pulled them slowly away from Alex and rested them on her skirt. "I did see, but I don't know."

Alex's face looked both confused and excited.

"I . . . well . . . I don't know either, but I saw it too. It was beautiful, don't you think?" Alex said this sentence carefully but with a smile ear to ear. He wasn't making it up, the comet did exist!

"Yes, but I would prefer that we keep this between us—as our secret." Phoebe looked into Alex's eyes again; it was like looking into the clearest sky.

Just then, a group of boys from Phoebe's class came running past. "Ooooh, our secret," cooed one of them, and they barreled through the door. Phoebe's face turned from apple to beetroot-red.

"Class is starting," called Mrs. Canaverel, looking quizzically and accusingly at Phoebe and Alex on the bench.

"Bye," said Phoebe, and she got up and ran through the door.

Alex wondered how long Mrs. Canaverel had been in the doorway and listening to their discussion. Those sorts of discussions were unsafe if heard by the wrong ears.

❖

That week seemed to go on for an eternity. To an eleven-year-old, time moved with a sense of freedom and unrestricted ease. It stretched itself so that every second of anticipation over the Championships was over-examined by all of Alex's year group. Every practice, rehearsal, and attempt were a strain on the passionate souls performing them.

By Thursday night, Alex was exhausted. He didn't know if he would be able to get near enough sleep to keep his eyes open and to make his limbs move for his performance the next day. He wasn't particularly nervous about the performance; he had done things like this so often in front of family and friends and on The Nexus that he had it down to an art.

Alex's exhaustion came from overthinking. There were two incredibly important things running over and over in his mind. The first was the box and all it stood for: the name, the missing lock, the comet, and the eagle. What did all this mean and what should he do next? Was he going crazy? The second was the coming change: He knew one of his friends would be chosen in the Championships, and he knew The Clan was coming to an end. Alex had always hated endings.

His father was already safely in bed. He had been far away tonight, really far away. This usually worried Alex, but today, because he'd also had his focus elsewhere, he felt that it was the least of his worries. As he sat there, perfectly still in his bed with so many thoughts in his mind, he wondered if this was something like what his father went through every day.

At some moment, it was not clear when, as Alex's head hit the pillow and the candlelight flickered to a dim, his thinking turned into dreaming. Alex never dreamed at night.

❖

Alex sat perched on a dune above a pink desert. A turban was wrapped around his head, and a light linen cloth covered his body from the blistering sun. He had never felt heat like this before and hoped he wouldn't again. Alex had never been to a desert; he had never been told what a desert was like other than when his father had described it.

He looked around him as pink, purple, and gray sands on sweeping hills melted like butter into each other for as far as the eye could see. The sky and the sun had a pink-orange hue due to the sand and the heat in the air, and in some directions the earth looked like it was dancing around reflections of heat. No one else was here; Alex was all alone.

He felt calm, as if he could sit here for hours if the sun were a little cooler. He wished he could turn it down like you would do with a dial on an oven.

Suddenly, Alex felt something cold and slippery slithering below the sand under his leg. He looked down to see a brown-and-green-striped serpent. He jumped back so quickly he could hardly tell how his body had known to function in that way at all.

The serpent's pink, slitted tongue jutted out of its mouth and flicked quickly in the air twice before retreating into its mouth. The serpent raised its body as if it had two back legs it was standing on, but it was raising to look and not to attack.

"Hello, Nova," said the serpent through its tongue and sharp fangs.

"Hello," replied Alex.

"Follow me." The serpent flashed its two dark hoods that sat on either side of its head; its red eyes were mesmerizing. It lowered its body back down to the sand and started slithering in the shape of an S down the sandy slope. Alex noticed the serpent was longer and looked a lot stronger than when it first appeared; it was big enough to swallow him whole.

Alex descended the steep, sandy mounds and followed the serpent through the valleys between the sandy hills for what could have been a minute or a week, it was hard to say. The sun stayed in the same place behind him, and his feet felt like they barely touched the ground as he walked.

Slowly, Alex could see a black line appear on the horizon, as if he were using a black, felt-tipped pen to outline the color.

"Where are we going?" Alex asked the serpent as he looked back over his shoulder and saw that the sun was now just a slice of tangerine on the valley floor behind him.

"You'll sss-see," said the serpent in a slippery way.

Alex stopped. "No, I won't go any further."

Annoyed, the serpent slithered back around Alex. Its entire body was a fat, blubbery wall that surrounded him. Alex was afraid.

The serpent once again sat up, and this time it towered over him. It was much, much bigger than before. It was perhaps taller than any building Alex had ever seen.

The black felt-tip on the horizon began to draw in the rest of the sky. Everything but the red, prying eyes of the serpent and its white fangs went dark. Alex let out a small whimper, right before the serpent launched itself forward toward him, jaw extended, ready for its supper.

❖

Alex awoke and sat bolt upright, sweat drenching his pajamas and bedding. The serpent was gone.

The window in Alex's room had burst ajar, and something heavy and metal clanked on his floor. He could hear the flapping of wings and momentarily the silhouette of a bird against the moon, the comet, and the night sky.

He didn't bother to get up, his eyes grew too heavy. Leaving the window open, he fell asleep again. This time with no serpent or desert to be found, only darkness.

CHAPTER 2

The comet had been in the night's sky for almost a week. Nothing was shared about it through The Nexus. No one, apart from Phoebe, had acknowledged seeing it. No one had mentioned an extra-large bald eagle, either. Perhaps everyone was too busy with the Championships. Perhaps it was all a dream, like the serpent in the desert.

Alex pushed all of that aside for the time being; he also had other concerns on his mind. It was Championship Day. He got out of bed, had a shower, and dressed in his school uniform. He had ironed it the night before, so it was extra pressed and ready for his performance that day. Ironing wasn't his strong point, but he always tried his best, as this was another task he was afraid to have his father do.

It was the morning of the Championships, and Alex felt fresher than you would expect given the night he had. He was usually a heavy sleeper, but that wasn't the first night this week that he had been awakened unexpectedly.

He could hear the communicator on in the front room. Alex walked out to see his father staring at the front of the screen, intently eating a bowl of cereal that was swimming in too much milk. He always managed to get food for himself in the morning, and Alex wondered if it was just out of habit.

... and in their finest dress, Creston's reigning Champions prepare for their three-hour trip from Castlegar across the sparkling Kootenay Lake and through the mountains today to see their family, friends, and community, and to of course watch this year's Creston District Championship. Lisa Anne Donaldson, the famous harpist; Eliza Berry, the young flute player; Jeremiah Stokes, the world's greatest skier ...

The communicator showed fleeting images of the Champions and rambled on about the other, older Champions returning to their proud parents and homes after years of performing in the capital. Alex wondered how they could manage being away from their families for so long. He knew, as it was always mentioned on the communicator, that it was too much of a risk for them to travel frequently because of the virus. Alex had always thought it strange, as often the contestants who returned showed little or no emotion when seeing their families. Maybe they were working hard to stay strong for the capital, he mused?

Alex opened the refrigerator and poured milk into his bowl of cereal before sitting next to his father and saying, "Morning, Pops." His father didn't blink, he just ate and stared.

... the crowds watching their departure are cheering loudly. Keen to cheer for their Champions but also in anticipation of today's Creston District Championship. Everyone is on the edge of their seats to see who the new arrivals will be to the city gates. I'll be traveling in the Champion bus and

will keep you informed upon our arrival. Back to you at The Nexus Live Studio. Dacaan Evermore...

The travel of the reigning Champions to Creston was never shared, just their departure and arrival. Alex wondered why that was. They hardly ever saw rest of the districts, and then only on the broadcasts from Castlegar or the other districts' Championships that played throughout the year.

Finishing his breakfast, Alex picked up his and his father's bowls, grabbed his bag with his gear for the performance, kissed his father on the head, and said farewell before leaving the house. Alex had pre-arranged with the neighbors who lived across the road, an elderly couple with no children, called Mr. and Mrs. Huddersmith, to pick up his father and take him to the Community Arena later today where the Championships would be held.

Alex left the cabin and took the winding path through the old, red cedar trees as he made his way toward the lake. He liked to run his hands across the hard and jagged tree trunks as he walked down the path, stepping on their cones and pines. It made him feel connected to them. Alex needed some time before his performance to just clear his mind. He had agreed with Cassia that they would meet a few hours before the Championships to just chat and relax. He was worried this might be the last time they would get to do something that was almost second nature to them both.

He got to the river but couldn't see Cassia. He checked his communicator, but she hadn't sent a message. He sat on a big rock at the mouth of the river that fed rushing water into the lake. He breathed in the fresh air, listening to the birds tweeting overhead. Alex often came here with or without Cassia to clear his head. Sometimes when he felt sad about his mother or worried about his father, he would take a trip down to this rock and sit in silence.

Alex picked up a handful of small, flat rocks and started throwing them into the water. Five skips was his average and fourteen was his best. He was always trying to break his own record.

"Is it going to be fifteen today?" Cassia had arrived with a bright, beaming smile on her face. She was also wearing a clean, pressed school uniform. The uniform was in the Creston Elementary School colors of blue and yellow. Girls wore skirts and boys wore pants, but apart from that there was very little in terms of difference in their attire.

Outside of their school uniforms, Cassia and Alex were opposites. To start with, Cassia was obviously a girl, and an outgoing one at that. Cassia was only slightly shorter than Alex. She had long, dark-brown hair that was always braided in various styles, with sun-kissed copper streaks that made her bronze skin look radiant in any kind of light. Alex had never known anyone else to have such perfectly matched skin and braided hair, and they suited Cassia, as they were as unique as her personality. Cassia had a medium build and an edginess to her that made her handsome and unusual for a girl. She wasn't a traditional beauty, but she was striking, and you could feel her presence.

In comparison, Alex often felt quite small next to Cassia in both stature and personality. He often wondered how they had become friends, given their complete differences. Cassia lived for music, Alex preferred silence and the sounds of nature. Cassia was loud and outgoing, whereas Alex was friendly but shied away from crowds where possible—he preferred their small group of friends. Cassia got poor grades, because she rarely paid attention, whereas Alex got some of the highest grades in their school. Cassia was fiercely competitive, Alex was only competitive against himself.

Frustrated, Alex threw another stone on the water. The lake was extremely still today and perfect for stone skipping. One, two, three, four, five...

"Give me one of those, and I'll show you how it's done," Cassia joked, and she threw one toward the water that landed like a tank, spiraling down to the rocky depths almost immediately.

They both laughed, looking at each other and then looking out at the water. They sat silent for a time.

"What happens next, if one of us goes to Castlegar?" asked Cassia softly, much more softly than she would usually speak. She was looking down at her pink, polished fingernails, and her hands were fidgeting.

Cassia rarely showed softness. When her father had been taken to Castlegar for his mechanical skills to work as a matter of urgency, he had left her as the eldest of her siblings and to help her mother take care of them. Cassia was just seven when he left. Her mother cried a lot and retreated from the world after the first year of the Creston Championships when he didn't return like she had hoped. Five to ten skilled workers were taken to Castlegar at the time of the Championships each year. They rarely came home, and when her mother inquired with the Dacaan Diplomacy Office, she was told he was to remain in Castlegar indefinitely. For years her mother had retreated into herself, leaving Cassia to fend for her brother and twin sisters. More recently, Cassia's mother was coming back into her old self and supported Cassia, especially knowing her daughter's singing talent and the potential that she might go to Castlegar and could bring news of her father back with her at least once a year. Cassia secretly despised her mother for thinking of her as a tool when she had done so little to help her and her siblings when their father left. She would happily see the day when she would go to Castlegar and be able to send hope and money back to her siblings, but nothing else.

After Cassia's father left, she and Alex had grown closer. They were both the head of their households, and they had a responsibility far greater than most other children at Creston Elementary. Although they didn't talk about it much, they supported one another. They had a secret bond that no one else could understand.

Alex sat thinking again about Cassia's question. He knew that it would be heartbreaking if they were to leave each other, but he would never want Cassia to give up her dream. The world was a difficult place, it had broken up families and separated friends. As the Regime said, 'The youth are our Champions,' and it had been drilled into every child through their years in school that 'Sacrifices must be made for the greater good.' Alex had always cared about the greater good. About the people that remained in the world following the virus. It was important for them to do as the Regime said and 'Honor Mother Dacaan and pray to thee.'

"We will do what we must," responded Alex.

He reached out and stilled Cassia's fidgeting hand with his, and they looked at each other. He looked into her deep, brown eyes and gave one of his smiles that only lifted half of his face. She gave one of her mischievous smiles in return.

As if reading each other's minds, they kicked off their shoes and stuffed their socks in them, placing them safely on the big rock they had been sitting on. Alex pulled up his pants, and they began galloping like horses down the side of the lake, laughing, careful not to splash each other in their meticulously pressed garments.

Alex and Cassia had spent their youth on this beach, swimming in the summer out into the water as far as they could go just to challenge themselves. In the winter, they would walk down the shore past the point where the lake tapered off and turned into a second lake they called Duck Lake to go skating on the ice. They had grown up watching the great red-bodied salmon with green heads that jumped up the river to spawn in the fall, careful not to interrupt the bears fishing for their afternoon meal. They would play hide-and-seek in the forest and pick bluebells in the spring.

Their childhood had been filled with memorable moments, like the time Alex got stuck in a tree, and he was left stranded for over an hour before help arrived. There was the time Cassia dove off a small waterfall into a watering hole that many of the children jumped into in the summer, and her swimming suit came off, leaving her embarrassed in front of her friends. There was the summer the Regime had given every child in Castlegar a new bike, and they spent hours on the trails going as far out as to the tall electric fences that surrounded them, learning every inch of the perimeter of their district, wondering what existed beyond but thankful that they were safe inside.

That morning, Cassia and Alex spent what they didn't know were the final hours of life as they knew it: laughing, splashing in the water, telling stories, and skipping stones.

❖

After drying off and retrieving their shoes, Alex and Cassia walked to pick up both Ariadne and Niall before heading to the Championship Center.

When they arrived at Ariadne's house, her mother was hugging her and kissing her at the door, with tears running down her face. Her father stood behind them with a proud but solemn look on his.

"Good luck, Ariadne, you will do us proud no matter what," shouted her mother a little too loud and with a crackle in the final words as Ariadne walked down the path to her friends. Ariadne rolled her eyes as she got closer, to signify her embarrassment, but the group could see that she was welling up.

Cassia gave her a hug as soon as she got close enough, and then almost forcefully pushed her out again, holding each of her shoulders at arm's length and remarked, "Wow, Aria, you look incredible."

Ariadne did look exceptional that day. Her fuzzy hair was pulled up into two balls on the top of her head, with clips in the shape of silver flowers at the front of them. She had put on a little makeup, which made her look older and hold herself differently. Her eyes were lightly dusted with a light blue eyeshadow, and her lips had a dusky pink shimmer on them. Because she was performing her gymnastics routine, she had on her blue-and-gold-breathable track suit and a pair of white running shoes that she would wear to the Championship Center. She would, of course, change into her stretchy body suit when she presented.

The sides of her mouth curled up at the compliment. "Thank you, Cassia, you look perfect as always," she replied.

"I know," Cassia responded, laughing, and the three of them walked down the street toward the Evanses' house to pick up Niall. Niall's house was quiet and dark when they arrived. It was a small, thatched cottage, unlike most houses in the area, and was covered with climbing green foliage and roses. It looked beautiful like this every summer.

"I messaged Niall just before leaving the house, and he said he was ready," chirped Ariadne.

Niall's curly, red hair appeared in his bedroom window. They saw it again bobbing past the latticed window on the stairwell, and then the door opened. His parents didn't say a farewell, and his face looked somber as he closed the door, flung his backpack over his shoulder, and headed across the front garden to the group. Niall's parents didn't always get along, and they weren't always supportive of Niall.

"Howdy, folks, ready for the big day," Niall mustered, a sentence that should have landed with much more enthusiasm than Niall delivered it with. He gave a shifty smile and looked up past a gelled curl to see the groups response.

"Ready as we'll ever be!" replied Ariadne in an overly

enthusiastic way to help in lifting the spirits, but the mood had shifted.

An awkward silence sat with the group as they made their way to the Championship Center. Nervousness pulsed in the air around them.

❖

The grounds of the Championship Center had been reformed like never before. Each year, the decorating and planning committee for the Championships got together weeks in advance to plan a new theme and set up displays that were only unveiled on the day.

The Clan gasped at the beauty when they arrived. This year, the outside was decorated in shades of multicolored festival. Usually the theme was a single color with a single concept. Two years ago, the theme had been red raspberry, and last year the theme had been orange sunset.

"Well, I'll be darned," said Cassia, breaking the silence of the group. "I would never have expected this one."

"They've really gone all out this time!" replied Ariadne.

Inside the Championship Center, the decorations continued. There were hundreds of children between the ages of six to eleven practicing their performances. Some were twirling batons, others playing with a soccer ball; a group in the far corner was playing a song on woodwind instruments. It was a hum of activity.

Feeling they were running late, The Clan found a spare place on the stands to put their bags and began unpacking and getting themselves prepared.

"If I don't get a chance to say it later, good luck today

everyone. You're all winners in my eyes!" Niall winked as he said this with an emotion that straddled the line of sarcasm and support.

"Good luck!" responded everyone in the group at slightly different times, and almost just as quickly as they had gathered earlier, they all disbanded. Cassia ran to claim a space behind the stands that was quiet and secluded, and she put in her noise-canceling headphones before belting out her scales to warm up. Niall ran over to the other soccer players on his team and joined them in passing the ball back and forth and doing small tricks. Ariadne went to the gymnasts' section on the sprung floor in the middle of the room and began tumbling passes.

Alex took his bag and walked to the storage room near the far exit door. It wouldn't do to practice his illusion performance in front of the group, or they would see what he had in store. Alex was one of the final acts in the Championships before the judges announced winners. In previous years, the crowd had done one of two things toward the end: either they had disbanded having become restless after a full afternoon of performances or they had watched intently to see if one of the final acts could potentially be the one to steal the day. Alex prayed for the former.

He pulled his props out from his bag: a newspaper, a piece of string, a bouquet of fake flowers, a hat, a magic wand, a rabbit—of the stuffed variety—and a lighter. Looking down at the items, he realized that his performance from this angle looked terrible. It was how he was going to perform it that mattered, he reminded himself.

Alex had been practicing for weeks and had perfected

all parts of the presentation. When his father was up to it, Alex used him as a supporting act as he practiced at home. His father would hold what he needed him to hold and clap when he asked him to clap. Today, Alex was promised a short table to hold his items, and he would rely on the audience for the clapping if he were lucky enough to impress them.

Alex ran through his act once more and felt confident. The string he pulled was taut, and it remained short, but then with the newspaper obscuring the view, he pulled the string out so it became ten times longer. The bouquet of flowers would start off as stems that he would light on fire, and then with the flash of his wand would turn into flowers. The big finale would be the empty hat, and with another flash of his wand, the rabbit would appear. It was the standard illusion performance recommended by the Regime, and it had sent all the props and instructions on how to do it. Most had seen this exact performance or something similar more than once, but it was still a crowd pleaser.

Slightly embarrassed at how basic his performance would be, Alex remembered that he, in fact, didn't want to win, didn't want to go to Castlegar, and only hoped that his father and friends would enjoy the short performance and then forget about it.

❖

The time for preparation was short-lived. The rehearsal had ended, and all the contestants were sitting in anticipation with bottles of water and some jelly sweets as they waited. The reigning Champions had arrived from their long journey from Castlegar and were styled by their entourage before heading down a red carpet. There were glamourous women in the most stylish dresses and men dressed in tuxedos with bow ties. The Communicator Live Crew ran frenzied behind them, and their entrance was projected on a screen inside the auditorium. The Champions all did a short performance when they arrived at a flowered backdrop just next to the Championship Center entrance and took their cordoned-off seats in the private area upstairs and to the sides of the stage. They were always separated from the crowd.

The big moment was the arrival of the queen. Queen Jocelyn was loved by the people, and she attended every single Championship. That day, she was dressed regally with a beautiful, emerald-jeweled crown perched on top of a nest of crimson-red hair. She smiled and waved and gave a short speech to the cameras before her entrance.

"People of Creston, it is our pleasure to welcome you here today for the Thirty-Eighth Championships. The children of this village have worked tirelessly to perfect their performances today, and everyone in Dacaan is eager to see what they have in store. Thank you to every one of you who has sacrificed and who will sacrifice for the greater good. And to your reigning Champions, welcome home. Let the Championships begin!"

Cheers seemed to echo across the valleys, bouncing off the mountains, and reverberating down the rivers. People were watching from their homes and in select public spaces with communicators playing live.

The Clan sat together as they waited. As the queen entered and sat down, the introductory performance began. The Clan looked around at the stands and pointed out Ariadne's parents, who had obviously been staring at her and started waving at the group. They saw Cassia's mother trying to keep her siblings in ordered.

"Alex, where is your father, is he coming?" asked Ariadne.

"Yes, he will come with Mr. and Mrs. Huddersmith closer to my performance," Alex responded, and adding, "He gets too distracted when he sits through the Championships for too long."

Niall's parents were also missing, but no one asked their whereabouts.

The Championships that year felt more professional than any year previous. The day started as usual with a short scrimmage by the soccer team that Niall played on. They played five-a-side, and it was for individuals to showcase their talents and skills. Niall really shone; he was by far the best player in the match.

The following performances started with some of the younger children, each getting two minutes to do their best to stand out and show their talent. Moving on to the older children, the talent only increased. Some of the performances were exceptional. Cassia had the voice of an angel, and not only did she sing but did a contemporary dance that left no dry eye in the audience. Ariadne did her floor routine, flipping up and down the stage in ways the human body shouldn't be able to move. They were both exceptional, and, although he was biased, Alex was sure that they were the best performances of the day.

At roughly ten past four, Alex noticed his father, accompanied by the neighbors, enter the auditorium. He gave a wave and smile in their direction; his father seemed in great spirits and fully aware, which was good to see.

As if his father's arrival was a ticking hand of a clock, he knew his turn wasn't far away. His hands got clammy, and he began taking deep breaths.

The next performance ended, and Alex could hear his heart beating so hard he was sure it would jump out of his chest. But it wasn't his turn yet. Over and over, applause, announcement, but not his name.

Alex sat trying to compose himself, listening to the clock tick. Then he heard it, his name. Never before had the sound of his own name brought so much distress.

Cassia gave a huge whoop as he took his steps up onto the stage. He looked around, seeing many familiar and unfamiliar faces. Faces of the reigning Champions from Creston and of the queen herself. He couldn't be sure, but he thought he saw her wave at him. He didn't have time to think about it. Seeing the table, he placed his props on it. The audience fell silent. Just breathe, Alex told himself.

Trick one, Alex took the piece of string and newspaper. He walked down into the crowd and asked a small girl to give a pull on the string. Walking back on stage, he put the string behind the newspaper and pulled. But rather than pulling longer and longer, to Alex's dismay the string turned into a fresh bouquet of flowers. This wasn't how the trick was supposed to work. Alex stepped back, almost knocking over the table with his props. A few people clapped, but there were murmurs in the crowd. Alex could feel his blood pressure rising.

Trick two, Alex took the stem of the bouquet of flowers and set it on fire. But, unlike in practice, the fire started to swirl and ravel up the stem, and then exploded into what seemed like a thousand multicolored flowers. Baffled, Alex stepped backward again. The crowd started cheering loudly, and flowers were held up by many women in the audience.

Success! But how?

From the crowd, Alex noticed the person he feared the most in all of Dacaan: Cravelda, the head of the Regime. She had a sour look to her but always spoke in sweet melodic tones that often sounded forced. She sat next to Queen Jocelyn—she was always next to the queen—and where she wasn't smiling, the queen made up for her negative demeanor with her own cheerful expression. Cravelda at that moment stood up, looking shocked. She wasn't cheering or watching the crowd's reaction to Alex's performance but was staring straight at him with a look that Alex could only associate with the word DANGER.

From stage left, the producer said, "One minute, you're almost up."

Alex refocused; he had one more act. He took off his hat and showed the crowd that it was empty inside. The smiles and wide-eyed excitement that he saw behind the stage lights were overwhelming. The audience was so excited at this performance they had never seen before. What next, they were all thinking. Alex was thinking the same.

Alex took out his wand and waved it across the top of the hat, one, two, three times and then hit the top. Suddenly, more rabbits than he had ever seen came jumping out of the hat onto the stage and into the audience. The children started grabbing the rabbits and holding them or chasing them across the floor. It was pandemonium. Alex looked over at Cravelda, who was furiously talking to one of the patrol. As the crowd erupted in applause once again, Alex ran off the stage. What had just happened, and what would happen to him? The Regime and Cravelda weren't amused—that was for sure.

Offstage, Cassia, Niall, and Ariadne had come to meet Alex.

"What was that?" asked Cassia.

"I have no idea," responded Alex.

"Let's head back to the bleachers," Ariadne suggested.

The Clan walked around to the bleachers and sat down next to Alex's father and the neighbors. The audience had been sitting, waiting for the management team to pick up and clear out the rabbits, and because it took some time, the excitement began to fizzle out. Most of them were on their communicators, voting for their favorite performances along with the rest of Dacaan. Alex noticed a faint look of concern on the neighbors' faces as they came closer.

Alex had been the final performance of the day, and there was a short intermission as the judges tallied their scores to announce the Champions.

"Pardon me," announced Alex to the group as he got up and made a beeline for the restrooms, trying to move quickly enough so that no one would follow.

To Alex's relief, the hallway was virtually empty. He didn't actually need to use the restrooms, but he needed space to clear his head, and the room was empty of people. He had always felt calm in these restrooms, they were mint green and felt very therapeutic. Alex walked up to the sink and splashed water across his face. He stood with his head down and watched as the water swirled clockwise, as to be expected. But not everything had been expected today.

Alex lifted his head and said to himself in the mirror,

"What actually happened out there?" forgetting himself for a moment as he presumed he was alone. But as he looked up, an image behind him in the mirror revealed he wasn't alone at all. It was the patrol that Cravelda had been speaking with.

Startled, Alex jumped back and to attention. "Apologies, sir, I thought I was in here alone."

The patrol said nothing at first, walking forward and washing his hands. He looked at himself in the mirror and twisted his coarse, black mustache.

"What did happen out there, boy?" the patrol asked.

Silence took hold of the room.

"Well, I had practiced that performance for months, and well . . . it didn't turn out as I had expected," was Alex's feeble response.

The patrol laughed as if the whole situation amused him in a wicked and unkind way.

"I am sure that Cravelda will want to speak with you later," was his response as he purposefully brushed into Alex's shoulder and then pushed through the door on his way out.

The hair on the back of Alex's forearms stood up on end.

❖

The final speech was coming to a close. It was given by the mayor of Creston, who was thanking Queen Jocelyn for joining them and the Regime for its support. He was thanking all the participants who joined in today's performances, but only two Champions would be selected to leave for Castlegar.

Phoebe, the small girl with who Alex had spoken with on the bus, scuttled across the stage with two envelopes. As she turned around, she looked up at Alex, directly in his eyes, before scuttling back offstage again into the dark.

"And the Champions are . . ." started the mayor. He hesitated, and his tall, white eyebrows stood firmly to attention. The old gentleman had been the mayor for as long as they could remember. He had kind eyes, was short and round, and wore his shiny, embroidered garments not just on the day of the Championships but all year. He was a man who was strong in his convictions, a man of disciplines who never faltered. Which is why this moment stuck out like a sore thumb.

Resuming at a slower pace, the mayor began, "I have the winners of the Thirty-Eighth Championships in my hands. The first winner is . . . Ariadne Lawson, please come down to the stage."

Ariadne's face was a look of both shock and excitement. Ariadne was extremely talented, but she was not one to ever boast about her successes and rarely was she put on a pedestal. Her parents and The Clan all stood up and gave her a hug each before she ran down the stands. This was of course a surprise because she was a year younger than the others but she excitedly somersaulted across the floor before walking up onto the stage to claim her prize.

Handing her the trophy, the mayor pushed her toward the microphone.

Proud and triumphant, Ariadne shouted, "Thank you, Creston, I will not let you down!" She held up the trophy as the applause in the building grew to a deafening level.

The mayor motioned for her to step off to the side on the stage.

"And the next winner, it would be no surprise to us all . . . for the best illusion act I think Dacaan has ever seen, Alexander Kerr!" announced the mayor.

The cheering of the crowd and their jumping bodies were like a blur to Alex. His father grabbed his hand, and they embraced before he walked down the stairs and toward the stage. People kept clapping him on the back, shaking his hand. He couldn't believe this moment was happening, it wasn't supposed to happen, he didn't want it to happen.

Alex got to the stage and climbed the steps. The mayor smiled and said to him, "Well done, boy," before shaking his hand so hard that he thought his arm might actually come off of his body.

What frightened Alex the most was that at some point in his ascent to the stage, what had happened really sunk in. What he had done was more than illusion. What he had done he did not understand. What he had done was something he never wanted to do again. What he had done was dangerous.

The crowd started chanting, "A-lex, A-lex, A-lex." The heat from the lights on the stage was unforgiving. Alex wished that he could just disappear in that moment—it would be the best illusion act they had ever seen—but he didn't. Why couldn't he just will that to happen, he thought confusedly?

Behind the microphone, Alex looked across the quietening crowd. He looked at his father, friends, and community he had known for so long. Ariadne ran across the stage to be closer to him, as an act of support to show him that she was there, and reached out to give a small squeeze on his shoulder. He took a long breath in; he knew what he needed to do.

"Thank you so much for this honor..."

The crowd erupted into applause again, and the mayor had to yell for them to quiet down before he could continue.

Alex felt a lump in his throat. There was a bead of sweat trickling down his face. He felt dizzy.

The crowd was quiet again as Alex spoke into the microphone.

"Thank you so much for voting for me and for this honor... an honor which I regrettably have to decline."

The crowd went so quiet that he could have heard a pin drop. People were looking around confused like they didn't understand what he had just said. Alex looked across at the mayor, who was shaking his head in confusion. Alex tried again, this time more forcibly.

"I will not be your Champion, I will not go to Castlegar."

For the first time in thirty-eight years of the Championships, a contestant had successfully executed a magic performance. For the first time in thirty-eight years of the Championships, a contestant had denied his win. The last thing that Alex remembered was a sinister smile taking over the face of Cravelda as she looked at the patrol, and Alex thought he saw her mouth the words "You know what to do."

CHAPTER
3

Alex didn't sleep well again that night. Flashbacks from the Championships were pouring through his head at lightning speed. 'What happened and what does this mean?' were questions that ran over and over in his mind.

Getting out of bed, Alex walked over to sit in a wooden chair by his window and gaze out at the stars. The moon was barely a slice now; the comet was much brighter, though. Still, no one had mentioned it apart from Phoebe. Did no one else see it? So much had happened in just a week. More things of significance had happened to Alex that week than had happened in his entire life. The comet, the eagle, the Championships, the suspicious illusion trick, his refusal speech, the box...

Of course, the box. Alex had almost forgotten the box with everything else that had happened. He got up from the chair, working hard to not let any of the wooden floorboards groan under the weight of his steps. Alex knew that his father slept lightly, and he didn't want to disturb him. He walked over to the closet and opened the door with ease.

There it sat, the same carved, wooden box with the name Nova written on the top. The box seemed to come alive tonight. It had red-and-blue-painted motifs all over it, with golden accents that twinkled in the moonlight as Alex held it up to the faded light. He sat down on the floor with his back against the wall just under the window.

He pulled hard at the box again, hoping that it might force open, but no luck. The clasps were tightly bound, and—given it looked very old—its wood and seams were sealed shut. Alex was extremely curious at what was inside the box. Perhaps it was information about his father's past life before the amnesia, or perhaps it was information about his mother?

Looking around the floor close to him, Alex was hoping that he might find a loose screw or something that would help him in getting into the box. Out of the corner of his eye, he did notice something shiny under his bed.

Alex crawled across the floor, setting the box to the side of him. He reached out his arm to grab at whatever it was lurking under the bed. He felt like he had to stretch his fingers to get them further toward the object, and then, as if it had come closer toward him, Alex felt a cold piece of metal in the palm of his hand.

He was a little shocked by the item's sudden appearance right where he needed it, but Alex brushed the thought aside. Much less abnormal things had happened to him recently. Pulling his arm back from under the bed, Alex unfolded his hand finger by finger and saw that the shiny item he now possessed was a key.

Alex didn't recall having a key that looked like this before. It was gold in color, and it had a long stem and a short handle that looked like a shamrock. Alex decided it was obviously worth a try and brought the key closer to the box. As if propelling light on its own, the box began to glow, as did the key. Alex dropped both and scuttled away, startled. Was this a dream again?

The box and key sat glowing on the floor. Alex was paralyzed with fear, but he did not feel threatened. Rather, the box and the key felt like they were inviting him in.

Alex moved back and sat squarely under the window in its dim light, looking in front of him and trying to plan his next move. Curiosity overcame nerves, and he inched forward again to slide the rather fat key into the rather slim hole. He turned the lock clockwise until it made a loud clunk, and the lid of the box made a cracking sort of noise that a wooden box that had not been opened for some years might make. It popped open but only by a few inches. The light that had been emanating from the box was now flowing out of it. It looked like the sort of mist that would settle over the lake after a hot summer day when the air cooled. Alex tried to move backward slightly, but the mist had already begun to wash over him, and it had a lovely, refreshing coolness to it. It looked like it had now filled his entire bedroom floor.

Mustering up enough courage, Alex flipped the lid of the box backward so that it fell on the floor behind. He wished it hadn't have fallen so loudly; he was sure his father would be up soon enough. The mist seemed to subside, and Alex looked into the box, but only saw its felt-lined bottom. It was empty. He turned it upside down and shook, but there was nothing.

"You've finally opened it, Nova," said Alex's father, who seemed to appear from nowhere.

Feeling nervous already, Alex jumped back again.

"Yes, I was curious . . . I . . . I couldn't sleep," he tried to explain.

Alex noticed that his father looked present. This always made him feel a sense of relief, but right now, more than ever, he was thankful.

"Father, where is this box from?" he asked.

Alex's father walked toward his bed and sat down. Alex picked up the box and sat next to him on the bed with one leg cocked to the side so that he could look at his father while he was talking. Alex wanted to find out everything he could, and he liked staring into his father's eyes when he was more lucid, because these conversations were so important.

"What happened yesterday, at the Championships . . . it was Happenstance," began Alex's father. He too looked straight into Alex's eyes in a way that seemed as if he were searching for something. "It was always you, Nova, now is your time," he continued, as if it made any sense.

Alex sat there wondering whether his father was as aware as he thought, but he decided he must continue. He had remembered the Championships, which had surprised Alex. The thought of the Championships and Cravelda's face made his stomach twist in circles again.

"Why do you call me Nova, Father?" was a question he had wanted to know for most of his life. He wondered then why he had never asked it before.

"It is your true name, your true destiny. It was only a matter of time before you found it and it found you," responded Alex's father, who rested back on his hands for a moment.

"Father, I don't understand," Alex pleaded, "you aren't

making sense, please explain what is happening to me. I'm frightened, Father."

"Son, don't be frightened. You are much stronger than you think, and your time is coming. You must go soon, let the box be your guide."

As he looked up toward the ceiling, Alex could tell that his father was retreating. He was going back into his mind, into that place that he inhabited for the majority of his life, like a turtle shrinking back into the home it has in its shell.

"Father, don't leave me, I need you," said Alex softly.

"I'm sorry, Nova, I am always with you no matter what. Perhaps one day things might be different," said Alex's father before getting up from the bed and walking to the door, turning right back to his bedroom.

Alex fell backward into his feathery pillows with tears in his eyes. He threw the box on the floor, and the key fell out of it. Then he drifted off into a dreamless sleep.

❖

Alex awoke, and before he could really understand what, where, or who he was, he heard the sirens. They were louder than he ever remembered. The communicators around the house were flashing red and said 'Alert!' over and over again.

Startled, he jumped up, ran over, and pulled on a pair of slacks and a T-shirt that were laying on the shelf in his closet. He picked up his backpack and ran out his bedroom door. He raced down the hall and saw his father sitting in bed, gazing out the window in the sunlight. Alex glanced at the clock on the bedside table. It was past midday and he'd overslept.

"Father, get up, quickly!" Alex said as he rushed to his father's chest of drawers and threw some underwear, socks, and linen clothing onto the foot of the bed. Alex's father had always worn linen in the summer. Alex hated the feeling of it, but he always made sure that his father had the things he liked the most.

Alex's father obediently got up, got dressed, and together they rushed down the hall to put on their shoes. Alex put two bottles of water, two bananas, and two granola bars hurriedly in his bag before going outside, locking the door, and rushing down the street.

The sirens had been a precautionary measure installed before the Championships, before the virus, the floods, and the wars. Alex was used to the sirens; they had been drilled into him since birth. 'Hear the siren, run for the highlands' was the motto repeated time and time again in school and during commercial breaks on the communicator. They had said the motto only yesterday at the Championships.

Alex remembered three times that the sirens went off for fear of a new outbreak of the virus. Once when a young baby had a fever, and his parents didn't know what to do with him; once when the butcher's son came up with a rash all over his body; and once when an older lady who was friends with his neighbors developed a hacking cough that was unlike anything heard before. In all cases, the subjects in question were taken from Creston to the infirmary, never to be seen again. Their families were taken from their houses to Cranbrook on the outskirts of the district. In the case of the butcher's son, the people of Creston had to throw away all their meats, and the butcher was closed down indefinitely, only for a new butcher to be established by a new family sent by the Regime to the village.

There was one time the sirens rang for a flood: The Sanca River had burst its banks along with many others in the district, due to excess run off that year. The water had threatened to climb up the banks and into their log cabin, but it had not quite made it. The basement had somehow not flooded, but many neighbors had suffered that year.

Never had the sirens gone off because of war, of course, since the Regime had decimated all opposing nations taking its people in and making Dacaan the only country with human inhabitants in the world.

Typically, sirens were drills, and there were usually four of them each year, one at the end of each season.

As he ran, a thought came to Alex's mind that their last siren drill had happened recently. There had been one at the start of the year, and then if he remembered correctly, there had been one on the day of Cassia's birthday, which was on the final day of April. It was now the 25th of June, so it seemed rather close to the day of the last drill. Perhaps this wasn't a drill, thought Alex.

Alex saw Cassia and her family. She also had her backpack on, and she was corralling the children. Her mother looked anxious and was doing very little to help.

"You okay over there?" asked Alex.

Levan, the youngest boy with a cowlick, came running over. Alex scooped him up in his arms.

"Come on, Levan, you are used to these by now, please be brave," joked Alex, trying to make light of the situation as he wrapped the boy around onto his back.

He could feel Levan shivering in fear, a feeling that made him turn his own fear into strength. Alex had to be strong, for Levan, for his father, and for himself.

Together, the Kerrs and the Maddoxes went to the village center and then made their way up the gray cement stairs to the highlands. There were many families also on the stairs, which had two hundred fifty steps in total, and it was often hard for everyone to move up them quickly. Some of the older people and children were much slower, but the lazy drone of the siren getting louder during the climb fueled adrenaline inside of them as they pushed themselves to get to the top as fast as they could.

At the top, the Obelisk stood at the entrance before the cave. Alex could see its tall sphere pointing upwards with the star at its apex. From the town, the Obelisk stood like a beacon of hope for those below. When people of the district stood in front of the church, the cross of the church perfectly aligned with the star of the Obelisk, and many would worship in that very spot, muttering, 'Peace to the Realm' and 'Mother of Dacaan, we honor thee.' The very spot where the worshippers came had an indentation from where so many had knelt to pray from the times even before the Regime, when the world was not safe and the rulers were not kind. Many felt lucky to have the Regime, for the security it instilled and the support it gave. The people saw the coming of the Championships as a renaissance—it was something that gave purpose to their lives.

From the town, you couldn't see the cave that sat back in the recess behind the Obelisk. It was where the people of Creston had hidden during the wars. They had lived with only candlelight and dried food for weeks. There was a waterfall at the back of the cave that provided water, and it was said that when rations had run out the people had eaten creatures like bats and mice, which also inhabited the dank dwelling. Alex and most of the children of Creston were frightened of the cave. Very few would ascend the stairs without the siren. It was considered a kind of holy ground, and it was a sin to go there unless the siren called for you.

After some time, the people of Creston had all made it to the top. There were hundreds of inhabitants of the town, but the highlands plateau was spacious. There were white daisies all over the grass and more on the edges of the cobblestone courtyard that radiated from the Obelisk in a series of grays and whites and some reds. Rhododendrons flanked the banks that rose up behind the cave, providing an array of pinks, purples, and whites.

After drinking in the scene, Alex and Cassia together noticed something unusual and looked at each other with concern in their eyes. Cravelda, the patrol, Queen Jocelyn, and both the Champions were standing at the mouth of the cave.

Alex and Cassia both pulled their families to the side of the stairs, and they lingered at the back. Like many others, they used the railing that arched its way around the cobblestone path to boost their position so they could see. Cravelda, the patrol, and Queen Jocelyn were elevated on the bandstand for all to see, and the winners and other Regime patrol were stood below in a semicircle at the entrance of the cave.

Standing on tiptoes, Cassia turned and said to Alex, "Aria and Niall are up there."

After Alex refused the Championship trophy the

night before, the third-place winner, Niall, was announced, so he and Aria would be going to Castlegar together. Alex was pleased that they would at least have each other there. The Recruit had also been named, and this year the Regime had carefully selected eight from the Creston District to leave for Castlegar and other parts of Dacaan for the good of the Realm. To work, to serve and to never be seen again.

Murmurs were running through the crowd; this was not usual. The Regime and the Champions always left on the same day as the Championships. They had never stayed back. There had also never been such a regal group at the sirens. Alex could not recall a time when the queen and Cravelda had been at the highlands. He was sure that he along with everyone in the crowd was thinking, why now?

"People of Creston," Queen Jocelyn spoke with strong words and with emotion, "thank you so much for taking the time to join us here in the sacred grounds of the highlands today."

Queen Jocelyn was the people's queen. Everyone loved her for her elegance, beauty, and kindness. Her hair was deep and vibrant with a large white shock that ran through it, which had always been there and not set in just due to her age. She was not old, however; she was perhaps a few years younger than Alex's father, but the years had been kind to her. Alex had always noticed when he saw her at the Championships or on the communicator that she moved with grace and had a gentle demeanor. She wore a deep-blue dress. She usually wore blue, and no one could deny that it was her color; it made her light-gray eyes sparkle. Her crown was silver with red and amber jewels encrusted in it.

She continued, "I'm sure many of you are wondering why we are gathered all together here today, this is not something that we typically do." She paused, her voice faltering ever so slightly at the end of the sentence. Queen Jocelyn had a commanding presence. When she paused, you paused, you listened to her silence.

"We come together here today to make two announcements, they are important for both the safety of your district and the future success of the Regime." Queen Jocelyn took a moment to breathe as a gust of wind rushed through the crowd and picked up her long ringlets, tossing them to the side. This pause made a statement, it allowed the crowd enough time to let the gravity of the situation settle in. Apart from a crying baby in the front, and a shallow cough from an old gentleman propped up against the Obelisk, there was silence.

"As you know, the Regime and I only want the best for our people. It is our duty to ensure your safety and to deliver your happiness. When we think, we think for Dacaan; when we serve, we serve Dacaan; when we fight, we fight for Dacaan. Peace to the Realm!" announced the queen, her voice making a startling shift from emotional to triumphant, lifting applause from the audience around her who were also echoing "Peace to the Realm!"

"It has come to our attention that there are evils among us that threaten Creston, that threaten your well-being and your families, which we cannot accept. It is, of course, our duty to work against these threats for your district and we must fight the fight together that will provide hope for our prosperous future," she continued in a fierce and unforgiving tone. The crowd was cheering, and there were many older people who were shushing the others to hear better.

"People of Creston, both the virus and magic walks among us," roared the queen, and the crowd began in a chorus of discussion at this statement. A few sobs from adults were now audible, and there was a commotion to the front right of the audience where Alex could see people picking up a woman who had presumably fainted up from the floor.

Alex thought he could see a slight twitch of the queen's eyes toward Cravelda, who was taking turns between looking at Queen Jocelyn and through the crowd. She was holding on to Queen Jocelyn's arm. Alex was glad he had put on his hat before leaving the house as he ducked from her view when her eyes swept through the audience.

There was a patrol at the front who was holding a large stick with the three flags of Castlegar, Creston, and Dacaan arranged on the top. With a look from Cravelda, he bashed its metal stem on the ground three times to silence the crowd and so the queen's speech could continue.

The queen now changed her expression and her voice once again and continued, "People of Creston, we must now work together to defeat this evil. You must support the Regime as we work to rid the virus and magic from Creston once and for all."

The crowd began to clap and chanted the words, "Rid-the-evil, rid-the-evil, rid-the-evil." It was a chant that was rarely made but always remembered. Alex and Cassia did not join in; they squatted down on their perch to talk discreetly.

"Do you know what this is about?" asked Cassia with a raised eyebrow that meant she had already answered her own question.

"You don't think it could be me," replied Alex with growing concern that pierced like barbs through his body.

Everyone knew from the time they were young that magic was an evil that no one knew but everyone feared. Magic was responsible for the wars and the end of the other civilizations in the world. Magic was the reason why the virus had killed so many people in the years before. Magic was like a dark shadow that had cast itself from the evilest enemies of Dacaan and had become a force in and of itself. But the Regime had rid Dacaan of magic, and it was something that had not been seen for years. The communicator often showed a short video between programs of a triumphant Dacaan and magic in the form of a black cloud being banished from all the districts.

Alex thought back on his illusion trick. He thought again about how the trick had gotten out of control, and how he could not explain what had happened to cause the rabbits to jump out of the hat. Real rabbits, and so many of them. Had he done that, was that magic?

"Alex, why did you reject going to Castlegar? You know that the Regime expects every child to go there if they win the Championships. And what did you do to change that illusion trick? I've seen it so many times before by kids like Big Tom and Jacob Jackson, and they always made it look the same. This time it was different, this time it looked real." Cassia stopped with a look of concern in her eyes.

The metal stick rammed on the hard ground again three times, summoning silence. This time, Cravelda stepped forward into a spot in the bandstand that was lit by the sun, it was almost like the clouds had opened theatrically, like the curtains on the stage in the Championship Center with the spotlight poised on the ground for the new act.

Cravelda began, "People of Creston"—her voice was colder and less ceremonious than Queen Jocelyn's—"first of all, it has come to our attention by an informant that one of your own has the virus and has not yet brought themselves forward. This is not acceptable."

The crowd had gone silent again; unease seeped through its people. Cassia had risen again to watch and listen to Cravelda, but Alex stayed in a crouched position, slightly shielded by his father's tall frame. He didn't want Cravelda or the patrol to see him.

"This young girl has put both herself and the rest of you at risk, and we ask her to step forward on her own terms immediately," summoned Cravelda.

As if in unison, the parents in the crowd grabbed onto their daughters by their hands and around their waists. A few notably touched the foreheads of their little girls and looked at them with fear on their faces.

None of the girls in the audience stepped forward. Alex could hear the chirping of crickets in the thickets around them and could hear the rustle of the leaves in the trees. He looked briefly from side to side to see the spectacular drop below them. From this vantage point you could see the town below, the church, and the river that ran to the lake. The hill was extremely steep. Alex was sure that he could tell which log cabin was his own, but as all the roofs were the same, it was hard to determine and would take a minute or two longer to decide on.

Without the need for the metal pole to draw the attention of the crowd this time, Cravelda carried on, "We have asked, and you have not listened. You have endangered not just your own life but the lives of the people of Creston and of the district. For this reason, I will call your name, and you will step forward for the patrol to immediately take you to the infirmary. The patrol will also remove your family from this group and will take them to a new house. We all know the rules, we all know the gravity of the situation."

Cravelda stopped for a moment and pulled a piece of paper from a pocket in her dress.

"Phoebe Garlast," barked Cravelda.

Two sounds came in the next moment: a cry of a mother in despair from the back left of the group and another sound from the back right close to the stairs. "No."

Cravelda looked first at the mother and pointed for the patrol to march through the crowd and forcibly take Phoebe and her father, mother, and little brother away. Phoebe's family was pushed into the cave along with Phoebe, who was almost immediately wrapped in a light orange, plastic jumpsuit with a breathing apparatus on the front. The color was slightly lighter than the color of Queen Jocelyn's hair.

Immediately after, Cravelda looked in the direction of the person who had pleaded "No," and her eyes locked with Alex's. Cravelda made that horrible smirk. Alex hadn't meant to make a noise, but it had sort of slid out. He had seen Phoebe just days before. When her name was revealed, he had peered over toward her and her family and saw that she looked completely fine. Nothing visibly showed that she had the illness.

Alex could see Niall and Ariadne's faces at the front. They saw him, too, and were whispering to each other with concerned expressions on their faces.

Cassia grabbed Alex's hand and said, "They are going to try to take you next."

Looking back down at her paper, Cravelda began to speak again, only this time her voice was much deeper.

"The second matter that we must attend to today is that of magic." Cravelda paused to brush her nose. Alex was too far away, but perhaps a small insect or feather had brushed against it. "It is illegal to practice magic in any part of Dacaan, and for those who are found to perpetrate the crime, well, they must be punished in the most severe way."

A rush of exclamations and murmurs ran briefly through the crowd again.

"In Dacaan, however, we believe in justice, and we believe in the law, so a full investigation will go into the circumstances in which the perpetrator has come across magic and used it against the Regime," explained Cravelda. "So without further ado, we ask the young boy who has committed this heinous act against the law to come forward."

Again, the crowd rustled, and parents now pulled their young boys close to them for fear of what was to come next. Alex's father's fingers touched the back of

Alex's hand, but he didn't look at his son's face. The crowd was quiet.

Growing impatient, Cravelda looked toward the back of the crowd, toward the stairs. "Will Alexander Kerr please step forward?" she demanded, pointing her finger for the patrol to begin their rush again through the mass of people. This time, they were rushing with their obsidian swords toward Alex.

CHAPTER 4

In all his life, Alex had never felt a moment that lasted so long. Often, he had felt that time would slow down, but this time it seemed to almost stand still. Everything was moving in slow motion. He saw Cravelda's finger pointed directly at him, as if her whole body were pointing itself.

The Champions behind Cravelda stood up with surprise and bewilderment. Alex noticed Queen Jocelyn raise her hands up to her face in shock, as if she wanted to cry or run into the crowds herself, but the patrol stopped her. Alex was surprised by her break in demeanor but had no time to think further on the matter. The crowd parted to avoid the patrol as they rushed forward with their dark-black, obsidian swords poised to attention in their hands. The swords were usually tied behind their belts, and Alex couldn't remember a time he had seen one so close, and never had they been coming at him in anger. Through the years he had watched them wielding at enemies in historical documentaries when the Regime fought the wars, but he had never thought that one day they might be wielded at him.

Alex's father turned around and looked him straight in the eye. He didn't seem to move at the slow speed as the rest of the scene, and he grabbed his son by the back of the neck and pulled him close.

"Listen to me, you must go now, go back to the house and take the box, Nova. It is not safe for you here anymore. Do not come for me, do not worry about me. I will be safe. This will all make sense soon, I promise. I love you, Nova." Alex's father turned back around to resume his position.

It was then that Alex heard it. High above the confused noise of the crowd that sounded like a record playing backward, he heard the swooping of wings.

"Nova, you must come, jump on," said a voice behind him. Turning around, Alex was shocked to see the large eagle that had flown alongside the bus. "There is no time to waste here, Nova. Jump on my back."

Alex hesitated but had no time to waste, as the bird had said. He realized this was his only hope and jumped on the back of the massive bird, soaring high into the sky. He grabbed on around the neck of the large eagle, the place where its soft down met its strong, dark, feathered frame. Alex had wondered many times in his life what it would be like to fly, but he had never dreamed of this. It was so silent up in the air, so peaceful. The air rushed over them, caressing the sides of his face and his forehead. When they caught a gust, the eagle lifted higher into the air naturally, while then effortlessly reversing itself. Alex could feel the strength of the eagle below him. It was powerful, it was old.

For a moment, Alex looked back at the crowd, who had all sped up into real time. The patrol was running down the stairs from the highlands, Cravelda was banging her hands against her thighs in complete anger and frustration, and the rest of the crowd was generally standing in shock, apart from one person he saw stumbling down the side of the mountain and through the woods ahead of the patrol. Could that be Cassia?

As if it already knew the plan, the eagle swept down toward Alex's cabin and perched on the ledge of the balcony to Alex's room. Alex rarely locked this door, as it was hard to get to since the cabin was on a rocky ledge on its westerly side. He jumped off the back of the eagle and ran into his room.

"Quickly, Nova," commanded the eagle as Alex went.

Inside, Alex picked up the box and put it in his bag. He also picked up a change of clothes and ran to the kitchen for another handful of granola bars, some boxes of orange juice, and more bottled water. His bag was small, and the box took up most of the room. There wasn't enough time to properly plan or pack. He ran quickly into the washroom and picked up his toothbrush.

Running back to his bedroom where the eagle sat, he was about to take off once again when he heard a loud knock at the door.

"Alex, it's me, Cassia."

Startled, Alex dropped his bag and ran to unlock the door. Cassia bolted in and locked it behind her.

"How did you get here so quickly?" he asked.

"Seriously, Alex? It doesn't matter . . . quickly" responded Cassia, looking slightly frustrated that he would ask something so ludicrous at such an urgent time as this.

Then Alex saw them, the patrol that were running down the street toward the house. Their black-and-silver-handled obsidian swords were glinting in the sun's rays. If the pair didn't leave in a few minutes, they would be leaving a different way with the patrol.

"Quickly, this way," said Alex as he pushed Cassia to his room and out onto the balcony.

Without any other questions and with a lot of bravery, both Cassia and Alex climbed onto the back of the eagle and soared up into the air. They were flying away from the patrol, away from Creston, away from their entire lives. Alex's predictions had come true.

❖

Alex had never seen Creston from above before. He had seen Creston from the top of the steps at the Obelisk, but not any higher. Right now, in that very moment, Alex wondered if he and Cassia were farther up in the sky than anyone from Creston had ever been. He knew that in Castlegar they had planes and helicopters that flew in the sky, but did they really touch the clouds like this? Alex wondered how much farther they needed to go to touch the stars or the comet he had seen.

Although so many things had just happened, for a short period of time Alex, Cassia, and the eagle remained quiet. Cassia, too, was looking around with a startled expression on her face. It was hard to consider the gravity of the situation when you were soaring so high up in the air that you were a part of the sky. Although Alex knew that clouds were made of water droplets, something he had learned in Grade 7 Sciences class, he was still in disbelief as they flew through the towering columns of misty vapor. They had always looked like cotton wool balls to him, and he expected their consistency to be just that: wooly.

For several minutes, the eagle swooped its wings and veered left and then right and then left again. Alex and Cassia held on tight for fear of falling off, but there was no need to be afraid, they both knew they were safe with the eagle. He had, in fact, rescued them after all; he was currently their best and only hope.

Breaking the serenity of the flight, Cassia pointed forward. Following her finger, Alex looked down and saw the reality of their world from quite literally a bird's-eye view. Behind them was the district of Creston and the Obelisk that could be seen vaguely in the distance. The perimeter fence that encircled their district and the exclusion zone around it with the various watch towers was outlined like an island in a sea of green forest. Alex had always known that other districts like Creston existed and saw some of their Championships on the communicator, but they had, of course, never been to them. Below them, Alex and Cassia could now see several other districts up the shore of Kootenay Lake. Beyond the lake, the sequence of perimeter-rimmed districts continued for as far as the eye could see. Many more than had ever been described in their geography lessons in school. Alex saw a white column somewhere in the middle of each and assumed this was their Obelisk or church. Each district was far enough away from the others that it was self-contained, buffered from the rest.

Cassia pointed again, this time in the other direction. Behind the mountains that Alex could see from his bedroom window lay another sea of green. In the center of it was a tall building with many towers and gleaming rooftops. Below the building was a city of every color under the rainbow. It stood alone with no other districts close to it.

"Castlegar!" exclaimed Cassia.

"Yes, that is the City of Castlegar," replied the eagle, as if Cassia had asked a question.

"You talk?" Cassia's question wasn't necessary, as the eagle had already proven that was the case.

"My name is Osiris, I came to bring you to Happenstance," said Osiris the Eagle. Osiris was a wise eagle—the wisest of all the eagles, in fact.

"Where is Happenstance?" asked Alex.

"Unfortunately, I nor anyone else can properly answer that question," said Osiris.

"So, you have stolen us away from our home to take us to a place, but you don't know where it is," retorted Cassia smartly.

"You were not meant to come on this journey," stated Osiris, who sounded irritated by Cassia's comment but unsure of what to do with her.

"Well, wherever Alex goes, I go," snapped Cassia. "He can't make it without me."

To that Osiris laughed. "You are a very strong girl. What is your name?"

"Cassia."

"Well, Cassia, I am very pleased to announce that Nova is stronger than both myself and you combined, he just doesn't know it yet."

"Why do you keep on calling him Nova? His name is Alex, so you should call him by his real name," stated Cassia matter-of-factly.

"The young man on my back is Nova. He is only

beginning to know it, but he will understand it very soon, and you must support him if you are going to stay by his side," said the giant eagle as he started to make a dip down toward a space between two districts. Alex could see smoke coming from the space below them.

"Is that Happenstance?" Alex asked Osiris.

"No, this is a stop that we must take on the way there. We will rest the night, it should be safe."

Alex had hardly noticed the sun nestling itself on the mountaintops. The sky shone the color of cotton candy pink, orange, and mauve as they descended.

❖

The smell of bonfire was the first thing Alex noticed. Smoke slithered like a gray snake into the air and dissipated into nothing but a strong odor. Osiris worked his way around it as he prepared for his landing.

On the ground were about two dozen men. As they approached, the main thing Alex noticed about them was the amount of facial hair and the odd-looking garments they were wearing. It was actually quite hard to see them from the air until you got closer and could distinguish hats, pipes, and swords.

The men seemed to know Osiris. One of them was waving both arms frantically in the air and pointing for Osiris to land farther away from the camp and the fire.

"Who are these people?" asked Cassia in awe.

"The Nomans," was all that Osiris said as he landed on the tall, soft grass. Alex wondered if he was more used to landing in trees, because they came down with a sudden thud that threw both Cassia and him to the grassy ground.

The man who had been gesturing came running over and pulled Cassia up from the grass first and then offered Alex a hand, which Alex politely refused.

"We've been waiting for you, suppers on the spit," said the gracious man, who was wearing jean overalls and a green-and-tan-plaid shirt. No one in Creston wore these sorts of clothes.

"Oh, and beg my pardon, my name is Christian Davies. Most around here call me Davies, but you both can call me whatever you'd like," explained the stranger. He seemed overly keen at their arrival. "It's great to see you've arrived safely, Nova," continued Davies, who didn't seem to like silences. "And who is this lovely young lady with you?"

Davies grabbed Cassia's hand and gave it a kiss. Her face flushed with a bashful smile, which Alex was surprised by.

"Cassia Maddox," she replied after being caught slightly off guard. "It is a pleasure to meet you, Davies."

Cassia smiled—a seal of approval—and followed Davies as he headed toward the camp. Alex followed closely behind her with Osiris.

At the camp, the men gathered around to make their acquaintance. They all seemed to be very light-spirited like Davies and smiled from ear to ear to see their guests.

"Osiris wouldn't stop talking about you," said a short, dumpy man with a weakly grown beard. Alex guessed the man might have been about twice his own age but half the age of the rest of the camp. He also couldn't help but notice that he wasn't wearing any socks or shoes, as were none of the other men around him.

"Leonard Shrewsbury, most of this lot call me Shrew," the dumpy man said, offering out his hand.

Alex realized that he rarely shook hands, as he knew most of the people he was used to seeing in Creston.

The group exchanged names and welcomes and sat on a circle of flat stones around the fire. Three wild turkeys were on spits above the fire, and Davies spent a lot of his time both talking and turning the meat. He treated it as if it were his masterpiece, moving it back and forth from the flame, so that the meat cooked just perfectly.

Alex had so many questions, but he decided it wasn't the best time. He could tell by the furrow lines on Cassia's forehead when she looked at him that she was equally perplexed. The group asked many questions themselves, and as the night approached and the sun had completely set, Alex noticed that a majority of the questions were about Creston, their upbringing, what they thought of the Regime, had they been to Castlegar, and so on. Cassia gave most of the responses with some interesting stories, often getting a hearty laugh from many of the men, while others seemed to have more somber expressions.

In a quieter moment in the evening when a few of the men had gone to patrol the area, Alex dared to ask Shrew a few questions.

"So, which district are we in?" He felt like this was a polite and nonintrusive start.

Shrew lifted his eyebrow a little and looked around the faces of the others who were close enough to hear them, before slowly starting to speak.

"Right now, you are in Nolandia, the space between districts."

Alex had never heard of Nolandia before. In fact, nothing was ever said about this land between lands. Alex had always thought of it as the scary unknown. Like a black void that belonged to no one and meant nothing. Now he found out that it had a name and even a purpose—to house the Nomans—and he liked that.

"And which district did you come from?" he continued, eager to uncover more unknowns.

"I'm from Penticton, a district close to Creston in the Okanagan Valley," Shrew began, saying every word in a much more considered tone than when he'd been the question asker.

Alex tried to recall one of the Penticton District Championships he had watched a few years ago; they had strong talent and eager spirits in that community.

Shrew continued, "I've been in these parts of Nolandia for more years than I can remember. We don't keep time too good, you see. This is just one of our homes, us Nomans are nomads, you see. We go wherever the wind blows us and wherever they won't bother us." The man's reply left Alex with more questions again than answers.

"Why did you leave Penticton?" asked Alex, thinking faster than his mouth could control itself.

Shrew stopped at this question and looked at the others, who all went quiet and looked toward them. Alex made a gulping sound that he hoped was too quiet for the rest to hear.

"Go on, tell 'em, lad," said a man named Sedwin, who was one of the taller men of the group. His head was shaved around the sides, and he wore a silver bun on the top.

Alex noticed that Shrew looked uneasy as he adjusted his position on a log he was sitting on slightly behind the rest of the group.

"They took my family, all eight of them. It was a cold night in November, and my sister had become ill. A neighbor in passing must of heard her coughing and thought that it was all of us, you see. The next day she came down with a fever, and we were all worried about her, she was just a fragile thing. It was another two days, and the illness took her." Shrew paused for a minute to gather himself.

"My mother called for the district doctor. We had thought she was just sick, but we didn't ever think it would happen that way. She died, you see." He hesitated again before inhaling loudly. "Then the patrol came with their obsidian swords, and they took her body and buried it behind the house, and they took us and piled us all on the back of a cart to take us away. They thought we were all sick, you see. They thought we had the virus."

Sedwin circled around the fire that was now simmering and walked toward Shrew. He patted him on the back. "Go on, lad," he muttered.

"They was gonna take us to Castlegar. We were afraid and it was dark. I'm the second eldest, and my little brothers and sisters were shivering and crying. So, they took us up the path and then the cart just stopped, and Sedwin here was there in the middle of the road, yelling, telling us to run. Well, I picked up young Finlay, and my mother and father tried to help the others. We tried to get them away, but one by one the patrol caught them. But

I was saved. It was Davies and Marcelle who grabbed me from some bushes and told me to run. I felt ashamed leaving my family, but Davies told me it was the only way to save them. We've been trying to save them ever since," he stopped abruptly as if all the breath had left his body.

"Be free, be people, be Nomans," they all murmured as emotion washed over the camp.

After a few minutes, Osiris decided it was time for bed. "Nova and Cassia must rest. They have a big journey still, and who knows what lies ahead of us."

"Come with me, young'uns, I'll show you yer tent," said Sedwin. He had an accent that Alex could hardly understand; he had never heard it in Dacaan before.

The pair got up and went to their tent. They thanked Sedwin, who asked them to 'hollar if they needed anything.' They kicked off their shoes, slumped their bags on the floor, and sat on the bed.

Alex remembered that he had packed granola bars and decided to open one, offering the other to Cassia, who happily accepted. Neither of them was used to spit-roasted turkey, so they were over the moon with the bars' familiarity.

"What a day," said Cassia as she flopped herself back onto the bed. She lay there staring up at the top of the tent. Through the vent they could see one or two stars sparkling overhead.

Silence filled the tent. So many thoughts raced through both of their heads. Everything was exciting and new, but also terrifying. They had arrived in a strange new world that was so different from their creature comforts. Alex knew that he could never return to Creston. He thought about his father and tears came to his eyes, so he rolled onto his side to hide his real emotions from Cassia.

"Are you ok?" Cassia said. Alex had always thought she was slightly too intuitive.

"Yes, of course," he muttered.

Feeling confident that the tears weren't going to expose him, he sat up and swung his legs onto the floor and looked at Cassia.

"You can't stay, Cassia," he said. "Your family needs you, and it is not safe."

"Well, I could say the same for you, mister," she retorted, with an emphasis on the word you.

Just then, Osiris entered the tent. He could hardly fit through the entrance and had to sidestep to get himself through. He looked even bigger when inside the tent. If it were a few weeks ago, Alex realized that he would be terrified of Osiris. It was still hard to believe that a bird could talk and be friends with a group of humans. It was also hard to believe there were humans living outside of the districts and who seemed to be thriving.

"Nova is right," said Osiris, "you cannot continue on his path with him. At the moment when the moon sets we will take Nova to the moonbow, and then, Cassia, I will return you to Creston safely."

"That will not be possible!" exclaimed Cassia. "Whether both of you like it or not, I will be going with Alex. His path is now my path too."

Cassia looked across at Alex with serenity in her eyes. He knew that she would not take 'no' for an answer.

Osiris ignored her as if she had said nothing. "Nova, do you still have the box?"

Alex reached down the bed and pulled the box out from his bag, thankful that it was still there.

"I would recommend you open it now, Nova, so that you become familiar with it," Osiris said, nodding his head that it would be all right.

It was then that Alex realized the key was not in the keyhole. He rummaged around in his bag and even tipped it upside down, but there was nothing, and then he remembered how the key had slid from the keyhole and fallen to his bedroom floor. He looked up at Osiris.

"I . . . I left it in my room," he said with shame in his voice.

"Well, I must go and retrieve it immediately," said Osiris with little hesitation. He turned around to head straight for the door.

"I'll come with you," said Alex.

"You cannot, it is too dangerous. I need you both to take some rest so that you are ready before the moon sets. I will wake you."

Alex felt embarrassment wash over him; it was a feeling he was getting used to. He was disappointed, and he thought of his father who had asked him to do this one task. He had failed. Angered, he got under the sheets, facing away from Cassia as he knew that tears were now running down his face, but this time they wouldn't stop.

The loud swoop of Osiris's wings as he took flight and the word 'Goodnight' from Cassia were the last things Alex remembered. Cassia blew out the candles, and they both fell into a deep sleep.

❖

Alex awoke to shouting. In the few seconds it took for him to open his eyes and alert himself to his new surroundings, he knew there was trouble. There were sounds of people moving and objects being knocked over in camp and the sound of birds in the sky.

"Cassia, wake up." He couldn't believe she was still asleep. He went over and shook her to get her attention. "Something's happening. Get your things, quick!"

Cassia was groggy; it took her a few minutes to properly wake up. Alex remembered this from when they were kids and they would have sleepovers at each other's houses, or from when they went camping with Niall and Ariadne in the summer. She was always the last one to get up, and boy don't you dare talk to her for at least an hour when she did finally wake up.

Alex grabbed all the items in their tent and put them into either his or Cassia's bag. He couldn't see very well because it was still dark out, but there was just enough light coming through the top of the tent from the stars and what he believed was the comet.

"Where are we, what's going on?" grumbled Cassia.

"Well, not to alarm you, but we narrowly escaped Creston yesterday as the patrol were chasing me. We flew on the back of an eagle named Osiris—who talks, by the way—and we are now in the camp of Nomans who live in the empty space between districts, Nolandia."

As if on cue, Osiris entered the tent to add, "And we must get you both out of here immediately. The Regime saw me at your house, Alex, and it has followed us. We must leave for Happenstance at once."

Cassia shot up out of bed with the sound of Osiris's booming voice, realizing the gravity of the situation.

All three of them ran out of the tent and saw that most of the Nomans were packing up their things to get ready to leave.

"Nova, Osiris, Cassia, we hope to see you all soon. Have a safe journey," said Shrew as he flew past at an alarming pace.

A light dew had settled on the grass in the fields around them. The fire pit let off a small trail of smoke now from embers that were soon to go out. Above them, the sky was getting brighter in the east, and the moon was sitting at two o'clock behind a cluster of streaky clouds. The comet shone bright to its right.

"Nova, open the box, it's time," commanded Osiris.

"Should we not leave first?" asked Alex. There was a sound in the distance of squawking birds and a mechanical whirring that couldn't be ignored. It was loud and ominous. Without having to ask, Alex somehow knew it was the Regime.

"No, we need to open the box first so that we can escape. The helicopters are far enough away. I tricked them on the way here and sent them in another direction. But we don't have long," responded Osiris.

"Helicopters?" asked Cassia sleepily. She looked bewildered.

"The patrol use them to control the skies, but they are slower than me, don't worry." Osiris seemed surprisingly assured at their situation, given the pending attack.

Alex was afraid. Everything was moving so quickly, and it all felt out of his control.

He dropped to the ground and grabbed the box.

"Here," said Osiris, dropping the key from his beak.

Alex put the key in the box and turned it. Again, the

light shone from the box, and a mist began to seep out of it.

Cassia jumped back, startled, while also watching intently.

"You must give it the command, Nova, hurry," said Osiris.

"What command? I don't know how to use it, and there is nothing inside," said Alex, frustrated. He put his hand in the box, and to his surprise there was something in it on the bottom. A piece of paper. Alex was shocked that it just appeared in such a way, but he pulled it out in any case and realized it was an old scroll. He opened the scroll and read the words to a poem he had never seen before.

"If you want to take the chance, say"—Nova stopped but saw Osiris nodding his head approvingly—"take me now to Happenstance."

Suddenly, the scroll peeled itself from Alex's hands, rolled itself up, and shot firmly back into the box. The box lid shut with a bang, and the key pulled itself from the lock and crawled to Alex's arm where it turned into a gold band, which was surprisingly warm on his skin.

Alex looked over and saw that Cassia had both hands over her mouth in shock. He also couldn't believe his eyes.

The box then lifted into the air, and it hovered in front of them before dissipating into even more mist and forming a bridge from the ground to the sky. The bridge was a variety of colors like a rainbow, only in dark monotones of bluish-gray. It was beautiful.

Osiris squawked louder than any bird Alex had heard before.

"I have called for the other eagles. The patrol will see the moonbow and will be on their way, so we must distract them as you make your way up it. Go quickly!" barked Osiris. He had made an order, not a suggestion.

Osiris walked toward Cassia and picked her up by the back of the neck like a cat might pick up its kitten.

"You are waiting here until I return," he muttered oddly, as he couldn't fully speak with his beak full. He moved to place Cassia on a rock near a tree out of sight.

"No." Alex replied in the most forceful tone he had made in his life. "Drop her, Osiris. Cassia will be coming with me . . . if, Cassia, that is still what you want to do?"

"Yes," was all she could reply as Osiris released her from his beak and she tumbled into the grass.

"Your wish is my command," responded Osiris, bowing toward Alex in a way that Alex found quite strange. No one had listened to his commands so readily in his life.

Cassia rushed over to Alex, and they embraced, looking up toward the sky.

"Are you sure this is what you want? It could be dangerous," Alex said to Cassia.

"Yes, Alex, you need me, and you know it," said Cassia toughly, letting go of him and shuffling her bag on her shoulder.

Looking back to Osiris, Alex said, "Thank you. We appreciate everything you've done for us, Osiris."

Osiris gave a small bow once again. "Until we meet again, Nova."

Osiris briefly watched as the pair made their first steps onto the moonbow and into the sky before flying in the opposite direction.

Holding hands, Alex and Cassia ran together as fast as they could with the sounds of birds and metal clanging as the battle took place in the skies behind them. The sun was rising higher in the east, and the moon had almost disappeared. This was the way they made their escape from Dacaan to Happenstance.

CHAPTER 5

When Alex awoke, the sun was shining through the trees. He felt patches of warmth on his skin, and when he opened his eyes the sun mottled his vision. He put his arm up to his forehead and tried to gather himself.

Cassia was lying close to him. She, too, was beginning to wake up and look around her.

The pair was surrounded by thickets of purple flowers that invited them to drink in their odor. A breeze was blowing from what felt like below the hill where they were perched. It blew up across them before sweeping into the skies above. Below them was a sandy beach, more sand than Alex had ever seen before. They got only a little sand in Creston at the beach on Kootenay Lake, as it was mostly rocky. The water was also foaming in toward the shore in a way that Alex had never noticed. He loved when the winds blew and the lake near his house would angrily swell up and down. He remembered a time when there had been a storm, and he and Cassia sat on their rock where the mouth of Sanca River met the lake and watched as the waves dared to splash up all around them. But right here and now there was no storm, and there was something different about this water. It looked almost emerald where it kissed the bay and deep navy quite soon thereafter where it stretched out farther than the eye could see.

Cassia stood up. "Well, this is different," she commented. She always had a knack of stating the obvious, and Alex often chose not to answer. He shot one of his crooked smiles her way, revealing his feelings of both excitement and apprehension.

Together they turned around to look behind them, and, to their surprise, there was a rainbow. It wasn't like the moonbow. Rather than shades of gray, it was beautiful and bold and shining red, orange, yellow, green, blue, and purple. It was so close to them that Alex thought he could reach out and touch it.

"I wonder if we start walking if it would take us right on back to Creston?" asked Cassia with a sigh.

"Cassia, you didn't have to come," replied Alex, feeling a huge amount of guilt about a number of things. Cassia had given up the security of her home and her family to be here in this place with him. He didn't even know where they were or whether they were safe.

"Alex, I don't want to talk about that again. I chose to be here with you, and you tried to stop me, but I wanted to come," said Cassia as she gathered her bag that was in a thicket close by. She opened it up and started rummaging through. Cassia always had a way of causing a commotion with something around her when she was frustrated.

Alex, too, went over and picked up his bag and opened the leather clasp. In doing so, he felt the band on his arm and remembered that he had not exactly put it on himself. Rather, it had found its way to him. He sat there for a minute just staring at it. It didn't look like a key; it looked like a piece of jewelry that one of the Champions might wear to a Championship. He noticed it had markings around its outside that looked perhaps like numbers. To inspect it closer, he took the band off and peered at it and then put it in the grass for a moment to go into his bag and get a bottle of water. He realized just how thirsty he really was and gulped the water down until the bottle was gone. He offered a second bottle to Cassia, which she accepted.

Turning back, he looked down to the grass where he had put the band just a moment before, and to his surprise it was gone. He started moving the grass around him, picking up small, flat rocks and throwing them aside. He checked in his pockets and all over himself, but he couldn't find it.

"Whatcha looking for?" asked Cassia.

"The armband . . . or the key . . . or whatever it is. I took it off for a moment and now it's gone!"

Cassia came over and started looking.

Alex picked up his bag, and just as he was about to tip it inside out, he noticed that the armband was now a key, which sat in the keyhole of the box.

"Look, silly, you left it there, in the keyhole, where a key lives," scoffed Cassia, who was also looking slightly dubious.

Just as she said that, the key started to rattle around in the hole.

"What should I do?" asked Alex.

"Well, open it, silly," said Cassia, who seemed to be getting more used to these abnormal events than Alex was. She had always been braver than Alex, like the time she jumped off the roof of her house into the snow when he'd been too afraid.

The key stopped wiggling, giving Alex a little more confidence. He grabbed ahold of it and twisted it again in the box and opened the lid. A small amount of mist trickled out over the grass around them, but not as much as before.

Alex hesitated, looking at Cassia for a moment, and then put his hand inside of the box, which felt like it was a lot deeper than it looked from the outside since most of his arm was now inside. Alex moved his hand around for a moment and felt another paper.

Lifting it out, he unfolded the paper. It was a map, and it looked in good condition. It also looked more ancient than anything Alex or Cassia had seen in school as it was different colors of beige and brown. The top of the map read *Happenstance Island*, and there was an X in the middle of the map with the words 'You Are Here.' Above the X was a depiction of a beach with 'Founders Cove' written above it and the blue imprint of water with the name 'Emerald Sea' on it.

Cassia pointed out toward the water and said, "That's it, that's the Emerald Sea, and this is Founders Cove."

Pointing at the map and looking up again, she continued, "How does the map know where we are?"

Ignoring her question, Alex looked farther down the map and in looking at the place in its entirety, he realized that the other places were slightly faded so that they could not entirely read where they were meant to go. Overwhelmed, Alex rolled up the map and placed it in his backpack. He would look more closely later.

"Cassia, I'm hungry, and we will need more than the granola bars in my bag," said Alex, feeling frustrated.

Coming from Creston and having visited no other places in their lives, Alex and Cassia were used to running to the deli for a sandwich or the bakery for something sweet. There was also always food in their houses, which was mostly provided by the Regime, who helped in bringing supplies from other districts. Creston was well-known among the districts for its salmon and hardwood, which they would swap with the Regime for the other districts' goods. These items were rationed, but Alex loved the days when the ship would arrive at the harbor and they would receive new stock. He always cooked a dinner of roasted meat on those days.

"Well, I'm hungry too, but I don't see anything around, so chuck me a granola bar," said Cassia.

The pair sat snacking on their granola bars. Alex was dissatisfied.

"My hair smells like that campfire from last night," complained Cassia, who had untangled her braids and was sniffing them and crinkling her nose. She looked down to the sparkling water.

"I'll make you a deal," she chirped.

Alex always knew when she was cooking up a plan because she had this suspicious look in her eyes. It reminded him of a fox that he once saw sneaking up on a rabbit before pouncing. He nodded for her to continue.

"Let's go for a swim, and then let's head over the meadow toward those trees. The coastline looks like it wraps around, and we are on one side of the island from that map, so surely if we move inland we will find people, some shops, and some food."

Knowing that when Cassia made up a plan she wouldn't take 'no' for an answer, Alex replied, "Okay, but no pushing me in this time."

The two left their bags and went running down the hill through the tall grass, kicking their shoes and socks off as they went. They had often gone swimming in just their undergarments when they were young, but as they got older, Alex had noticed Cassia was increasingly shy with these things. Alex took off his T-shirt and pants and stood at the edge of the water in his boxer shorts, looking outwards so that Cassia didn't think he was staring.

"Come on, slow poke!" she yelled as she went running into the water.

Alex followed her, and they both dove in. Coming up out of the water, he coughed and sputtered, as did Cassia.

"It tastes like salt!" he exclaimed, having never been to the sea before.

The shock of the salty water was quite alarming, but he smiled at Cassia and they splashed each other and jumped around with a frivolity they hadn't felt since their last time in the water in Creston.

"Children, come here at once," yelled a strange voice from the shoreline.

Alex and Cassia immediately stopped what they were doing to look up and see who it was and whether they were in danger.

Looking back toward the coast, they saw a man coming down the same path they had descended just a few minutes before. He must have run straight past their bag and things. Alex worried about the box but saw that the man's hands were empty.

The man was quite tall, and he didn't entirely look like

any man Alex had ever seen before. He had a hunched back and a round belly around the middle. His dark, black hair and long facial hair were quite disheveled.

Fearful of the stranger, the children stood submerged in the water. Cassia looked toward Alex for reassurance.

"Tidings to Lady Luck!" the stranger exclaimed. "Now, what are you doing in there, wee ones? You must be freezing! Come on now, we must get you dried, and I've got a lovely picnic just up the way with the family."

Feeling nervous, Alex couldn't think of what to do but yell, "Who are you?"

"Well I'm Barnaby O'Neill of course. You can call me Barnaby. Me and my family are from Founders Cove here, the cove that you are swimming in now," he replied to ensure they understood that it wasn't him who was the one out of place, because he in fact lived here and they didn't.

"That's the name that the map gave us," said Cassia to Alex. "He has food, and he looks nice enough." She started to walk out of the water, covering herself so the others wouldn't see.

"Would you both mind turning around for a minute," she said, shaking her head.

"Oh, yes of course," replied Barnaby, turning promptly.

Alex could feel his face going slightly red at the thought of Cassia's modesty.

He looked the other way down the coastline. According to the map, that direction was east, and it had beautiful columns of rock and many flying birds that were cawing and nesting in cliff faces. Then Alex noticed it. A girl with violet hair on the rocks—or was it a fish? He squinted but couldn't quite make it out.

"What is that over there?" he asked Barnaby.

"Oh, that's our mermaid, Giselle, she's no bother," he replied, heading up the hill as if seeing a mermaid were nothing.

Alex turned back and heard her song as it picked up in the wind and echoed hauntingly in the cove. It was both mournful and mesmerizing. He wished he could hear the words. She glanced up slowly, locking eyes with Alex's stare, and dove into the water.

After a few minutes he turned back, and Cassia was dressed and already talking to Barnaby as they walked back toward their things on the hillside. Alex rushed out of the water, grabbing his clothes on the beach, feeling he needed to stay closer to Cassia to make sure she was safe with this man that neither of them knew.

As Alex got closer, he noticed that the man wore a knife in a belt on the side of his body, and he grabbed Cassia's hand and pulled her back toward him.

"What are you doing, Alex—that hurt me!" she yelled at him.

"We must be safe, we don't belong here," Alex responded.

"Why, yes of course, young sir, you do in fact belong here now. One of you holds the key to Happenstance, and you can't get entry without the key. I saw you arrive on the rainbow a little while ago and as my wife was already packing a picnic. We decided to head this way, to Founders Cove to come and find you," said Barnaby with a jolly smile on his face. He had the reddest cheeks that Alex had ever seen, and although he was rather ugly in appearance, there was a kindness to his eyes that implied his good nature and good intentions.

"How did you know we were coming?" asked Alex, who was trying to piece together what he had just heard from Barnaby.

"Well, the rainbow almost always means that someone new has arrived, and well, I didn't know it was going to be you, but I knew it was going to be somebody new. I'm the troll here, you see. Founders Cove has the most rainbows on the entire island of Happenstance, so my job is to look for rainbows and the newcomers who have come here on them."

Cassia and Alex looked at each other, perplexed.

"There are others?" questioned Cassia.

"Well yes, not lots, but a few, and we need to support them when they arrive so that they can find their way," said Barnaby, who now turned around and continued walking up the hill toward their things.

"Where do they find their way to?" asked Alex, trying to understand more of what Barnaby was saying and trying to find out more about where they might be headed.

"Well, that is always the question, and we will find out soon," smiled Barnaby over his shoulder as they arrived at their bags.

Cassia began piling up her belongings and clipped her bag shut. Alex had left the box open, to his surprise, so he closed it and pulled the key from it. The key came alive in his hand again and crawled up his arm to clasp back onto it.

"Ah, so you're the one with the key," said Barnaby, and he added, "I must say, I've rarely seen two arrive together unless they are family—you must be siblings, I presume?"

Cassia looked at Alex with his very different appearance to her own and laughed.

"No, I'm just a friend. My name is Cassia," she said, holding out her hand. "Very nice to meet you, Mr. O'Neill."

"Oh, it's Barnaby," he said, smiling, and shook Cassia's hand with one of his hands over the top of her own.

"And I'm . . . well . . ." started Alex, looking at Cassia. He was about to say 'Nova' because it seemed that everyone already knew him by this name, but he hesitated. "My name is Alex."

"Well, it's a pleasure to meet you both," said Barnaby. "Now come on, you both must be hungry."

The trio walked for just a few minutes farther up the hill before they could see it.

"There's my lighthouse, right over there, and my family," said Barnaby.

A tall, white-and-red-circular building rose from a grassy cliff ledge like a beacon. It was beautiful, and Alex and Cassia had never seen anything like it before. Alex was surprised they hadn't seen it from the water, but perhaps they just hadn't been looking for it.

A woman who looked somewhat like a female version of Barnaby was stepping out of the door at the bottom of the lighthouse, holding a wicker hamper under one arm and a young baby in her other. A small, scruffy dog came bounding out toward them and started barking excitedly before licking their ankles and hands as they leaned down to pat its head.

"Ah, you found them, Barnaby, and you've got two—splendid. Well, tidings to Lady Luck!" said the lady with the same jolly smile and red cheeks as Barnaby.

"Yes, that's exactly what I thought. We've got lucky and got two today. This is Cassia and Alex," said Barnaby.

"Well, hello. I'm Siobhan, and this is little Paddy," said Barnaby's wife. "I hope that I've made enough eel and pickle sandwiches."

Alex and Cassia shot a worried look at each other at the thought of what the sandwiches contained.

Siobhan spread out a blanket in the grass and placed the hamper down. Everyone found their place on the patchwork blanket and kicked their shoes off. Placing the plates and napkins among them, Siobhan then proceeded to take out the eel and pickle sandwiches.

"I wasn't expecting two," said Siobhan.

"Don't worry, we can share," said Cassia, looking at Alex knowingly.

Cassia picked up one of the plates and a napkin and accepted a sandwich, which was perfectly cut in half so that the two could share.

Siobhan also pulled out some cheese, crackers, and olives, which Cassia tucked into and put on their plate.

"Bon appétit," said Barnaby as he ravenously began munching into his sandwich.

Alex and Cassia had never heard this saying before, but they responded with "bon appétit" and smiled wearily before picking up the sandwiches. They were just hungry enough from the long journey and the swim that they were willing to taste the unappetizing meal, even if just a bite.

Alex bit in first, wincing a little as his teeth cut through the center of the sandwich that contained the eel. Trying not to chew too many times, he quickly swallowed it down in one gulp before realizing it was actually not that bad after all.

"Very tasty, thank you," he said to Siobhan before looking toward Cassia and nodding his head.

"The two of you have never eaten eel before, have you?" said Barnaby with a smile in his eyes, since his mouth was now madly crunching on the cheese, crackers, and olives.

"You see," Barnaby started before wiping the back of his arm across his face, "things in Happenstance seem to be different to other places where people like you come from. We eat different, we talk different, we look different, and we do different. You'll learn to understand over time, I'm sure. But there's one thing in Happenstance that all the people have, and that's the same belief." He reached down onto the blanket and touched the hand of Siobhan, who was cradling their young babe.

❖

After an entire day with the O'Neills, which mainly consisted of eating and talking, Siobhan showed Alex and Cassia to their room in the lighthouse. It was a modestly sized room with bunkbeds on one side and a seating area on the other with two seats and a table. It would be perfect for the two of them. The most splendid thing about the room was the fantastic view over the Emerald Sea to the west as they watched the sun set.

Alex offered to take the top bunk thinking that it would be the chivalrous thing to do, but Cassia had already decided she would take it. She slung her bag up and was already climbing up the side of the bunk.

Little Alfie, the dog, had also made up his mind that he would be taking the bottom bunk and was curled up at the foot of the bed.

Alex reached into his bag and pulled out the box with Nova on it and sat in a chair facing out the window. It looked like Cassia had already fallen asleep, so he wanted to take some time alone to sit and think.

He ran his hand over the carved wood on the box and over the name Nova. How had his father known about this name, and had he kept the box down in the cellar for all these years? Why did he wait until now to give it to him, and how had the eagle known to come for him?

Alex had always been different from the other children he knew. He had never struggled in school, and he liked to get caught up in his thoughts. He wasn't outgoing like Cassia, Niall, and Ariadne. He could spend time with them or his father or himself.

Growing up, he had spent a lot of time thinking of his mother. Because she had died when he was little, he didn't even remember her. There were many times when he held back tears when he thought of his mother and often—although he would never admit it—those tears were tears of anger. He was upset that she had left him, left him with his father who he'd mainly had to take care of for most of his childhood. And then he would feel angry at himself for feeling this way. Alex had always wanted what other children had: a stable family where the mother would cook the dinner and the father would teach you how to fish.

Now, it seemed, that all of what Alex had known about his life and his past could be wrong, or at least some of it. And his life certainly wouldn't go back to whatever it was before. He reached in his bag and pulled out his communicator, hoping he might have received a message from his father, although it was unlikely as his father stayed away from technology.

"Well, you won't be using that here in Happenstance, young man. It won't work," said Siobhan as she entered the room.

"Oh, I didn't realize," said Alex, looking down at the device and feeling even further from his father than ever.

"I've brought a warm mug of chamomile tea for you, my dear," said Siobhan in a hushed voice, "and I see there that Cassia is asleep. I'd brought her one as well." She slid the tray of tea including a teapot, cubes of sugar, and a small carafe of pouring milk onto the table in front of him.

"Thank you, Siobhan," said Alex as he slowly awoke from his thoughts.

Siobhan had the baby wrapped tightly around her chest in a sling. He, too, was sleeping.

"Well, perhaps I'll join you if you wouldn't mind," she said, and before he could respond, she sat down in the other chair facing toward him.

Siobhan poured the tea into the matching cups that sat on matching saucers. She put one lump of sugar in each and gave a small pour of milk before stirring them both.

"I thought it might help you sleep. Well you, not all of you need help with that," said Siobhan as she nodded in Cassia's direction at the top of the bed. Cassia was lying there making no sound at all. She hadn't even taken off her day clothes.

"You've both had a very long day and had a long ways

to travel. I know it's a lot for most that come our way, but you've done very well. Both of you have," said Siobhan, looking into her cup as she was speaking before glancing up at Alex to make sure he was following.

"Yes, it certainly has, and thank you and Barnaby again for your hospitality," said Alex, a little unsure of what to say as he, too, was feeling sleepy. He was, however, happy that Siobhan was there. There was something relaxing about her presence and her doting on them that he enjoyed. It made him think of what having a mother would be like.

Siobhan looked down at Alex's lap, at the box he was holding. "Now, what have you got there, sonny?" she asked.

"It's a box, my father gave it to me . . ." Alex hesitated, realizing he shouldn't give too much away if Siobhan didn't know about a magical box like he had in his lap.

"Well, it certainly is beautiful, and it must be a very prized possession of yours if it made the trip all the way to Happenstance," Siobhan responded with a soft smile.

Alex smiled too, thinking of his father and of how happy receiving this gift from him made him feel. He felt like it connected them on a deeper level that he didn't quite understand yet.

Sitting there in comfortable silence, Siobhan seemed to notice that the sun was gone and the last of the light was fading with it over the horizon. She reached into a deep pocket in the apron on the front of her dress and pulled out a match. She struck the match and lit a candle that sat on the table in front of them. The candle threw off more light than Alex had expected.

"Siobhan," started Alex, feeling his eyes grow heavy

and wanting to hear a story like his father would often give before bed and knowing that she would very well tell him, "tell me the story of Happenstance. What sort of kingdom is it?"

"I'm glad you asked me that question," said Siobhan.

She drank her tea down and tipped the bottom of Alex's cup so he would too. She then held her hand out and walked Alex toward the bottom bunk and tucked him under the covers. Alex didn't mind that he was also still in his day clothing. He realized he didn't have much to change into.

"Many, many moons ago, before Dacaan was Dacaan, there was a war. It's a war that you've probably not heard of before. There was good, there was evil, and there was everything in between. During this war, evil was more powerful and prevailed over good. It destroyed the people, the land, and everything that we know is just. But, evil could not win the stars, and without the stars, evil could not exist." Siobhan stood up for a moment to rock the baby as it murmured, perhaps at the grave tone that entered her voice and the room.

"Can you tell me more about the stars?" asked Alex when Siobhan returned to his bedside and as he buried his head further in his pillow.

Pushing a short, blond lock of hair behind his ears, Siobhan continued, "The stars wouldn't fight the evil because without darkness they, too, would not exist. So, they struck a deal. The stars would create a new world, and evil could have the world. What you now know as Dacaan. So, it was agreed. The stars created Happenstance."

"So, Happenstance is a place for good?"

"Happenstance is a place for magic and good, yes," replied Siobhan. "As evil took over the world and created the Realm of Dacaan, it fought off magic because magic was too powerful. So magic found its way to Happenstance."

Seeing Alex falling asleep, Siobhan pulled up his blanket a few more inches to nestle him in. She went to the window and closed the curtain and blew out the candle. She walked toward the hallway and Alex could see the outline of her body before she walked through the door.

"But where is the evil now . . ." Alex tried to ask a final question, but she was gone and so was he, into his dreams.

❖

Alex was in the desert. He faintly remembered being here before, but the memory was not vivid. There were hills of sand all around him, and they glimmered under the hot midday sun in purple, blue, and fuchsia-pink colors. It was beautiful and reminded him of the colors on the top of a birthday cake that his aunt had made him when he was just five years old.

The sun was so hot in the sky. He had never felt so hot before, and he worried that he would melt into a puddle and seep into the thirsty grains of sand. His mouth was drier than it had ever been before, and he felt like everything around him felt the same way. The sand that stretched as far as the eye could see was dazzling but hungry for water.

Suddenly, he noticed the sun was setting at an alarming rate. He welcomed the reprieve from the midday heat but didn't want to be alone here, in a place he didn't know in the dark. Out of fear he began yelling, "Hello, hello, is anyone out there?" but there was no reply.

Down in the valley he saw some movement, and, feeling like he couldn't stand a second longer being alone, he ran down toward it. As he got closer, he saw that it was an antelope with curly horns.

"Don't come closer," he thought he saw the antelope mouth at him.

He couldn't help himself; he ran and ran and got closer, almost close enough to touch the beast who curiously didn't move like most wild animals might do when they sensed a quick movement.

As he approached, behind the animal a black ink stain marked itself on the horizon and dyed the sky maroon. In the cloud was a beast he had seen before. It had yellow and red eyes and a forked tongue. It stood up in the sky and opened its jaws wide to reveal large fangs.

"Noooooooo," yelled Alex as he pushed the antelope away before the serpent's mouth descended slowly to engulf it, leaving himself in the line of the serpent as it came closer and closer.

❖

"Alex, wake up. It's just a dream," said Cassia, who was shaking Alex.

Alex opened his eyes. He was sweating and could feel that his body had been lashing out. He looked around and remembered the O'Neills' lighthouse and the bunkbeds. He was surprised, as the sun was already shining through the curtains. It felt only like a moment ago that he had gone to sleep.

"Are you ok? What happened?" asked Cassia, who looked at him worried, still holding on to both of his shoulders.

Alex sat up, feeling slightly embarrassed by his nervous disposition.

"I'm fine, thank you. You're right, it was just a dream," he said as he got up and went to the window to open the curtains and look outside in the morning light. There were a number of white and gray gulls swooping up and down over the edge of the coast, and below the window Alex could see a little patch of garden that Barnaby was watering.

"What was the dream about?" asked Cassia. She wasn't going to let it go.

"I can't remember," he lied, not wanting to talk about it any further.

There was a knock at the door. It was Siobhan, and Alex felt relieved that she'd interrupted the conversation.

"Good morning, you two. Breakfast is on the table, and there's been a letter from the Wizard Oberon for you that you should read at once," said Siobhan, and with that she made a turn to leave abruptly.

"The Wizard Oberon?" questioned Cassia. "Who's that?"

"A Wizard Oberon is a man who has magical powers," said Alex, thinking of a story his father had once told him that at the time he had thought was one of his confused ravings.

The pair packed up their things once again—they were getting used to it—and headed down to the table where Barnaby already sat with a newspaper called the *Happenstance Chronicles*. On the front page read 'Arrival

Cove Disappearance' next to 'Comet Signals New Dawn for Happenstance.'

"Morning," said Barnaby with a somewhat sterner tone than what Alex remembered yesterday.

Alex and Cassia sat down at the kitchen table, and almost immediately in front of them were bowls of porridge with honey, nuts, fruit, and thick cream to choose from. The pair were relieved, as they weren't quite sure what to expect after the sandwiches yesterday.

Barnaby got up and picked up two letters from a small, wicker tray on a cabinet near the door. He gave one to Alex and opened one himself.

They all sat there quietly, except for the baby who was in his high chair, making bubbles in his mouth with his porridge. Cassia went to him and picked him up to rock him, which he seemed to like a lot as he tugged on her hair. Cassia was used to this, having helped to raise so many siblings. Alex thought he saw a tear in her eye, but she brushed it away and looked intently at him and at the letter.

Alex and Barnaby both opened their letters and looked at each other.

"Is there trouble?" asked Siobhan with a concerned look on her face.

Alex was surprised by Siobhan's question and reaction, given their discussion and her insisting during one of yesterday's conversations that Happenstance had only good people.

"Well, I'd better get my things, Siobhan. Looks like I will be gone for a wee while," said Barnaby. And with that, he got up from his cushioned window seat and headed behind a curtain into the back room. They could all hear a lot of rustling and things being tossed around.

"Excuse me," said Siobhan as she scooped up the baby, who immediately began crying. She followed Barnaby into the other room, where a hushed but heated discussion began.

Cassia was quiet as she sat down in one of the wooden chairs. "Alex, are we in trouble?" she questioned, looking at the envelope in Alex's hands.

Alex looked down at the note with the name Nova on the front. He opened it up and read the contents. Without looking at Cassia, he responded, "Yes."

CHAPTER 6

"WE NEED TO get away—and fast," said Cassia, who was running ahead of Alex in the dark, down a twisted path with tall bushes on either side.

The road was bumpy and wasn't trodden on often. There were many rocks and tree stumps to contend with. Alex assumed as he stumbled along that there were very few nighttime explorers who went down this path.

"Slow down and be quiet," said Alex to Cassia, frustrated that she wasn't following the plan. They had discussed it at dusk—while he was looking for dry wood—that they would escape when Barnaby fell asleep during that night.

Barnaby and Siobhan had given the two a warm welcome the day before, and for that they were grateful, but they were concerned at Barnaby's change in mood and frightened by the knife he held around his belt pocket. They'd decided that since they were just a day's walk from his home, if they escaped to find the Wizard Oberon themselves it would cause the O'Neills less concern, and they would both in turn feel a lot safer.

Alex had written a note for Barnaby and slid it through the side flap of his tent as quietly as he could before they left. He knew that Barnaby hadn't risen because he could hear the troll snoring loudly even as they departed the camp. He had again thanked Barnaby for all his help but insisted that they should not be the reason for his and Siobhan's upset. He thanked him as well for the two flasks of water, cake, and two eel and pickle sandwiches he had taken to help the pair over the next day and said that he would be sure to repay him. One day.

Alex and Cassia were now about half an hour away from the camp that was so cozy with its fire and tents. Alex was beginning to wonder if they had made the right decision. The plan was to run until the moon was in the middle of the night sky and then find some bushes to sleep under until first dawn, when they would run on farther to ensure that Barnaby couldn't keep up with them—should he, of course, decide to chase them.

There were crickets in the tall grass, and Alex was sure they were close to water, maybe a pond because of the smell of rushes and lilies in the air. The pair ran until they came to a clearing with stone cliff faces in front of them. There was a path, and as they entered, they soon realized it was much like a maze twisting and turning and forking and looping.

"What if we are going the wrong way?" said Cassia, who was starting to get worried. "These rocks remind me of the cave at the Highlands."

Both children began to think of the tales of animals that lived in that cave.

Slowing from a jog to a walk, the two moved forward with more care. Bats occasionally fluttered past overhead, and the sound of what they could only assume might be a coyote or a wolf howling haunted them from a distance.

The air was stale and murky due to the rocks around them, and the two had to push through some parts where the rock walls got narrower. They could feel damp moss and lichen growing out of the crevasses.

"I don't know, Cassia, do you think we should go back?" But almost as soon as he said it, Alex thought about how cross Barnaby had been that day and was worried what he might be like if he were to get really angry. Going back didn't seem like an option at all.

"The moon is almost in the middle of the sky, and I'm tired. We should sleep at the next opening," replied Cassia.

Good idea, thought Alex.

It took longer than they had wanted to find a clearing, and the stress of the escape, plus the fear of what was lurking around them, took a toll on Cassia. All of a sudden, she pulled her backpack from her back and threw it onto a rock and slumped her body down.

Alex could hear her crying. He felt frustrated, there was no time for tears, but he sat down and put his arms around her to console her. He looked up and down the rocky passage and felt that with the two rocks on either side that guarded them this could potentially be a good place.

"Shhhhhh . . ." He started trying to do what he'd seen mothers do with their children on The Nexus. "What's wrong, Cassia?"

"I . . . I'm just worried that I've made a mistake. I wanted to come with you . . . to help . . . but I am letting you down," Cassia sniffled, and her tears made a wet mark on the shoulder of the woolen, pullover sweater that Alex was wearing. He didn't mind.

"Of course you aren't letting me down," he responded, really meaning every word he'd just said. "If it weren't for you, I don't know if I'd be brave enough for all of this."

Cassia obviously didn't believe what he was saying and just cried harder. "I just feel awful for leaving my family and our friends. They must be so worried about us, Alex. I know that I'm only going to let you down. I'm not strong enough for this. And we are now in so much trouble. The Wizard Oberon wants us and we don't know why, who knows what might happen to us?"

"Cassia, you didn't have to come, but I'm so happy that you did."

Cassia looked up at him with tears in her eyes, which he could see only because the moon was shining down on them, casting a million little stars over her irises.

"You can go back if you want, go back to the O'Neills and take a rainbow or a moonbow or whatever . . . but go back," Alex said, still holding Cassia in his arms. She was so close he could see her lips glistening.

"Of course I don't want to . . . Alex, don't you get it? I have to be here. I just need you to know that you mean everything to me," she replied.

Alex was shocked but also not sure of what to say or do, so they sat there with the words lingering in the moment in an unintended embrace.

Suddenly, as if angered, Cassia got up and brushed away her tears. "I'm fine, you see," she laughed awkwardly.

Alex was about to respond, he wanted to pull her close to him again, but the moment passed. The pair were suddenly surprised by a light that came off the armband under Alex's sweater. The armband unlatched itself and started to clamber like a crab with many metal legs down into his hands. It occurred to Alex that it had taken very little time for him to get used to something completely extraordinary. Perhaps everything extraordinary became ordinary when you got used to it?

Looking at Cassia, he swung his backpack around and pulled out the box, which was also now shimmering. The armband morphed into a key as it crawled into the lock, which Alex twisted open before slipping his hand in.

This time what he touched wasn't a paper. It was cold and metallic.

Alex pulled it out and noticed it was a small whistle. "What should I do?" he asked Cassia.

"Well, what do you do with a whistle, silly?" she laughed at him.

Alex blew silently on the whistle; it seemed an odd thing to do in the dark of night. But the box had helped him before, and he didn't think now was the right time to defy it. They were lost in the middle of the night, after all.

Sitting there, watching the box, Alex and Cassia waited for something to happen. It didn't. So, Alex took the whistle and blew a little louder. This time the notes seemed to pick up in the wind and carry off in a sort of bluish color down the rock-walled pathway before dancing like the northern lights into the sky.

Within moments they could hear it: a rush of wind and the sound of buzzing. Something, or someone, was coming. Cassia grabbed on to Alex again.

"Well, you almost made it," said an unfamiliar, airy, female voice that reached their ears before she did.

❖

Gwendolyn Liathras was the most beautiful thing Alex had ever seen. She was very petite in human form and small enough to fit in his hand when she flew in the air. When flying, she had wings the size of a butterfly's that shone with a pearlescent glow. She had long, rainbow-colored hair that tucked behind her pointed ears and hung to the smallest part of her waist. Gwendolyn had an aura around her that lit up her surroundings. She wore a textured, green, two-pieced garment that looked like it almost lived on her like a leaf did on a tree. She was so dazzlingly different.

Cassia didn't show the same goodwill toward Gwendolyn that she'd shown toward Barnaby. Of course, it was late, and she had been upset and tired. Alex decided to take on the basic introductions and discussions.

"I've been looking for you both for some time. I could sense your arrival at Prospect Rock." Gwendolyn eased into conversation right away as if she knew them both for years. She arrived as a ball of light in her true fae form before fluttering to walk in her human size as she approached them in the passageway.

Alex was surprised by her arrival but didn't feel afraid.

"She's a fae, it's all right," he whispered in Cassia's ear as he remembered another tale presented by his father of the fairy people—or fae—with wings who could fly. They were kind, but many were known for their tricks.

Gwendolyn wasn't the type to offer smiles freely, and she had a stern demeanor. The box had obviously been the one to present the whistle and call for her, so Alex presumed this introduction was a welcome one.

"Yes, I am not here to hurt you, I'm here to bring you

to Kismet. My name is Gwendolyn. You don't need to be afraid," she said with a knowing look on her face.

"This is Cassia, and my name is Al—"

"Yes, I know who you are," Gwendolyn said, interrupting him. "Your name is Nova."

After the unorthodox introduction, Gwendolyn turned back into fae form. She was circling the two and hovering, looking them up and down. With a flick of her hand, she closed the box and the key scrambled back to Alex, this time clasping back on his arm for safety.

"Please make sure to keep this box out of harm's way. Now, follow me," she said, and her glimmering light was quickly out of sight around a rocky corner.

Alex and Cassia picked up their things and ran after her.

"Doesn't she know we have legs?" scoffed Cassia.

Alex was still perplexed by Gwendolyn. It was odd to see a person who could change size, but he was in awe of seeing a person who could fly and who had wings. He was also still taken aback by her striking beauty and wasn't sure if he should look at her or not. Could she read his mind that he was thinking of how beautiful she was?

They turned a corner, and Gwendolyn was waiting there for them.

"I thought you were both tired. Come on, we haven't got all night," she said and buzzed almost out of sight again.

"Well isn't she a hoot!" exclaimed Cassia in a mocking tone. "And you can close your jaw when you are speaking to her. Don't you know it's rude?"

Cassia stormed on ahead as Alex's cheeks grew warm in embarrassment.

Gwendolyn didn't slow her pace and the path seemed to rise, which made it harder to navigate on foot. Alex and Cassia were panting and out of breath but tried their hardest to keep up.

Eventually, they got to a steep incline with a warm light offering solace at the top. They must almost be there, thought Alex.

"Come on, you two," said Gwendolyn at the top of the hill.

"Easy to say coming from someone with wings," quipped Cassia coldly.

As they got to the top of the hill, they could see it. A beautifully lit village nestled snuggly in the treetops, sitting in the sunken crater at the top of the rocky mountain they'd been walking up.

"Welcome to Kismet, Land of the Fae," said Gwendolyn as she began her descent, flying above a set of stairs lit by candlelight.

Cassia, who had before looked like she had a face filled with sour grapes, was now smiling in excitement at what lay before them. She looked at Alex with a smile.

"After you!" he said to her as the pair started down the many steps.

At the bottom of the stairs, they walked along another well-lit path between the trunks of the trees. A number of small faces, all appearing quite young like Gwendolyn's with sharp-pointed ears, looked down from their treetop abodes as Alex and Cassia made their way through. Some of the children waved, to which Alex and Cassia smiled back.

After some time, they arrived at the center of Kismet

where what looked like the largest and oldest tree stood. There was a man at the bottom of it.

"Come, say hello to my father. You will stay with us for the night," said Gwendolyn, who then flew away.

Alex had rather wished Gwendolyn would have stayed to make the introduction, but that didn't seem to be her way of doing things.

"Hello," said both Alex and Cassia together as they approached Gwendolyn's father.

"Hello to you both. I am Anthony Liathras, King of the Fae, and you will stay here with us for the night. But come, it is late for you, Nova and Cassia. Go to your beds, and we will speak more in the morning."

With that, Anthony flew away, sprinkling some dust over the pair on his way, making them shrink in size. Two hummingbirds came to pick them up and take them to their treetop rooms.

Both Alex and Cassia were too tired to protest.

❖

The next morning was a blur. Things were not like at the O'Neills' where life to some extent seemed similar to life in Creston. Breakfast was served in their rooms at daybreak, and they were washed and dressed with the help of the hummingbirds, who had taken them to their room the night before. After eating their breakfast, they rode on the backs of the hummingbirds and flew to the top of the tree they had stayed in. All around them was a buzz of activity in Kismet below, but, while they were in the center of it, the canopy was quiet.

Both Gwendolyn and her father were already there, meditating in the morning sun.

"Welcome, Nova. Welcome, Cassia," said King Anthony, gesturing for them to sit.

Again, Alex wondered how he'd known their names before meeting them and how Gwendolyn had known the night before. It was as if they were expected in Kismet.

Both Anthony and Gwendolyn sat on great swirls of multicolored leaves and flowers. Alex and Cassia sat on smaller pods made up of the same greens and colors. Alex wondered if the father and his daughter would usually sit up here or if it was just for the purpose of entertaining their guests. Looking out above the canopy and above the rocky crests, Alex thought he could just about see the Emerald Sea and thought the white and red barely visible in the distance was the Founders Cove Lighthouse.

"The Wizard Oberon has summoned you, my child. You must go to him, and quickly," said King Anthony.

Gwendolyn walked nimbly across the bed of leaves and put in front of the guests another tray with hot tea, fruits, and flowers on a plate. Alex wondered if they were edible.

"In case you are still hungry and thirsty," she said as she dropped off the tray.

Alex and Cassia picked up the tea and drank. Neither were altogether used to waking up this early and having a second breakfast so soon.

"Yes, we have been summoned," replied Alex, before gingerly asking, "and how did you know this? How did you know who we are without having met us?"

"We fae have our ways," responded Gwendolyn with a wry smile.

"Plus," added her father, "news travels fast in Happenstance, Nova. We've been waiting since we saw the comet, the sign of your arrival."

There was a silence. But why have they been waiting for me?, was the thought that ran through Alex's head.

As if she heard his thoughts, Gwendolyn said, "Happenstance is fading, magic is fading. Lady Luck's prophecy is coming true, and she saw you, Nova."

Gwendolyn took a calm sip of tea from her cup and with a tinkering sound placed it back down in her hand that held the saucer.

Alex was stunned; he didn't know what to say or to think.

Cassia looked over toward Alex. What they were discussing were important matters and she, for once, hesitated before speaking her mind.

"All of this is new to us," began Cassia slower than she would usually speak. She was directing her conversation to their hosts, while occasionally glancing at Alex for approval. "For years we have lived in Creston, we have been supported by the Regime. Alex has been called Alex our entire lives, and now there is a box with the name Nova and many people who can fly and do magic that call my Alex, well, Nova. And we walked on a moonbow and arrived in Founders Cove in a new world called Happenstance. Well, we are just trying to put everything together, and it's rather difficult. We don't know a Lady Luck and her prophecy, and it isn't our problem everything is fading."

Alex wished Cassia hadn't said the final sentence.

Both King Anthony and Gwendolyn wore looks of disapproval. Silence fell over the group, and only the chirps of golden finches could be heard above the canopy. Alex noticed the song and was surprised that a place like Happenstance would have the same creatures they had grown up with in Creston.

Behind them, there was a rustling in the leaves, and a new but familiar voice sounded, "There is much for you to learn. The problem is your own, as well. You must go to the Wizard Oberon at once, as King Anthony says."

It was Osiris. He was climbing up the branches to the top of the canopy to meet with them. A rush of relief for seeing another familiar face came over Alex. He knew that Osiris was on his side and that Osiris could help them.

"Osiris, we were worried about you. We left you in the battle, and there was no way to know what had happened once we had walked across the moonbow," said Cassia, who was still emotionally charged from her confused rant about their situation. She ran over and threw her arms around Osiris, who pulled away slightly wincing.

"You're hurt," said Alex, noticing that where his wing was closest to his body near his neck, Osiris had an open wound and above his eye another gash.

Gwendolyn summoned a hummingbird to get medical supplies, and Osiris nodded his head in thanks.

"Yes, the battle was fierce, and not all eagles made it home safely that day." He bowed his head for a moment and hobbled toward another branch.

"What we are facing now, Nova, is a time of great change. Your arrival is the catalyst that we have been preparing for," said King Anthony. There was gravity to his voice.

"But, why me, why now, and what am I meant to do—I'm just a boy," replied Alex, confused and getting increasingly frustrated.

"You will know much more soon enough, but you are about to embrace your destiny," said King Anthony. "We are all born incomplete with a yearning to make ourselves whole. Following our destiny is what slowly completes us. We make choices in life, whether we like it or not, and they take us on a path toward completing our destiny, and your time to make and important choice is now. The process has already begun, Nova. You are here in Happenstance, aren't you? You are much more significant than you think, and there is much more to the world than you know. But all of this takes much explaining and will take time and training. The Wizard Oberon awaits."

Alex got up from where he was sitting. "And what if I say no," he responded as King Anthony was about to pour tea and Osiris was hobbling to a comfier position in the canopy. They both stopped abruptly, but it was Gwendolyn's fierce—almost piercing—eyes that got him first.

"If you say no, Nova, well then perhaps the darkness just might win for good," said Gwendolyn somberly as she walked to her father and helped pour his tea. Cassia grabbed hold of Alex's hand and held it tight.

A new fae arrived in the canopy, or had he been there the entire time? He was striking like Gwendolyn, but he had a much fiercer look to him. He looked strong, and his eyes locked on Alex, making him feel uneasy.

"I will take them," the fae said, looking at King

Anthony and then Gwendolyn like he had something to prove.

"No, it is my duty to . . ." began Osiris, who was quickly cut off by King Anthony.

"Yes, Luca Alwin, you must take them. Osiris, you are too weak right now to safely fly them both. You will meet them at Serendipity as soon as you can, but for now both Luca and Gwendolyn will escort them."

Osiris sat down with a loud sigh. He knew, however, that he had no say in the matter. They must get to the Wizard Oberon as soon as possible. It was true, he was not strong enough right now.

"When shall we go, then?" asked Alex.

"As soon as possible, gather your things, as it will take another day to get to Providence and from there the steep ascent up Glass Mountain to the school," replied King Anthony.

Whether they were ready or not, Gwendolyn removed their trays with the fruit and breakfast snacks. In a whirlwind they once again gathered their things, were transformed back to their normal height, and were gone.

❖

In the light of day, it was even easier to see the beauty of Kismet as they climbed the stairs to leave. Flowers of every color hung from the trees, and a variety of birds with long beaks, short beaks, tall necks and legs, short necks and legs, and unique calls were on every branch. It was more beautiful than any of the elaborate decorations the Championships had put together before, because it was real and living and pure. It was also so different from anything that Alex was used to and could have possibly ever imagined in his small life in Creston. Even the images made up in his mind from his father's stories couldn't compare to this.

Thoughts from the meeting in the canopy were spinning through his head. Why was everyone calling him Nova? What was all this talk about his destiny? Why were there so many expectations over him? Could he really be what they all thought he was?

At the top of the ridge, Luca indicated that they would walk above rather than below in the twisted maze of rocky paths they had taken the night before. The upper path wound across the rocky ledges, and there were series of intricate rope ladders and bridges swinging over deep gorges.

Alex was thankful that neither he nor Cassia were afraid of heights. They had been used to climbing trees and jumping from the rocky cliffs into Kootenay Lake, so this was something they could stomach. The height here was much taller than they were used to at home, of course, but they both knew to not look down.

It didn't help that both Luca and Gwendolyn shrunk and were flying quickly and quite far ahead. It didn't bring much confidence to Alex and Cassia who had to brave the path alone.

After a few hours, the group came to what looked like the end of the rocky cliffs. They climbed down and entered into a woodland. The woodland was shaded and a little chilly, so Alex and Cassia put their sweaters on. The woods were also darker, and it was harder to see where they were headed and what lay in front of them.

Alex noticed that Luca spent the majority of his time

showing off and flying circles around Gwendolyn. The pair almost ignored him and Cassia, who they were meant to be chaperoning.

Cassia asked for a moment to sit down when they came to a clearing in the woods. It was a beautiful place to stop, and the sun shone through the tall evergreen trees to a mossy cluster of rocks. Alex offered Cassia one of the sandwiches they had taken from Barnaby when they left camp the evening before. He couldn't believe it had been such little time ago! He also offered one to Gwendolyn and then Luca, but they declined politely, looking somewhat perturbed by the smell and the contents within the bread.

"It's good, honestly," said Cassia through a half-chewed mouthful that made it even more unappetizing.

She smiled, giving Alex a smile. "More for us, then."

"Come on you two, we haven't got all day," said Luca, looking annoyed that they were stopping to eat so soon after having only left around half a day earlier.

"We aren't far from Providence, we can get there by nightfall, and if we hurry we can take a ferryboat rather than swimming across the river," promised Gwendolyn with a kinder air to her voice.

Alex and Cassia liked the sound of a ferryboat, so they picked up their things and started walking again.

"For two travelers who have never traveled before, we are trying our best to keep up!" chimed in Cassia.

After another half hour or so, the forest cleared and there were grassy plains below them with a river that ran like a fork at the bottom. In the distance, Alex could see a dock with the ferryboat below and was relieved to see that this option was still available to them. He loved being on boats and his feet were pretty sore, so it seemed like the best possible option for them.

"Come on, you two," scoffed Luca, rolling his eyes at Gwendolyn with every intention of showing his disappointment at their slow pace to the entire group.

Alex watched as Luca ran toward an old tree stump covered in moss and climbed up on it. He began twirling in a circle before becoming a stream of light and shrinking into fae form. He had been trying to impress Gwendolyn all day. He bounced across and flew around her head, landing in her hair close to her ear and whispering something.

Alex noticed that Gwendolyn looked down to the ground away from Luca. Sadness cast itself across her face for just a second, but it was long enough for Alex to see.

Embarrassed that her face had betrayed her, Gwendolyn shot an angry look at Alex, and turned her back as she walked toward the river.

❖

As they arrived closer to the ferryboat on the river, Alex noticed that it was actually a waterfall that fed into it. They were at the bottom of the river's descent from the steep cliffs and at the start of its horizontal journey across the plain. It reminded him of the mouth of the Sanca River next to his cabin in the woods in Creston, and he felt a pang of longing for it and for his father.

Luca had begun a narrative that was directed at Alex and Cassia but was meant for the pleasure of Gwendolyn. He was boastfully explaining where they were, and it was aggravating.

"... and as you'll see, the force of the Hope Waterfall from the Northern Kismet Mountains flows down through the Fortuity Forest and accumulates with the underground water system that rises above the rocky bedrock, which is the foundation of the Prosperity Plains. It flows as Hope River toward Providence ... Watch this." Luca stopped for a moment and pulled two long hair pins from Gwendolyn's head. He ran his hand across them so that they magically became longer and formed into two half-rectangular shapes. Pointing the pins forward in his hands, he walked ahead until they were pointing out to opposite sides of him.

"Water witching," said Gwendolyn, embarrassed and trying to explain to the others. "It comes in useful sometimes when you need to find water."

Gwendolyn said this through a look of frustration as she grabbed her pins and shook them back into their normal size. She put them back into their rightful positions in her long, colorful locks.

"Water witching? Wouldn't it be useful when you aren't standing in front of a river already?" laughed Cassia, looking at Alex.

"Precisely, water witching," said Luca contritely, ignoring Cassia before continuing. "At Providence we will go into the town for the night before our climb up Glass Mountain. Not long now!" He finished with an annoying smile on his face.

Alex had noticed that for some time Luca was annoying him. Perhaps even angering him. He had an air of boastful arrogance that was just irritating, and the way he only addressed Gwendolyn, even when he was speaking to all three of them, was selfish. He wished Luca would just go away and leave them to continue their journey without him. Fury pulsed through him.

Luca started running down toward the boat, pinging off of rocks and uneven ground as he went and, in that moment, just vanished completely out of thin air. He was gone.

"Luca!" screamed Gwendolyn with a look of fear and confusion on her face as she rushed toward where he had been.

"Where did he go, Alex? He's disappeared in plain sight!" cried Cassia.

In the midst of it, Alex looked down and saw his armband was glowing and felt hot—hot enough that it was burning. As Alex was rushing toward the site of Luca's disappearance, he was trying to pull it off. Something didn't feel right.

Suddenly, a voice from behind them came booming, "It's time you both come with me!"

At first they thought it might be Luca, but swinging around quickly, Alex and Cassia saw who it was first and then jumped back with a start. It was Barnaby O'Neill looking frightfully angry and coming toward them, brandishing his pocketknife in one hand.

CHAPTER 7

The ferryboat didn't move as quickly down the river as they might have hoped. Alex looked down to the stern of the boat into the eyes of Barnaby O'Neill, who quickly looked past him up the river and continued to paddle.

Gwendolyn and Cassia were sitting at the front of the boat with a blanket around them. Alex couldn't tell who was consoling who. They were both in a state of shock. No one had managed to find Luca, and they had since left and were halfway to Providence by now.

Alex wondered how afraid they should be of Barnaby. A couple days ago, he had seemed to have such a kind heart. He had offered them his home, his food, and the comforts of his family. He didn't even seem like the same person now, making Alex wonder if this was, in fact, the temperament of trolls and whether they had made a mistake in trusting him before knowing him.

But everything was happening so quickly since their arrival in Happenstance, so they really had no choice. Alex also worried, however, that if Barnaby was so convinced on taking them to the Wizard Oberon that perhaps the Wizard Oberon was also wicked and of greater concern to their safety. Then he thought of his father, who had given him the box and told him to leave. He didn't trust anyone more than his father.

Alex scratched his head and looked over the boat at his reflection in the water. He looked the same; he could tell even as the water reflected a rippled image of him in return. His golden hair with its white streak was still the same, his blue eyes were the same color they had always been. His nose, cheeks, ears—everything was the same, but he felt so different, and he felt so tired. Alex sat back from the water, slumping himself into the side of the boat. He was sitting on a big pile of rope.

"So, are you going to apologize then, young man?" demanded Barnaby of Alex. He said it loud enough and in a deep enough tone to make Alex shift in his seat uncomfortably, but the two young women at the front of the boat were far enough to miss out on the conversation.

"For what, the sandwiches?" replied Alex in a slightly sarcastic tone that was unusual for him. He genuinely wondered what he should apologize for. He and Cassia had escaped Barnaby for their own safety.

"Trolls don't like to be deceived," said Barnaby, "nor do they like to be betrayed, and you've accomplished both in a very short period of time."

"Yes, Barnaby, we escaped and left you, but you weren't so far from your home, and we decided that since you seemed . . . well . . . so upset with us and our trip to the Wizard Oberon that we should just leave you." Alex stopped for a minute to catch his breath. He was frustrated, as Barnaby was grinning from ear to ear in a slightly sinister way. "And then you came, and you made Luca disappear, and now he's gone, and you are taking us on a boat against our wishes after having come at us with your pocketknife."

Barnaby started laughing. It was a low, deep, belly-rumbling laugh that made Alex's hair stand on end.

"If you think it was me who made Luca disappear then you really have a lot more to learn, Nova," he replied, and with that he turned around and continued turning the oars in the boat, but with a backward motion. He was still chuckling to himself.

Alex crawled up the boat to the girls. He was upset and frightened. What did Barnaby have in store for them? Alex knew that he needed to protect the girls and himself, but he wasn't sure what he should do. He didn't know Barnaby or the Wizard Oberon's intentions and was now doubting having even come to Happenstance. Everything was so different from the world he had lived in for eleven years, and nothing felt right.

Alex looked down and felt a burning sensation where the bracelet had been on his skin—hot and red.

"Gwendolyn, what will Barnaby do with us?" asked Alex, trying not to look afraid.

Cassia swung her head around. Her hair was blowing with Gwendolyn's in the breeze. For a moment, Alex thought he saw anger in her eyes that was directed at him, but she masked it with a smile.

"Yes, I'm worried, he seems to abhor us, and he already sent Luca to . . . well . . . to . . . nowhere. Trolls are known to have a wicked temper," Gwendolyn said, looking back toward Barnaby then forward again, pushing her body forward on the boat so that she was as far away from Barnaby as possible.

"It doesn't make sense," she said. "I have never known

a troll to use magic. They typically stay away from it. But this sort of magic is so strong, much stronger than any of the faes or I know how to use. It is a type of dark magic."

Gwendolyn looked away, and as the river bended, she looked back down it for something, for Luca. She continued, "I've never known a magic so strong that it makes someone just disappear. Luca didn't deserve that." She had a look in her eyes that showed a mixture of anger, sadness, and confusion. Then in a moment of absurd anger, Gwendolyn shrunk and flew back to Barnaby and started buzzing around him, pulling his hair and biting and hitting his face.

Barnaby began swatting at Gwendolyn, but she got roughly a dozen good jabs in before his large, hairy hand knocked her to the belly of the boat, where she returned to her full form.

"Keep away from me, fae, or your journey will end here—as will hers," he said, pointing to Cassia at the top of the boat. "I only need him, the Wizard Oberon needs him, and it is my duty to get him there."

"And how do you think the Wizard Oberon will respond when he finds out that you've used dark magic? Everyone in Happenstance knows that dark magic is a criminal act," responded Gwendolyn, now standing up in the boat with a sort of controlled power as though she was already playing judge and jury in this matter.

"Well, let's let the Wizard Oberon decide whether I am guilty or not," said Barnaby with an equal response of authority.

"Well then, perhaps you do not know, troll, that making another citizen of Happenstance disappear is dark magic or that a citizen of Happenstance is not allowed to use magic against another citizen?" retorted Gwendolyn, dismissing Barnaby as if he were childish and altogether uneducated. "And trust me, if I could, I would." She spat, turning away from him.

Alex wondered if perhaps the laws about making people disappear in Happenstance weren't clear. He only knew that people didn't disappear out of thin air like this in Dacaan unless they were taken by the patrol to Castlegar.

Barnaby sat down again and started rowing slowly, shaking his head. It seemed to Alex that trolls could be quite awkward at times and disagreeable when things did not look in their favor.

"None of you understand what is happening here, you are making assumptions," Barnaby responded in a gruff voice.

"What do we not understand? I feel like I don't understand anything these days," said Cassia from the front of the boat.

"Perhaps it's just that us trolls aren't very good at explaining," Barnaby responded then, rolling his eyes. He stood up, making the boat shake considerably, and the rest felt they might capsize.

He continued, "I don't know magic, I don't know dark magic. I had the pocketknife in my hand because I was cutting the rope on the boat. I don't know what happened to your friend, and I do not intend to hurt any of you here unless you get in the way of my mission again."

"Well, that sounds like a threat if ever I heard one," said Cassia in her know-it-all manner.

"None of you understand me, see. It's like we are talking in two different languages," said Barnaby, slumping back down once again in the boat and sloshing water over the sides around where they sat.

Feeling as if Barnaby was in some real stress around the topic of their understanding him, Alex decided to approach him again in a different way.

"Why must you take me to the Wizard Oberon, in that case?" Alex said slowly and calmly to diffuse the tensions on the boat.

"You saw the letter, you got one yourself," snapped Barnaby. "I was asked to, and what the Wizard Oberon asks for you do."

Picking up on the renewed peace, Gwendolyn chimed in, "Well, it's one thing to obey the Wizard Oberon—we all must do that—but it's another to kidnap and frighten Dacaanian children and make a fae disappear."

"I did not kidnap them. You know as well as any fae that the job of the trolls of Happenstance is to offer any children who arrive here safe board and passage, and that is exactly what I am doing," he said, faster than his lips had a chance to catch up with his pace in rowing as the boat accelerated.

"Plus they stole my sandwiches. Never in all my days have I hosted and fed people in my own house and been treated so poorly." Barnaby finished his rant with small but audible sobs, which made Alex feel terrible and made Cassia's eyes tear up. It was strange to see such a large man cry.

"We have been awful, Barnaby, we are so dreadfully sorry," said Cassia, inching closer down the boat. "We thought that you wanted to hurt us or eat us."

"Now, why would you think a thing like that," said Barnaby through sniffles.

There was a silence while Alex and Cassia sat and thought.

"As soon as you received the letter, your attitude toward us changed," replied Alex.

Barnaby wiped his tears and slapped his hand on one of the oar handles roughly, so that it splashed in the water.

"I didn't want to leave my family. I don't like traveling, you see, but it is part of my job and responsibility to support the Wizard Oberon and to pay my duty to Happenstance. I also found out that you were the famous Nova, and it made me worried. I know that you have a powerful magic inside of you. Osiris told me. And nothing good comes of magic. Look at what happened now to your friend Luca. And, then what you did to me, leaving me at the camp, of course I am upset—as you would be!" said Barnaby, starting to sob again.

Gwendolyn rose again in the boat and looked back and forth between Alex and Barnaby, trying to make sense of everything.

"Well, if this is the case and you don't deny it, then, Nova and Cassia, you owe Barnaby an immediate apology," stated Gwendolyn.

Cassia's guilt made her move quickly up the boat, and she wrapped her arms around Barnaby with as many I'm sorrys as possible, while Barnaby patted her shoulder.

"Barnaby, I'm so sorry, however can we repay you?" said Alex.

Barnaby smiled and waved his hand in the air as if to bat back Alex's offer. Alex felt silly in fact, and he couldn't believe how wrongly he had judged such a gentle soul as he looked at Barnaby smiling with tears still streaming down his face, wrapped in Cassia's embrace.

Gwendolyn moved down to the middle of the boat as if she were taking the floor once more to speak, and she looked down directly at Alex. "This doesn't change the issue about the disappearance of Luca and the dark magic," she said in an accusatory way to Alex.

Cassia moved toward them both with her eyes and mouth open in surprise, knowing that the puzzle was solved.

Alex looked down and felt a burning sensation where the bracelet had been on his skin—hot, red, and now incriminating.

❖

Barnaby had tied up the boat along the dock at the harbor front at Providence. Alex was surprised that a river could possess a harbor front as the river that they had been traveling on didn't seem wide enough, but where the river forked there was a wide opening. The banks of the river were now covered in a gray-colored stone, and many other boats of relatively similar size were parked up or being untied to go upriver. Alex didn't remember any boats having passed them on their trip from Hope Waterfall, and he was sure that he wouldn't have missed them going past since the landscape had been mostly the waterway and the rest unremarkable riverbank and rushes.

Barnaby had taken Gwendolyn along the dock and asked Alex and Cassia to wait for them to return. Alex could see them down the dock; Gwendolyn was pacing while Barnaby leaned against a wooden railing.

While they were waiting, Cassia was rambling on about how terrible it had been that they misjudged Barnaby and stolen his sandwiches, while she munched away on dried fruit biscuits that Gwendolyn had left for them. Cassia had a way of talking uncontrollably at times, especially when she was upset, and Alex didn't need to say anything apart from nod his head.

Alex was, however, much more focused on their new surroundings. The dock wasn't anything like they were used to at Creston. It was painted in a multitude of colors, which were not jarring but lovely on the eye. The boat next to them was light blue, and it belonged to a fisherman. There was a rod, some nets, and a trapping cage in its hull. A large straw hat sat on the seat without a driver. There were a handful of fishermen on other boats, however, and Alex thought that they were human, or maybe troll and some could be fae, he wasn't quite sure. They all moved delicately along the dock and on their boats, as if their bodies were moving in some sort of unison to the unheard music of the river.

Barnaby and Gwendolyn returned to the boat.

"We will rest here tonight before we make our ascent up Glass Mountain so that we can ask around for Luca," said Gwendolyn on their return. Alex noticed that her eyes darted sideways at him when she said Luca's name, and he felt an even deeper sense of guilt than he had felt earlier about Barnaby.

"Are one of you going to explain what is going on?" said Cassia. "We think it is time," she added, as if she and Alex had discussed and agreed to her asking this question before, but they hadn't.

"We will discuss later. Right now it's not safe to talk about such things with others who might not understand," said Barnaby, looking with shifty eyes around the dock at the various people.

"Wear this," said Gwendolyn, conjuring up a set of different clothes for the pair.

"Where did that come from?" asked Cassia. "Did you use magic?"

"Shhhhhh," warned Barnaby, "lots of folks here in Happenstance use magic, but they don't talk about it like that."

Alex looked at the clothes, feeling that he would fit in much better with the surroundings in them, and so would Cassia. Although they weren't to his taste, he was sure he would feel less awkward in them.

"Go on then, no one's looking," said Barnaby, turning away, as did Gwendolyn. The two in the boat faced away from each other, stepping into their garments.

Alex was thankful that the other fishermen and boatmen were far enough away or weren't paying attention.

Once redressed, Barnaby lifted first Cassia, then Alex, out of the boat one by one onto the dock with one hand. He was definitely a strong man, and now that Alex had seen him cry, his strength felt less oppressive to him.

The four of them walked down the dock. A small and slender man with a long, thin nose, who didn't look like he owned a boat but who might be looking to use one, came rushing past them as they walked.

"How do you do?" he said as he brushed between them, paying little attention to who they were, and to Alex's pleasure and surprise not seeing them as out of place.

"Hello," said Barnaby back to the man, but the man

didn't have enough time to have heard him as he was rushing by quite quickly.

"Goblins for you," Barnaby grumbled.

At the end of the dock was a long pathway that led to a square. There was a statue of a woman with curly hair and droopy eyes. She was sitting on a creature that looked like a serpent but with a broader body and flaring nostrils. Alex had a flashback to the serpent in his dreams, and his hair stood on end. The woman was pointing up behind them, and Alex noticed a large, snowcapped mountain in the direction of her fingers. It was so large that he was surprised he hadn't seen it before; they had been traveling on the boat for so long in that direction that surely it would have been there in plain sight.

"Glass Mountain," said Gwendolyn. "Don't worry, it didn't just appear, it has always been there, but you can only see it when you get closer to the statue here at Providence. It is hidden and protected as it holds the most valuable possessions here in Happenstance, the Constellation Library, and the Serendipity School of Magic. It is where we are headed tomorrow."

"Wowzers!" exclaimed Cassia, not able to hold back her emotions. "And what about this lady?" She pointed to the woman on the horse.

"That's Lady Luck riding Dragmar Gregorius, Happenstance's most famous dragon," said Gwendolyn with a look of pride on her face. "Lady Luck is the mother of Happenstance and chose the good to come to Happenstance from your world."

Ignoring the many other questions that could come next and instead focusing on the interesting fact, Cassia ran toward the statue and rubbed her hand on the animal's leg. "What is a dragon?"

"Well, I guess it is like a serpent that flies and breathes fire," responded Gwendolyn, looking slightly bemused that she had to explain this to Cassia.

Alex had a fleeting memory of Dragmar Gregorius from tales his father had told him over the years and realized again that his father had not just made the things up that he had told him. These sorts of validations made Alex proud of his father. His father obviously knew more about their world and this other world than many others.

The conversation died down as Barnaby approached a peddler who was selling fruit and bought them all apples. Alex wasn't hungry, so he put his in his bag. He noticed the box was shining ever so slightly, so he zipped the bag as tightly as he could before slinging it once again over his back.

As they walked farther from the dock and across the square, more of a crowd seemed to emerge. Some Alex could discern were goblins like the man they had gone past by the boats, and others were trolls like Barnaby. There were a few humans and many fae walking in human form. There were also other beings that he had never come across before, but he didn't want to ask.

Cassia was walking ahead of him, eating her apple. Her eyes were big, and her head was darting from side to side as she was looking around and taking everything in. Alex ran up to her and whispered in her ear not to stand out so badly, but she mainly ignored him.

"Look!" she exclaimed with a shrill of excitement, pointing toward an animal on the other side of a road, which she went running out into and almost got run over by a horse and cart.

"Watch where yer going!" yelled the man driving it. Alex was reminded of Sedwin of the Nomans.

Cassia navigated the road more carefully this time, and Alex followed in close pursuit. He saw that she had found a pet shop with animals of all kinds, including small exotic birds like the ones in Kismet with their colorful plumage. There were large black-and-white-striped cats, gray wolves, and many animals Alex had never seen before. Cassia was focused on what looked like a baby horse with a horn on its head that was out in the front of the store, bouncing around in the air. It was interesting that none of the animals were chained up like in Dacaan. Alex had seen animals that were sold as livestock or taken as pets in Creston, but they were almost always caged. He thought back on his own furry Mr. Gray, who could come and go whenever he pleased. He did stay around, even though he spent most nights out hunting in the moonlight.

"She's not interested in you," snapped a croaky, old voice from the doorway. Alex and Cassia walked closer to the door and saw a woman with warts on her face and a crooked nose. She had old looking skin, old enough that it looked as if it was no longer alive as it had a grayish-green pigment. She wore a black hat with a crisp, pointed top and black garments and black pointed shoes. All black.

"What, it's like you've never seen a witch before," croaked the witch.

"We haven't," said Cassia without thinking, and Alex

elbowed her in the side. She was sometimes too assertive for her own good.

"Newcomers then," said the witch with a sly smile as she got up from her small wooden stool to approach them.

Alex and Cassia didn't say a word and tried not to take a step backward so as not to be rude to the witch.

"Well, I'm sure you are making your way up Glass Mountain then, and heaven knows, you might get to meet our Wizard Oberon," said the witch with a lighter voice, which she appeared to put on to sound kinder.

The witch could sense that the children were frightened and gave them a repulsive smile that showcased her terribly crooked and not-so-white teeth.

She continued, "About the young unicorn, my lady, our animals here in Happenstance choose their humans, the humans don't choose them, and you work together in unison, not in ownership."

It was at that moment Alex noticed a golden snake that before had appeared as a necklace unravel itself and slide down the neck of the witch, along her arm, and toward them.

"Beg our pardonsss," ssss-ed the snake, "we haven't introduced ourselves, yet. I am Sleasta and this is my witch, Legara Tarsworthy. It issssth a pleasure to meet your acquaintance."

"Pleasure to meet you," responded Cassia, and just before they could make their introduction, they heard Barnaby and Gwendolyn calling their names.

"We must go, but I am sure we will meet again soon," said Cassia.

"Perhaps not," responded Legara.

And with that, Alex and Cassia rushed back through the crowd to find the others.

"Come on, you two, there is a tavern just up Elmar Street. I know the owners, so we shall stay the night there," said Barnaby.

Alex and Cassia were taken through the crowded streets. There were smells they had never experienced before and yelling from stall owners in a language that was not known to them. There were shops with the most beautiful stones and shining crystals and groceries that sold a variety of foods, fish, and meat that Alex could never have imagined. There were bakeries with ornate pastries and one shop that appeared to only sell candles and fresh cut flowers. Alex noticed a newsstand with a front page heading of 'The Phoenix has risen, Happenstance has a final hope before fading into darkness' and wondered if this had to do with the comet in the night sky, the phoenix his father often spoke of.

After some time, the group rounded a bend and saw a sign for 'Elmar Street.' They walked another few hundred feet down the road, and on the corner sat the 'TumbleWeed Tavern and Guest House.' It looked clean and cozy, and Alex was looking forward to sitting down and perhaps having a real meal. They had been on the move for some time.

Barnaby opened the heavy, black door and was greeted almost immediately by the tavern owner with a big hug and a pat on the back. The owner gestured greetings to the rest of the group, as well.

The tavern owner turned out to be a cousin of Barnaby's, Shea O'Donnell. He had a wife and two children of similar age to Alex and Cassia. The children almost pulled the pair's bags off their backs and ran with them upstairs, presumably to their room. Alex did not like to part with his box, but a nod from Barnaby showed that they were in good company and everything should be trusted.

Shea showed the group to a table in the far back of the tavern that had a red, velvet bench seat wrapping around in a square and surrounded by wooden cladding—most of the tavern was wooden. A big, roaring fire stood the middle of the room with a hearth that came down from the ceiling and up from the floor. The dual-aspect windows at the front of the tavern gave a spectacular view of the outline of Glass Mountain as the sun set and shone off the parts of its snowcapped peaks.

The people in the TumbleWeed Tavern were a reflection of the mixed crowd out on the streets, but the majority were trolls. They were loud and boisterous, with many sloshing silver-looking goblets and talking excitedly with their friends. The tavern had an inviting air to it.

"Four boar-steak roasts with all the trimmings," said Barnaby to Shea, clapping him on the back after they'd caught up about their families and lives for some time. A sturdy-looking lady came around with four silver goblets of frothing ale, placing them firmly in front of them so that the brew sloshed over the sides and on to the hardwood table.

Cassia looked at Alex. Neither of them had drunk ale before as children in Dacaan didn't drink such things, although they knew Ariadne's family let her have a single glass of wine at birthdays and at Christmas dinner each year.

"You don't need to drink those if you don't like," said Barnaby with a laugh.

"No, thank you, we will try it," said Alex, nodding at Cassia, who took a big gulp through a winced face.

Alex picked up the heavy goblet of frothy liquid and took a sip but soon realized how bitter the taste was. He put it back down as elegantly as he could, wiping his mouth with the back of his hand to make it look like he was satisfied.

"So, you want to know more," said Gwendolyn. It took a moment for Alex to realize that she was picking up on the conversation that Cassia had started back at the dock.

"Yes, we would like to know more," admitted Alex, granting the approval as Cassia seemed much more subdued at the moment.

Barnaby looked around and deliberately leaned in, pushing Alex on his back slightly so that he leaned in too. "We are safe here, but we must be careful," he explained.

"Nova, everything you know about your life as Alex is fabricated," said Gwendolyn, taking on the role of the narrator even though Barnaby had opened his mouth first to make the start. "We cannot tell you everything right now, but you are Nova. You are a descendent of the first people of Happenstance and you possess magic that Dacaan, and even our world, does not understand. You have a chance to change life as we know it, and that comet you saw, the Phoenix, is only the start of it. We are taking you to the Wizard Oberon Silver, who has been the protector of Happenstance since time began here. He will share more with you, but for now we need to keep this to ourselves. Happenstance is safe, but its people are fearful of what is to come. They know that there is a war brewing, and they know that the evil Regime must be overthrown, as Happenstance is fading. Your arrival could be our last hope, but with war there comes great misery and injustices that these people fear." Gwendolyn stopped and looked at Barnaby, who had been mostly drinking his beer while she was talking.

"We do not know if the Regime has something to do with the fading of Happenstance and of our magic here," said Barnaby gruffly.

"Why has this been kept a secret for so long, and what am I meant to do? I don't know how to use magic," said Alex.

A table with a few humans stirred next to them and the group sat in silence for a moment until they felt it was safe again to start talking.

"We have told you enough for now, Nova—in fact, we have probably told you too much, young man. We must leave the rest to the Wizard Oberon," replied Barnaby.

Alex didn't know how to respond to this new information. Surely, it was all a big mistake. The rabbits at the Championship and the magic box: sure, he had done something that was out of the ordinary, but he didn't know how. How could they think that he was capable of saving Happenstance if he didn't even understand what he was doing?

Shea arrived again with the same barmaid, and they placed four plates in front of each of them at the table before rushing on to serve the other guests around them.

In front of Alex sat the biggest plate of food he'd ever seen.

"Now, what you have here," said Barnaby, happily jiggling his fat belly, "and I know because I've had it so often, well you have wild boar, creamed mushrooms, cabbage with fennel, onion puddings, and . . ."

Barnaby's voice trailed off, and he dropped his three-pronged fork, which fell with a clatter on the table.

Alex turned around and saw that coming to their table were Shea's two children. The boy was carrying a box that was shining brightly—too brightly. His heart sunk, and he thought of the conversation they just had about keeping things quiet. The loud, jolly laughs and discussions around the tavern went silent as the boy approached the table.

"Nova, is this yours?" he questioned with a quizzical look on his face, and his eyes bore into Alex's. The boy dropped the box on the table in front of them, and the band that was on Alex's arm betrayed him and crawled over, latching itself into the keyhole for all to see.

CHAPTER
8

"WE NEED TO go, now," said Barnaby, pushing Alex from behind and ushering Cassia and Gwendolyn along the narrow hallway to the back exit.

They had slept the night at the TumbleWeed Tavern and Guest House, but Alex had spent it with one eye open. Toward daybreak, he awoke to an orchestra of birdsong outside his window and had opened the curtains to see a quiet crowd in the cobbled streets below, all looking up toward the guest house windows above the tavern.

Something felt out of sorts with the birdsong; it was a deep melody that felt ominous. It wasn't the joyous harmony he might have heard outside his home in Creston, with small birds washing themselves in small pools in the rock garden and zipping around with an excitement for the day ahead.

At the end of the hallway, the four met with Shea, who was polite but looked aggravated that it was so early in the morning and that they had caused him so much grief in his well-known establishment. Barnaby knew that, although all what the people wanted were answers, Alex's safety was the priority, and he reminded his cousin of this.

Shea opened the backdoor and with a smile said, "If

there is ever anything that you need, Barnaby, which any of you need, please let me know."

Shea went to close the door, but Gwendolyn stopped it. "If you hear anything of my friend, Luca, please send a message to the Wizard Oberon."

"I promise, I will do," said Shea, looking slightly irritated that Gwendolyn had brought Luca up for probably the tenth time that morning.

And with that, the four went through the door, and it closed with a loud bang. Alex hoped that no one out the front had heard anything, and he was relieved to hear no movement from the crowd. But in the silence, something didn't feel right.

"Isn't it funny that the birds have gone silent?" said Cassia.

Alex looked up and saw a murder of crows in a dead tree above them. It was the only tree he had seen in Providence—or perhaps since he'd arrived in Happenstance—without leaves.

"We must get to the . . ." started Barnaby, but Gwendolyn quickly shushed him, having noticed and paid attention to the tree and to the birds.

"It is not wise for us to be so obvious in our coming choices." Gwendolyn carefully selected her words to be deliberately deceiving but nudged Barnaby on his shoulder.

The night before, when Alex's box was discovered, he had rushed to his room with it, leaving a tavern of quiet onlookers behind him. In his room, he'd decided that the key had made its decision to go into the lock, and that it was important for him to listen to the key and to open the box. From inside, he had pulled out a long, heavy garment with a tie at one end. He'd decided to sleep with it that night and thought that this was less interesting than the other items the box had provided, but it was certainly practical given the colder climate they were in now and the even colder weather they might expect on their climb up Glass Mountain.

At that moment, Alex was feeling tired and cold and decided to unravel the garment from his bag.

"An invisibility cloak." Barnaby clapped his hand over his mouth as soon as the words came out, but it was too late.

The crows began their dark, brassy melody and started flying in a dark, circular funnel in the sky. They began flying so fast and so closely that you could hardly discern the individual bodies—they had become one. The air beneath them created a vacuum that almost pulled Alex off his feet and into it.

"Run!" shouted Gwendolyn, who had shrunk and was flying ahead of them, showing them a path at the end of the small garden through the backstreets.

With the cloak in his hand, Alex followed behind the rest.

"Quickly, Alex," yelled Cassia, who was in front of him but had turned around to see that he was trailing farther behind. She waited with her hand out, and as soon as he was close enough to touch it, she shot off again around a corner.

Alex could feel a wind blowing around him and the cry of the birds inching closer. The suction from the pull of the birds was making it harder and harder for him to run forward and keep up with the group. He turned a corner and saw them ahead, going around another corner.

Cassia was waiting around the next bend at the top of a flight of stairs. But the pull was too great, and Alex was left stranded.

Fear ran through him, and then something like a surge of lightning shone from within, and he turned toward the birds in defiance while wrapping the cloak around his neck. And then everything was white.

❖

Alex woke up, and he wasn't in the backstreets of Providence anymore. He was on a ledge of a rock, and evergreen trees were all around him. The sun had moved closer to midday in the sky, and he could see the rooftops of Providence below him. He could tell because he noticed the Hope River, dock, and the statue in the main square. He could see the sword of Lady Luck pointed up toward where he sat, and he knew he was on Glass Mountain. But how had he gotten here?

Looking around him, he noticed that the sun was shining down on his face, and he welcomed its warmth; it was cold up here. He snuggled into the rock and sat with his back against another lichen-covered rock for a moment, gaining his bearings. Little flowers of white, pink, and purple sprouted up in the grass around him. They made him feel warmer too.

Alex noticed there were birds singing again, but that their song was kinder. There were no black crows anywhere to be seen, and for this he felt thankful, but he thought he heard something.

There was a stirring in the woods below him, and he noticed that toward the cliff face there were stairs up to the ledge that he sat on. He walked over to it and looked down but couldn't see anything. Maybe he had dreamed it up.

There was a small trickle of water seeping down the side of the cliff. The water sparkled in the sunlight and looked clean and fresh. Alex cupped his hands and let it run into them. He splashed the first handful of water over his face, it was cold and fresh, and then took a big drink of a second cupped handful. He'd pulled out his water bottle and was starting to fill it when he was startled by Barnaby's voice.

"Well, I can see you were worried about us, lad," Barnaby scoffed as he climbed the final step to the top of the cliff. Cassia and Gwendolyn were close behind him and came running over.

Cassia almost leapt toward Alex and wrapped her arms around his neck before saying, first earnestly and then repeating herself, gingerly, "You disappeared on us, you disappeared on us."

"We thought you'd vanished like Luca had. It's such a pleasure to see you," said Gwendolyn with more of a softness in her voice than Alex was used to.

"I thought your cloak would make you invisible, not make you fly," said Barnaby, with one eyebrow cocked.

"I'm sorry, I don't know what happened or how I got here," said Alex, trying to explain himself. "I'm very pleased to see all of you." He wrapped the cloak around his arm.

Alex looked at Barnaby, who seemed the most upset with his disappearance but who smiled at him, turning soft. They were all looking at Alex's cloak.

"This time it has worked in your favor, but you're going to need to control that, Nova," said Barnaby.

"Control what?" Alex replied.

Gwendolyn looked at Barnaby, a fleeting look of concern washing across her face. "We must get him to the Wizard Oberon at once. Perhaps he can help us with Luca as well?"

"Isn't it such a coincidence that we've all ended up here," said Cassia, doing that thing she did where she would fling her arms out horizontally and twirl around, looking at the sky.

"No, it isn't," said a voice that belonged to none of them.

Startled, Barnaby pulled out his small blade and dropped into a fighting stance with one leg in front of the other. They were all on edge since last night and the reveal of the box, and then the attack of the crows.

"I called for you, for all of you, and you've arrived in your own way," said the voice again. It was an old voice, a cold voice, a voice of authority.

"Who are you? Come out at once!" exclaimed Barnaby, who was in no mood for a new intruder.

"I am not a who, I am a what, and I am right here in front of you," replied the voice.

Alex was the first to see it. Behind some vines on the cliff face were two eyes, a nose, and a mouth. He noticed the mouth first because of the scraping sound the lips made as they spoke. It was a rock face.

"Nova, as you know, the Wizard Oberon has asked for you, and you must come this way at once. I will also grant entrance to your friends," said the voice in a demanding way.

"What do you mean you 'called for us'?" asked Alex, who was trying to understand the meaning of all of this.

"None of you are taught in the old ways, in the ways of our mind," replied the rock face. "So many years of neglect, what a disappointment."

"What are the old ways?" asked Cassia, walking closer to the rock face as her curiosity overcame her fear.

"The old ways were back in a time long before you were born, when all creatures were in tune with the world around them. You now rely so heavily on sight, taste, touch, sound, and smell, but there are more than those five senses. You are all capable of so much more and Nova even so much more than that, but even you, Barnaby, can find the old ways helpful." The rock face's eyes wandered over to the troll, and its face looked like it gave a slight nod. "You must open your heart and open your mind, but this is not the time to start learning such things."

"How did you know my name?" asked Barnaby gruffly, annoyed at the rock face for singling him out.

The rock face laughed for some time in such a way that irritated the entire group.

"Don't you think I would need to know your name to summon you?" the rock face responded.

"I didn't hear you summon us, we just arrived," retorted Gwendolyn, who felt her knowledge of magic should not be lumped together with the rest.

"Don't you listen, Gwendolyn, soon to be queen of the fae?" The rock face laughed again as Gwendolyn blushed. She hadn't shared that information with them before, so she looked down at the ground in frustration at having been exposed.

"Don't you think it's funny that you all ended up in

this one place, here with me even though you were apart? That isn't a coincidence," the rock face said, amused with himself. There was a silence before he continued. "I know more about your past, present, and future than you currently know and more than you will probably ever know. I know that Nova, who currently calls himself Alex, and Cassia have come from Creston in Dacaan. I know that they arrived at Founders Bay and were taken in by Barnaby and his kind wife. That they were found by you, Gwendolyn. That your betrothed, Luca—" the rock face explained before being cut off by Gwendolyn.

"Where is he, where is Luca?" said Gwendolyn, upset that another one of her secrets had been revealed and not on her own terms.

Cassia looked with sympathy at Gwendolyn, who was now standing there with all of her carefully wrapped secrets and emotions exposed.

"That is for you to find out," replied the rock face.

"Well, if you know so much, then why won't you help us? Why won't you tell us where to find Luca?" said Barnaby in frustration. He was huffing slightly under his breath. Alex had never seen him like this before.

"I cannot alter your course, you must find your own path," said the rock face, somehow looking bemused even though its expression was made of limestone.

"Then why have you asked us here?" asked Alex curtly.

"We must get you safely to the Wizard Oberon, and there are dangers now in Happenstance, so you must be careful. Who knows what might have followed your friends," replied the rock face.

Alex's armband now climbed into his hand and again

became a key, but not the same key that it had been when it was meant to open the box. This was different.

Below the rock face there now revealed a door slightly obscured by some ivy and behind the freshwater that drizzled down from the ledge of the cliff. Alex wondered if his eyes had deceived him before or if the door had just been too hidden to notice. It was made of stone, and there was a discernible silver handle and keyhole.

Alex walked over, slid the key into the keyhole, and opened the lock. The door was extremely heavy, and he had to get Barnaby's help to push it open.

Behind him he heard it—the squawk of a crow. Of more than one crow. They must have followed Cassia, Barnaby, and Gwendolyn up to the base of the mountain like the rock face suggested.

"Quickly," urged the rock face, "you will be safer inside. Just try to avoid the dragon."

"A happy dragon?" asked Cassia with fear in her voice.

"Not now, Cassia. Inside, quickly," said Gwendolyn, grabbing her arm and pushing her and the others into the darkness. She closed the door behind them before the crows swooped to get inside.

❖

Inside the mountain was the sound of dripping. It wasn't as cold as Alex expected, given that they were now sheltered from the wind. It again reminded him of the cave in Creston, and a cold shudder ran down his spine. He could tell Cassia was feeling nervous, too, as she was walking close to Barnaby and looking around at every dark crack and crevice.

After a few minutes, their eyes adjusted, and it didn't look as terrible as it might have.

"Well, it's not bad, but it's not quite what I had in mind when I heard we were going to the Wizard Oberon," said Barnaby, trying to make light of the situation.

"Do you not usually take this route?" asked Cassia, trying to keep conversation going, as she hated the quiet and she especially needed distraction now.

"There are many footpaths up Glass Mountain that most normal folk will take, so this is new to me," replied Barnaby.

"And me," said Gwendolyn, looking around like she was out of her comfort zone for once.

The group stopped for a moment to look at her. She was a soon-to-be queen, and their perception of her had now changed somewhat.

"I'm sure this is not the sort of travel someone like you would be accustomed to," said Barnaby to drive the point home.

"Listen," she replied, "I didn't want you to think differently of me. I am not that sort of princess. I believe that a queen-in-waiting is stronger in the face of danger than sitting and assessing a court, not that we do that in the fae world in any case." She gave a flick of her hand that said she had finished the discussion. Alex got the sense that she most certainly didn't want to talk about the second revelation the rock face made about her pending nuptials to Luca. Perhaps all of this was reason for the sadness he saw on her face before, but why be sad if you were going to be queen and have a doting future king at your side?

Alex thought maybe there were more secrets that she was keeping, but now wasn't the right time to pry further.

The group carried on. Gwendolyn was the one brave enough to now forge a path ahead of them. Her courage matched her need to show that she was not to be mistaken for weak or too noble, and Alex appreciated her good nature. She was more warrior than queen-to-be, that was a fact. She was in fae form and shining her light ahead of them so that they could see.

"Alex, your cloak," said Cassia, pointing to its many embroidered threads that now formed hundreds of small stars that shone brightly, helping to illuminate the pathway.

"Would you like to wear it?" he asked her, about to take it off and drape it over her arms. Although it was not cold in the cave, he felt it was the least that he could do for a friend who not only traveled to a different world with him but who was traveling into the depths of it.

"No, Nova, it is your cloak, and only you can use its power," said Barnaby, taking off a wooly coat that he had been wearing and dropping it onto Cassia's shoulders instead.

"Well, if it's a cloak of invisibility, then why is Alex not invisible right now?" asked Cassia, happy that she had Barnaby's coat but annoyed at not being allowed to try on the magic cloak.

"Nova knows, whether he knows it or not right now. It's like what the rock face said," Barnaby concluded with a laugh.

"Well, the cloak seemed to not just make him disappear, but it transported him. How do you make sense of that?" continued Cassia, feeling comfortable in her general ramblings with Barnaby now.

Alex watched how they interacted with each other. He realized that she felt the same feeling he himself had back at the lighthouse when Barnaby's wife brought him tea before bed and told him a story before tucking him in. Cassia didn't say it, but Alex knew she missed her father.

The path ahead snaked in a variety of different directions, carved around rocks and beautiful waterfalls that seemed to drop from the heavens but from places where no light could be seen above. Alex noticed that it felt like they were going downward rather than upward, and he just hoped they were going in the right direction.

"The rock face mentioned a dragon, is it Dragmar?" Alex muttered. He didn't want to show that he was somewhat frightened at the thought of it.

Gwendolyn stopped ahead and turned around to look at them. In the moment that she had turned, Alex saw a coldness in her eyes that he had not seen before. Her appearance had changed, becoming less ethereal and more commanding, perhaps because of the darkness in the tunnels or because he now knew of her importance.

"When Happenstance was created and its earliest people arrived, it was a place of equal balance, and people grew to not be afraid. Everyone put love first," spoke Gwendolyn in a way that led her words to reverberate around the walls of the tunnel.

She turned around a sharp bend that led to a series of circular stairs and continued, "It wasn't until the time when humans first arrived here in Happenstance that discourse began, and the harmony with which we once lived began to be disrupted."

"What disharmony? We all get along," replied Barnaby with a laugh. He wanted to keep the mood light.

"Of course there is not harmony, troll," replied the princess in a tone that only a queen-in-waiting could offer.

She turned around curtly, calming her demeanor, and continued, "Humans live in fear because they all crave power, and they know that power can destruct. This craving for power and fear made its way to Happenstance with their arrival. Although only good humans who were chosen by Lady Luck came to Happenstance, they are creatures of habit, and their past infected their future. First, there was fear. They feared the other inhabitants of Happenstance even though they did nothing ill-willed toward them. There was a fear that their new home had more powerful inhabitants because they possessed innate magic and very few humans do. This is what power teaches you, to question and fear others. That is how power thrives."

Gwendolyn paused for a moment to navigate the final stair, which was partly destroyed, and then helping the others up it by staying in position so that her light beamed down. They continued forward down the path.

"Dragons were the first creatures that humans grew to fear. The dragons had lived here harmoniously for years. The humans, however, were worried that the dragons might attack them and burn their villages, so they decided to go kill the dragons. The fairies, the trolls, the goblins, the witches, and the other inhabitants of Happenstance tried to speak with the humans, but they didn't listen. Well, they didn't all listen," continued Gwendolyn.

"What happened to the humans who didn't listen?

What happened to the dragons?" asked Cassia, always wanting things to be explained quicker than possible for the explainer.

Gwendolyn waited for a few long moments to let what she had said before sink in, and because she had never been the type to give into others' demands.

"Three things happened. The first thing was that the dragons retreated into their caves, because they did not want to suffer the same consequences of men and their power that they had suffered for thousands of years before on what is now Dacaan. The second thing was that the humans decided to chase the dragons into the mountains to kill them all." Gwendolyn took another pause; her voice had been wavering, and Alex could sense her emotions again.

"And the third thing," Alex said to prompt her in a consoling way, to show her it was okay to go on.

"The third thing was that the other inhabitants of Happenstance created a movement, which resulted in war, in fact, to help protect the dragons. The humans that fought with the movement became the Wizard Oberon's as a reward, and the bad people were cast away from Happenstance, back to Dacaan. Or so the tale goes," finished Gwendolyn, this time with a sound of triumph in her voice.

"The War of the Dragons," said Barnaby. "Well, that isn't how I was taught it. I had thought those humans had entered Happenstance to take the dragons, but the people of Happenstance sent them back to Dacaan, and the dragons remained hidden in the mountains to stay out of the way of all other creatures who might mean them harm."

"The final part is true, yes, the dragons remain hidden to avoid conflict, but the rest is what they teach you to soften the blow. You can't always believe what you are told," replied Gwendolyn, this time in a much kinder way to Barnaby.

"Then why should we trust what you've taught us now?" asked Cassia in a way she often did that made the recipient of her question feel upset.

Gwendolyn swung around with her piercing eyes, but at seeing the naivety on Cassia's face, she calmed once again. "You shouldn't, but it is up to you as the pupil to take your own view of my truth."

And with that, Gwendolyn darted up the path ahead of them, turning off the need for further conversation.

Alex allowed Gwendolyn's words to dance around in his head before digesting them as he walked the path ahead. There was just one thing he couldn't make up his mind on based on what Gwendolyn had said: whether to be more or less afraid of Dragmar Gregorius of Glass Mountain.

❖

After some time, Alex wondered what point in the day it might be. When they had entered the cave, the sun was approaching the middle of the sky, but he couldn't know without the sky to guide him.

He once again reached into his bag to pull out his communicator, but the battery had died, so he couldn't check the time. Feeling frustrated, he threw it back into his bag. Happenstance was most likely on a different time to Dacaan, in any case. It might have a different time system altogether, for that matter.

Alex was starting to feel frustrated. He also couldn't discern whether they had moved that high up the mountain. Although they had climbed some stairs, it also seemed they had gone downward at points. It was hard to know where, if anywhere, they might be. He was thankful when they turned around a corner and entered into a big, open space that was filled with light. Looking up, Alex could see that light was shining through a ceiling of crystals that hung from the rocky roof in a myriad of different colors including green, blue, pink, and purple. They were sparkling in patterns like stars in the night sky. The colors shone through the crystals and laid a mosaic pattern of color on the floor and walls.

"This must be the Constellation Library," exclaimed Gwendolyn in awe.

"Wow, this is something else," said Cassia, walking forward to look up into the air.

"Careful, lassie," said Barnaby. He grabbed the back of his wooly coat she was wearing to pull her back from the edge.

It was hard to see at first, but there was a great precipice in front of them, and further along the edge of it was a long rope ladder to the other side, which had a wider landing and area for them to stand.

"Come on then, let's get us across to the other side," said Barnaby, leading the way this time as Gwendolyn dropped to light the path for the others.

Barnaby stepped out on to the rope bridge. It swayed sideways a little, and he had to cling onto the rope railings that were draped with a hessian material. He looked over the edge.

"Whatever you do, don't look down," he said with a laugh. A bead of sweat glistened on his brow.

Cassia was next, and she caught up with Barnaby as quickly as she could. "What's down there?" she asked, trying her best to keep her eyes forward.

Barnaby didn't answer. He grabbed her hand and pulled her along faster. Alex accidentally knocked a small rock over the edge. He and Gwendolyn watched as it fell, moving through the light that shone through the crystals, then into the dark abyss. They heard no sound of the rock landing below.

"You'll be all right," said Gwendolyn softly, to overcome the anxiety that Alex was now feeling. Gwendolyn was, of course, fine flying, but Alex didn't have that option.

Barnaby and Cassia were about three-quarters of the way across the bridge before Alex started his crossing with Gwendolyn just in front of him. His heart was racing. Had he ever felt this frightened before? But then his fears grew; he could feel someone else behind him. He could hear them, smell them, sense them. He felt paralyzed with fear.

"Hello, Nova."

❖

Alex whirled around with a fright and stumbled back on the bridge, making it sway. He was pleased that the hessian sidings were there to protect him from the drop, but still he was not ready for what he saw: an old woman with a pointed hat and long, rectangular glasses propped up at the very tip of her short, pointy nose. Everything about her seemed to be at the sharpest of angles. Her eyebrows ran in a straight line from the bridge of her nose up to the temples on her forehead, and she sat vertically on a wooden broom hovering in the air. She was a witch.

"Where have you been, my child? I've been waiting for you for some time, and the Wizard Oberon has asked me to bring you to him at once. There is little time," said the witch.

"Who are you, and how do you know the Wizard Oberon?" asked Gwendolyn, flying in front of Alex to protect him, although she looked very small and not intimidating at all.

"Well, perhaps the question is, who are you?" the witch asked.

Gwendolyn was in no mood for games. "I asked you first, witch," she all but growled in a much louder tone than one might expect from such a tiny person.

"Well, I am of course Persephone Tarsworthy, witch and protector of the Constellation Library," she replied, as if there were no need to explain anything else.

"Oh, of course, my apologies," responded Gwendolyn, taking full form.

"You know her?" asked Alex in surprise.

"Yes. You know me in fact, too. Well, you don't know, but we've met," responded Persephone, who also came off her broom and walked on the bridge. Alex wondered if the bridge could hold all their weight.

"Are you the sister of the pets shop owner in Providence?" asked Cassia from the far side of the bridge.

"Yes, quite so," replied Persephone. "But, I also met

Nova when he was a baby. You would have been too small to remember."

Alex was shocked to think that in his childhood he would have met someone like Persephone, a witch from Happenstance.

"Persephone Tarsworthy, the most famous witch in Happenstance," said Barnaby as he doubled back on the bridge and kneeled in front of her, putting his hand to his heart to show appreciation.

"Oh, get up, you fool," responded Persephone, "I do not respond well to trolls kneeling at my feet."

"Apologies, I thought—" began Barnaby, but the witch interrupted.

"Yes, that's the trouble, you thought," she said in quite an abrupt manner. "But you didn't think that your return to this side of the bridge might cause some structural issues?"

And with that, she hopped back on her broom as a quick response to the groaning sound of the bridge below their feet.

"Hop on, child, and be quiet please, you wouldn't want to wake Dragmar Gregorius," said Persephone to Alex, and he did as he was instructed, jumping onto the back of her broom and in turn allowing safe passage for all to the other side. He wasn't sure how easy he felt on the back of a broomstick and decided it was best to hang onto her sides and close his eyes so that he did not look into the chasm below.

"Is Dragmar Gregorius around?" asked Cassia as she rushed hurriedly with Barnaby across the bridge.

"Shhhh, not now, child," said Barnaby, who clearly

didn't want to think about what lurked below as the bridge seemed less safe than it had just minutes before.

Once all were on the other side, they headed around the wall, which opened up onto a massive octagonal-shaped room with books lined up on either side of its walls and up to the starry, crystal ceilings. At what looked like every fifth level, there was a row of green plants that cascaded over the edge of a walkway. Ladders ran up the outsides of the bookshelves for people to climb up, although it could be presumed that Persephone would fly when necessary.

Alex had never seen so many books and was surprised both at the beauty of the place and at the fact that so many books existed.

"I thought all the books were burned by the Regime," gasped Alex, looking up and around.

"Well, we claimed as many copies as we could before that happened. We focused on acquiring the originals, of course," replied Persephone as they both dismounted the broom, and she walked over to a large desk covered in pages and quills.

"The Constellation Library is the largest library of books in the world. My job is to ensure that it does not just sit and decay. A library is a living thing, of course, we can't just let writing die, we must write too," she said, picking up one of the quills and putting it in an inkwell. "I've been writing your story as you've grown, Nova. We are just coming to your quest, and I believe that it shall be a fantastic one."

Alex decided not to respond to this remark. He was so often confused by who knew what about him and what he even knew of himself, that it was best to question less and continue forward. At least for the time being. He was saving the majority of his questions for the Wizard Oberon.

"Well, there is no time to wait dawdling here," stated Persephone, clutching her broomstick. "To the elevator, the Wizard Oberon awaits us at the top."

She rushed toward the middle of the room where a tall, golden cylinder shot up into the daylight.

"Come on then, all of you, no time to waste. Jump in," she said, walking through a door into the elevator.

Once they were all inside, she pushed a button that read 'Serendipity School of Magic,' and up they shot at lightning speed to the Wizard Oberon who was awaiting them.

CHAPTER 9

The Wizard Oberon was old and gray. His hair was long in all places, and you could barely see his pale eyes through it. They were similar in color to Alex's but had seen so much more. Although he was old, he was tall, and although he looked slim, he was strong. His blue hat sat back and flopped in its own weight on his head. He wore overly large and long-flowing, blue clothing that mostly covered all parts of him, apart from his hands and his feet where white gloves and brown shoes did the job. He hadn't said a word since their arrival when he had nodded his head to the witch and to the others in the group, before looking Alex in the eye and turning and walking away.

"Go," pushed Persephone with both her broomstick handle and her word.

Alex followed the Wizard Oberon, still unsure whether he should feel excited or frightened. Both feelings toiled inside of him like a great knot.

The Wizard Oberon crossed a great square toward a gleaming, white pavilion that held front porches decorated with twisted columns. Alex could see people in similar blue dress to the Wizard Oberon. They were slightly obscuring themselves behind the columns and topiary, but he could tell that their eyes were upon him. For some reason, he felt that many more eyes than even the ones he could somewhat see were watching and soaking him in.

Alex stumbled slightly on a stone on the floor but tried to keep up pace with the Wizard Oberon, who was walking very quickly despite his age. Did everyone in Happenstance move quickly, Alex wondered. They headed up a spiral staircase, and, suddenly, they had moved inside. They then walked down a hallway with tall pictures of other wizards, who looked similar to the one in front of him, although some were bald, some were fat, some were women, and some had different skin tones. But all wore the same jeweled regalia around their necks.

The Wizard Oberon walked around a corner and disappeared into a room. Alex walked in and then rushed around it looking for him, thinking that he had simply not walked fast enough, and that the Wizard Oberon had taken off as there were no other doors. Suddenly, the door he'd just walked through slammed behind him.

"You've wasted much time, Nova," came a voice from behind him. It was the Wizard Oberon.

Alex was caught off guard. "My... well, my apologies. I came as quickly as I could," replied Alex, not knowing what to say but feeling affronted.

"Yes, well, there's no time to discuss such matters now. It is about what lies ahead that is important," said the Wizard Oberon.

The Wizard Oberon walked over to a tan leather chair, which had an animal skin draped over it and was perched beside a fireplace. He gestured to the matching chair across from it, and Alex sat too. The chair faced out a window, and Alex saw fluffy, white snowflakes floating slowly to the ground outside.

There was a moment of silence between them as Alex settled into the seat and looked nervously into the fire.

"Might I ask, sir, what I am late for?" said Alex in the politest way that he possibly could. He realized he rarely called people 'sir' and felt awkward. He didn't know how to act and noticed more specifically that his hands felt out of place, so he chose to sit on them. The Wizard Oberon had a commanding presence, and although the room was snug with the fire crackling, he presented a cold front that made Alex shiver.

"Well, you, young man, are late for your quest of course. Your destiny awaits you," replied the Wizard Oberon in frustration.

The Wizard Oberon snapped his fingers, and two cups and saucers with hot tea appeared on the marble tabletop that stood between them. He snapped his fingers again, and a silver pot with sugar cubes and a silver spoon appeared next to the steaming mugs.

Alex hadn't been sure of what to expect when meeting a Wizard Oberon, but at the same time nothing seemed out of place. The Wizard Oberon was confident and sharp with his words, and he was obviously magical. Alex felt he didn't know what might happen next around this Wizard Oberon, and it filled him with an excited exhaustion. Or perhaps his tiredness came from the mint tea that he was sipping. He had been traveling for days now, he thought as he sunk more comfortably into his chair.

"We have been waiting for this moment for a long time in Happenstance, young man. We are ready here at the school and with the Council of Elders." The Wizard

Oberon paused to stir two sugar cubes into his cup before continuing, "But the fact of the matter is that the people of Happenstance are not, and nor are you."

The Wizard Oberon was sipping his tea and looking intently down his long nose toward the boy sitting in front of him. Alex had never felt so small or insignificant in his life and was sure that the Wizard Oberon was scrutinizing him. Alex hoped his quick attempt this morning at combing his hair back meant that he did not look too scruffy. He had, however, been through a crow attack, an unexplainable shift in time and place, and a trek through the underbelly of a mountain, so he could only presume that his hair was now disheveled. He set down his tea and ran his fingers through it in an attempt to compose himself in front of the Wizard Oberon.

"You see, sir"—he had said it again, but it seemed he couldn't help it—"I think that you have found the wrong boy. I am Alexander Kerr from Creston, and my life is altogether . . . well . . . insignificant. You are wasting your time, I believe, sir," Alex mustered timidly. For some reason he pictured himself sitting there in front of the Wizard Oberon looking like a small mouse.

"Oh good heavens, young man, we have very little time for this. Has your father taught you nothing?" rebuked the Wizard Oberon, and he set his tea back on the table so that the liquid sloshed everywhere as he stood up abruptly.

"Well, my father has amnes—" started Alex, but who was again interrupted by the Wizard Oberon.

"Jacob was one of the smartest of humans. The things he told you were not untrue, they were confused by that wretched virus given to him by the Regime," said the

Wizard Oberon as he walked over to his dark mahogany desk that sat behind their seating area. Alex watched as he picked up a handful of scattered papers and slotted them into some sort of order before bringing them back over to Alex.

Alex was taken aback by the fact that the Wizard Oberon mentioned his father and provided reassurance that the suspicions he'd had about the stories his father had told him were true. Alex remembered the many moments of lucidity his father showed, but the confused stories of the stars, the otherworld, and magical things Alex had before thought were all just that—confused. Of course, Alex had been surprised that a number of the things his father had mentioned were, in fact, part of Happenstance, and it suddenly dawned on him that his father had perhaps once been here and had known the Wizard Oberon.

As the Wizard Oberon approached him with the papers, Alex piped up again, "The Regime gave my father the medicine for the virus, you mean. So that he could survive. It would never give him the virus, it has been trying to protect Dacaanians from it."

Shaking his head and closing his eyes, the Wizard Oberon set the papers softly down in a now much more consoling way into Alex's hands. "You have much to learn still, Nova, and I am here to teach you. Let us start now."

❖

It took the entire evening for the Wizard Oberon to explain. They were uninterrupted apart from the top up of tea, the arrival of biscuits, and a light meal for their supper. Alex said very little but listened as hard as he could. He heard so many important things about himself, his life, Happenstance, the Regime, and his family that he was worried it would be too much, and his mind would simply give up trying to hold onto everything. He also worried that if some things were so contrary to your beliefs, that they just don't stick. Your thoughts can't explain them, and it would take time to really sink in. Some things the Wizard Oberon said were shocking, others harrowing, but mostly what he heard made him sad. It was a sadness that sat at the pit of his stomach like a coarse coil of metal mesh melding its way through his intestines. Alex felt that his world had been turned upside down in just a few hours. Everything he thought he knew and understood seemed wrong. Everything that made him feel safe seemed to be his enemy.

Yet, the Wizard Oberon had provided him with clarity. He knew who he was now and was certain of a bigger objective on what must be done. It was terrifying to think of the quest that lay ahead, but it also filled him with the same sense of purpose that a sword must have when wielded.

"Come now, Nova, it is time that you get back to your quarters. The others will be wondering where you've been," said the Wizard Oberon, who also looked tired from their prolonged discussion. The Wizard Oberon winced ever so slightly as he stood up from the chair and walked past the great fireplace, which was now just smoldering with embers of the logs that had fed it before.

The Wizard Oberon walked Alex back down the vast hallways but took a different direction than before, and they walked through a courtyard with a beautiful array of snow-dusted topiary hedges and sculptures dotted throughout. Alex noticed the dragon on the far side. He thought of the story Gwendolyn had told about the dragons and realized that their existence in the mountains was not so unlike his existence in Creston. At least the dragons chose their fate, even if it was a cruel one. Too much was spinning around like a tempest in his mind; he needed to rest.

At the other side of the courtyard, Alex could see in the frosted glass windows that sat behind a portico that his friends were inside, along with many others. He could hear them talking and laughing and having a very jolly time.

"I'll join my friends here, first."

"We will resume discussions tomorrow after breakfast. I will see you then, Nova," said the Wizard Oberon as Alex walked up toward the door.

"Where shall I meet you?" asked Alex, looking to the left toward where the Wizard Oberon had been just moments before, but he had vanished. Alex didn't have the mental capacity to think about where the Wizard Oberon might have gone, so he sat down on the frozen ground with his back to the wall, his knees bent up, and his hands on the back of his head. Now that he was alone, he let the tidal wave of emotions he had been holding back wash over him and let out a rumble of small sobs and a waterfall of tears just as the door burst open.

"There you are, we've been wondering where you were," said Barnaby.

Alex was not prepared for the arrival of the others and quickly wiped his eyes. He stood up, looking away from them, but he couldn't get his emotions past Cassia.

"Alex, are you all right?" she said, putting a hand on his shoulder.

He brushed it off more viciously than he'd intended and walked a little further away. "It's been a long day."

Cassia and Barnaby looked at each other before Barnaby gave a little nod.

"Well, I'd better be off," he said. "I'll see you both in the morning." And with that, he headed off, leaving Alex and Cassia to themselves.

Cassia walked a little toward Alex, just into his line of vision, and gave a sheepish grin before turning and gazing up toward the night sky with him. The comet was gleaming above them.

"Can you see it?" Alex asked, wanting her to say 'yes' so that for once he would feel less alone in all of this. For once he would know that she truly understood that coming here wasn't just a fun escape but something much, much more important.

"Yes, I can. Barnaby said it was a comet, and it's the most beautiful thing I've ever seen," she replied, looking at him again with a consoling smile on her face.

"Could you not see it back in Creston?" Alex asked.

"No, I couldn't," she replied.

They stood there for a few minutes more, looking up at the stars but thinking about each other.

"Come on," interrupted Cassia, who liked to spend less time in her own thoughts than Alex did. "I have something I want to show you before we head to bed."

She grabbed his hand and walked him around the courtyard portico to a door on the far right. A hallway led to a second door and another outdoor area that was lit by the stars. It was a semicircular theater with a stage that ran deeper than Alex had ever seen before, and the seats projected like rings around it. It was magical to see such a place at night, when no one else was there and the light of the heavens lit up the white marble, giving it an otherworldly feeling.

"Come on, slow poke," said Cassia, who was already running down the path toward the stage in front of him.

Alex smiled and followed her. Cassia had a way of making any situation exciting, and for a moment Alex was back in Creston, running through the snow and sliding out on to the frozen lake with her. He picked up a small handful of powdered snow, pressing it hard to form it into a ball and throwing it playfully her way. She laughed and threw one back at him before falling on the stage. Alex fell next to her. Lying on their backs, they started waving their arms back and forth to make snow angels.

Not wanting to get too wet in the snow, Alex sat up with a big grin on his face and looked down at her, watching her frantic arms rushing up and down with her closed eyes and silly smile.

"Thank you, Cassia," he said, not quite sure where the words came from.

She sat up and brushed the snow out of her braided hair. "For what, silly?" she asked sheepishly.

"For following me to this other land, for being there for me, for understanding me better than I understand myself," he replied.

In true Cassia style, she responded with a smile and then looked out over the rows of seats in front of them.

Cassia looked down; she didn't do well with compliments. "Well don't thank me yet, it feels like all of this is far from over."

Fresh snowflakes started to fall again, fluttering like feathers around them.

"Imagine if we were at the Championships again but this was our stage," she said, picking up on a shared feeling that was emanating between them.

Alex thought back over the Championships. The look on Cravelda's face when the rabbits ran loose, the trial at the Obelisk, and the taking of Phoebe and her family.

"Cassia, there is something I need to tell you, well, some things," Alex stammered, looking over at her and wondering how he could best condense the many hours of information that he had been told by the Wizard Oberon down into a time frame that Cassia would appreciate.

"Go on," she said with a curious hesitation in her voice.

This time it was Alex who paused, trying to gather himself and his emotions once more.

"The Regime is not what we think it is, Cassia," he started, testing this sentence and realizing that without context it would most likely seem absurd to her.

"We are children of the Regime, Alex, it is all we know. How could it be any different?" said Cassia in a learned defensive tone. "It feeds our families, it keeps us safe from our enemies, it protects us."

"The Regime has been taking the people of Creston from their districts and using them as slaves. It has been keeping us caged like animals so that it can take our produce." Alex then added with a new burst of emotion, "The Regime gave my father the virus, Cassia."

"Wait, what do you mean? We both know the Regime helps our ill and praises our most successful through the Championships each year, and we know that the Regime helped in curing your father," she responded with a troubled look on her face.

Alex stood up and walked in front of her, offering both hands to help her up off the cold ground. His fingertips had started to tingle in the cool air, and a light breeze ran through the stadium that sent chills down his spine. In that moment everything, including the chimes swinging in a distant garden, the moonlight, the comet, the warmth of Cassia's body below the icy exterior of her fingertips, felt so amazingly real and recognizable in a way that Alex had never known before. Even though the moon hung in the sky above, he felt more awake than ever.

Cassia stood up close in front of Alex. He could tell that she was in denial of the things she had just heard, because he had been too. That is why it had taken so long for him and the Wizard Oberon. The only times that Alex had spoken in the first few hours were for questions of defiance, the next few were for questions of interrogation, and the final were for questions of concern. It wasn't until the Wizard Oberon was adequately convinced that Alex had unraveled the powerful clutches of the Regime from his mind and had understood the gravity of the situation that lay in front of them that he had allowed Alex to leave for the night. For Cassia, it would take some time to digest the information and come to terms with it. Alex knew, however, that what he told her next would change her mind about the Regime faster than it had taken for him to change his, and mostly because it was coming from his lips.

"Cassia, Queen Jocelyn was once married to my father. They were the king and queen of Happenstance," he paused, looking into her eyes and then looking up to the sky to stave off more tears. "Queen Jocelyn is my mother."

❖

Alex was running through the sand. It was hot on his feet, and he wasn't wearing any shoes. He was concerned that his feet would blister and melt into the fragments of rock below him. A memory he felt not in his head but deep in his bones told him to run; it told him he wasn't safe here although the setting was familiar and beautiful. The sky was the brightest, most brilliant blue, and the sun was too large. Perhaps it had come closer to Earth and that was the reason it was so hot. He imagined that this must be how it feels to sit inside an oven. The sand below his feet was crimson-red, and he looked at the imprints his feet were making behind him. He couldn't tell if the imprints were bloodied or just blood-red. He didn't know where he was running, but he was running away. He had to get away; it was coming for him, so he must be faster.

Ahead, Alex could suddenly see a glimmering on the sand, beautiful and hopeful but, most importantly, fresh. Water. He realized he didn't know how thirsty he was until he saw it. His forehead was sweating furiously, and sweaty drops were sliding down his face into his mouth. His tongue felt heavy and full of sand, although his mouth was closed. It was coarse and felt foreign in his body. But he had hope. If he could get to the water and drink enough, he might be able to run farther and make a faster get away. In that moment, that water and that escape were all that mattered, although he couldn't quite remember what mattered beforehand. But that wasn't important anymore.

Ten more steps, and he'd be there. He was so close. He was leaping with all of his might forward, his body moving in involuntary and unusual ways, but using every muscle to continue on. He imagined that to anyone looking on he might appear more like a frog hopping along through the sand, but surely frogs couldn't live in such a hot and barren place. And then he was there. He made his final leap forward with his head down, ready to take a lasting gulp of water that would run through him all the way from his head down to his toes to cool his body and replenish him. He opened his mouth wide and had his heavy tongue out, ready to lap up the brilliant, cool liquid, but to his surprise he took a big mouthful of sand. Perturbed, as he already felt like he had a mouthful of dry sand before, he spat it all out. Looking up, he could see the water just a step ahead—he had mistaken the distance. He leaped again, doing the same thing and missed. He tried again and the same thing. Reality hit him, there was no water.

All of a sudden, a loud thunderclap sounded in the distance, and turning around, he saw the darkness coming. This is what he had been fearing. It had caught up and there was nothing that he could do now. He tried to back away using his hands and feet like a crab but fell again into the sand. Not knowing what to do, he covered his head and curled up into a ball, shivering from head to toe. He opened one eye to see a tall, dark, black serpent standing with its fangs protruding above him, looking down with a sinister smile on its face. Drops of rain were falling all around him but not enough to give him a drink, and now it was too late anyway.

"It's-s-s-s nis-s-s-se to s-s-s-see you again, Nova," laughed the serpent, bending down and flicking its tongue along his leg.

Repelled, Alex withdrew backward, but it was no use, the serpent was there next to him again.

"You think you can es-s-s-scape from me, child?" said the serpent, who was still laughing through a broad smile on its face. It began to circle around Alex, making him feel claustrophobic.

"What do you want from me?" said Alex, trying to sound as defiant as possible with every inch of his body.

The serpent laughed more and coiled faster around him, but in a wider circle. Alex noticed that the rain droplets began falling harder, and he opened his mouth, but in tasting one realized they were salty and not satisfying. He then heard a *thump, thump, thump* around him and opened his eyes to see that smaller serpents were falling around him like rain from the sky. They headed toward him and started slithering around his body. One got under his top, and he grabbed it and threw it as far away as he could.

"What do you want? Tell me!" he screamed, this time out of frustration, anger, and fear.

"I want what the res-s-s-st of them want," sissed the serpent.

And then, a strength suddenly pulsed through Alex's veins, and he stood up in the circle. The smaller serpents slithered away, sensing change, and burrowed themselves into the sand.

"You can't have me, I am not yours," said Alex, but from a different place. He was no longer the boy in the grips of the serpent but a voice from outside, looking down at the scene. He felt sorrow for the boy at first, but it was quickly overcome by a sense of pride. He felt much stronger than the serpent now.

Shocked by the sudden change, the serpent jumped backward away from the boy.

"Who are you, where are you?" asked the serpent, looking around but seeing nothing.

Inside of him, Alex let out an overwhelming emotion that had been swelling up from within. It felt like an uncontrollable light that was penetrating through him, and suddenly a wave of cold, blue water came rushing over the hill of the desert.

"No, what is-s-s that, noooo," said the serpent, beginning to slither away. But he was not fast enough, and the wave engulfed him and washed far into the horizon.

The boy that had once been there had vanished and had become something brand new, an unexpected new, but an important new all the same.

❖

Alex awoke to the sound of a gong. He propped himself up with one hand on his bed and the other shielding his eyes from the bright sun that flooded the room. He felt well-rested, as if something important had happened during the night that he couldn't remember but that had stuck with him like a badge of honor.

"Breakfast time, sleepy," said Cassia, throwing his clothes at him on the bed.

"Thank you, Cassia," he said, smiling through a sleepy, scrunched-up face. He liked thanking Cassia, she did a lot for him.

"You were sleeping like a baby this morning, and I didn't want to disturb you, so I spent a little time just sitting and thinking—you know how much of that I usually do," she said, smirking before a more serious look overtook her face.

"What were you thinking about?" asked Alex as he threw on the freshly pressed Serendipity School of Magic top and pants from behind a wall that blocked him from view. The top had an insignia on the blazer front pocket of a dragon with the name of the school embossed around it.

Cassia took a few seconds to respond. He knew what she would have been thinking about.

"Alex, or should I say, Nova, I believe everything you said, and I want to help you," she said, looking him in the eye as he came around the corner of the wall.

They took a moment to smile at each other, thinking about the strength of the bond that had grown and was growing between them. No one else had been through what they'd been through. But together the situation they were in felt less frightening, less chaotic, and that was precious. Something was changing for them both, and between them both.

"I knew you would," said Alex, feeling happy that she trusted him so much and that they were no longer living a lie.

He packed his things into his bag and set it in a big

wardrobe on the far side of their room where Cassia also put her things.

"You finally called me Nova," Alex said, twisting the door handle but not yet opening the door.

"Well you are Nova, aren't you?" Cassia replied, pulling her braids around to the side and adjusting her coat.

"Yes, I guess I am," he said.

CHAPTER
10

After breakfast, Nova met the Wizard Oberon. Well, he didn't know where to look, but the Wizard Oberon happened to just appear. With a wave of his hand, they were in a completely different setting on two great, stone chairs on another part of the mountain, but Nova couldn't completely understand where. It was windy, but they were warm under the sun. It was if they were in their own snow globe, but rather than the snow being inside, it was floating to the ground all around outside their bubble. Things like this weren't odd, Nova assumed, when you were in the presence of a wizard.

"So, child . . . Nova," the Wizard Oberon said, taking extra time to pause on his name, "you've begun to accept your destiny?"

Nova sat there, understanding that the Wizard Oberon knew more than most people might know about him, and not just the facts of the past. The Wizard Oberon looked down regally at the tops of the trees where small birds were singing and floating on the sharp wind. One of the birds looked black, and Nova thought of the crows, but he felt safe with the Wizard Oberon in their globe.

"What is *your* name?" countered Nova to the Wizard Oberon's question.

The creases in the old Wizard Oberon's face pushed together slightly. He took the great staff that he held in his hand, which was carved with many different animals that Nova knew, and also didn't, and tapped it lightly on the ground as if to assert his authority.

"You are learning, Nova, or at least, you are willing to learn," he said in response to this, and the two fell silent. Time and place made a merry dance around them.

Finally, the Wizard Oberon broke the silence and began on another one of his long missives. "My name is Oberon Silver. I am the Chief Counsel at the Council of Elders and current Ruler of Happenstance. I am very old. Older than ten of your lifetimes, and I have seen many things. I know many things. I know the stars, I know the gods, I know the evil. For some time, I have been waiting for you, Nova. Last night we spoke a lot about what has come to be, but now we must speak more about what will come to pass."

The Wizard Oberon Silver stopped for a moment and looked toward Nova to make sure that he was listening.

Nova looked at the Wizard Oberon and asked, "What must I do?"

"It is more what you must not do," said the Wizard Oberon. "It is easy to devise a plan, but it is important to understand it from the inside out."

Nova sat, thinking of what that could mean. The Wizard Oberon gave him time to ponder.

"But there are things that must be done, and they must be done properly. Firstly, you must prepare and train. Secondly, you must build up your confidence and strength, which will take time that we lack. And finally, you must face the Regime."

"But," continued the Wizard Oberon, "I know that he has been coming to you in your dreams, the Dark Lord."

"You mean the serpent?"

"If that is how you see him, then yes. He is coming to make you weak and to frighten you, to unnerve you. Whether it is when facing him, the Regime, or any other, you must not come undone. Lady Luck is on your side, and the gods smile in your favor, Nova, but as with any destiny, it is yours for the taking. Only you can choose what happens next," said the Wizard Oberon. He looked tired as he gazed out over the mountaintops.

A feeling associated with the serpent came to Nova. He felt strength.

"How will I know what should happen next?" asked Nova, feeling nervous once again that so much rested on his shoulders.

"You must follow your heart. I can see many things, but the power in you is so strong that you must face this on your own. I will, of course, be there to help you grow and to support you, but when the moment comes it all comes down to you," responded the Wizard Oberon with a furrowed brow that emphasized his concern.

Nova thought for a minute before saying, "What if I don't know what to do?"

"That is exactly the attitude you must not have," said the Wizard Oberon, getting down from the stone chair that he had been sitting on. "One day, Nova, you will be stronger than me, and when that day comes it will be my end, and it will also be a new beginning. Dacaan has been in a state of chaos for too long now, and Happenstance is fading. It is up to me to help you make things better, we only have this one chance, and it can only be now." The Wizard Oberon looked tired as he got closer to Nova before waving his hand again.

In the next moment, Nova was somewhere completely different: a school classroom with a chalkboard and a teacher's desk in front of him. He looked around, wanting to ask the Wizard Oberon more questions and worrying about the things he had just heard, but the Wizard Oberon wasn't there. A bell went off, and a dozen children who looked his age ran into the room.

"Nova!" came the familiar voice of Cassia, and she winked at him as if it were their little secret about his name. She came bounding over to him enthusiastically and sat in the desk next to him.

"I was looking for you, where did you go?" she asked.

"I was with the Wizard Oberon, but he just disappeared," he responded and noticed the many eyes gazing at him, including the green eyes of a tall, dark-haired boy sitting in front of him.

"No one sees the Wizard Oberon," said the boy, and murmurs ran through the class of children sitting all around Nova and Cassia.

The boy turned around and stood on his chair. "Who are you, anyhow? I haven't seen you, or you, before in Serendipity."

But before either Nova or Cassia could respond, a gray-haired woman came in through the door. "Silence, children. Callum Hughes, come down from that chair immediately, or you will be asked to join the headmaster again."

The woman, who was presumably their teacher, came

marching in and put a briefcase down with a thud. She clicked the top latch open, and out popped a piece of chalk and a chalkboard eraser of their own volition, and they flew to the board. The etching sound the chalk made on the dark green chalkboard was shrill and high-pitched. By the looks of all the children around Nova, the sound was hurting their ears equally.

Welcome to Magic 101. I am your teacher, Mrs. Borealis. Today we will be learning about Telekinesis. The chalk squiggled to a stop and dropped into the small, metal shelf below the chalkboard, landing face-side-up on the eraser.

"You, in the middle there, with the blondish-white hair—stand up!" said Mrs. Borealis, pointing toward the center of the class.

Nova looked around to find the child in question.

"Yes, you. I'm pointing at you, my dear," said the teacher, wiggling her long, bony finger at Nova.

The children all began to giggle as he awkwardly stood up, swaying around from side to side. He didn't understand how he could have just had such a serious conversation with the Wizard Oberon Silver on the side of a mountain about his quest and about the future of the two worlds, but also be so afraid in a classroom of children his own age. Nevertheless, he had always hated being singled out in school, and this had not changed, apparently.

"And what is your name, young man?" asked Mrs. Borealis, who was sitting assuredly on the edge of her desk with one leg crossed over the other.

He looked down at Cassia, who nodded her head to him. "My name is Nova, Nova Kerr," he said, realizing that was the first time he had introduced himself with this new name or even said it out loud, and it was jarring coming out of his mouth. The sound felt somewhat foreign to him.

"And, young man, we have not seen you before, I don't believe, so please grace us with more information about yourself. Where you are from, perhaps, and why you have chosen this class?" continued Mrs. Borealis.

"Well, I'm from a town called Creston, and I don't know why I have chosen this class. I didn't choose this class, in fact, and the first time I had even heard about it was when your chalk wrote its name on the board," said Nova, honestly hoping that now she might leave him alone and choose another student in the room to question.

On hearing this, a stern look washed over Mrs. Borealis's face, and she hopped down with the click of her two heeled shoes landing on the floor. She walked slowly down through the desks closer to Nova. Giggles had erupted through the classroom at first but quieted as Mrs. Borealis broke rank.

"So, we have a funny one here, I see," she said to Nova, looking into his eye with an anger that suddenly converted into a cheery type of kindness.

"No, no, Mrs. Borealis, I think you have it all wrong. Alex, I mean Nova, would never have meant to be rude in your classroom," said Cassia, trying to defend her friend.

"And who have we got here, then?" asked Mrs. Borealis with a sickly sweetness in her voice that was only for show.

"His girlfriend," interrupted Callum, looking around the classroom for support from the other children.

"Callum, one more time," said Mrs. Borealis, whipping an angry glance his way.

The laughter died down once more.

Mrs. Borealis rapped her fingers on Cassia's desk, signaling for her response.

"My name is Cassia Maddox. I am friends with Nova, and we have come from the same place," she said, and cooing sounds started around the class, followed by a flare of more giggles.

"Well, since you've both been so forthcoming with this information about yourselves, then why don't you be our guinea pigs?" said Mrs. Borealis, walking back toward the desk. She plucked a shiny, red apple from her bag and put it on the desk in front of her.

"You first, girl. We'd like to see what you can do. Focus on the object, and make it levitate with your mind," she insisted, poising the apple in perfect position.

"I . . . I don't know what you mean. What would you like me to do?" asked Cassia, who didn't understand how that could be possible.

"Well, young lady, use your magic like you know you can. Don't be shy in front of your classmates," replied Mrs. Borealis. "Just use your mind and think of the apple moving up, up, up."

Cassia looked over at Nova, who shrugged his shoulders somewhat. She winced her eyes closed, furrowed her face, clenched her fist, and thought about the apple floating. She opened her eyes again, but nothing had happened.

The classroom erupted with laughter and hand pointing.

"Silence, children, silence at once," yelled Mrs. Borealis, "perhaps I should pick one of you instead."

The room went silent again.

Nova, who was already standing, said, "I'll try."

Murmurs ran through the children as Mrs. Borealis replied with a sly smile on her face, "Yes, please do, Nova."

Nova did something similar to what Cassia had done just a few moments before. He concentrated through his entire body, but just as he opened his eyes, he opened his hands, and there was a blast that jolted him back in his seat.

The apple was now mush all over the blackboard and in Mrs. Borealis's thick hair. Her desk had been pushed back, and she had fallen to the ground in the process.

Getting up and brushing much of the apple mess from herself, she said in a raised voice, "Young man, whatever has gotten into you? This is not the sort of behavior—"

But she was cut off by a male voice louder than her own, "Mrs. Borealis, please come with me outside for a minute."

Flustered, Mrs. Borealis said, "If you will excuse me for a moment, children. Please open your books in front of you and start reading from the first chapter. I will be just a moment with Headmaster Simmions."

Through the glass to the outside of the classroom, Nova could see that Mrs. Borealis was shaking her head and was apologizing to the headmaster. This was the first time he had seen something like this, as usually when there was trouble in a classroom and a child was misbehaving, the headmaster would take the child away and not reprimand the teacher.

Inside the classroom, the children had all opened their

books, but Nova knew that they were whispering about him. The boy in front, Callum, turned around and was elbowing a friend beside him who had curly, light-brown hair and freckles.

"What were you thinking? We aren't meant to use that sort of magic indoors," he said, looking Nova up and down.

"Children our age don't usually have that sort of magic though, Callum. My brother in the senior year can't even use that sort of magic yet," said Callum's freckled friend.

"Well, you might not be able to, Roger, you are weak, but I can," said Callum, looking at Nova.

"Leave them alone," said a girl with short hair that hung in tight ringlets with beautiful ribbons running through it.

"Why would I, Esme?" said Callum, brushing off the girl's request.

"They are new here. You should show them respect—not everything is a battle," she said to Callum.

At that moment, the door burst open, and Mrs. Borealis rushed back in. "My apologies, class, and to Mr. Kerr."

The bell rang and the children stood up, putting their books in their bags or under their arms and putting their coats back on.

"Looks like we will have to discuss this later," said Callum in a menacing way, picking up his things and leaving with Roger.

"Ignore him," said Esme as Callum left the classroom in a rush, slapping many of the other boys on the back as they headed down the hallway. "He is just a bully, and a weak one at that."

"Thank you," said Cassia, who introduced herself and started talking with Esme as they headed out of the classroom.

"Can I have a word please, Mr. Kerr?" said the same voice in the classroom from earlier. It was Headmaster Simmions.

"Yes, of course you can," replied Nova with a gulp as he followed the headmaster up the hall, unsure of what might await him.

❖

Nova sat down in the headmaster's office. It was filled with an assortment of books and other collectables that seemed fitting for a man in charge of a school like this. The room was warm, and there was a beautiful, colorful tapestry with birds of all shapes, sizes, and colors. Many plants with a variety of flowers and fruits growing in large terracotta pots lined the window. The room wasn't as big as the Wizard Oberon's that Nova had been in last night, but it was commanding. It had a small fireplace at the far end and seating against latticed windows that showed an accumulation of snow on the outside. The view out the windows was that of the school grounds, and Nova could see the stadium and the courtyard with the topiary bushes that he had been in with Cassia the night before.

The headmaster sat down in a white chair below a lamp that dangled overhead and indicated for Nova to sit in the chair next to him.

"And how did your first class go, Nova?" asked the headmaster, whose voice was loud but also soothing and deep.

"It wasn't as I had been expecting, although, I guess I hadn't been expecting anything as I didn't know I would be here," he responded, wondering if his response would come across as rude.

"Nova, the Wizard Oberon has told me about you, and it is my job to protect you. On behalf of myself and Mrs. Borealis, we are terribly sorry for your treatment this morning. She wasn't informed that you were here yet, and it won't happen again," said Headmaster Simmions, pouring two glasses of water and pushing one toward Nova.

"It's not a problem. The Wizard Oberon said that I would need to go through training, but I had no idea what it would be," Nova responded. "And I am new to magic. I didn't know that I had it until recently."

"No, of course you wouldn't, as you are from Dacaan," replied the headmaster before taking a big gulp from the glass of water in front of him.

The headmaster continued, "Children of Dacaan are taught that magic is evil, and technology is how to connect to the higher power. You must spend time controlling your magic, and Mrs. Borealis is a fine teacher who can help you in doing so."

Not sure how to respond, Nova said, "Thank you, I look forward to spending more time in her class." Although he was slightly precarious after his ordeal with the apple this morning, to say the least.

"Have you had a chance to read the rest of your syllabus?" asked the headmaster, who was now sitting sideways in his chair, looking with his head cocked on a skew toward Nova. He reminded Nova of a bird.

"No, I haven't, sir," he responded.

"Well, isn't that something," said the headmaster

before snapping his fingers and having a handful of papers appear, which he handed to Nova.

"The Wizard Oberon has insisted on these classes for you before you go back to Dacaan on your quest. Even though we have very little time, it is important for you to prepare," said the headmaster with an assured nod of his head. "Now, of course you have Magic 101, Weapons and Wands, Spells and Charms, Flight, oh, and Basic Survival."

"Basic Survival?" repeated Nova.

"Yes, in Creston you are cushioned from the real world, and it is important to understand how to live and protect yourself in nature," said Headmaster Simmions.

"And Cassia..." began Nova.

"Cassia will join the same classes as you, but she will take a lot longer to find her magic—that is, if she can find it at all," replied the headmaster. "I will spend this morning speaking with all of your teachers directly so that there are no repeats of today's, shall we say, episode with Mrs. Borealis."

"Yes, thank you for that," responded Nova.

"Now, you must go and mingle with your classmates. That, too, is essential for your learning, Nova." Headmaster Simmions rose from his chair and opened the door for Nova to leave through.

"Thank you again, Headmaster Simmions," said Nova as he left down the hallway.

❖

Nova rushed outside to find Cassia. He saw her on the far side of the grounds, speaking with Esme near a large tree with branches that were dusting the ground around them. Not wanting to call attention to himself, he grasped his books and the syllabus given to him by the headmaster and walked quickly past the other children. He was pleased to have spoken with the headmaster, but he did wish that he could change what had happened in Mrs. Borealis's class. He didn't like drawing attention to himself.

As he walked, he had the feeling that the children were grouping closer around him. All of a sudden, one of his feet got caught and he tripped, letting his books fly forward in front of him and the papers float around like butterflies in the air overhead. The children started laughing again, and as Nova rose to his knees, he saw Callum standing with his arms folded in front of him.

"Not so tough now, are you?" the boy said, picking up one of Nova's syllabus papers. "Basic Survival?" He laughed in a taunting way that made the other boys laugh menacingly and the girls giggle and whisper to each other behind cupped hands.

Callum rounded up the boys once more, giving each other low claps before they ran away as the bell rang and all the other children headed toward their classes.

Cassia had noticed the commotion and went over to help him with Esme by her side. They helped him to his feet, and Nova dusted off his trouser legs that were covered in mud and wet snow. He felt embarrassed and could feel his cheeks getting warm even though the snowflakes that had started to drop on them were cold to the touch on the crisp, sunny winter's day.

"Ignore them, they are bullies, and bullies don't

deserve our time," said Esme, walking in the direction of her next class.

"See you later, Esme," said Cassia with a curt smile in her direction before looking back toward Nova.

"I didn't ask for any of this," he said, feeling embarrassingly frustrated, a combination that he had felt in his first year of school in Creston. He thought he had got past this humiliation in school.

"Well, if it isn't angry Nova coming out to play?" replied Cassia with a smile. She was always good at mocking his emotions in the right way to make him snap out of it and see how he really looked from the outside.

Nova smiled even though he didn't want to. Cassia was the only person who made him smile, no matter what.

"I guess I am the new kid," he said reluctantly, "and really all of this is for a bigger cause."

"Precisely, young man," said a voice from behind him.

Nova and Cassia swung around to see an elderly man with a cane and in the same long garments and regalia that the Wizard Oberon wore. His skin was marked with age, and he was hunched over with a dark robe draped over him, which looked heavy on his frail frame. Standing next to him was a young boy who looked like he'd been pulled through the mud. He had straw stuck to brown patches around the bottoms of his trouser legs that Nova noticed as he got closer to him.

"You two are late," said the man with a voice of authority that Nova imagined had one day sounded much more commanding.

"Oh, we are very sorry. We are new, and we lost track of . . ." stuttered Cassia.

"Silence," interrupted the old man, "we do not have time for rambling. Please follow me." With that, he turned and headed quite quickly —much faster than you might expect for his age—toward a set of beautifully gilded gold, black, and silver cast-iron gates, which Nova hadn't noticed before on the far side of the yard. The old man pulled a lever which, again, looked too heavy for him, and the gates began to screech open. Nova assumed that the man must have one day been quite strong and that it was the sort of physical strength that stayed with you even when your body began to cripple.

The old man opened the door and behind it was a ring of muddy, trodden ground. Nova didn't want to step on it, but to avoid further embarrassment he decided that this wasn't the time or place to worry about muddy shoes. The young man who appeared to be an apprentice picked up a rope and flung it over a long railing next to the wall of the ring.

"Welcome to Flight for Beginners. I am Professor Delvoy!" said the old man in a triumphant manner as he elevated above the mud into the center of the ring.

Cassia's jaw dropped open. They had seen a lot, but to see an old man who looked quite frail flying against the background of the sky in front of them was quite out of the ordinary. Nova wondered when Happenstance would stop throwing surprises their way.

"Haha! Young masters, welcome indeed," came the booming voice of Barnaby as he entered the ring from a door that stood in a tall tower to the right.

"Barnaby, it's great to see you," said Cassia, who was fond of Barnaby. It showed, as she was grinning ear to ear.

Barnaby brought his fingers together and blew against

them, letting out a loud whistle, and Nova could hear the sound of galloping coming from within the tower. Out ran two full-grown unicorns. Nova had seen horses before, but typically they were brown or black or mottled in color. These horses were beautifully white, and although they were running on the ground, the mud didn't seem to dirty their coats. They had long white manes and what Nova knew as their telltale pointed horns on top of their heads.

"That, young man, is a unicorn, and that there on top of its head is an alicorn," said Professor Delvoy, looking at Nova as he looked at the horn. "It is where they hold their magic, their power of flight."

Cassia clapped her hands together in excitement.

The unicorns stood between Barnaby and the young apprentice. They were fidgeting somewhat and scratching their hooves on the ground as if they had a huge amount of pent up energy inside of them, and they let out little whinnies as the troll and the young man patted them on the side.

"Elevante," said the young apprentice, who was clearly familiar with the animals and knew what to do and say.

With that, the two unicorns rushed forward and around the outskirts of the ring, kicking up mud behind them before looping up the walls and into the sky. They flew up past the clouds and away to where the group on the ground could no longer see them. Cassia's face was at first excited like it had been when they saw the baby unicorn in Providence, but it was now concerned at their disappearance.

As if their departure had been of no consequence to the others apart from Nova and Cassia, Professor Delvoy continued, "Today you will learn some of the fundamentals of magical flight. You have now met two of the animals, but come, let's meet some more."

Professor Delvoy flew toward the door that Barnaby and the unicorns had come out of that linked the ring to the tower, and he landed on the solid ground once inside. The rest followed him while walking through the mud, with Cassia rushing ahead.

"Will you teach us how to fly like you do, Professor Delvoy?" she asked.

"Yes, but it took me over three hundred years to perfect," he scoffed, looking her up and down. "For a mere human, it would take a lifetime."

Nova ran up and walked slightly behind Barnaby and the young apprentice. "Barnaby, it is a pleasure to see you. I didn't know that you'd be part of our classes."

"I won't," said Barnaby with a smile. "School is not something that us trolls have ever been good at, but the animals—I've always loved the animals, and me and Professor Delvoy have known each other for years."

Nova turned toward the young apprentice. "And I don't think we've been properly introduced, my name is Nova," he said.

"Yes, I know who you are," snapped the boy in an angry way.

Nova had hoped that he would perhaps make at least one friend today and was surprised at this response.

"This is Peter. He's been the stable hand working with Professor Delvoy for some time now. He has something special with the animals," replied Barnaby, trying to placate the situation and provide some comfort to Nova.

"I am more than just a stable hand, sir," spat out Peter

in an even angrier fashion. "I hand raise most of our flyers here at Serendipity. I train them, I love them."

And with that, he shot forward into the tower and stood to the side of Professor Delvoy, who was opposite to the others.

Nova again felt frustration trickle into him. Did Peter find out about the class this morning? Did he speak with Callum who told him not to like Nova?

Barnaby half patted and half pushed Nova on the back so that they entered into the tower. The bright from outside made it so it took a moment for Nova's eyes to adjust to the new darkness, but as soon as they did he looked around and then up to his surprise. This was no normal stable like the farms in Creston. He had expected a low ceiling and perhaps steps to take you up to the top of the tower, but instead it was hollow in the middle with a series of open pens up the sides of the walls holding more unicorns and other feathered animals than he could count. From outside you couldn't hear it, but the sound of squawking and flapping and carrying on by the animals echoed up the middle of the tower.

"We have over two hundred animals here in Aviary Tower, with over fifty unicorns. The biggest herd in Happenstance," shouted Professor Delvoy. "They've been here the longest. We've had unicorns in Happenstance since it was created, since they were forced to leave your world because they were threatened by man. Now the tarakeets, they have perhaps the ugliest look of all the animals, yes, those ones over there"—Professor Delvoy pointed up toward a gray-feathered bird that had small, beady, yellow eyes rimmed in red—"but they are known to be the kindest and gentlest of our animals, so please do show them compassion. They had a hard time in your world before, as they were almost extinct."

"There are the hummingbirds that of course live with your friends, the faes, and there are commodores, cormorants, falcons, pigeons . . ." Professor Delvoy walked forward, paying little attention to his students but rambling on about the different species in their midst. His voice was softening in tone and was now hardly audible amidst the raucous around them.

"Aren't they absolutely wonderful," said Cassia, whose mouth had been open in awe since they first saw the unicorns outside.

"Yes, they are," responded Nova, who was enthused but less enthused than Cassia. He noticed that he was being watched by Peter, who still stood close to Professor Delvoy.

"Cassia, do you think I might have done anything to offend Peter while we've been here, or do you think he would have known what happened this morning?" he asked, still looking in the direction of Peter while whispering in Cassia's ear.

"Who is Peter?" she replied before looking in the direction of Nova's gaze. "Ahhhh, the stable boy. No, why would you say that?"

"Pay attention! You know nothing, and you must know everything in a short period of time," shouted Peter in such a way that the rest of the group was startled, and Professor Delvoy stopped his monologue about his creatures.

"Good heavens, child, what in Happenstance has come over you?" exclaimed Professor Delvoy, looking at him with a quizzical look on his face.

"We've put so much time into training the animals, and these humans are not even paying attention to your lesson," responded Peter, who was obviously quite upset.

"Nova and Cassia, might I remind you that this is a private lesson, as no other child in Serendipity has such little knowledge about flight as you both. It is up to us all to make sure that you learn as much as you can in a very short period of time before you go to face the Regime," said Professor Delvoy in a crisp and precise manner that allowed for nothing less than their full attention.

Both Nova and Cassia bowed their heads, feeling humiliated for being told off and for being caught out in not listening to the lesson.

"Ungrateful, that's what he is," muttered Peter under his breath.

"I beg your pardon, young man?" questioned Professor Delvoy sternly.

Rather than repeating himself, Peter continued, "He is not prepared, and he does not have enough time. He is weak, and we must find another."

"That is not fair," said Barnaby, whose fists were clenched in frustration.

Professor Delvoy held his hand up to Barnaby before responding, "That is not for you to say, Peter. If you would like to continue training with me, then you will learn to hold your tongue in the future. Now please, go and call our two flyers back. They have been outside long enough and will need grooming. We will continue this lesson without you."

Obviously flustered at the Professor's remarks, Peter picked up a bag that held brushes and other grooming items and stormed toward the door. Barnaby and Professor Delvoy began talking together in hushed tones. Something came over Nova, and he ran toward Peter—he wanted to confront him on the way out.

"Peter, I am sorry if I upset you. I don't know what I have done. If this is about Callum and Mrs. Borealis's class then I am truly sorry, I didn't mean to cause anyone harm," said Nova to the back of Peter's head.

Peter stopped and waited for a moment, his silhouette shining with the sun in front of him. He turned around so that his face was just visible in the light. Nova could tell he was still angry as he took steps closer to him, and with a curled lip, he replied, "You are a fraud. You have stolen what I have been working for my whole life by just being here, and the most frustrating thing is that you don't even want it, you don't even care."

"But I don't even know what you mean. How can I take something from you if I don't know what it is that I've taken?"

"This is the problem with you, Nova. Your eyes are open, but you cannot see." And with that, Peter turned around and walked briskly out of the Aviary Tower.

CHAPTER

11

"Y‍OU MEAN TO say that you haven't spoken with the Wizard Oberon about Luca?" said Gwendolyn angrily, looking at the snow-covered topiary in the courtyard. Her hair had a pinkish tinge as it shone in the sunset, and her eyes looked despondent, but there was also something else set deep within them that showed another emotion Nova couldn't quite put his finger on.

A feeling of guilt ran through him as he thought about what had happened in the woods just a few days ago. He worried that there were too many things out of his control right now. All along, he had felt he was heading toward something, being pulled toward something, and now that he had found it he knew he needed the strength to be at one with it. Nova knew that the college was exactly where he needed to be to learn how to control himself better, since he didn't understand this power that was coursing through his veins. Even if the other pupils hated him, he needed to focus and put everything into his training.

"Gwendolyn, I'm so sorry, there have just been so many things—" started Nova, but Gwendolyn stepped away, not wanting to hear excuses. There were no excuses.

"There must be a way to bring him back. If it was so

easy to make him disappear then it must be easier still to bring him back," she said, as if willing it could action it.

"I will speak with the Wizard Oberon tonight. He of all people will know what to do," said Nova with a glimmer of hope. The Wizard Oberon had an unfathomable strength, but Nova wondered how far that strength could go.

Gwendolyn stood in the courtyard looking at Nova with a renewed but fleeting look of compassion on her face. He wondered if she loved Luca at that moment, as her eyes swelled with tears. She leaned forward in the dimming light and kissed Nova on the side of his face, closer to his eye than to his lips. He could feel his cheeks flush and tried not to look awkward as he stared into her enchanting eyes.

"Nova, you are the chosen one. You know that, and it will take time to figure out what that means, but my trust is in you—I know that we will find him." Gwendolyn shrunk and flew off down the hallway.

Nova was left in the snow-covered courtyard and saw on the far side of it the shape of a woman with long hair. Was it Cassia, he wondered?

"Cassia, is that you?" he half shouted, but the figure ran away, and he felt a pang of guilt that perhaps she'd seen too much of his previous exchange. But he would speak with her later, and everything would be ok.

Nova looked around at the shadows cast from the buildings around him. The snowy topiary gave a menacing look with its sharp branches and thorns all around him. He felt a chill down his spine and decided to walk through the ornamental maze to head to the Wizard

Oberon's room. He needed to discuss Luca with him immediately.

As Nova began to take further steps, the shrubbery around him that had at one point been at the height of his knees shot up in front of him and blocked his way. He felt like he was getting suffocated by thorns and the walls were caving in. He started running down paths, turning left and right toward where he thought the exit was, but he only came up against higher and higher walls of green, thorny foliage. What was happening?

Suddenly, in front of him he saw something: a male figure with pointed ears. Perhaps this was the figure he had seen in the courtyard right after Gwendolyn had left. He was frightened at first, thinking that the figure was perhaps going to come toward him, but it started running around a corner, so Nova decided to pursue it. He began running, but just as he thought he was getting closer, the figure would disappear around a corner for Nova to chase once again. He was, however, starting to catch up, and he thought that the figure was perhaps Luca. A turn of the figure's neck around one corner exposed his face and Nova realized *it was Luca*.

"Luca, come back, why are you running from me? We have been looking for you!" shouted Nova.

Feeling frustrated, he began to run faster toward Luca. He wanted to bring him back to Gwendolyn like he had promised, and this was his chance. But every time he turned a corner, Luca looked back with more fright on his face and ran even faster.

"Stay away from me," Nova thought he heard from Luca in front of him.

"Don't you want to come back, where have you been?" asked Nova, starting to feel tired of the pursuit.

He wondered where they were. They had been running so far, and the courtyard that he had been in was not that big. They must now be in a different place, but where? It felt dreamlike and unreal, although the thorns that occasionally scratched his arms and the cobwebs cast across branches that tickled his face said otherwise. He looked up. Above him it was dark, and the stars cast their light.

All of a sudden, Nova rounded a bend and saw Luca in front of him. The fae was at what appeared to be the center of the maze, and there was a tall figure in front of him. Nova recognized it even in the dark, for it had a towering frame and a shimmering, emerald-green-and-black body in the dark night. It was the serpent from his dreams.

"Luca, run! Get away, please! Fly!" he yelled, knowing that the serpent posed a real threat. He feared that Luca, who was a very strong fae, would still stand very little chance against this tall serpent.

To Nova's surprise, Luca didn't move. He knelt in what looked like an act of submission to the towering reptile above him. The serpent coiled around him and began to slither toward Nova slowly and steadily, with its tongue lashing at the air in front of it.

"Sssssssooooo," said the serpent in a high but menacing tone, "you've come to ssss-eeeee me again."

Startled, Nova stumbled backward and fell to the ground. Although this felt like a dream, he remembered that it had started in the courtyard, he hadn't been asleep. Could this be real?

"Let him go," shouted Nova in an act of defiance, and

to his surprise, he mustered enough courage to run past the serpent's head and down past its slippery body toward Luca.

He grabbed the back of Luca's shoulders and turned him around, but Luca's face was missing. All Nova could see was a reflection of the stars above him. Suddenly, Luca disappeared once again and became a cluster of circling crows that twirled like a cyclone up into the night sky.

Nova started yelling, "Luca, Luca, come back to me."

"It's no usssse, child," sissed the serpent, "he is not there."

The serpent slithered back toward Nova and began wrapping itself around him like it had done around Luca and like it had done in his dreams before.

"You do not frighten me," stated Nova, but his voice faltered, making his statement insincere.

The serpent laughed. "Of course I frighten you. I am the monster in your dreamssss, I am the monster in your non-dreamsss. Here's a riddle that might help you," said the bemused serpent. "Finding me is easy indeed. I am greatest before I die and am powered by the sun during the day before becoming at one with the night. What am I?"

Nova realized that he was wearing his backpack, so he ripped it from his back and grabbed his box from inside. His armband turned into a key and crawled to the box. Nova opened it, and a flood of light came pouring out, making the serpent jump backward into the shadows.

The serpent laughed once again. "Didn't you hear me, boy? Your light won't help you."

Nova reached in his box and pulled out an object that was somewhat heavy to the touch. It was a dagger with a bone handle and a sharp, silver blade. Nova pierced it into the serpent's body at the closest point to him, making the serpent recoil backward into the dark.

"Ssssso, you want to fight me, boy?" laughed the serpent after licking its wound. Nova realized that the small indentation the knife had left was not very deep in comparison to the serpent's rather large body, and only a small drop of blood seeped out.

The serpent stood up in front of him. It was intimidatingly tall, and it flared the hood around its head. It had all but blocked out the starlight, and it opened its mouth as if it were about to lunge down and devour Nova. So he held up the dagger. To Nova's surprise, he felt a strong force pushing him back. He looked up and saw the serpent was no longer there, but a beam of blueish light and dust was coming out of the dagger. The serpent had retreated, this time farther than it had before, and Nova felt that the balance of power had shifted.

"Nova, come away from there at once," he heard a stern, gruff voice coming from behind him. He looked back and saw the Wizard Oberon. The courtyard in that very instance had reappeared. Nova looked around, but the tall walls of the maze were gone. The serpent had vanished, and the sky had changed back to dusk.

"Young man, follow me," snapped the Wizard Oberon, and he turned his back and started walking.

"What are you? You are darkness," said Nova toward where the serpent had been, and he turned to follow the Wizard Oberon.

❖

Rather than making their way up to the Wizard Oberon's quarters, they headed down into the underbelly of Serendipity through a series of hallways that were lit by torches and had ornate mirrors lined on either side. Nova noticed the Wizard Oberon's reflection did not appear in those mirrors, but he didn't have time to think about that. The halls eventually graduated into damp, earthen-and-stone walls. Nova felt nervous at their descent, mostly at the fact that he did not know where they were headed. Perhaps they weren't going toward the Constellation Library where they had met Persephone?

The Wizard Oberon didn't say a word to Nova during their walk, and he strode with a quicker pace than before. Nova wasn't sure if the Wizard Oberon was angry with him or not. He had already been frightened by the episode with the serpent, but what he really worried about was the Wizard Oberon being disappointed with him.

Finally, they arrived at a small, circular opening that was tall and showcased ten crowned kings carved into the rocky walls. They were angular in their look, but they were imposing and almost lifelike in an uncanny way, given their cobbled exterior. Nova felt that their eyes were looking at him. He thought he heard a murmur, but the Wizard Oberon was not fazed and was still in a hurry, so they carried on. He moved his left arm in the air commandingly, and an entrance appeared. He turned back and waved his hand for Nova to come quickly as his eyes darted from side to side to make sure they were alone.

Nova entered through the space, and it was like they had re-emerged above ground at the school again. Although there was no natural light, he was taken aback by the five crystal chandeliers that ran down the center of the room. Sturdy, mahogany, semicircular tables ran around the periphery of the room, and there were deep blue, velvet seats with gold-and-pale-blue cushions in a variety of chaise lounge and armchair shapes. He had never seen a room so ornate or elaborate in his entire life. Up the walls were oil-painted portraits. Nova could tell they were all from Happenstance and from days gone by based on their outdated dress and hairstyles. Other paintings showed interesting scenes that featured unicorns, trolls, dragons, fairies, witches, and much more. There were busts and ornaments that looked like they were made of marble on the tables and a few shelves.

"You will wait here, *child*, and don't touch anything," came the Wizard Oberon's voice, interrupting him from his innocent musings. Nova noted that the voice was angry.

The Wizard Oberon rushed through a door on the left side of the room without knocking. Nova could tell that the many voices already coming from that room were in a heated discussion, and they halted at the Wizard Oberon's entrance.

'Silver, old chap, we've been waiting for you.'

'Is the child here?'

'Shhhhh, lower your voices,' the Wizard Oberon said.

Bang. The door closed with a start. Nova was left alone in the beautiful room, but he felt apprehensive. He sat on one of the circular chairs in the middle of the room and looked around at the paintings on the walls. It was like each one told a story that was intriguing and inviting. Nova noticed that some of the paintings covered the wall that they had come in through, and the door had vanished. It was as if no entrance existed. He also noticed that the pictures on that end of the hall looked considerably older than the paintings at the other end. The paintings also stopped at the far end, and there was empty space as if there were more to be hung.

After some time, curiosity got the better of Nova, and he got up to walk toward the older paintings. He started with what seemed to be the oldest. The colors were darkened and somewhat subdued. It was as if they were fading. The settings were in the clouds, and there were celestial objects in the background with winged, semi-naked figures in the foreground. In the back, right-hand side and behind it was a picture of former Dacaan, the Dacaan before the Regime.

Suddenly, it was as if the cloud in the painting was drifting away from Dacaan, and swirls of creatures were coming out of it. Nova stood squarely in front of the painting and reached his hand out as if to touch it. He reached out only so far as to imagine his fingers touching the canvas, and he imagined himself inside it. He closed his eyes.

"Once upon a time, there was darkness."

Nova opened his eyes, startled by the voice, as no one had been with him before. He looked all around him, but there was nothing. Turning back to the canvas, he saw that a dark-skinned woman with wings had stepped forward in the painting and was speaking to him. The characters had moved from their original positions, and all he could currently see was the woman in her white robe on a cloud, the Earth, Moon, Sun, and stars behind her.

She continued, "Evil had prevailed in the war of the Stars, and it had won Dacaan."

A dark swirl of clouds cast itself around Dacaan, making the sound of thunder and lightning. Nova wondered if he would be discovered by the Wizard Oberon and looked behind him at the door where the meeting was taking place, but he could not hear anything so turned back around.

"This Evil knew that it could manifest itself in many ways on Earth, and it did so in the form of Power. It rooted itself into many things, and among them Humans. Humans had once been a peaceful, nomadic people who were compliant with the circle of life and saw their existence as lesser to the world, to nature, to Magic, and to the Stars. Humans didn't know what Evil was, so they didn't know to fear it. But Evil told them if you would like to rule the world, you can. Let me help you. You will have everything you have ever wanted, the best lands, food, possessions. And the Humans agreed to join forces with Evil."

The woman telling the story showed a look of concern on her face and now pointed toward a newly formed cloud.

"But not all Humans agreed, some didn't want to join the side of Evil, and a war ensued. The Stars agreed with Darkness that Happenstance should be formed, for good to live. And so it began, the great migration. Evil made the Humans within its power fear those who didn't obey and whom Evil itself feared. Lady Luck helped in bringing first the Good Humans who had sided with the Stars to Happenstance. Evil then began to victimize the Magical Beings on Earth, and so began the migration of Fae, Trolls, Dragons, Unicorns..."

"But trolls aren't magical," said Nova, interrupting the woman without meaning to.

"Trolls have made the choice to subdue their Magic. Shall I continue?"

"Yes, of course, that was foolish of me," responded Nova, embarrassed both to have asked what seemed to be such a foolish question and to have asked a woman in a painting.

"No questions are foolish, child, only non-questions are foolish," said a bust of a man to Nova's side, which he wasn't expecting to also speak.

"Thank you." Nova bowed to the bust, feeling the response was most appropriate for such an object.

The woman continued as the scene in the painting began to resemble more of what it was when she had first started, "And so, the Magical Beings escaped the world. This allowed Evil to gain more Power and more strength. And so, Happenstance came to be, a land of Good and Magic."

And then the woman stopped talking, and the painting stood still as if nothing had ever happened. Nova looked at the bust, expecting an explanation, but it, too, stood there inanimate.

He walked away to continue looking at paintings on the wall and was next drawn to a much smaller but sad painting. It was dark in color and showed a scene inside an infirmary with sick and dying patients and their doctors. Once again, like with the earlier scene, the painting came to life, and a young child who was sick and lying in a bed began talking and telling his tale.

"For hundreds of years, and to this day, Evil possessed Humans and Humans wielded Power like a sword for its Evil master. But, over time there became a vicious cycle. When Evil spread further across the world, more

Humans sought Power and there was conflict. Wars began, people fought, starved, and died all in the name of Evil. Then, one day, one Human realized they must design a weapon to combat all insubordination. A Virus that would kill all who did not have powerful medicine to help in saving them. A Virus that would strike fear in Humans and force them to face a life where they could trust only their oppressor. And, as it was conceived, so it was done. The Virus was unleashed, and it killed thousands, and made millions fear."

The scene in front of Nova was now animated with the people in the infirmary beds looking dazed and confused and crying out in pain, with doctors and nurses scrambling around to help them.

"And for those who were not killed by the Virus, they suffered from the new plague, Amnesia. Eventually, once controlled, the Regime used it as a systematic weapon against its enemies so they posed no further threat."

The scene in front of Nova once again came to a standstill. He felt shocked. The Wizard Oberon had alluded to all this, but could it be so? For so many years? He had been surprised at the wisdom shared with him by such a young child, but he assumed that child had lived many years, even if in a painting, so had seen many things.

Nova thought of the children who had been taken from Creston for fear of the virus and imagined them in those beds in the infirmary. He thought of his father and his amnesia, and he thought of Creston itself and how he'd never seen the outside of the district until his escape to Happenstance. Everything was winding itself together and illuminating his mind.

Nova looked up at the other pictures on the walls.

There were men who stood with swords and reminded him of the Nomans he had met on his final night in Dacaan. He looked at scenes of battles and men dressed in uniforms, like those of the Regime killing common Dacaanians and Nomans.

There was a rustling behind the doors where the Wizard Oberon conferred with the Council. Nova stopped for a moment, fearing that he would be found out for snooping at the works, but he wanted to know more. He rushed down past the doors, past more busts and paintings of times and things that looked much more familiar to him as he moved farther along. And then he came to the final painting on the wall. It was a mother with a young boy. Her face was covered with dark, crimson hair with a streak of white running through it, and the baby was jolly in her arms, reaching up to grab an emerald necklace. Although her face was obscured, Nova could tell she was beautiful. They were sat in a room made of bricks, and behind them stood a man with one hand over a fireplace, poking the logs. It was presumably the child's father.

For some reason, the painting brought a tear to Nova's eye. The painting felt familiar, but it felt far away.

"Nova, you've found me," came the mother's voice, soothing, soft like a whisp of air.

Taking a step closer, Nova looked at the young child, who had now come to life and was looking directly at him, smiling. It had a white streak in its hair like its mother.

"I've been waiting for you to find me," said the voice of the woman, who had now pushed her hair back to reveal herself.

"Queen Jocelyn," said Nova, startled. Since his discussion with the Wizard Oberon about his mother, he had wondered how he would react. There was a silence as she pushed her hair behind her ear.

"I, Nova, am your mother. I know that I have not been there most of your life, but that doesn't mean I don't think about you and love you in every way." Queen Jocelyn smiled at him and caressed the face of the child in her arms, who was cooing and giggling.

"You saw me, at the Championships, and you said nothing," said Nova, suddenly angered by her confession.

"Nova, things are not as they seem. It would not have been safe for me to make my connection to you known. Your father and I have done everything that we could to help you, and we are so grateful that you have made your way here, to Happenstance, now," she replied, stroking the small cowlick at the front of the baby's face.

Inside, this made Nova feel a warmth and a tenderness like he was now in her arms, and she was holding him and loving him.

"Mother, why did you leave?" he asked with a timid anger.

"You were taken from me, and I was put into servitude by the Regime. I did not leave, Nova," she responded, looking lovingly into his eyes.

Nova could hear some commotion behind the doors where the Wizard Oberon was speaking with the Council.

"Well, bring the boy in. We haven't time for this, we must expedite the plans at once."

Alerted, Nova tried to reach into the painting slowly, longingly.

"Do not trust anyone, Nova. We will meet one day, I promise," spoke Queen Jocelyn before becoming still once more. Nova's hand touched the painting, but it had gone still, and the hair once again obscured his mother's face. Looking to the back of the photo, he wondered who the man had been, stoking the fire and staying silent all of that time. Was it his father?

"Nova, what are you doing over there? Come here at once," commanded the Wizard Oberon, who was apparently still in a foul mood.

Nova begrudgingly left the painting and his mother and headed toward the open door held by the Wizard Oberon. Inside the room was a large, oval table with many men who looked old and distinguished, much like the Wizard Oberon. He wondered if they, too, were wizards as many wore similar blue clothing. He noticed that one was a fae, King Anthony, Gwendolyn's father, who nodded at him when he entered. One was a troll, and there were two with horns of different size and shape. He saw the witch, Persephone, who he had met in the Constellation Library and who he smiled at, but she looked forward somberly.

The room had a tired feel to it. The air was stale, and the mood was sullen. Nova wasn't sure what he had walked in on. He, too, brought a feeling of sadness after the conversation he'd just had in the room outside.

"Nova, welcome to the Council of Elders. We have come together today to talk about, well, to talk about you," explained the Wizard Oberon.

Nova wasn't used to a room full of people discussing him. Although he had changed his name, he still found it hard to believe that he had some significance on the grand scheme of things that would require a Council of Elders to speak of him.

"Hello, it's a pleasure to meet you all," said Nova, looking around the room and feeling somewhat intimidated.

"As you know, Nova, and we do realize that a lot of this is to some extent new to you, but the Regime must be stopped. Magic is fading and so, too, is Happenstance, and the Regime is to blame. We must stop the enchanted chalice that has been draining magic from your world but that is now draining our own. Things have gone too far, and it is up to us in Happenstance to intervene. We have informants on the ground already, and we are making plans, which you are central to," the Wizard Oberon paused, looking at Nova to make sure that he was listening.

"Yes, I do understand this, but I don't know the plans, and I don't know what you want me to do," replied Nova, feeling frustrated that he was being asked to partake in something that he hadn't been included in.

"You will find out in time. First off, we need you to take your lessons seriously. I heard that you had some troubles in a few of your classes today, and you have a lot to cover. Most humans take years to learn the powers of magic," the Wizard Oberon said with a slight frown on his face, "but I know that you are not just any human."

Nova had been standing when Persephone waved him over to sit on the far side of the room next to her, which he did. He was surprised that someone whose outward appearance looked so wicked could also be quite kind.

The silence grew, and Nova realized that the Wizard Oberon was awaiting a response, although he didn't seem to remember there being a question. "Yes, sir, I will study as hard as I can."

"Good," responded the Wizard Oberon, "and we will be forming a team of Guardians, including other children who are at the top of their class. Callum, Roger, Peter..."

"No, I... I can't..." responded Nova, instantly regretting that he said anything.

The Wizard Oberon stopped and turned on his heels to look at Nova. He had been pacing back and forth, much like he had been the other night in his quarters when he was relaying important information. An unsteady silence grew between them.

"Happenstance has been here for hundreds, no, thousands of years, young man, and I have been here for its duration. The point of its creation was to separate good and evil. It is a place for people both normal and magical to come together. There will be no animosity here, there will be no ill will, and there will be no choosing of allies. Any being from Happenstance is your friend, not your enemy. The enemy is the Regime, and we must fight it together," declared the Wizard Oberon, and Nova was too nervous to defy such a statement.

"Yes, of course, sir," he responded nervously. "I will do as you ask, and of course Cassia will join us."

"No," the Wizard Oberon responded with some force, and his cape swooshed around as he faced Nova with terrifying eyes.

"Cassia has come all the way to Happenstance with me. She is taking the same classes with me. We will be ready together," responded Nova in defiance.

"She is not you, Nova. Humans from Dacaan are

weak, and she will take more time than we have to prepare. She will be a hindrance to us."

Feeling a bravery bubbling inside him, Nova responded, "She is, in fact, stronger than me and more able than me to fight the Regime."

There was a silence in the room and murmurs toward the back.

"If she is to pass the final tests then she will join you. If not then she stays, and it is that simple," snapped the Wizard Oberon.

Nova smiled, feeling that he had won a much more epic battle against a much more angered Wizard Oberon than he had actually fought.

"Now, child, we must discuss the serpent," said the Wizard Oberon, and the Council shuddered around him and started murmuring more.

Nova was quiet. He didn't want to talk about the serpent because it frightened him, but he felt like he would have little choice but to follow the Wizard Oberon's lead.

"Was this the first time you saw it?" asked the Wizard Oberon of Nova.

"No."

More murmurs arose around the room, and Nova looked around to see wide eyes and fear on the faces of the people who he preferred to see as his support.

The Wizard Oberon rapped his staff on the ground. "Silence!" he summoned.

"Tell us, boy, tell us about the serpent," said the Wizard Oberon, and the room grew quieter and somewhat colder. Nova shivered, not knowing where to start or what to say.

"It comes in my dreams. It first came to me in a dream in Dacaan, the same week of the comet."

There was a gasp this time but no murmurs, just more uncomfortable silence.

"It usually comes in the desert, and I am running, and it is hot, but it eventually finds me and it, it tries to eat me."

This time there was shuffling in some chairs and then the room fell quiet again.

"And has it always been a serpent?" asked the Wizard Oberon.

"No," replied Nova, "there were crows too. They were only there this time, though."

"And is this only in your dreams?" asked the Wizard Oberon, turning and walking toward the front of the room as if he were going to walk through the wall.

"I've been awake twice now. Once with just the crows, and another time with the serpent." replied Nova, and an eruption of murmurs coursed through the Council.

"And how many times have you seen this in Happenstance?" asked the Wizard Oberon, and the room became louder. Nova looked around and wondered if he should respond, since there was so much anxiety within the group, but he looked at the Wizard Oberon and knew he must.

"Twice, once in Providence with the crows and once here at Serendipity this afternoon. It was in the courtyard."

There was a frenzy in the room as the noise escalated and the elders discussed what they had just heard. The Wizard Oberon rapped his staff on the ground again and shouted for silence.

"We will adjourn this meeting until tomorrow morning. Evil is here among us, and we have little time," declared the Wizard Oberon, packing up a file on a desk in front of him.

"No," said Nova. Surprised, the Wizard Oberon looked up at him.

"What more could you possibly have to say, young man?"

Nova made a gulping sound. He was nervous but knew it must be raised. "There is a fae that has disappeared."

"What do you mean disappeared?" asked Persephone, who had twisted in her seat to look at him.

King Anthony stood up with shock on his face. He touched a hand to his stomach as if he were in some sort of pain. "Which fae?"

"We were at the river and Luca, well, he just vanished into thin air."

The room erupted again. The Wizard Oberon rapped his staff and there was instant silence.

"Fae don't just vanish, young man. Who did this? You do realize that this is a punishable act, and the perpetrator must be found immediately," asked the Wizard Oberon.

Sweat ran down from Nova's brow and his hands felt clammy. Nova knew that what he had done was a crime, but the guilt within him sat heavy as a stone. He had to unburden himself, no matter what the consequences.

"It was me," he responded, and more gasps rumbled across the room. "I made him disappear, I used dark magic."

CHAPTER 12

Nova made his way back to the halls without going outside. He knew that Cassia, Barnaby, and Gwendolyn would be at the main hall like the night before, and he found comfort in their ambivalence. They didn't need to hear his confession, not yet.

The meeting had come and gone like everything in Happenstance, with little warning. One moment Nova was running from a murder of crows, the next he was back at school being mocked by the other children, and then he was learning about the art of flight and meeting all sorts of new creatures like unicorns. Even meeting his mother for the first time came with no warning. The meeting with the Council of Elders hadn't gone as planned, if he could have planned it in the first place, that is.

On top of it all, Nova hadn't had a chance to properly speak with the Wizard Oberon about bringing Luca back from wherever he might be. He had tried to take some time to speak with the Wizard Oberon but was brushed off because the elders had more to discuss—alone.

He was now snaking alone down the myriad of hallways. He hoped that he had taken the right paths, although they seemed to have a mind of their own and there seemed to be many more twists and turns in the underbelly of Serendipity than were necessary. He had just arrived at the hall of mirrors he and the Wizard Oberon traveled through earlier when he heard a sound. He stopped and looked around him but saw nothing. He took three more steps, and then he heard it again—three more steps behind him. He stopped and turned around but saw nothing. Or did he? There seemed to be something in the shadows that was reflected by one of the mirrors. He turned around, startled, and remembered the dagger in his bag, so pulled it out hurriedly and held it in front of him.

"Who's there?" he shouted into the dimly lit hallway.

Nothing.

"Well, whoever it is, I've got a dagger," Nova heard himself say and instantly felt silly for it. He had, however, been through a lot with the serpent and the news of evil in Happenstance, so he rationalized in his head that his words could be justified.

As he pirouetted with the dagger in front of him, he heard the steps again, but each time coming from different directions and with different flashes of dark in the various mirrors in the hallway.

Nova felt tired; it was exhausting being afraid so often. A bead of sweat dripped from his forehead, and he wiped it away in a frustrated manner. Then came a laugh. Not a slippery, wet, amphibious laugh like the one from the serpent, but more of a croaky, feminine cackle that was suddenly, unbearably close to him.

"Well, I'm no angel, but I've never been greeted like that before," came the voice.

It was Persephone Tarsworthy, the witch. She was

unexpectedly in front of him, larger than life with her black, crooked hat tilted down in a way to make her immediate appearance less severe.

"Mrs. Tarsworthy, you frightened me," said Nova, bewildered and slightly annoyed.

"Well aren't you the young man with a dagger pointed at me?" replied Persephone.

Nova pointed the dagger down, feeling once again embarrassed at using it.

"Haha! Well, I hope that I am not going to disappear this time," laughed the witch.

The words stung Nova like a sharp bee sting. He felt ashamed.

"You are much better than that dagger, young man, but I guess you have a lot to learn still, and we have not enough time to properly teach you," she said, eying him like everyone seemed to, up and down with a look of disapproval.

Nova put the dagger back in his bag and zipped it up. "I wanted to speak with the Wizard Oberon about bringing Luca back from . . . well . . . just back. Do you know what might happen?"

"Yes, the Wizard Oberon must use dark magic to undo your dark magic, and he isn't in the least bit happy with it. As I'm sure you know, Happenstance is fading, and so is his magic. It will take a huge amount of his energy to do this. But what's done is done, and we must move forward," said Persephone rather matter-of-factly. Nova thought it strange to be so matter-of-fact about the disappearance of a person and the use of dark magic, but he was so pleased to hear that what he had done could be undone that it didn't matter.

"So he will come back, just like that?" Nova questioned with a curbed enthusiasm.

"Well, there are risks. When you cross over to the other side, it is often hard to ensure that all of you returns. We must wait and see."

"If you don't mind, Mrs. Tarsworthy, I'd like to get back to my friends and get some rest. It has been a long day with lots of *unexpected* events."

Noting the emphasis Nova placed on the end of his sentence, Persephone replied, "And of course you must be afraid of what might happen to you because of all of this?"

Nova stopped. Obviously, the thought was on his mind, but he felt selfish for even considering it. He was, of course, due a punishment for such a heinous act, but he wasn't sure if at that moment in time he could hear it.

Persephone continued, "King Anthony has asked for you to be pardoned. He believes that it is one thing to use dark magic and mean it, and another thing to use it unintentionally. The Wizard Oberon agrees that you will not be punished, this time. But it cannot happen again."

"I am . . . grateful. I deserve punishment, I really do, but I will do everything to control my magic, and that is a promise. But I do need help."

There was a pause, a noted interruption for Nova's apology and cry for help to fully become absorbed.

"In any case, my dear, you cannot go yet. I will need you for several more minutes at least. Follow me." And with that, she was gone like a flash. Nova couldn't find her anywhere until her hand jutted out from one of the mirrors and grabbed his.

"Come with me, it is much faster this way." And then they were gone, into the mirror.

Nova had never really considered what was on the other side of mirrors, but now he knew. It was a long series of reflections of rooms and hallways, and everything was upside down. Nova couldn't tell if he was currently upside down or right side up, but perhaps it didn't matter?

Persephone seemed to know exactly where they were going, and soon enough Nova was in a room that was familiar. It was the elevator that took them down to the Constellation Library.

"There is something that I must give to you. I've been keeping it safe for some time," said Persephone as they piled in the elevator, and she pressed a button that said '4962.' Nova couldn't remember which number they'd pressed to come up before, but there were so many numbers that were completely out of any order that was discernible to him, so he just held onto the railing as the elevator made its descent. It seemed that they went farther down then they had gone up the other day. After some time, the elevator came to its landing place and signaled their arrival with a *ding*.

The door opened, and Persephone headed out first into a room that didn't look anything like where they had been before. The stained glass windows made it look something like a church. Everything seemed extremely dusty, and it lacked the grandeur of the large library that they were in the other day. Nova noticed that many of the books looked very old and were locked behind glass cabinets.

"Where did you get all of these books from?" he said

in awe, marveling at the names on them: *Robinson Crusoe*, *Alice in Wonderland*, *Hamlet*, *Beowulf*.

"These old things. The Constellation Library and this room here hold all the books preserved before the book burnings in Dacaan. Some of the best masterpieces are in this room," Persephone responded.

She looked over, and noticing Nova's quizzical face she added, "These are the books the Regime thought might be too dangerous and decided to burn. It then created its own set of books, mainly for standardized learning—twenty-two in total, to be precise." Persephone reached under her robe and pulled out a large set of keys to open a lock near the entrance where they came.

"Why would the Regime think that a book is too dangerous?" questioned Nova, trying to digest the information. The books that he was used to taught him and the children of Dacaan the history of the Regime and the world, of the skills they would need in order to reap the land and produce the items necessary to share with the other districts.

"It is what the book allows the reader to do," responded Persephone, who was mumbling under her breath as she scanned a section of books, apparently looking for something more specific.

Still feeling unsure, Nova continued "What would a book allow a reader to do?"

Persephone was frustrated, and she kicked her heel into the ground and waved her hands in the air. Nova muffled a laugh, but Persephone didn't hear.

Snapping out of her irritation as she looked up and saw what she'd been searching for, Persephone plucked it from the shelf with her bony finger, as if it were planning to escape her once again, and refocused her attention on the conversation.

"A book can allow a reader to do nothing or to do everything." She hesitated a moment. "It is important to know that books are always riddled with intent and perception. It is up to the reader to come to their own conclusions. But sometimes the words on a page can evoke thoughts and even actions in the reader. Reading can cause change, and that is where the power lies."

Persephone seemed pleased with that response, which only left Nova perplexed.

She walked toward him with the book she had found, gazing down her sloped nose and over her glasses at him.

Nova looked at the book and felt like his eyes were playing some sort of trick on him. It had a faded brown, matte cover with silver and gold images and writing. Because of the images, it reminded him of the box that he had received from his father, and he wondered if it was a matching set, which made his heart almost stop. He reached forward and wiped the dust away, much like he had done when he first received the box from his father, to again discover his name on the cover: *Nova's Quest*.

They stood there for some moments as Nova tried to take in the significance of what was in front of him, and he wondered how it had come to be. Was this book about him? He was afraid to touch it but wanted to open it and find out.

"Take it, Nova," said Persephone as gently as a witch could say, and she handed the book toward him.

Nova took it into his hands. The book wasn't big in size, but it had weight to it. He wiped more of the dust off and noticed that the same light shone from it as did from the box at times. But it didn't frighten him like the box had done, because he was now familiar with this sort of thing. He felt comfortable holding on to the weight of the unknown.

"Well, open it, dear," said Persephone insistently, and she again reached under her robe and pulled up a small pocket watch to check the time. "We'll miss supper if we don't hurry up."

"Yes, of course," said Nova hurriedly. He turned the front page back, and more light trickled out, but this time it danced in small beads around him like it was embracing him.

The front page began with a short message, and he read the lines out loud, "To our dearest Alex, if you have made it this far, we are thankful and know that you are in safe hands. If you have made it this far, it most likely means that we are not with you, but we wanted to share your story and some advice to help you with your coming quest. You now know that you are actually Nova, and that you are Dacaan and Happenstance's last chance. It won't be easy, and you face a long road ahead. The path will not be clear, but always choose wisely. We love you, Mum and Dad."

Nova reread those final six words again under his breath, and a tear trickled down the side of his face. He looked up, hoping that Persephone hadn't noticed, but she was already on the other side of the room and pulling down additional books from cabinets.

He opened more of the book and saw chapters of his life—chapters that until a day or so ago he hadn't known about: his parents, his birth, his childhood, and his quest. He read through and couldn't believe how true to life a lot of it was, and he wondered how true to life some of the earlier writings were that he couldn't remember. He flipped forward and noticed that many of the pages were empty, only a fragment of the book was actually written. He turned back to the page where the writings finished, and a few pages before there was a chapter titled 'Nova's Arrival in Happenstance.' A tingle ran down his back. He flipped again to the final words before the blank, white pages and saw that the book had written about his confession to the Council of Elders and about him standing there reading this book. It lingered eerily on a sentence: 'Nova flipped through the pages, bewildered and unsure as to how the book knew what it knew before slamming it shut.'

Persephone looked over. "Yes, I had assumed you might have that reaction. The book is more than just a real-time account of your life, Nova. It will provide clues from your past to help you take the right direction in your future. The map will tell you more about where to go next. Did you find your map?"

Nova stood for a minute, still feeling eerily confused by the words forming in the pages below and wondering if it was writing his emotions and his thoughts right then and there. He slammed the book shut. Oh.

"Yes," he finally replied, "I found the map in my box, but it only showed me where I was, and not where I needed to go."

The witch tutted, "Well, my dear, you must give magic to receive magic, as we say here in Happenstance. Now come, that is enough for this evening. Take these and leave at once."

And with that, Persephone put some more books into

Nova's arms and pushed him through an old, hardly visible mirror that hung on the wall, and he was gone.

❖

Cassia had saved Nova dinner, but he hardly ate it. He took a few mouthfuls of brussels sprouts and felt like spitting them out, but he gulped them down distastefully. He had hardly heard what Barnaby, Gwendolyn, and the others were discussing. Gwendolyn had given him a sideward glance as if she were asking 'Have you spoken to the Wizard Oberon yet about Luca?' King Anthony hadn't told her; Nova was surprised. Although he didn't feel like he had the strength, he knew he must say something.

Jumping out from his seat unexpectedly, Nova stood up to address the group. "The Wizard Oberon will bring Luca back."

Gwendolyn's eyes filled with tears. She opened her mouth to ask a question, but Nova took off, feeling rather unheroic and ashamed. He tucked his books under his arm and headed to his room. He couldn't tell them the risk that Luca might not be himself when he returned, not yet.

Once there, he sat on his bed with his quest book and the others in front of him. He reached into his backpack and pulled out the box inside. He was right, the designs did match. His mother and father had planned this together. What did that mean?

He opened the box, and the telltale light shone from it. He reached in, but there was nothing there. No cloak, no map, no dagger. He stuck his whole arm in, and again nothing. Had he lost those items that had so magically appeared before?

He sat there and wondered about the map. He tried to visualize its details in his head: size, color, and weight. Then he pictured the places that were on it: Founders Bay, the coast, the lighthouse, the Emerald Sea, and the compass on the side to discern north from south and east from west. He reached in again and felt a scroll. Hoping that it was what he wanted, he pulled it out. Unraveling the scroll, he saw that it was indeed the map, and it had all the locations he saw before but also the new ones he'd come to recently: Destiny Rock, Kismet, Fortuity Forest, Hope River, Hope Waterfall, Providence, and Serendipity. But the rest of the edges were blurred. He held the map out taut on either side and looked it up and down. He flipped it over and shook it, but nothing.

Then he had an idea. He started to think of Happenstance. He said in his mind that he wanted to see Happenstance, the full picture, and he thought of the place itself: the fresh air, blue skies, snowcapped mountains and rolling hills, the people, and the animals. When he opened his eyes, there it was.

"Knock, knock, knock. Are you going to show me what you are doing, Nova? Goof!"

It was Cassia at the door. Nova felt the need to hide what was in front of him, but he'd been caught and there was no time. He wasn't sure how long she'd been there and what she'd already seen.

"You were conjuring," she said in the smart, proud way that she liked to speak in when she was right about something.

"No, I wasn't," replied Nova, unsure of what exactly she meant.

"Yes, you were, Nova. I can read, too, and I've been reading about conjuring after the class you missed this afternoon. It's when you make something appear from nothing. You will something that isn't there to be there. You've done it before, so it's good that you at least know what you are trying to do this time."

"What do you mean? What else do you know about it?" asked Nova surprised at how much Cassia was learning given she didn't like school at all in Creston.

"The rabbits at the Championships, silly. That was conjuring. Of course, most start with basic magic like levitation, but you are a natural," Cassia said smugly to him, as if in knowing his art she was a part of it.

"And my escape from the crows...Luca..." said Nova despondently.

"That is teleportation. Well, the escape from the crows was at least," Cassia said, proud of her newfound vocabulary.

"And...Luca?" Nova asked again.

"Well, that's a dark magic. We aren't even meant to learn about that. No one apart from Wizard Oberon does that, Nova." Cassia eyed Nova as if she were gauging his reaction to this statement, and she was confident in her own. Nova certainly wasn't confident with that statement.

Cassia rounded the end of the bed and sat in front of Nova and his possessions. He could tell that she wanted to touch the books, but she was holding herself back. There was a tension between them.

"Nova, you do realize that I've seen the box and your

map before. You do realize that you used to share things with me?" Cassia suddenly snapped.

"Yes, of course I do, I still do," he responded.

"No, you don't. You keep on disappearing. You have been seeing people like the Wizard Oberon and Persephone and getting things like these new books. You've been missing classes, and then you hardly even talk to me. We came here together, and I'm doing everything to stand by you, and I want to support you, but you need to let me in," Cassia said and inhaled deeply, as she had made her speech at such a speed and with such frustration that it appeared she'd forgotten to breathe.

Nova stood up and pushed the books to the side and sat with Cassia. He cocked his knee up on the side of the bed and took a moment to pause, because he didn't want Cassia to be upset. He didn't want to do anything to hurt her; he was so happy to have her in Happenstance with him.

"Cassia, you are the one thing in this place that makes sense to me. Everything feels so weird and new right now, and I am just trying . . ." He stopped for a minute, trying to choose his next words. "I'm trying to do what is expected of me. I'm trying to do what's needed of me, and we don't have much time."

Cassia's face changed in mood. She looked pleased to hear the words from Nova's mouth, to know that he also was struggling in their new reality.

"I'm sorry, Cassia, please don't hate me," Nova finished, hoping that he'd said enough to her to make her understand.

"Please, don't," started Cassia, who did that thing where she tossed her hair to the side and closed her eyes as if this helped her concentrate better. "I didn't mean what I said, I just..."

Nova grabbed her hands and smiled at her, and then he pushed her shoulder so that she fell onto the duvet on the bed. They both laughed. Nova had a flashback to Creston, to their final night splashing in the water.

He decided to take the lead and explain more to her. "Cassia, as you know, I am being asked to go on a quest, and I would like for you to come with me. I don't know how dangerous it is, but we need to face the Regime. Things aren't right, Cassia, nothing is right."

"Yes, I know," responded Cassia gingerly, "everyone knows."

"What do you mean?"

"Esme and I met up after class, and I asked her why she thought the boys treated you so badly earlier. She explained that all children of Happenstance grow up being told about the 'Coming of the Phoenix'—a time where one child will find out that they will lead Happenstance's most important quest. They grow up learning magic and practicing all of the things being taught at the Serendipity School of Magic in case they are the one. Now that everyone finally knows you are the one, they're jealous," Cassia said.

"But that isn't my choice. I didn't want to become Nova, it just happened!" he snapped.

"Well, they don't know that, and if they did, they probably wouldn't care. They are dealing with their own issues. Apparently, they also feel disappointed that you have come from Dacaan and haven't had formal training. That the future of their world and ours depends on someone with little or no education. They think they are better than you, that you don't deserve it."

Cassia leaped over the footboard of the bed and into the light, which cast a long shadow on their bedroom floor. A huge smile covered her face.

"Nova, it is your chance to prove them wrong. Read your books, work hard, oh, and come to classes! Trust me, you will make them see soon enough." And with that, she grabbed her own textbook and headed off down the hallway.

Nova looked out the window and then looked back on the bed. For the first time since he'd arrived in Happenstance, he felt that he was in charge of his own destiny. His parents had left him something behind. He thought of his father and his mother coming together at a time when everything was right, at a time when his father was still unaltered by the virus and his mother was still with him. He wished he could go back in time. He missed his father, and he wondered how he was.

Sitting in front of him was the map and the book. Nova had the power now to go to places unseen and write his own destiny, but he didn't know what to do with it. Then, a tempting but dangerous idea sprung into his head. He hesitated, worrying that it could be too dangerous, but then decided he needed to take charge of himself. He needed to do what was right. It would only be for short time anyway!

Picking up the map, Nova noticed that his journey to Providence and Serendipity had lit up new parts of Happenstance that were blank when he'd first looked at the map and it had only shown Founders Cove. He closed his eyes and ran his fingers back and forth along the coarse paper. He thought back on the place he called home, a place that he knew, that he had belonged to. He realized that he knew so much about so little. The smell of brown, trodden leaves in the crisp air on an autumn night; the sound of the stream that ran with all its might in the spring after the winter's mountain runoff; the taste of fresh dolly varden, his favorite fish. He thought of his father, his peppered, graying hair, his blue eyes that matched Nova's, which most of the time stared off into the distance. He thought of the moments of clarity and love.

Opening his eyes, Nova looked down at the map. It had worked. The map that had only been half complete with the parts of Happenstance Nova had been to suddenly had the curved grayscale of what looked like a moonbow in the middle of it. On the other side was Creston. Excitedly, Nova set the map to the side and opened his book to the end of his current story. A cold tingle ran down his spine again as he looked at the words '... he set the map to the side and opened the book... Nova wanted to travel home,' but he ignored that and asked the question that he had been skeptical of asking.

"Can you take me back to Creston?" he asked the book once again, with his eyes closed.

And once again, Nova opened his eyes, and other than the question he had just asked appearing on the page in front of him, nothing had happened. His armband, however, was glowing. Nova thought back on how it had been so easy to escape the crows the other day, and he wondered how he had done it.

"Take me back to Creston," Nova said as a command, this time much more forcefully.

Nothing happened.

Frustrated, Nova tossed the box, the map, and the book into his backpack and threw them on the floor. He fell back on his bed with gut-wrenching homesickness clawing inside him. He just wanted to see his father, just for a moment. He wanted to ask him about the book, about the box, and about his quest. Most of all, he wanted to make sure he was okay and hug him.

"We meet again," came words from his window.

Nova sat up like a shot. He had heard a swoosh of feathers and the scratching of talons before he heard him speak.

"Osiris!"

"Yes. I just arrived and thought I would come to you at once, Nova," the commanding bird perched on the windowsill said with a serious voice.

"Are you recovered now?" asked Nova, looking at his wing but noticing no more bandages.

Osiris ignored the question. He was not the sort of bird who liked speaking of ailments. "They are coming for your father."

Nova was taken aback. The pain that he had just felt over his father and his home was already sitting in the pit of his stomach, and these words spoken by Osiris were like a knife twisting inside of him.

"What do you mean? Who is coming?" Nova asked in staccato notes. He reached down and picked up his bag to put on his coat.

"Cravelda, since you left Creston she has been searching for informants, and she believes your father is one of them. With just cause," responded Osiris, shifting from leg to leg on the windowsill as if he were walking the floor, pacing to clear his head.

"But my father has amnesia, what do you mean?" Nova responded.

"Happenstance has a series of informants who share information about the Regime and what is happening in Dacaan. Your father and your mother have been sharing information for years, that is how I knew to come for you after your father gave you that box." Osiris gestured with his eyes to the brown corner of the box that jutted out the side of the bag.

Nova pushed the box more firmly inside and clasped the bag together.

"We must go at once to save my father," he said, walking toward the windowsill and ready to jump on his feathered friend's back.

"No, it is too dangerous, and there is more at stake. They will take your father to Castlegar, and the Wizard Oberon has instructed that we must go only when you are ready."

"I'm tired of everyone telling me what to do and when to do it. My father is in danger, and I must go to him at once," snapped Nova, upset that Osiris had told him such important news but didn't want to help him.

Osiris turned his back on Nova and flew out the window, saying on his way, "I'm sorry, Nova. I wanted you to be the first to know, but it is too dangerous to go. I will not risk it for either you or your father's sake."

As the bird flew away into the dark blue sky, Nova said, "Well, I will risk it."

Nova flipped back in the book to his seventh birthday. It was easy to find because he knew the date. That day he had spent with his father; they had baked and laughed and joked, and when the cake came out of the oven it was half burned, but it didn't matter. That was one of the best days of his life. Nova thought of his father, alone and in trouble. He reached into his bag and draped the cape around his shoulders.

Nova closed his eyes one more time, and this time his plan worked.

CHAPTER
13

"It's not safe for you here, Nova. You must leave at once."

Nova was overwhelmed at hearing the voice of his father, who was lucid and well-dressed in a denim top and darker denim pants. The smell of black coffee filled the air, and Nova felt a fleeting security in the embrace of the log cabin.

He walked over and wrapped his arms around his father. He noticed that his father didn't look as tall as he once did. Nova wondered if he himself had grown in the short time he was in Happenstance.

"Haven't you missed me, old man?" he asked with wetness around his eyes, his body's reaction to happiness.

"Of course I have, son. I've missed you every moment that you've been gone." Jacob pulled him back and looked at his face with a smile, before pushing him away, "How did you get here? No, we must not discuss it, you must leave right away. I wouldn't have told Osiris if I'd thought he would bring you here."

"No," said Nova, stopping for an instant to gather his thoughts. He was disheartened that his father was so eager to get rid of him when he had just arrived, but he understood his reasonings. "Osiris informed me, but he told me not to come. I came on my own."

Nova's father circled the table and looked out the window near the door where they stood. He pulled the drawstring on the blinds so that the metal edge banged on the ledge, and he twisted a plastic rod so the slats pointed down. He lifted a slat open and peeked his wandering eye through one last time, just to be sure they were alone. Nova hadn't noticed before how much those simple blinds were like a shutter to their world.

"How did you come, then? Another moonbow? Did the Wizard Oberon open it?" Jacob lifted his arm and looked at his watch.

Nova thought this odd and wondered if his father's lucidity was subsiding.

"The next moonbow isn't scheduled for over a week, and it's closer to the Rossland District. I believe that is where the Wizard Oberon will most likely have you enter," he said in a frenzied way that worried Nova.

"I didn't take the moonbow, Father," Nova replied as he opened the fridge and grabbed a can of cream soda. He sat down with a slump at the table, sliding his bag onto it. He wondered what time it was in Happenstance. He could tell he had arrived here in the morning, because the sun was filtering in through the curtains on the other side of the house as it threw light onto the dining room table. Nova often saw the room like this before he left for the school bus. He pulled off his coat while noticing it was much warmer here than at the snowy college.

Nova felt no need to explain how he'd arrived back in Creston further, and he felt pressed for time as his father rushed to the window above the sink and pulled the small curtain across before frantically scanning the perimeter of that side of the house.

"Father, I'm not ready." The words came out of him flippantly, like they weren't meant but were only said to cause a reaction.

Jacob stood at the sink with hands on either side of the basin and lowered his head. "You *must* be, Nova."

With the inflection on the word 'must,' Nova knew what his father meant.

"It's all come so quickly. You only gave me the box a couple weeks ago, and I've only just learned about Happenstance and my quest. I can't do it," he said, feeling somewhere deep inside that his words were betraying him.

"You must," repeated his father, turning around this time. "Your mother and I, we did everything we could to prepare you for this day. When it was possible to."

Nova felt a wave of sadness flood through him. In all these years, his father had never mentioned her. They never talked about her; it was a sort of taboo. But now that he had said it, the anxiety around their secret washed away, making room for sadness. Nova wondered how many times his father had seen her arrive at the Championships in all her ceremonial attire. They had been so close, but so far. Did they still love each other? What had happened? Looking at his father, Nova saw that his face gave no clues.

"You must trust your instincts, Nova. Plus, you must read the books and listen to your teachers. Learn everything you can before you face the Regime. You are stronger than you or I even understand right now," Jacob said, looking at Nova for a moment up and down like he didn't know him, before another jolted look of concern rushed over him as he heard a sound outside.

At first it was a sound in the distance, the gentle crackle of gravel like popcorn under rubber. It drew closer quickly.

"Father, run. They are going to take you!" cried Nova in despair.

"I . . . I wanted to tell you something important, Nova. It's something that you will soon find out about me . . ." started his father, but the sound of the doors opening on the vehicle outside, and the heavy boots acting as the tenor to the soprano notes of steely, high-heeled shoes, interrupted him. It was Cravelda and the patrol.

Nova peeked out the front window to confirm their arrival. "Tell me another time, Father. Leave quickly, through the back window."

"I will be fine, Nova, you will see me in Castlegar soon enough. Now go, leave how you came".

Nova turned around to his father again, and he saw him sitting on the couch in the front room, staring vacantly at the wall.

"Father, quickly," he urged, but it was too late, his father was lost. Nova tried to force him to get up, but his father had fallen too far into his own mind to respond. Tears streamed down his face; his plan to save his father hadn't worked. He had to save himself.

Nova picked up his things and rushed toward his bedroom. The footsteps were now at the front door and there was a heavy, metallic banging as the patrol forced their entry.

Sitting on his bed, Nova felt the comfort of the place he called home melt away as he heard the door finally give way. He opened his bag, pulled out his cape, and grabbed the map and book. What if it didn't work again, what if he couldn't get back?

"Round him up," came Cravelda's voice from the doorway, and he heard the patrol storm across the peaceful front room. His father let out a gasp, and for a moment Nova thought that he was going to rush back in and fight them to save his father, but then he heard it.

Click, click, click, click, click. The sound of heeled shoes. She was coming down the hall, and Nova's room was the first stop on the right.

Nova racked his head. How had he done it before? What had he done? He closed his eyes and thought of Happenstance and the room that he had been in before he left. He thought of the people and of the Wizard Oberon. He opened them again, nothing.

Click, click, click. Meow. It was Mr. Gray in the hall. Cravelda's shoes stopped, and, from what Nova could tell, she bent down to perhaps stroke the cat, who let out a hiss and scurried quietly on his soft paws into Nova's room. Mr. Gray ran straight over to him, purring softly.

Click, click, click. Cravelda was just a few steps from entering his room. Nova closed his eyes again and thought of Happenstance, of the lighthouse, of unicorns, of snow. He opened them again, nothing.

"We've taken the informant to the van. Do you want us to search the house?" came a voice following in a pair of heavy boots in the hall.

"Yes, check all the rooms and the basement. Who knows what is hiding in there," she responded.

"Yes, ma'am," came the gruff voice before it shouted to the other patrol outside, "Search the property."

Nova didn't know what to do. Should he try to leave through the window or hide under the bed? He tried to push Mr. Gray away, but the cat came back purring even more loudly, rubbing his arched back against Nova and flicking his tail. Nova tried to ignore him and closed his eyes, thinking of Happenstance again. He opened them, but he was still in his room.

Click, click. There she was. The light illuminated her from behind, and the odd, angular shape of her form-fitted, ankle-length dress and tightly tied bun on her head was terrifying.

"We meet again, Alex . . . or should I say Nova," grinned Cravelda, and her face drew back in a sneer that exposed white, crooked teeth and pink gums.

"Leave my father alone," said Nova with less gusto than he'd hoped for.

"Ha ha ha ha ha!" she laughed mockingly. "I have no reason to, you are not in a position to make demands, child."

She walked to the middle of the room.

"Did you know that your father was keeping secrets rather than sharing them? That he was protecting you against my orders?" she said.

"I don't know what you mean, my father has amnesia from the virus you gave him. And, if he were, then of course he would be. I am his son," said Nova angrily.

"Ha ha ha ha ha! My spies tell me that you have a lot to learn, and I guess they are right," was her stinging reply.

Spies? Nova wondered who had been watching him. Was it the crows? Feeling the need to protect himself, he pushed the map and the book back into his bag.

"Patrol!" screeched Cravelda, looking over her shoulder, and she turned back to Nova with a more muted smile on her face.

"Now, what have you got in that bag, young man?" she asked with a new look on her face that lit up her eyes in excitement.

Nova clutched the bag and swung it behind him. He couldn't lose the only things that his mother and father had together given him.

Two of the patrol came stomping back down the hall and stood at the door of the room. Cravelda looked over her shoulder at them before again turning back to Nova.

"Seize him and take that bag!"

The patrol began taking steps toward Nova, and were just about to pounce on him, before he let out the cry "Mother!" He had just a moment to see Cravelda's eyes open in a knowing yet startled way before he was gone once again.

❖

Nova sat on a stone-cold floor. He was somewhere he had never been before, he knew that much. He was in a room that was much more opulent than anything he had ever seen in either Creston or Happenstance, including Serendipity.

The floors below him were marbled with white, black, and green swirls. There was furniture of mirrored glass all around him, and the room gleamed white and light gray with accents of pastel colors. A grand, four-poster bed sat on his left-hand side, and on his right was a sitting area with plush blue, pink, and purple seating holding several fur throws and cushions. Decorative ornaments adorned the hard furniture surfaces.

Nova got up to investigate further but was wary of who might be inside, so he trod quietly and carefully. To the left-hand side was an open door, and he saw that light was pouring in from an open window. As he drew closer, he saw that it was, in fact, a balcony with tall columns of gleaming white and flecks of gray. It was beautiful and sanguine.

That's when he heard it.

As sweet as a songbird, the notes played in their chorus. The sound was ethereal and played by an instrument he hadn't heard before. There was a delicate plucking of strings that let out undulations of sound. It was the sound of the crest of the wave as it ebbed and then the sound of the breeze blowing the arms of a weeping willow tree. It was beautiful sadness encapsulated in a melody. Then he heard the soft and gentle voice, a voice that spoke of love lost in both its pitch and tone. It paired itself with the gentle melody.

Turning the corner again quietly, he stood to take in what he saw. Behind the sheer curtain that played to its own tune in the breeze sat a woman upon a small, cushioned stool. Between her legs and her arms sat a tall, bow-looking instrument with several long strings that ran from metal fingers at its top to metal fingers at its bottom. The woman was wearing a mint-green dress embossed with golden flowers, and she wore a butterfly comb that pulled back a silver streak in her crimson hair. It was his mother.

The melody, the song, the gentle breeze, and her. It all made Nova's heart flutter like a butterfly in the wind. He lost all fear of being found and just stood there, listening, as she sang her beautiful song and continued to its next verse.

I think of him, upon my knee,
His face I always wish to see,
I hope that we will one day be,
Free to be together.
Stormy nights and winter's day,
They do with me as they may,
As long as he might have his say,
And be brave in any weather.

The tune stopped, and she got up and walked to the banister to look out. The sunlight flooded down like it had created a spotlight just to showcase her.

Nova quietly walked closer to the balcony and let out a small noise as if he were clearing his throat.

She turned around and stood there, looking.

"Mother," said Nova, and he headed toward the balcony. He wanted to speak with her, to tell her he understood and that it wasn't her fault. That he loved her.

"Mother." He said it louder now and went to grab her, but it was as if he weren't there. His arm ran straight through her. He let out a small whimper.

"Nova, you are not meant to be here," came a voice from inside the room. Shocked as he had thought no one else was there, Nova turned around to see little Phoebe and her mousy-brown hair behind him. He remembered how the Regime had taken her to Castlegar the day it almost took him too.

"Well, what are you doing here?" he asked her as she pulled him back into the room with force.

"I'm helping you. You're lucky I was there to hear your

call," she said gruffly, and he was surprised that his mother didn't hear her, either. "I cast a temporary spell so that we are invisible. No one can know either one of us are in here. You'll ruin the plan."

Phoebe grabbed his arm and led him out into a hallway that had servants busily scurrying around. Nova looked back over his shoulder and tried to pull away, but Phoebe's grip refused to loosen. He noticed again that none of the servants could see them.

"Where are you taking me?" he whispered.

"You don't have to whisper here," she responded, agitated and still gripping his arm. "Now, follow me. Since you are already here, I'm going to show you why you need to take things more seriously."

Nova realized after some time that they were finally outside of the building and in a manicured garden that, to be quite honest, resembled the inside. He wondered if the flowers in the garden were cut to be dotted around the inner halls that he had just walked through. The entire building had been perfumed with a melody of sweet aromas, contrasting with the more rustic scent of cedar that he was used to back in Creston, or the smell of books and antiquities in Serendipity. He looked up and realized he had been in a castle. Its turrets and spires looked so tall from below, and he tried to look at each balcony but couldn't see his mother.

Letting go of his arm now that they were outside, Phoebe waved him toward an alleyway that was dark and cobbled. She led him through the twisted streets, and he noticed how much color was painted on the faces of the women and some men and how elaborately they dressed. They looked like those plucked flowers from the gardens they had just walked past, and he wondered what birds they had in Castlegar that allowed for such extravagant feathered fashion.

There were also all on their communicators as they were walking and were hardly aware of each other as they tapped on their screens, not engaging with their present company. Nova thought this was rude but not at all unlike how he might have pictured the people of Castlegar to act. Busy with their outrageously colorful lives.

"Are you going to tell me where we're going?" Nova urged, feeling out of his comfort zone and wondering how long Phoebe's spell would last, given that he was so obviously not from this place. He knew he would stand out like a sore thumb in his school uniform.

"You'll see soon enough," Phoebe responded with a frustration in her voice.

"How did you know I would come here and that I would be in that room? How did you know to cast the spell?" Nova asked, hoping to unravel some of the mystery from their meeting.

"That is my job, that is all of our jobs—to help you," she responded, looking briefly back at him to judge his reaction.

"Who are you talking about, whose job is it to help me?"

"When you are in Dacaan, it's the informants' job. Haven't they told you?" replied Phoebe, looking back again with a question mark on her face.

Nova felt frustrated again. "No one tells me anything."

Phoebe led them around a cart full of hay and pigs in the road in front of them, and they arrived in a large, circular plaza with various birds and people in it.

This time she hushed her voice. "There are informants all over Castlegar and on Earth, working with the Wizard Oberon and Happenstance. We have all been waiting for this moment, for your arrival, and for you to help us in taking our first steps to overthrowing the Regime."

Nova wasn't sure if he should also respond in a hushed voice or not, since he was told not to before, but decided it was better to be precautious. "What do you know . . . what do I need to know?"

Phoebe stopped and looked around at Nova. "Have they really told you nothing? We are so close to the moment, surely you should know more."

Agitated, she grabbed for Nova's hand again and pulled him forward, before releasing it and picking up speed as she walked across a large opening that Nova knew was the plaza. It was where most of the messages came through The Nexus, and he noticed screens everywhere. A main stage was to his left.

Nova felt they were walking very fast, and he was worried that he wouldn't keep up and would lose Phoebe with so much going on around him. Every so often he would see a flash of her mousy hair bobbing through the crowd, and he would rush to keep up. He didn't want to lose her, and he didn't want her to stop sharing more with him about all the things he didn't know.

The crowd seemed to taper off as they got to the other side of the plaza, and Nova could see that the buildings became more tired-looking. He had never noticed this area when he watched The Nexus. The people around him were wearing similar types of clothes to the people he had seen before, but theirs looked more threadbare and ragged, like they were old and needed a good wash.

"Where are we?" Nova asked.

"This is the Dundrells," replied Phoebe, looking squarely into his eyes. "It is where all the Champions are brought, and also the lucky people like me who get out of the infirmary."

Nova didn't understand for a minute and had a fleeting thought of Ariadne and Niall. Were they here, and would they spend the rest of their lives this unhappy?

He looked around at the people who had no smiles on their faces. None were Ariadne and Niall. Most of the people wore hats with wide brims to keep their eyes from view, and they walked quickly like they were going somewhere, unlike the people on the other side of the plaza. Those people were just walking to, well, walk. Those people had an air of elegance, charm, and a confidence of character, whereas the people he saw here didn't wear smiles on their faces, and the flashes of their eyes that he caught showed a deep-rooted fatigue that made Nova's eyes swell.

Not wanting to believe it and not yet fully comprehending it, Nova started, "But the Champions are always glowing and look happy when they come back to Creston or when they are shown on The Nexus. They don't look like these people—"

Phoebe cut him off. "Well, they are these people, and it's good that you've seen it. It's good that you understand. Not everything is as it seems."

Nova had heard that sentence a few times before. Not everything is as it seems. He wondered what else was completely contrary to his beliefs.

They started walking up a set of stairs that was painted in all the colors of the rainbow. It was beautiful, but it wasn't clean. It didn't look marvelous like the stairs in the castle and its gardens or like the elaborate shops and houses that surrounded the castle side of the plaza.

"You need to erase all of the things you know about the Regime," began Phoebe.

She was keeping an exceptional pace and speaking without any faltering in her breath despite the stairs they were climbing.

"All the Regime does is take and conceal. It wants you to think it is helping the community, and that without it we would be terrible wretches with nothing to eat and no safety from invaders or the virus, but it's not true. It created those lies to keep us locked up in district cages. It has us performing like trained animals."

"Why don't people in the districts know? They have the right to know what is going on," replied Nova.

"We've tried," said Phoebe, who added emphasis to her statement with a hand gesture that signaled the weight of the burden of knowing and yet not knowing what to do.

"People believe what they want to believe, and they are afraid, afraid that the Regime will take their families away. So, they keep quiet and pretend to not know. More must be done before we can truly get the people to understand, and it all starts with you."

"What starts with me? What do I need to do?" asked Nova, desperately wanting to understand his place in all of this and how he could help.

"You must do what the Wizard Oberon tells you, when he tells you."

With that, Phoebe started taking the steps two by two and rushed up to the top of the long staircase. Nova tried his best to keep up, and once he got to the top, he folded over and began huffing, because he was out of breath. He turned around to look at the steps behind him, and he saw a view that was magnificent. The castle with the sacred flaming chalice next to it was set against the green foliage of the forests with the river running through and the town around it. He assumed Creston was northeast from where they stood.

"Wow, isn't it beautiful," he said, genuinely in awe by what was in front of him.

"Beauty can sometimes be pretty awful if you ask me," Phoebe said, spinning around and walking off.

They came to an arched entrance, and there was a path in front of them with rows of trees on either side, which swayed in the wind. As they headed farther down the road, Nova noticed two old and dilapidated buildings that looked like they could be abandoned. On the front of the one on the left read 'The Factory' and on the front of the one on the right read 'The Infirmary.'

Looking at Nova's puzzled face, Phoebe said, "This is it. This is what I wanted you to see."

"You wanted me to see two abandoned buildings?" questioned Nova.

Shaking her head, Phoebe responded, "I wanted you to see the penitentiary but best to not risk that. Come on, we'd better head inside."

Nova followed as Phoebe quietly opened the front door to the factory building and headed in. Inside, the entranceway was dimly lit, and it was clean but old. The carpet was threadbare, the glass chandelier was cracked, and only certain bulbs lit up. The wallpaper was fraying from the walls. Nova could hear a buzzing sound from within as they rounded a corner that opened onto a huge floor containing machinery and workers—the unsmiling people that they had seen on the far side the plaza.

"When you win the Championships, this is your reward," Phoebe said with a smirk that pointed downward on her face.

"What is this place?" asked Nova, looking around and wondering what he was seeing exactly.

"This is one of the workhouses. There are many more, of course, and there are the mines and shipyards. A lot are closer to other satellite cities from Castlegar, like White Rock. It is on the coast, so perfect for the Regime's trade networks," said Phoebe matter-of-factly. "Come on, we don't have much time before the spell wears off."

She spun around, and they headed outside and then through the door of the second building. Inside was a lady dressed in a dreary-looking white color with a red cross on her head, sitting in a wooden cubicle that read 'Reception' above it. Going past unnoticed, Phoebe led Nova down the hall and opened two swinging doors for them to walk through. They entered an open room filled with beds of people sick and writhing in pain.

"This is where the Regime sends those with the virus. The virus is inflicted by the Regime, of course, and these people will most likely either not come out of here or end up like your father. There are only a few who turn out okay, and they end up working at the factory next door, but they will never go back to their villages again unless they've lost their memory and it's safe." Phoebe looked around at the many people, and Nova could sense a sorrow in her voice as she spoke.

Thinking back on the photograph outside the hallway

where he had met the elders, Nova was sad to see so many people in such a terrible situation. He found it hard to stomach that the Regime was at fault for passing on the virus and making people this way, and a sickness swelled up in his throat when he thought again of how it was to blame for changing his father. It must pay for what it's done.

This time Nova was the one to turn to leave. He angrily pushed through the doors and headed back past the reception desk.

"Excuse me, young man, you are not allowed to leave here," said the woman.

Startled, Nova stopped in his tracks.

"Run!" cried Phoebe as she pushed him through the front doors out of the building, but it was too late. The alarm had sounded, and the patrol who had been silently guarding the perimeter grabbed them both and forced them back into the building, taking them to a room that was unoccupied.

"What are your names?" they asked.

"My name is Nova."

Phoebe rolled her eyes, and the patrol's lips curled up with satisfaction.

CHAPTER
14

The floor was cold and damp. There was a dripping sound from the side of the cell where the small-slatted window sat above, and water streamed from its barred, frosted glass. A sound of scuttling came from the darkest parts of the room, where Nova assumed rats and other creepy, crawly things were scratching around on the hard, concrete floor.

It was easy to appreciate wide, open spaces and the freedom to roam them when you were no longer in them. Now Nova realized how constricting it could be to feel alone and trapped. Not having the power to control the things you do or where you go was suffocating, and Nova noticed that his breathing was much shallower.

Thoughts swam like fish through his mind. Where was Phoebe? What was this place? What did they intend to do with him?

Their capture had all happened so quickly. One moment they were walking invisibly around Castlegar with not a worry in the world, and in the next they were seen, they were discovered. The full weight of how dangerous the Regime really was sank into Nova. It settled inside him like a heavy weight, and anger bubbled up from his core.

Nova pulled himself up off the floor and moved toward the bars of the cell. It was hard to see what was farther down the hallway. There were dim lights that lit it, and he could see that he was in one of several barred cages. He wondered who else might be inside the rest.

"Phoebe," he whispered, and he heard a movement from down the hall.

"Phoebe!" he shouted louder, and this time he heard several heavy, steely footsteps coming from the opposite direction before two loud bangs hit the bars on his cell.

He rushed back into the darkness to hide himself from the patrol who walked closer. At first he thought there was another person sitting behind him because of a whimpering sound that was echoing against the four cell walls, and he swiveled around. But he realized he was alone, and the noise was coming from him. He also felt a throbbing coming from his head, and he wondered what it could be.

The patrol hung around for some time, looking in the cell to try to see Nova. He rattled in his pocket and Nova could hear the patrol's keys jingle. He could see the silver glimmer in the dark. Was he going to come in?

Seconds passed before the patrol pulled out a flashlight and shone it around the cell, exposing to Nova all its musty edges for the first real time. He saw a big rat on the far right scurry through a hole much smaller than it, and there were some small beetles that weren't affected by the light passing them as they made their way around the ground they called home. It occurred to Nova how lucky they were to come and go. He also wondered why they would choose such an awful place to live.

"Well, if it isn't our prize pig," the patrol muttered in a way that sounded like his tongue was heavy in his mouth.

Nova said nothing, but he felt frightened. He had never spoken with someone who had so much power over him. Someone who was one turn of a lock between his freedom and his oppression. He felt uneasy at the sound of the man's voice; it was the voice of someone who saw an animal in a cage and not a human. To the patrol, Nova was not an equal. This wasn't in the sense of how the Wizard Oberon or any of his elders would speak to him with superiority because they knew more than him. This was in a way that said, 'I own you.'

The patrol continued, "You are our best prize, yet. We have already sent the crows to tell Old Lady Cravelda, and she is going to be really darn happy that we have you here. You know she's been looking for you, and we already have your father. What a *magical* little collection."

Nova noticed how the patrol put an emphasis on the word magical as if it had its own connotations, and it was rooted in a deeper meaning.

The patrol took a step backward and switched off his flashlight, which had been shining directly on Nova. He turned on his heels before walking slowly back to where he came from.

Think, Nova, think.

Nova's mind went blank at first. He was always used to having thoughts racing through him, teasing him, pestering him. Even in Creston he had thoughts when he wasn't meant to, when it was banned by the Regime. But right at the moment when he needed them, he was betrayed. Betrayed by his own mind.

He closed his eyes and just sat. He started to tune

into the rhythm of his surroundings. Long hallways with cells, dripping, scratching, patrol boots, bodies moving across cement floors, and whimpering just like he did. Sad but muted cries and low, fast breathing. The air stank of despair.

Nova opened his eyes and started moving slowly and quietly to the parts of his small room that the patrol's light had shone on. He wasn't afraid, nothing in here was going to hurt him. It was what was out there.

He ran his hands around and touched the smooth shells of his many crawling friends. He didn't want to hurt them, but it couldn't be helped. Is that how the patrol felt about him, too? No, the patrol had intent. He almost knocked over the small footstool when he got to it, and his heart rate accelerated at first, not knowing what it was. He must have missed seeing it before. On top of the stool sat a beaker of water and a plate of something that smelled inedible. Nova took a small sip of the water, feeling thankful for the slightly rusty-tasting liquid that ran down his parched throat. He gulped more of it down but then decided to save some in case he didn't get any more.

He moved farther around the cell and on the opposite side of the room found the mound of hay that the patrol's light had touched briefly. He pulled himself up on it.

Why did his head feel so heavy?

He curled up into the bed, closed his eyes, and fell into a deep sleep.

❖

Nova opened his eyes. He wasn't sure how long he had

been asleep, but his situation hadn't changed. The first thing he noticed was the smell of must, damp, and filth. The second thing he noticed was the sound of the drip, the patrol's boots, and whimpering from cells farther down the hallway. The third thing he noticed was a new tray on the stool. A shudder ran down his spine. Had someone been in here?

He crawled over to it and put the fresh water to his lips. At least he knew there would be more. The food looked even more inedible, but he took a bite. He spat it out back onto the side of the tray; it tasted vile and like nothing he had ever tried before. While he felt hunger in his belly, he knew that he could not eat that. He wondered how long it might be before he would have to.

He still felt woozy, but he was feeling much better than before. He noticed that he could see the cell more clearly now: its four corners, the cracks in the walls, and the little critters that moved around in it. He saw on the far wall that someone had written something, so he got up to investigate. His legs felt heavy, and he wondered if he could make the few steps across the room, but he did. As he got closer, he saw that there were lots of scratched notes and messages from those who had, sadly, been here before.

Nova ran his fingers across the marks on the wall and read them by the small amount of light and by what his fingers spelled out to him.

'Cravelda must die'
'Ella D was here'
'Down with the Regime'
'You are not alone'
'There is no escape'

Nova slumped against the wall. He felt both happy to feel less alone but miserable that others had been here. He thought over the things that they had said, and the final message stuck in his head—there is no escape.

Bang, bang, bang.

Nova had been so caught up in his own thoughts that he hadn't heard the patrol approaching.

"Yard time," the patrol boomed.

Nova wasn't sure what that meant or what to do, so he brought his knees up to his chest and sat there against the wall.

"Get up immediately, Inmate Two Sixty-Three," barked the patrol.

Nova stood to attention, and the patrol reached into his pocket and pulled out the keys. He went through the loops on his chain until he found the right one and rattled it in the lock. He turned it around twice and pushed the heavy, barred door back. Nova felt exposed. He knew that the patrol had the luxury to do what he wanted with him in this enclosed environment. In the short space of time that Nova was in there, he grew to feel that it was his space and that it belonged to him and no one else. He also felt safer with them out there and him in here.

Seeing that Nova wasn't coming forward, the patrol walked through the door with his heavy boots. Nova noticed how clean he looked against the dirt of his enclosure. The patrol grabbed his arm and pulled Nova forward. His grip was tight, but Nova also noticed that the patrol was strong enough to grip tighter, so he followed his lead.

Looking down the hallway, Nova saw several other children his age or younger coming out of their cells, assisted by similar patrol in matching black and red outfits. Nova noticed that they all had a chain of keys on their pockets, which glimmered like his own patrol's had as they moved about. He also noticed the obsidian swords they wore on their belts, and he felt a shudder wash through him.

"Eyes down, Inmate Two Sixty-Three," shouted the patrol, and Nova did as he said.

Once the patrol had brought all the children from their cells, they stood to attention. A command from behind came "Attention! Now march!" and the patrol did as they were told, marching in unison with their unused arms swinging while their other arms grasped tight onto their inmates. They followed each other down a hallway and up a flight of stairs.

Nova stepped through the door and into the light. His eyes took a moment to adjust. It was fresh and clean outside; he could hear birds singing, and the sun shone down on the small yard the children were brought to. The patrol continued to march with the children next to them and did ten laps of the yard before releasing their inmates' arms and heading back inside. Nova's head was spinning. It still hurt from earlier, and he didn't know what was wrong.

The children began talking with each other, and many came toward him, eyeing him. Nova didn't like this sort of attention and was embarrassed, as he was sure that he was dirty from being in his cell. He looked at the children around him and saw that their clothes were tattered and their hair was disheveled. He felt guilty for his previous opinion.

"Hello, my name is Gabriel. It's nice to meet you," said

a young boy who was only slightly shorter than Nova, but who had a nice smile to his face.

"What's your name?" said a girl to the side of Nova, without giving her own. She had long hair that she wore in two braids down her back.

Nova looked down at the ground. He didn't want to use the name Alex and deceive the others, but the last time he had given away his name so easily it had ended up backfiring on him.

"Give him some space," said Gabriel as he pushed the others back. "Go talk among yourselves."

Nova liked Gabriel. He could tell he was a natural leader, the type who could say little but who was respected. Nova had always wanted to be more like a Gabriel.

Gabriel took Nova to the far side of the yard, and they stood by a fence, looking out onto another field that was also partially surrounded by fence.

"That's where the adults go. There are five times as many of them as us," began Gabriel as he ran his hand through his hair so that it moved off his face. It was handsome and hung in just the right position no matter how it was moved. Even though it was dirty and dark in color, there were streaks of lighter honey color that glimmered in the sun. Nova wondered whether Gabriel's hair was usually this long or if it helped to date his length in the penitentiary.

"We are sent out in the morning before lunch, and the adults are sent out midafternoon. We do ten laps each day, and we get thirty minutes to chat with the others before we are called back into our cells. We then get served more gruel and water. They switch on the lights for the afternoon so that we don't go crazy with our thoughts, and then in the evening they serve us gruel and water again before the lights go out," said Gabriel in a cool way.

Nova shook his head in dismay. He couldn't make sense of it. Why would the Regime want to keep children like this?

As if he could read Nova's thoughts, Gabriel continued, "It takes us because we are too much of a risk to it. Some of us here are too vocal, some of us stand up against it, some of us know magic."

Gabriel stopped and looked at Nova from the corner of his eye, but Nova looked away, not wanting to look suspicious. He didn't want others to know about his magic, not until he had mastered it, at least. He rotated and faced back toward the penitentiary.

"What you are looking at is the Kids Penn—that's what we call it. And over there"—Gabriel pointed at a larger building to their left—"that is Big Penn. It is where we go when we are too old to stay in here. And, believe you me, most of us don't get out of here."

Nova looked up at the gray building that had what looked like black dust sprinkled all over it. The building in front of them was five floors tall, and he knew there was at least one floor below. He wondered how many children were here or had been here before.

"The Regime set up the Penn years and years ago, knowing that the Resistance were working with Happenstance. It was in its best interest to suppress the Nomans before coming up with the virus and the Championships. It was the easiest way to secure its power, snuff out the challengers, and set up a system of oppression in the guise of service. For so many years there have been uprisings, and each and every one is stopped before it even gets started. The firm hand of the Regime stamping it out before it catches fire. We are waiting for the sign for the real revolution." Gabriel nodded his head at the end of the final sentence like it would help in making the wish come true.

Nova again tried to divert his eyes so that he didn't draw attention to what he knew. He wondered how many signs there could be and whether he was connected to this one. If he were, then what could he do while trapped in here? He looked around at all the children who were talking and looking over toward him. Some were so young. They had started playing a game of hopscotch, first by scratching the numbered boxes on the ground, and then hopping along from one side to the other. Nova wondered if the yard was where they had gotten the stones to scratch notes on the walls.

Farther along the fence stood another boy who was looking out at the yard too. Nova's vision wasn't great as he peered down. Perhaps it had something to do with the pounding at the side of his head?

"Who is that?" asked Nova, wincing in pain.

"Ah, good, so you do talk," said Gabriel with a kind smile, and Nova blushed again, realizing how rude he had been to not say anything at all to someone who was being so kind to him.

Noticing his unease, Gabriel said, "It's okay. A lot of kids who come in here don't speak for days, or even weeks. I'm just glad you can."

Gabriel started walking down the fence toward the other boy. From a distance, Nova thought that he looked very similar to the rest, but as they got closer he realized the boy was older. He must have been older than Nova, in fact, and the eldest in the group.

"Vance, what are you doing down here alone?" said Gabriel, approaching him and giving him a friendly clap on the back.

The boy looked distant and distracted. He stared out into the grassy field ahead.

"Vance, I wanted to introduce you to a new friend who has just arrived," Gabriel said a little louder.

Vance came out of his daydream and looked at Nova. "Hello."

Nova responded looking sheepishly at both Vance and Gabriel, "Hello, I'm Nova."

"What's up with you today, my friend, cat got your tongue? You look discombobulated," said Gabriel to Vance. Nova didn't know if Gabriel knew magic, but he seemed like a magician with his words. If what he had just said even was a real word.

"It's almost my fourteenth birthday," Vance responded, looking Gabriel in the eye.

Gabriel's cool, calm demeanor faded for a moment, and he looked Vance up and down, shaking his head.

"It can't be," he responded with a weakness in his voice.

Vance looked down and kicked a small stone that was in front of his feet, then picked it up and threw it far into the space between yards. He looked unnerved and as if he might cry or had cried not too long ago.

"Guess what they do to kids when they turn fourteen, new friend?" he said, looking up at Nova.

Nova shook his head, unsure what could be any worse

than the situation they were in right now. He responded, "What do they do?"

"You get transferred to Big Penn from here. But, before you go there, you go to Cell Block Fourteen," Vance responded, shaking his head and looking at the floor again.

"What's Cell Block Fourteen?" asked Nova, glancing at Gabriel, who had a look of fear on his face.

"You tell him, G," said Vance, turning back to look out at the fields ahead. His corkscrew hair and tanned skin looked less grubby than the others, and for a split second Nova wondered why before being confronted with Vance's reality. At least he had found the means in here to keep himself somewhat clean.

"Cell Block Fourteen is where they put the patrols who go crazy or who commit a serious crime. Some of them have killed children in here, some children have tried to attack them. They don't like us, they have never liked us. When it's their job to do it, it's one thing, but when they have nothing else, it is another."

Nova couldn't take any more. He had to get out of this place and save the others.

"Perhaps there is something I can do to help," he said with a nervousness that ran through the final five words of the sentence.

Gabriel and Vance looked at him. They both knew. They knew his secret, or at least one of his secrets.

Then Vance replied, "Magic won't help you in here, they've made sure of that."

How could it be that he couldn't use magic here? Hadn't Phoebe used a spell before? The spinning sped up in Nova's head as thoughts danced at dizzying speed.

❖

He woke up and he was on an operating table. There was a woman with the same hat on as someone Nova had recently seen but couldn't remember. He felt dizzy, and it took him a moment to recall the woman at the infirmary reception desk in her white hat with the red cross. His eyes were blurry, but he was looking around, trying to take in his surroundings.

"You're one of the lucky ones, you didn't fall too hard and I'm guessing before that they didn't hit you too hard," said the woman, turning away from Nova and back to a table that had gauze, a needle and thread, and other things that he didn't want to look at.

Nova went to sit up, but his head felt woozy, and he fell backward onto his pillow. He tried to recall what had happened to him and what happened to his head, but he couldn't think.

"Where am I?" he said in a slightly slurred voice. Did that voice belong to him?

The nurse was cleaning things away, and she barely noticed him talking, but she muttered in response.

"You are in the infirmary. Now that you are better, they will take you back, don't worry. It's just down the road," she said in a mechanical voice.

"No!" exclaimed Nova, but he was still so woozy that the frustration in his voice didn't feed through, because it was too full of air.

He had something stuck in his arm that he tugged out. It hurt, but he felt freer. He sat up more slowly this time. He had to get out now if he could.

"You aren't going anywhere, young man. There are five

armed patrol outside in the hallway, and all I need to do is scream before they are here in a flash—you don't want them to hurt you again, do you?" she snapped. She came back over toward Nova and pushed away the trolley that held the gauze and medical equipment and again turned her back on him.

Nova looked around the room as much as he could. He was sitting in the middle of it, facing cupboards and a sink. To his left was a window. He wondered where it led and if he had enough energy to pull himself through it?

"And don't even think about that window," the Nurse quipped, and she packed up her things in a handbag and grabbed a coat as if she were about to leave.

"Wait, don't go," scratched Nova's voice.

"Why? I have healed you, so we both must go."

Nova wondered how long she had been doing this job, a job to fix people that she presumably cared so little about. He thought of the time he had fallen off his bicycle when he was young, and there was a gash on his knee that his neighbor, Mr. Huddersmith, had mended. How each stitch was perfectly sewn up, and how they had given him hot milk and cookies to calm him, and how he had been speaking with Mrs. Huddersmith about his love of the night sky so that he hardly noticed what was happening to him. They had, of course, numbed the area so that it was virtually painless.

Thinking for a second, Nova responded, "Do you not care about the people who you heal?"

The nurse stopped as she approached the door and turned to look at Nova. A darkness ran through her irises before she responded.

"Of course, I make sure people get healed. It is my

job," was her reply. And with that, she opened the door and walked out into the hallway, closing the door behind her but leaving it slightly ajar as she spoke quietly to the patrol.

Nova tried with all his might to pull one leg and then the other from the bed. He swung himself around so that his feet hit the ground below. It was like his body was asleep and being uncooperative. He looked at the window. How many steps might that be? Five, six?

He pulled himself to stand up and then felt uneasy and steadied himself on the bed. There was a mirror to the far-right side of the room, and he caught a glance of himself in it and noticed a big gauze patch on his head. He stood up and took a step. It was more of a shuffle, and he had to steady himself. He wondered if it were his injury or whether they had given him something that slowed him down.

Step number two.

Out in the hallway, he could hear the nurse saying her thank yous and goodbyes to the patrol and the click of her heels as she headed away.

Another step.

The door creaked open, and the sound of heavy boots filled the room. Nova wished his body would cooperate and tried to move as quickly as he could.

Two more steps, and his hands were on the window ledge. He then looked back, and a hand of a patrol was reaching out toward him. He looked down and saw that he was several floors up. What would happen when he hit the ground? There was no time.

He pictured himself as he fell from the windowsill, serenely, with nothing but air all around him, detached from everything. Time passing slowly as he fell to his imminent end on the ground below. It was more peaceful than expected.

He landed with a humph, but the feeling wasn't the hard, sharp connection he had anticipated. The wind rushed out of him, but he was on his back still looking at the cloudy sky above. He looked back up at the window and noticed that, rather than having sunk the ten or so floors he had expected, he had only fallen three or four, and he was now rising.

Sitting up, Nova felt the familiar feathers of a friend. He looked up at the white head and yellow beak of the bird he was flying on.

"Osiris, it's you!" he exclaimed.

"Yes, you are a lucky one, aren't you?" came a female voice behind him.

"Phoebe, how did you get here?" he asked with shock in his voice. He'd thought she was still in a cell in that horrible prison.

"I have my ways," she retorted with a proud look on her face. "Here you go. I'm sure you wouldn't want to leave without it."

Phoebe threw Nova's backpack his way. She did so rather half-heartedly, and Nova scrambled forward to grab it before it slid down Osiris' sleek, oily feathers as the group ascended upwards. Steadying himself, Nova tore it open and saw that the box and his other possessions were somehow still inside.

"How did you manage to get this?" said Nova, in shock of what was in front of him. He thought it was lost for good.

He looked over at Phoebe and added, "Thank you so much."

"Let's just say that not all of us get captured so easily," she scoffed at him and turned toward Osiris.

"Hang on, you two. The Wizard Oberon has opened a temporary moonbow, but we must get there as soon as possible," Osiris said as he flew above a puffy, white cloud.

"It's still daylight," said Nova, looking around. He realized he was surprisingly coming to his senses as the earth moved quickly below. He touched the bandage on his head.

"We must fly far from here, to the other side of the earth where it is dark. It is not easy for the Wizard Oberon to open a moonbow on a whim," Osiris responded a bit more gruffly than before.

Nova thought about the Wizard Oberon and wondered what he would say upon his return. He must be in trouble if the Wizard Oberon had had to open a moonbow. He knew they were only around once every couple of weeks, and he thought of the amount of magic the Wizard Oberon had to use in order to open this one for this specific purpose.

He worried about the discussions to come upon his return to Happenstance, but he had no other choice as the three of them sailed far from the sun.

CHAPTER
15

"I DON'T THINK I can do it," said Nova nervously, cracking his knuckles.

"Of course you can," responded Cassia, who was sitting on a waist-high pillar, her woven hair illuminated from behind by the moonlight.

"How do you know?" asked Nova, looking away from his knuckles and toward her. A thought ran through his head of how beautiful Cassia looked tonight, and then he shook his head as if to clear it away.

"I've messed up so many times now, Cassia. And, now that I've seen it, now that I've seen how bad it is, my quest to face the Regime seems completely absurd. I'm not ready," continued Nova as he paced back and forth across the small, concrete podium.

The two were back in the stadium they had come to on the first night they'd arrived at Serendipity. The air was even sharper and colder now, but they were used to it. They had always liked playing outside in the winter, building snow forts. It had never occurred to Nova then that one day they would be in a completely unexplainable, icy, and magical world.

"You know as well as I do that everything happens for a reason, and we wouldn't be here in this place together if there wasn't a reason why. Heck, Nova, I know it, everyone here knows it, why can't you see it?" said Cassia, who was swinging her legs in a way that made them look like they, too, were emphasizing a point.

"Yes, I know, Cassia, I just haven't had time to train my magic. I haven't had time to think. I've been here only a few days, and I've only just been told about my quest. Somehow I've also managed to take myself back to Dacaan and to Creston, where I almost got caught, and then did get caught by the Regime—I can't even save myself, so how am I going to save anyone else?"

Nova was keen for an actual answer here, if only someone could step forward and help.

"We need to spend the next few days doing everything we can to understand the plan and prepare like the Wizard Oberon said. You've hardly touched your textbooks or been to classes. Plus, you don't know yet what they want you to do exactly, silly," responded Cassia with a surety in her voice that made Nova feel some comfort. She was right, as usual.

Cassia jumped down from the podium, landing on bent knees, and then walked toward Nova and held out her hand. He took it, and she walked with him to the middle of the snowy stage.

"I want to show you something," she said, looking at him with a mischievous grin on her face.

Cassia reached into her bag and pulled out a long, thin object. It was a wand. Nova had seen those mounted on the walls of one of their classrooms, and had looked at many with various names for some time, but didn't imagine actually taking one.

"Where did you get that?" he asked with a hushed voice in case anyone saw them.

"I was given it, by one of our teachers," said Cassia smartly. "I wasn't just sitting around while you were in Castlegar, I'll have you know."

Cassia raised the wand so that it lay horizontally in the air with her outstretched arm over the top of it. She closed her eyes and lifted it slightly, tapping it down as if she were hitting something in front of her.

"Convivium!"

Opening her eyes, Cassia looked around, but nothing had happened.

"Oh," she said with a sudden embarrassment on her face, "let me try again."

"Are you sure you know what you are doing? I thought the teachers said it would take you longer to learn magic than the rest," replied Nova.

"Well, I'm a fast learner, and sometimes saying you can do it is half the battle. Plus, I'm not going to let people tell me what I can and can't do."

Cassia closed her eyes again, holding the wand in front of her.

"Convivium!"

Nova was looking at Cassia as she opened her eyes. He didn't want her to feel disappointed in herself like he had done. But, when her eyes opened this time, all he saw was awe and delight on her face.

He looked in the direction that her wand pointed, and out in front of the stadium were seats filled with well-dressed people. They were laughing and joking with each other, some with small binoculars and others eating popcorn, looking at them.

"How did you do that?" Nova said, amazed.

"I believed," replied Cassia, "in magic and in myself."

She walked toward the front of the stage with a huge smile on her face, looking out toward the crowd in front of them. It was absolutely wonderful and miraculous.

"They aren't real, of course, it is just an illusion. Better than yours in the Championships, I might add," she said with a smile and a wink. "I spent some extra hours with Mrs. Borealis, our Head of Magic, and she helped me with a few spells to accelerate my learning. I'm still a little rusty, and although it isn't inside me like it is in you, I can still make it work with the right tools." She flipped the wand so it spun around several times in the air before landing back in her hand.

"Show off," scoffed Nova.

Cassia pointed the wand out in front of her once again. "Finito!"

Just like that, the people in the stands disappeared.

Nova laughed.

"Well, I can't have you going to the Regime on your own and not bring something to the table."

"You're incredible, Cassia," said Nova, blushing. But it was true, she was. In his eyes she couldn't do anything wrong.

Nova walked toward Cassia and grabbed her hand gently to look at the wand in it. It was an excuse to touch her hand, really, and he pulled it and her closer to him. So close that the icy air from their breath intertwined in front of their faces and made a small cloud of miniature snowflakes.

They stood there like that for a long time, looking deep into each other's eyes. They were so close that Nova could see the gray and purple specks that twinkled in Cassia's irises in the moonlight. They had known each other for so many years, but had he seen that twinkle before? Had he seen her like this before?

Cassia brushed some fluffy snow from Nova's hair and gave a little giggle before she touched his cheek softly. The pair closed their eyes and leaned into each other, feeling each other's soft lips gently connect. That night, a new type of magic had found its way to Happenstance.

❖

Nova waited outside the chamber of the Council of Elders again. This time, rather than spending his time looking at the elaborate art that hung in the room, he listened in to their discussion, hoping to pick up as much information as he could about their plans and decisions.

So far, the meeting had been predominantly led by a female voice, one that he knew but couldn't put a face to. It couldn't have been any of the people who had been in the previous meeting, because it was much younger. Nova pressed his ear to the door.

"He is simply underprepared, that's all. He has more power than any of us could think of, but he doesn't know how to use it. It is unruly and dangerous, and we must push the quest back," said the unknown female voice.

Nova empathized with what she was saying but hated that he had let them down. He didn't like to hear those words of disbelief even if he, to some extent, felt them himself.

Responding to the female voice, Nova could hear the Wizard Oberon's deep, old tones resonate in baritone in the room. "He is powerful, but not powerful enough, yet. He is building his strength and this is the issue."

Nova could hear murmurs in the room that were muted but showed that the group was talking over these two points about both Nova's inexperience and inability all at once. He felt frustrated that so many people were focusing on him and talking about his inabilities. They had invited him here to speak more about his quest, and all they were doing right now was focusing on flaws.

But hadn't he been the one to bring darkness to Happenstance, hadn't he used dark magic to make Luca disappear, hadn't he willed himself back to Dacaan and ended up in the penitentiary? He realized their concerns were just, and he felt deeply ashamed once again. He was a liability to them all.

"We don't have time, though. Remember, we are losing strength every day with Happenstance fading. What if we wake up one day and all the magic is gone? It will have been too late," came another voice that sounded like it could be King Anthony.

There were more murmurs among the group.

The young female voice picked up. "Yes, you are right. I have seen his abilities, and with some support, however, we could do it. But we need just a little more time, and he must not go alone."

"Well, of course not," rebutted the Wizard Oberon, and there were more murmurs.

Another older voice of a woman, perhaps Persephone, spoke next. "King Anthony is right. Our window of opportunity is short and we cannot lose any more time. The comet showed us that we must act now. People on

Dacaan are suffering, and Happenstance is in great danger."

"Yes..."

"I agree..."

"We must make progress..."

A medley of voices all spoke up at once, making it hard for Nova to hear the full sentences. The Wizard Oberon rapped his staff to settle the room.

The young female voice started again, "It is not about if we should make our move now, in that case, it is about our course of action."

"But, we have been building these plans for years..." came a distant voice that petered off quietly so that Nova couldn't hear the end of the sentence.

"We have no time to change our plans," came another outburst from the far side of the room.

"Then we must unlearn our plan and start afresh," said the female voice once again.

"Bring the boy in. Let's first speak with him about his tutoring over the coming days, and tomorrow we will come together and rethink our strategy," said the Wizard Oberon.

Nova stood up and scurried backward from the door and turned the other way to look out the window. He didn't want them to see that he had been spying on the conversation.

The door clicked, and it was Persephone. "Hello, my sweet child, please join us," she said in a musical way, as if all were okay.

Nova entered the room. He already knew he was about to be reprimanded, and in such a large group of officials, it made his face turn red.

"Young man, please sit down," demanded the Wizard Oberon as he rapped on a chair at the front of the room with a stick, indicating where he must go.

Nova hurried over and sat as instructed. He looked around the room and saw the female speaker was Phoebe. How had she been invited and been so vocal in this prestigious meeting, he wondered? Nova sat in the chair and stared back down at the floor.

"Before we start, might I say, Nova, that we are so pleased to have you back in Happenstance, and we are so grateful that you have returned safely to us," chimed Persephone, trying to set the tone for the meeting—light and breezy.

The Wizard Oberon did not, however, look so whimsical about the matter. He got up and strode to the front of the room before beginning his missive.

"We are aware that you are early in your journey into magic and that the magic you possess is much more powerful than what an average child might ever understand in their lifetime. It cannot be, however, that you use your magic without thinking. The first rule in magic is to always control your power. Do you hear me, young man?" asked the Wizard Oberon, tapping his staff in front of Nova's feet in the space he was looking at on the floor.

"Yes, I hear you," he responded, looking up slightly before looking back down again.

"As I am sure you know, Dacaan, Happenstance, and your friends and family are in grave danger. People that you know have now been exposed because of your careless exploits with the Regime, and who knows what will happen to them next. The Regime is cruel and merciless, even with children . . ."

Nova thought of the children at the penitentiary and thought of his father's capture by Cravelda. He felt bile rise to his throat at the thought of it; the Regime disgusted him. He gulped the feeling of sickness back down, but the anger remained.

"Every step that we take henceforth must be together. Every action that we take must be together. Do you understand me?" continued the Wizard Oberon.

Nova took a minute before responding. He sat there as a thought came into his mind with laser precision and so much reason that he dared not dismiss it.

"Yes, I agree, Wizard Oberon Silver, and I am sorry for my misjudgments in how I should use my magic. I will certainly be more careful next time," he responded, and waited a minute as the Wizard Oberon turned around and looked at him, ready to continue his instruction on what Nova should do.

Nova, however, interrupted before the Wizard Oberon could say his next words and continued himself, "I do agree that I need your support and the support from others in fulfilling my quest. If it wasn't for Phoebe's help in Castlegar, who knows where I would be now."

Nova paused as more murmurs and some gasps ran across the room.

"But, in order for you to best use me, you must inform me, and in order for you to best inform me, you must include me. As you've said, we must move forward together." Nova stumbled across the sentence as it made sense in his mind, but he wasn't sure if it had come out altogether correctly.

"First of all, I need you to include me in all further meetings," he began before adding, "from the start."

Nova looked around the room and saw a smile light up on Phoebe's face and Persephone nod her head while a lot of the others talked among themselves. The Wizard Oberon had turned away from him and was looking at the front of the room.

"I did listen in on your discussions about me, and I appreciate everything that you are all thinking," continued Nova bravely, in a way he wasn't used to speaking. He stood up from his chair and looked across the room to the wise faces.

"I, too, am afraid that I am not yet prepared to face the Regime."

There were some gasps in the room, but Nova continued, "I do, however, have my own plan on how we should face the Regime that I would like to present to you."

"Yes, Nova, please share this with us. Don't be shy," said Phoebe over a loudening set of murmurs from around the Council.

The Wizard Oberon rammed his staff on the floor once more.

"Please continue, young man," was his response without turning around.

"I would, first of all, create a group that would support me and make up for my inadequacies at present, who can help me on my quest." Nova said. "Cassia will be one of those individuals, along with Barnaby and Gwendolyn."

"Preposterous . . ."

"Impossible . . ."

"The fae princess . . ."

Snippets of conversation stood out as the room burst into explosion.

"Silence!" said the Wizard Oberon, this time without ramming his staff on the ground.

Nova continued, "The second thing is that we must plan for how to spread a message that change is coming and that people must be prepared. Most people in Dacaan don't know there is a problem, they don't see the Regime as a threat. But there is power in numbers, and we need them on our side."

The room exploded into conversation again, and Nova sat down in his chair, not sure whether he had said the right thing or the wrong thing. But at least he had said it, and that was the main thing.

Phoebe stood up once again, and the Wizard Oberon turned around to face the group with a stern face. The room went silent.

"These . . . ideas . . . are unfounded," said the Wizard Oberon. "Nova, you are new to this, and while we appreciate what you have to say, there are many precautions we must take."

"But, Wizard Oberon, please . . . he could be on to someth—" began Phoebe before she was cut off.

"We will reconvene tomorrow at dawn. Nova, you will join us," said the Wizard Oberon, and with that, he stormed out of the room.

❖

Nova sat with folded legs in a sandy desert. He looked around and felt that he had been here before. The sand was hot, and the sun was even hotter. It hung above him in the middle of the sky like a light on a ceiling. He looked forward to the horizon and saw hills and mounds of sand all around him that rolled into the distance. There was nothing around, just him and sand.

How had he got here, he wondered?

He stood up and looked around. Pivoting and looking behind him, he saw that in the far distance was a black cloud. He felt frightened to the point of nausea, and a muscle memory deep inside of him told him to run, that safety would soon turn into terror and he must leave. NOW.

Nova turned around and started running. The sun was blistering, and he was thirsty.

Why are you running, stop running, you have no water, and there is nowhere to hide—is there?

Feeling conflicted, Nova slowed his running to a walk and looked back over his shoulder. The dark was coming.

You must face it, you must beat it—what other choice do you have?

The voice in Nova's head was saying the opposite to Nova's body, and it continued walking. STOP, NOW—what are you afraid of, you are strong.

Nova's body succumbed to the fierce direction of his mind, his feet stopped, and he turned around.

He looked at the black cloud as it twisted around, forming an eye in its center. A black cone stretched slowly down toward the ground, forming a point at its tip and causing sand to swirl everywhere around it. Nova took off his shirt and covered his eyes.

Something was coming. He couldn't tell what at first, because he couldn't see it, but he could sense it. Something made of flesh, and it was charging across the desert, causing more sand to twist upwards around the funnel that was winding its way toward him.

Then he saw it, a serpent with a black body that almost matched the menacing clouds above it. Its body was long and fat, and its eyes were yellow.

"You think you're sssssssmarter than me, boy?" quipped the serpent as it arrived and circled around Nova.

Nova stood there, fear running up and down him and making him unable to speak.

"Whatsssss the problem, boy, catsss got your tongue?" the serpent mocked him and coiled further and further around before standing up in front of him.

"I'm not afraid of you!" shouted Nova, knowing that he truly was.

The serpent burst into laughter. "Well, of course you are."

"No, I'm not," replied Nova. "I wanted you to come."

At this, the serpent laughed again, only this time twice as loudly.

"Why did you want me to come then, boy? You know that I'm going to eat you."

"No, you won't," replied Nova to the serpent.

To this the serpent opened his mouth as wide as it could. So wide that its jaw hung at a ninety-degree angle and almost touched its body, revealing a huge set of fangs with two prominent ones the size of Nova at the front.

"What do you think now?" said the serpent, returning to its laughter.

"Well, go on," said Nova with only a slight falter in his voice, "do it then, and be done with it."

The serpent pulled back a little, hurt that its attempt at intimidating Nova had not succeeded. But it wasn't long before it reared up again with its two white fangs glinting in the light and leaned forward, wrapping its mouth around Nova.

Nova let out a loud cry before pulling himself out of the way and driving his dagger into the back of the serpent's head.

Not expecting it, the serpent fell to the ground and released itself from the coil around Nova. Blood seeped from its thick, wet skin and fell into pools on the sand below.

"Never underestimate me," said Nova for the final time to the serpent as its body faded from existence. The clouds drew back and made way for mellow sun, and fresh greenery popped up from the ground all around him.

"I did it, I did it, I killed the serpent," began Nova, closing his eyes and pumping his clenched hands into the air in front of him.

"I did it, I killed it . . ."

"Nova, Nova—wake up," came Cassia's voice, "you've been dreaming again."

Nova opened his eyes, and he was back in the room he'd fallen asleep in across from Cassia. It had all been a dream. It was all fine.

"What happened, what did you kill?" asked Cassia, who was flicking her hair out of her eyes. She'd clearly been in a deep sleep herself.

"The serpent, it's gone," said Nova with a goofy grin on his face.

"You're silly, go back to bed," responded Cassia as she walked back to her bed in her pajamas.

"Wait," said Nova shyly.

"What is it?"

"I can do this thing, the quest. I'm ready," said Nova confidently.

Cassia walked back over to Nova and ran a hand down the side of his face, cupping his cheek and kissing it softly. Electricity hung in the air, and Nova pulled her toward his lips. This time their kiss lingered like it could go on forever.

Cassia pulled herself back and smiled.

"I know you're ready, Nova, I've always known you would be. But no one can save the world without sleep," she responded as she headed back to her bed.

❖

The next day, Nova felt a sense of confidence he didn't know existed inside of him. He woke up Cassia before waking Barnaby and Gwendolyn in the rooms down the hall, and he asked them to be ready to meet him downstairs at 6:30 sharp.

Feeling inspired to do something different, Nova slicked his hair back in the mirror—a look he'd always wanted to try but had always thought was not fitting his style. He opted to wear his pants rather than his slacks.

When he got downstairs, he was the first to arrive at the meeting point. He paced back and forth in an eager anticipation and look at the small birds that sung a beautiful morning song while bobbing in and out of the hedges.

Cassia was next to arrive. She'd left just a few minutes after Nova as she had been plaiting her hair already braided hair into its two even rows on either side of her head—to beat the morning frizz, she had often told him.

Barnaby and Gwendolyn must have met on their way down as they arrived together.

"I would have said it was nice to have you back if you hadn't of woken me up so early," scoffed Barnaby.

"What is it, Nova, what do you need us for so urgently that it couldn't wait until after breakfast?" said Gwendolyn sleepily but with no malice in her voice.

Gwendolyn was more herself since Luca returned and was being taken care of in the medical wing of Serendipity. She was the only one who had been allowed to see him, but she said that the doctors assured her he would most likely make a full recovery. Nova had felt a huge amount of relief when he learned the news.

Nova was still pacing somewhat; he felt giddy on his feet. "You all represent my most trusted people in Happenstance. You've supported me, you've helped me, you've protected me."

"Several times," winked Barnaby.

"As you all know, I have been asked to fulfill a quest. The Regime is corrupt, and it is up to me to somehow stop it."

Nova stopped in his tracks and looked straight into the eyes of each of his friends in front of him.

"I cannot do it alone, and I need the strongest people that I know to help me on my journey," he paused a brief moment before adding rather less confidently, "will you join me?"

"Yes, of course, I would expect to be there," responded Barnaby, bowing his head somewhat in Nova's direction.

"Nova, anything you need, I will be there for you," said Gwendolyn.

"You know that silly—you didn't call us here this early

to just ask that, did you?" joked Cassia, rolling her eyes in the direction of the others.

Nova smiled and began walking. "Please follow me, there is somewhere we all need to be."

He guided the group down the twisted hallway under the college that led to the boardroom and opened the door.

Many of the elders were sipping cups of coffee and tea and talking casually with one another. But when the door opened and they saw who had arrived, the room grew silent. Nova walked in and indicated for his friends to join him.

The Wizard Oberon turned to see their entrance and immediately said, "Why are they here? Please ask them to wait outside—this is a private matter."

"They will be my team, the group that I will rely on to help on my quest and to respond to the threats of the Regime," said Nova contently before adding, "They are the best and I need the best."

"Nova, we cannot agree to this group. We have much more acceptable candidates, and we have brought some of them along today. While we appreciate that you'd like to involve your friends in this matter, it is too grave a risk—as we discussed yesterday—you are still too green for this quest, and you will need those with much more ability," responded the Wizard Oberon sternly. "Please go at once."

Feeling hurt by the Wizard Oberon's words, Cassia and Barnaby started to walk out of the room. Gwendolyn looked at her father, and with a nod of his head, she began to walk out too.

"Stop," Nova said and turning to the Wizard Oberon, responded, "they *will* be joining me."

Nova's command was strong, and it shocked the room, including the Wizard Oberon who rapped his staff, indicating for everyone to sit.

Nova grabbed his friends by the arms, and they all stood toward the back of the room. Many of the elders gave disapproving looks as they walked to their chairs.

The Wizard Oberon began, "As we know, Happenstance is under threat, and Dacaan sits idly in the grips of its tyrannical rulers. For too many years we have been subject to the forces of evil. We have had to move to Happenstance not out of choice but out of need. We have made a new world here that has been peaceful, but which now faces its greatest challenge. We know that evil has already found its way into Happenstance, and in order to fully eradicate it, we must face the Regime."

The Wizard Oberon paused and brought a hand with outstretched arms up, which dimmed the lights and drew what looked like a projector that the classrooms in Creston might have had—only without a machine to power it.

The Wizard Oberon continued, but this time with visual cues in a way that reminded Nova of the paintings that came alive in the hallway just outside.

"The Regime has done many wicked things over its time. First, it was the virus used as a weapon to make those it needed quieted to fall ill. It is a virus that still plagues Dacaan today, with only one antidote that helps those who take it fully recover from the aftereffect, even amnesia, that lies in the hands of those in power."

Nova looked at Cassia, not believing what he had heard. His father could be cured. He needed to find a way to that antidote. Cassia nodded her head to show she understood his thoughts.

"The second," continued the Wizard Oberon, "is the treatment of the people in the infirmary, penitentiary, the Dundrells of Castlegar, and how the Regime exploits them."

The picture on the screen had morphed from the scenes in the hospitals, and of small children sick and being taken from their families, to scenes of the place Nova had recently come from where the people had lost their smiles.

The Wizard Oberon looked toward Nova. Nova felt uneasy.

"What Nova said yesterday was correct, we must find a way to inform Dacaan of the horrible things that the Regime is doing—without their understanding of the problem, there can be no solution."

Many turned toward Nova still with doubt in their eyes, or perhaps it was pity. But Nova felt a huge sense of pride in the Wizard Oberon's approval of his idea. He fought hard against a smile that was trying to emerge on his face. He didn't want to come across as overzealous.

Persephone's voice came from the crowd, "How are we going to draw attention to this? What can we do to inform them?"

Phoebe had entered late, and in seeing Nova at the back of the room, she had come toward him. She had a grin on her face that made her look like she had constructed something in her mind that Nova would like.

A new image of Dacaanians with scrolls being spread from hand to hand appeared on the screen. A system of message sharing from one person to another, sharing ideas. Making people think. It was exactly what the Regime warned them against, and it was dangerous, but it must be done.

"This is good, but I know what we must do," said Phoebe in a slow and exaggerated way that made the room pause.

She reached Nova and grabbed his hand. Cassia looked at Nova and then down at the hand Phoebe clasped with jealousy written across her face.

Phoebe once again spoke to the group, "We will free the children from the penitentiary."

The room broke into a chorus of voices.

"Free the children, but how?"

"It's unsafe..."

"There are too many patrol..."

The Wizard Oberon rapped his staff on the ground sternly.

"Nova, please join me at the front with your friends. Phoebe, you too," he commanded.

The group made their way to the front of the room and stood in a line behind the Wizard Oberon.

"As we all know, Nova is our chosen one, and we must believe in his choices for the quest. Phoebe will, of course, join him, as she is his guardian in Dacaan," said the Wizard Oberon.

Nova didn't know what that meant. He had never known that Phoebe had such a title, and he looked at her to see if she, too, was confused by the comment, but she only looked forward. The next in line was Cassia, who caught his eye as he looked at Phoebe, and then she looked away again, angrily.

"With very little time, and an altogether inexperienced group apart from Gwendolyn, I have selected two more advanced pupils who will support the group," said the Wizard Oberon before walking to the door and opening it.

Callum walked in, smirking in Nova's direction. It couldn't be! Nova was less than impressed with this reveal. The second was the young boy, Peter, from the Flight for Beginners class with Professor Delvoy, who had also shown malice toward him.

"But, sir, don't you think that this will be too many?" Nova said as they walked to stand in front of him and next to the Wizard Oberon.

"These two pupils have excelled in various areas of magic, and you will need them. Apart from them, we have instructed all of your teachers to grant focused lessons to you and Cassia so you can build up your understanding of magic."

Frustrated, Nova was about to interject once again, but Cassia spoke up instead.

"Thank you, Wizard Oberon Silver, for your support," she said in a voice that was much more meek than usual for Cassia.

"You have one week before you depart. The Regime is already aware of your magic and perhaps your intentions, Nova, and will most likely be preparing to see you again," said the Wizard Oberon.

One week was not a lot of time. Nervousness rushed over Nova.

"Council dismissed," commanded the Wizard Oberon with a final rap of his staff.

CHAPTER
16

THE NEXT WEEK rippled past both quickly and slowly. It reminded Nova of Kootenay Lake and the waves that ebbed from the winds before a storm. They were at the mercy of a greater power.

Nova was slowly becoming more comfortable at the Serendipity School of Magic, and in that week it really did begin to feel like home. He was having daily training with the Wizard Oberon and Headmaster Simmions. He was also having private tutoring with Cassia on the subjects that had been outlined in his syllabus, and he was making some great progress. His magic was being controlled better, and he was in more of a balanced mindset about how and when to use it. He could also now shoot an arrow, swing a sword, and tie a number of knots. He was told he was a very quick learner.

Thinking back on how magic wasn't possible in Castlegar, he was grateful for all the sessions he had. These were important lessons to learn, even if they weren't all required when he got to Dacaan this time. Nova tried not to think about when and where he might need to apply them, but he thought it was best to perfect them and to follow advice on how to prepare, regardless.

The Wizard Oberon was right, they had to work together.

Cassia and he had become closer than ever before, and although he hadn't found an appropriate time for another kiss, Nova knew that their bond was special. She had questioned him about Phoebe, he had responded reasonably, and she trusted him. She was also becoming 'a force to be reckoned with,' according to Persephone the witch, who was taking much of the credit due to her private tutoring on the use of spells. The witch even went so far as to say that Cassia had learned more in a number of days than many students learned over the course of their years at the college.

Everything seemed blissfully perfect when he looked at it. Nova was surrounded by people who cared about him and for who he cared about, and he was learning all the things he was destined to learn, and he was embracing his destiny. In a short space of time, however, it was easy to forget the bigger picture, and while all this preparation was happening in the background, Nova was pushing the thought of his quest further and further inside. Deep into a place where nightmares lived, leaving it to manifest itself into something else, while on the exterior this version of Nova was twinkling radiantly like a star. Even Callum's quips and Peter's coldness didn't bother him.

In the evenings after their lessons, Nova and Cassia would walk through the Bothreal Gardens on the far side of Serendipity where it was quiet. Hardly anyone else went there because it was somewhat tucked away like a secret. There were evergreen trees, lakes, and pathways in the snow that they had created. That week a brood of swans were settled on the lake. Having asked Barnaby, the pair found out that the swans were journeying through Happenstance on their way to warmer climes for the winter. Barnaby also explained how birds were the only creatures with a rite of passage between the worlds, and it finally clicked in Nova's mind how Osiris and the crows had made their way through.

Nova and Cassia appreciated what was happening between them in that moment. Although it was fleeting, it felt precious. They walked on the path around the lake, watching the regal swans in awe as the birds glided effortlessly across it. They would never be able to tell how quickly their webbed feet were paddling below the surface. Nova felt a familiarity to it. He found them remarkable.

One day, Nova walked with Cassia to the partially frozen lake, but the swans were gone.

"They didn't even say goodbye," joked Cassia.

"Tomorrow is our last day," said Nova.

❖

The Wizard Oberon asked all the pupils and the elders at Serendipity to assemble at the stadium the day of their departure. Nova was surprised to see so many of them in total—and a bubbly group at that—sitting in the stands when he arrived. He didn't want to say it, but they seemed older than the students of the same age at his school in Dacaan. Perhaps the weight of knowing magic made them more mature?

It was a sunny but crisp day. Sunrays cast patches across the stadium, making the light and dark project like fingers through the columns and onto the crowd. The stadium looked so different in the day and with people. It was altogether a different place from when he and Cassia were here alone. Looking down on the snow on the podium where they stood, Nova pointed to the spot where they had made snow angels a week or so ago. Fresh snow covered it, and to everyone else it was just a slight inconsistency with the flush snow that had settled across the stage, but to Nova and Cassia it was something else.

Cassia let out a small giggle, "I wondered who did that?"

The Wizard Oberon peered over at them gruffly and shuffled the papers he had prepared around in his hands, sliding his glasses farther up off the tip of his nose.

Like he had done in the chamber of the Council of Elders, the Wizard Oberon rapped his staff on the ground, and silence descended throughout the crowds.

"We have come here today to celebrate the departure of Nova and The Six. They have come together to form a sacred unity that will protect us from the evils working against both Happenstance and Dacaan, and we must ask Lady Luck to bless them with goodwill in order to ensure their safety on this most important of ventures," the Wizard Oberon boomed. His voice sounded stronger, more metered, and more determined than Nova had perhaps ever heard a person's voice sound.

The Wizard Oberon waved his hand for Nova to step forward, breaking from the line he was in next to Cassia, Barnaby, Gwendolyn, Phoebe, Callum, and Peter. He looked back and got smiles of approval from his friends while the two boys ignored him, looking toward the Wizard Oberon. Nova faced forward once again, looking out to the crowd. Over the past week, and notably after the announcement that Callum and Peter were joining Nova on his quest, the attitudes from the other pupils had changed toward him. They would smile at him, and some of them even offered their support in his learnings if he needed it. One girl had even offered her dessert after dinner, which he kindly refused.

The elders joined them, and one older gentleman who Nova knew as Mr. Cuthwright stepped forward. He had a body that was partially of a ram, with horns on his head and hoofed feet. He had in his hand a small bottle with a corked lid, and he passed it to Persephone.

Persephone walked forward and stood in front of Nova. She opened the bottle and uttered the words, "Ad astra per aspera."

Nova wasn't sure what it meant, but as she blew across the lid of the bottle, a blue vapor drew from it and first swirled across Nova and then back to The Six behind. Something instantly felt different inside him. He felt an uncommon strength that he was not used to that sat like a metal armor across his body. He looked back and saw the vapor twirl around his friends, and it drew itself into a tiara on Cassia. She looked beautiful with the band sat above her head and the jewel encrusted in it, shining like a purple eye from her forehead. It was her replacement for a wand gifted by Persephone for her brilliant work.

Next, there were men Nova hadn't noticed before. They came from behind them on the stage and put red cloaks over each of The Six. The cloaks draped over their shoulders and were loosely tied with golden broaches on the right-hand side of them.

"These cloaks and broaches," began the Wizard

Oberon, "are a symbol of the elder's protection and unity among each other."

Nova looked back, trying to catch eyes with Callum, who cast them away and pretended he was smiling at someone in the crowd.

"Bring the swords!" declared the Wizard Oberon, and the high-pitched sound of ceremonial trumpets sang their brassy notes as the thud of metal, clanking steps approached.

Having a brief flashback to the steely boots worn by the patrol at the penitentiary, Nova was relieved when he saw a legion of much friendlier soldiers in ceremonial dress arrive in the stadium. They circled on either side around the stage, stopping in front of the group. There were seven soldiers in total, and they each had a sword placed on their open palms, which they were holding at waist height. They walked up one after another, handing a sword and a belt to wrap around their waist to hoist the sword in place to each member of the group.

Nova was the last to receive his sword, but before the soldier came forward, the Wizard Oberon said, "Nova, son of the holy order, we grant you Orion's sword."

The crowd exploded in a cheer as the soldier presented Nova with the sword, and Nova looked up at the Wizard Oberon, who whispered, "I will explain more later, just be careful with it."

The sword felt heavy as the soldier handed it to Nova and wrapped the scabbard around his waist. He held it up in the air so that he could feel the weight in front of him, and the crowd's sound escalated. Looking back at The Six, he saw that they, too, were copying him. He held the sword pointed up in the air, and the others mimicked him once again, and the crowd exploded. Nova looked up and saw a white light shining from the tip of his sword into the sky, and he again looked at the Wizard Oberon for answers. The wizard indicated for him to put it back in his scabbard, which he did without delay.

The crowd's excitement had reached an altogether high. Nova could see smiling faces and cheering, and he felt a sense of pride. Nova couldn't let them down.

"And finally," continued the Wizard Oberon, "bring in the unicorns."

Mr. Delvoy, who stood at the front of the crowd, made an unusual whistling sound. At first Nova looked back at the entrance where the soldiers had come through but then heard ooh's and aah's from the crowd and looked their way. They were pointing to the sky, and Nova could see five unicorns galloping through the air. They looked majestic, and, although their steps were out of sync, they moved in unison, slightly up and then down. They navigated the invisible bumps in the breeze with their manes and tales floating in the wind.

Above them flew a large eagle, and he knew it was Osiris. The eagle flew quickly down to the ground past the unicorns , landing on the opposite side of the Wizard Oberon to Nova, but looked across at him and said, "You didn't think that you'd be going on your quest without me now, did you?"

"Of course not, I couldn't imagine not having you there," said Nova through a smile.

"I wonder which unicorn will choose me," said Cassia excitedly.

The unicorn that dropped down next to Nova was called Stannah. Nova had met her before in flight school.

She was recognizable because she had slightly flecked gray within her mane. Stannah was a strong and dependable unicorn, and Nova was pleased that she had chosen him. He looked back and saw that the most beautiful mare with the softest whinny, called Jayra, had chosen Cassia, and that she was happy, which made him smile.

Callum and Peter had two male unicorns, who were much taller than the mares Nova and Cassia had. They seemed happy with their choices too. Nova had seen Peter with his unicorn before, so wasn't surprised by this choice. Phoebe's unicorn had chosen her some time ago, and it rubbed its muzzle endearingly against her cheek.

Nova presumed Barnaby would fly with Osiris since he didn't know how to ride a unicorn. Or perhaps he was too heavy? And Gwendolyn could shrink and fly with any one of them or also ride Osiris.

The crowd was cheering and excited, and the Wizard Oberon rapped his staff for a final time to indicate that he wanted silence. The crowd took a few seconds to come to a hush.

"Nova and The Six face many tough challenges ahead, but with our support they will succeed. Tomorrow they will fly, but tonight we will celebrate in the great hall with a feast. Formal wear will be provided to all pupils," boomed the Wizard Oberon, and the crowd erupted. "Now fly!"

Nova, Cassia, Phoebe, Callum, and Peter mounted their unicorns while Gwendolyn, as expected, joined Barnaby on Osiris. The group rose off the ground in unison. As they did, the trumpets once again played their song, and the crowd whistled and cheered. Raising up and over the stadium, they could see the crowd getting up to watch them as they flew high into the clouds, waving before disappearing altogether from sight.

"The Wizard Oberon would like us to fly down through Providence. They had a live broadcast of today's ceremony and will also be celebrating tonight," yelled Nova to the group around him as they flew.

Nova flew closer to Osiris to speak with Barnaby and Gwendolyn.

"Do you think the people of Providence are still skeptical about me and about the quest?" he asked, thinking back on their night at the TumbleWeed Inn.

"Today is your opportunity to change their minds if they do," said Gwendolyn with the sort of confident look that only a queen-in-waiting could warrant, even if she was only the size of Nova's thumb.

"Yes, yes of course," responded Nova and nodded his head as if he had thought this all along, making Barnaby smile.

The unicorns and Osiris sped through the puffy clouds and moved down toward Providence with The Six and Nova on their backs.

They could hear it at first: a noise that echoed through the mountains and sounded almost as loud as the cheers they'd heard from the crowd at the Serendipity stadium. But, as they got closer, Nova realized that the reverberation of the crowd's noise off Glass Mountain wasn't all joyous. While there was some cheering, there was also booing and shouting.

Nova led the group to the square that held the statue of Lady Luck riding Dragmar Gregorius. The Wizard Oberon had asked the assembly to take place there so that the people of Providence could also see the college above. A space opened around the statue for the unicorns to land. Nova could see that some people in small groups where cheering while others were angrily waving their hands in the air and yelling. He looked at Gwendolyn again, and she looked back and smiled confidently.

"Maybe we should go, they seem angry, Nova," said Cassia, looking nervously toward him.

"No, we must stay. We need their support," responded Phoebe, looking disapprovingly at Cassia.

"We have to get them on our side, Cassia. There is power in numbers, and it must start here," said Nova.

"Well, do something then!" Cassia looked away, disgruntled at the united voice of Nova and Phoebe.

Nova got off Stannah and asked the others to do the same. The crowd quieted at his movement. He walked over to the statue and began to climb its large foundations after an initial boost from Barnaby. He clambered up to the top, but not as high as the mounted rider herself, wrapping an arm around her body for support.

The crowd was now silently waiting, and Nova looked out across it, at the angry faces, and felt his throat close up.

"Well, come on then, we haven't got all day," came a jibe from the far side of him, and the crowd erupted into laughter and began its conflicted chorus of cries and jeers once again.

Nova felt sweat form in beads on his forehead. He looked nervously down at the others.

Osiris squawked loudly at the crowd, "Silence! Show him some respect!" The crowd became still again. Some of the onlookers closest to the bird jumped back, and a babe in arms began to cry.

Opening his mouth, Nova hesitated, eating the words that were in his head like they were trapped in his throat, unable to come out. It felt like ages to Nova, but the hesitation was only for a moment. He closed his eyes and thought of the children he had met in the penitentiary, and of his father, before finding his voice.

"People of Happenstance, I know your concerns. Trust me, this is all new to me too. It was not so long ago that I didn't know I was Nova or that I was bound to a quest. I've spent days trying to understand what is happening in Dacaan and here in Happenstance. I have seen evil . . ." he paused as the crowd stirred at his mention of evil.

"I know you feel that safety is yours for the taking here in Happenstance, but it is not." Murmurs traveled across the crowd like the wind across a field of wheat. "Evil has already found its way here, and unless we believe in the same cause and come together to fight it, Happenstance will be lost forever."

The crowd was getting loud again. People's eyes had grown large and frightened at the thought of evil among them.

"Let him talk!" yelled a female voice from the back, and the crowd silenced.

Nova swayed slightly on his post before settling back into his message. "There is one thing that I am certain of now, we can only confront evil if we come together. I am just like you, I was happy with my life, nothing seemed wrong, nothing needed changing. But now that I understand the forces of evil at play and the innocents who are already suffering, it is time to stand up and do something."

The crowd was still silent, but the mood had changed. It felt like a warm wind gently comforting everyone in its presence all at once.

After a pause to take in this new atmosphere, Nova continued, "I am prepared to take on my duty, for you. My friends here"—Nova looked pointedly toward Callum and Peter as he said this—"have been brought together, and they have agreed to take on the duty of helping me on this quest. We can no longer sit and wait, pretending like everything is okay. We must unite, and we must fight together."

It took Nova several seconds to realize—because he had fallen into some sort of trance—that the crowd had erupted with excited cheers. Even the people who had been angry before were now clapping and nodding their heads in acceptance. They started chanting his name—Nova, Nova, Nova! He couldn't believe it.

Looking down, he noticed that The Six had pulled out their swords and were holding them in the air. He did the same with Orion's sword, and the spectacular light shone from its end high up into the clouds. The crowd roared with approval.

❖

Nova didn't particularly enjoy the banquet that evening. Not because it didn't have the most lavish spread of all types of culinary wonders, but because he had spent so much of the day in the spotlight, and he was ready to just rest.

The Six seemed to enjoy it, though, and Barnaby tucked into at least one whole plate of each of the various cuisines in front of them and drank at least two times the types of available wines and beers. Presently he was passed out in his chair. Gwendolyn didn't drink and hardly ate and didn't look at all herself, but Nova assumed she was just tired. It had been a long day.

The night was a formal occasion, and Nova had only ever seen the rest of the pupils in their usual Serendipity School uniforms. The boys were now dressed in tuxedos of deep black and gray, looking smart and polished. The girls were dressed in ball gowns of all colors of pastel, most of which puffed out at the bottom with a white underlay. The dresses were heavily embroidered with crystals and jewels and looked heavy to wear, but the girls didn't seem to mind.

Cassia stole the show. When she arrived and walked into the room, it was as if everyone had stopped and looked her way. Her usual hair that was plaited down the sides was now held up in a nest on top of her head, with a few strands that hung delicately against her bronze shoulders. She wore the tiara across the top of her head, and the color of it matched perfectly with her fluffy, lilac dress. Her lips sparkled pink, and her eyes wore a thin line of black that flicked out to a whisper on either side, making the gray and matching lilac in her irises flicker. She had on black gloves that rose to her elbows and delicate black shoes that popped out from under her dress as she walked. She was the most beautiful girl that Nova had ever seen.

The night wasn't just about eating. There was entertainment in the form of magic acts that were so much more superior to the illusion act Nova performed at the Championship it made him and Cassia laugh out loud.

Many around them who didn't understand the correlation thought it was out of character and quite possibly rude. But to them it didn't matter. Phoebe joined in on the joke and smiled. There were jugglers, singers, dancers, and musicians. But although it was all so lovely, Nova just wanted to be back in his room, thinking about the next day. Cassia tricked him onto the dance floor, and they danced for two slow songs. He did it mainly to make her happy.

Nova was one of the first to leave. He had begged Cassia to stay and have fun, but she wouldn't listen, and she joined him. They walked in the moonlight, Cassia with her shoes in her hands.

"I never realized how much these heels hurt if you wore them for an entire evening and danced in them," she laughed. She was giddy from the excitement of the evening, and she was half walking and half skipping with one arm wrapped around Nova's.

"Can you believe that we leave tomorrow?" said Nova in a way that changed the light mood that had previously been in the air.

"It was just a little while ago that we were just normal kids in Creston—now look at us!" she said, still with an air of frivolity.

"Crazy, eh?" said Nova. He had undone the bowtie around his neck. He was hot even though it was cold outside.

"Yah, pretty crazy. It wasn't long ago that you were Alex," she said, and a wave of emotion seem to fall over her. She shivered under her fur coat in the cold.

"You realize how much you mean to me," Nova said, using his index finger to tap her nose in a playful way.

Bashfully, Cassia's eyes dropped to the ground and then back up at him before she playfully said the words, "Back at you."

The pair walked for a little while longer, snaking in and out of the many halls and pathways, before ending up in the portico in front of the courtyard below their room. Nova wrapped his arms around Cassia and then twirled her out in front of him, catching her hand before she twirled too far away. He wrapped his hand over her head so their arms formed a semicircle, before dipping her back so that her head almost touched the ground.

"Why didn't you pull those moves on the dance floor earlier, mister?" Cassia giggled.

"I didn't want to make the others jealous," joked Nova.

They continued like this for some time, dancing and laughing in the portico. Nova picked up Cassia in his arms and swung her around, worrying that her feet would be cold on the ground.

It was weird that absolutely no one was around, since everyone was still at the banquet, and for those moments it felt like it was just their two hearts being together, alone and as one in the universe and under the sparkling stars.

Feeling out of breath from dancing and laughing, they stopped and sat on a bench, looking up at the night sky. Nova draped the coat over Cassia's shoulders and wrapped his arms around her too. She crossed her legs and tucked her toes into the warm jacket. It felt so natural now between them, their skin was used to the feeling of the other's. They had somehow changed one day over the past week from being two to being one. Nova wrapped his hand in hers so that their fingers were woven together.

He looked at her and drew his face closer to hers, and their lips locked in a kiss.

"We should do that more often," Cassia laughed.

"I've been nervous, I didn't want to rush things. We've been friends for so long, and I would never want to jeopardize that," said Nova with a very straight face that slowly curled into a smile.

"You don't have to worry about jeopardizing a thing," replied Cassia, and a sadness washed over her face.

Nova looked at her, wondering what was going on in her head at that very moment. What was she thinking? Perhaps he was mixing up her look of sadness for confusion. It was time to say things straight to her.

"I know I've said it before, but thank you again, Cassia, for joining me here. For everything. I wouldn't be as strong as I am today without you," Nova said, looking at her with something raw in his eyes that conveyed the deepness of his emotions. "In fact, I love you, Cassia. I always have. But now, well . . . you know . . . it's different."

Cassia bent her head forward, and at first Nova thought she was laughing before he realized that she was crying. Unbroken streams of liquid left white trails down her face when she looked at him.

"Don't thank me," said Cassia in a wispy voice as if she couldn't find enough air to speak.

"What do you mean, I have everything to thank you for. For being here with me from the start, for believing in me, for—"

Cassia cut him off. "I'm just doing what I have to do, Nova. I am doing it to protect my family, to protect my brothers and sisters," she responded in a pleading voice.

"I followed you that's all. I wanted to be with you," she continued.

Nova sat there, confused. What did she mean?

"Yes, that's why you are so important to me, I respect you for all of that. And that is what we are all doing—protecting ourselves, each other, and our families." Nova didn't understand where this had come from. Her mood had changed so quickly.

Cassia got up, her coat falling into the snow before she picked it up again and ran off.

"What did I say, where are you going?" yelled Nova as she hurried away.

Nova got up to run after her, but she had pushed his hand away as if she were pushing him away. He had come too close, and now he had ruined it.

"Just leave me alone, Nova, this was all a big mistake." And she was gone.

CHAPTER
17

The next day it was like nothing had ever happened.

"Good morning, sunshine," Cassia chirped as she rustled around, cleaning up bits and pieces in their room and preparing for their voyage. She was wearing her normal clothes, and she looked normal again, like she had completely forgotten the night before.

"Morning," responded Nova in a less enthusiastic tone. He had heard Cassia crying through the night, and he knew that something wasn't right. She did this, she had always been better at pretending than he was. It was like when they were growing up and played Guess Who?, a game that Nova found stored away in his basement and would play with Niall and Ariadne and Cassia. Cassia always won; she was always good at making you think she was someone else. She was always good at knowing when you were lying too.

"What's wrong? It's your big day today," she said as he walked toward the washroom. She gave his shoulder a light punch in a joking way. She was nervous.

"I just need to focus," Nova responded, closing the washroom door behind him. He felt conflicted, he wanted to wrap his arms around her and kiss her soft pillow-like lips, but he could tell that she was being off with him. Thoughts were still reeling around in his head from last night. He didn't want to be pushed away again.

❖

The Wizard Oberon, Persephone, and the elders were already there when Nova and The Six arrived. Peter prepared the unicorns and presented Stannah to Nova first, nodding his head in a form of approval as he did. It was a small gesture, but for some reason Nova knew it meant a lot. Peter didn't speak much; he conveyed his feelings through his actions, and he had always been cold toward Nova in the past. This was the first kind action, and Nova thanked the boy as he stepped forward and mounted Stannah.

"Not more pomp and circumstance today," said Phoebe, rolling her eyes at the Wizard Oberon and the elders.

"Some of us certainly had too much pomp that led to rather difficult circumstance after last night's festivities," joked Barnaby, who looked fresher than Nova had expected, but who was still rubbing his aching head.

Nova thought again about Phoebe. How long had he known her in Creston, and how long had she been living this double life? Had she always played a role as his guardian in Dacaan?

"No, we just came to bid you farewell and to let you know a few important things before you leave," replied Persephone in a soft way while she nodded her head toward the other elders around her.

"Thank you, Persephone, we appreciate your support,"

replied Gwendolyn, who was in full form next to Barnaby. Osiris flew in and landed next to them so that the whole group were together.

"You will travel via a rainbow at Commencement Lighthouse on the southern tip of Happenstance. Osiris and Barnaby, we trust you will know how to get there?" said Persephone.

"Yes, ma'am," replied Barnaby with an excited smile on his face. Nova wondered if he was always so jovial when he heard about lighthouses.

"There will be a moonbow just outside of the Rossland District, which is also your arrival location tonight. It will be open at ten o'clock, but only for ten minutes to ensure that you are the only ones who use it since it is so close to Castlegar. We cannot risk leaving this open, do you understand?" she said more sternly than when she had started the conversation.

"Yes, Mrs. Tarsworthy, we understand," said Callum. Nova noticed it was his turn to look nervous today.

"We also want to say that there might be times when you must separate, but remember you are working together, and you must follow the plans," said the Wizard Oberon in an even sterner tone than Persephone.

Nova had heard the plans now at least twenty times. He could recite them with his eyes closed. They needed to stick to time and to the plan and everything would be okay.

As if reading his mind, the Wizard Oberon continued, "The risks are high if you do not keep to the plan. You all know the plan, it is well rehearsed. We don't want any mavericks, do you understand?"

"Yes, we do. Our aim is to do you proud and complete our mission as discussed," replied Nova.

"We will see you tonight, don't worry," said Gwendolyn as if she were taking responsibility for the group's time keeping. Nova felt happy with that.

"We must go, time is of the essence today. I will help with the passage," said Osiris, and with that, he lifted off the ground and the mounted unicorns followed.

It took about an hour for them to fly to the lighthouse, and as they flew they saw the fading coastlines of Happenstance while the vast lands that kissed the Emerald Sea just vanished. Although they didn't have time to stop and rest, seeing this helped in reminding them all of the gravity of this quest.

The rainbow was vivid in its colors in front of them, all seven of them. It was their gateway to Castlegar, and although the skies were pristine blue with hardly any clouds, they didn't know what awaited them on the other side. Nova had clearly tipped off the Regime one week ago, and the Wizard Oberon had told them to be prepared as the Regime would now be expecting their arrival. Nova had also seen a number of crows over the past week, and every time they flew past him or sat on a tree with their cocked heads, watching him, he wondered if they were spies sent from the Regime.

Looking across at Osiris, Nova could see that Barnaby and Gwendolyn were deep in discussion as Barnaby kept turning to her small figure in his jacket breast pocket. Nova moved his body slightly to the side so that Stannah would fly closer to them.

"Are you two all right?" he said.

"Yes, we are of course," said Barnaby.

"This is the first time in our lives that we are leaving Happenstance, that is all," replied Gwendolyn loudly so Nova could hear her even if he couldn't really see her.

"I guess we just don't know what to expect. We were talking about our families and loved ones and the people we are leaving back home," said Barnaby. "Gwendolyn was thinking about Luca and her father."

A flush of guilt washed over Nova; he hadn't even considered their sacrifice. In asking them to join him, they were leaving the people who they held dear and putting themselves in grave danger. The quest that Nova had in front of him was not guaranteed to be safe, no matter how much they meticulously planned it all out.

Nova spoke loudly so that all of the group could hear him over the wind that rushed past, "I want to thank you all. Everyone is making a sacrifice, and this is not a journey without danger, and yet you have all agreed to pursue it with me. I will do everything in my power to keep us safe."

"No," called back Callum, who was flying at the front of the group. His counter to Nova's short speech brought a momentary awkwardness to the group until he added, "We keep each other safe."

Nova couldn't tell if Callum was saying that to dismiss Nova or to support what he'd just said. Either way, at least they were on the same page.

Although it was early morning on this side of the rainbow, as they arrived in Dacaan the sun was descending in the sky.

Osiris led them to a clearing in the woods on the outskirts of the Rossland District, which he said was close enough to Castlegar but in a location where they wouldn't be seen.

Once they arrived, a group of men came rushing out from the woods. It was the Nomans.

"Well, what a pleasure 'tis to see you lot already. We've been waiting all day!"

It was Davies, Shrew and Sedwin and the other men that Nova and Cassia had met before. Nova hadn't realized they would see them that day, and he felt an overwhelming sense of security in having them there.

"Ooooh, look at this beautiful mare," said one of the men, slapping the rump of a unicorn, and it reared up at him.

"I wouldn't do that if I were you," said Nova. "From where they're from they own us, and not the other way around."

Some of the men laughed, thinking Nova had just made a joke.

"Now, let's get these ponies out of the clearing and out of view. There's nothing like them in these parts, and we don't want any patrol seeing them. Especially not on such an important day," said Shrew.

They walked from the clearing and came upon a camp. There were many more men than Nova had met before, perhaps five times as many, and he wondered why they were all there together this time? They offered Nova and The Six some food and drink and to sit down and talk for a minute.

Shrew filled Nova a cup of bitter brew and served him and the rest of the guests mugs of chili.

"Now we know that that there Wizard Oberon of yours has plans for tonight," started Sedwin, "this is everything that we've been wanting for some time now, and we've come up with our own plan to help. We will be lighting fires to signal in each and every town the time for one of our lads to ring the district bell and summon the people."

Nova felt uneasy, this was not what was planned. What would the Wizard Oberon say?

"You'd need to be careful with that," replied Phoebe. "We need to get out of here before ten o'clock or the plan isn't going to work."

"Well, we will light the fires once you're gone," said Shrew.

After talking some more, Nova agreed on the plans, and he and The Six finished their meal.

"The men and I will wait here with the unicorns. You will need to go on foot from here," said Osiris. "Nova, you will need your map."

Nova reached into his bag and pulled the box out along with the map, unraveling it.

"We are right here, near Champion Lake, and to get to Castlegar you just follow the trail and then the river all the way down. It's about an hour's hike from here," said Shrew. "At some places, the river travels underground, so you just need to catch up with it farther on where it resurfaces."

The camp was alive with the many different men moving about, talking in small groups. Some were washing pots and pans down by the river. Others were smoking pipes, making the air smell a sweeter, earthier fragrance than it was used to. It occurred to Nova that these men could do as they pleased, that they didn't have to do what the Regime told them. They lived off the land, and they trusted each other. This was the life that they would fight to have others embrace in Dacaan. This was freedom, and he wondered how far they would have to go to fight for it?

❖

The sun was in a deceptive position, where it sped up its descent before tucking itself under the horizon so that the moon could have its turn.

Nova and The Six had set out from camp and were navigating the path along the river that led them into Castlegar. In a few places they had to stop and hide, as they heard patrol breaking the underbrush in the forests around them, but the large, mossy rocks along the river's edge provided much protection from being seen. Their footsteps in the bubbling stream provided cover from their scent being picked up by patrol dogs, which Sedwin had said were also in the area.

As Shrew had mentioned, they did come up against an area where the river tunneled underground.

"May I?" asked Nova, pointing to the pins in Gwendolyn's hair.

"Yes, you may," she replied, and Nova did the water witching trick that Luca had taught them back at Hope River. He pulled the pins to make them longer and walked forward with them pointing out from his hands until the direction of the water below them was indicated by their movement.

Nova was pleased that Gwendolyn seemed fine with him now. She still wore a sad expression on her face, however.

"Gwendolyn, I've noticed that you've been looking sad for a while. Is everything ok?" asked Nova nervously.

It took Gwendolyn some time before her answer. "It is sad when the people that you love the most leave you."

Gwendolyn rushed off ahead, naturally turning the conversation off and leaving Nova by himself. Nova was worried about her but decided that now was not the right time to talk further about such matters.

"I've come this way before, it's just around this corner," said Phoebe.

She was right. As they turned the corner, they faced the wide mouth of the drainage system in Castlegar, and they quickly rushed into it.

The damp smell and the scurrying sound reminded Nova of the penitentiary again. Phoebe indicated that they were safe down here, however, as this was a part of the city patrol didn't bother with. But Nova told them to keep their guard, as the Wizard Oberon had mentioned that Cravelda would most likely be waiting for their arrival and have extra patrol on watch throughout the city.

"It's a shame that the Chalice prevents magic from working and that they found out about my invisibility spell. They must have really upped the anti-magic enchantment in the Chalice in the past week," said Phoebe, who was flashing a wand in front of her but nothing was happening.

"Well, we will see about that, but for now it's useless," said Cassia, whose gem in her tiara was also no longer shining. She took it off her head and threw it into her bag.

Nova looked down at his armband, and it, too, wasn't

shining the same residual light as it usually did, but he was okay with it. As long as the plan worked, they didn't need magic. Not at first. They only needed the counter enchantment for the Chalice and looking down in his pocket at the vial the Wizard Oberon had given him, it was still glowing brightly. It had the power to defy the anti-magic of the Chalice and unlock it.

They wound their way through the tunnels. They were dank and very little light shone in, but it was the only way, and Nova took solace in the fact that they were safe. For now.

Phoebe suddenly stopped and put her finger to her lips to indicate that they needed to be silent. At first Nova couldn't see it, but she pushed on the ceiling above and lifted up a circular hole, which let the fading daylight flood in around them.

"Coast is clear. Nova, Barnaby and Gwendolyn, this is your stop!" she chirped, waving her arm for them to come over but not looking at them as she focused on what was happening above ground. She removed the lid completely and pushed it to the side above.

Gwendolyn had put a scarf around her hair to cover her pointed ears and wrapped her cloak further around her to cover the clothing she wore below. Barnaby had traveled wearing a thick coat, pants, and boots. He pulled the hood of his cloak over his head to cover himself, as he had much more hair and was already taller than the average human of Dacaan. At first, they would have to be as inconspicuous as possible, and although it wasn't as cold here as it was in Happenstance, Nova prayed that they would blend in.

The three walked over to the hole above them.

"I'll be back soon," said Nova.

Once they were above ground, Nova felt the gravity of the situation finally setting in. The plan was happening whether they liked it or not. There was no going back now. Nervous energy pulsed through them.

They had come up at a small street off the side of the square that housed the Enchanted Chalice. There were several Patrol which had been expected. Barnaby and Gwendolyn squeezed Nova's arm before heading off. As planned, they headed for the square and walked slowly across it. There was no one but Barnaby, Gwendolyn and the Patrol who then began moving towards them.

"What are you two doing here, its past curfew," sniped a Patrol.

Almost immediately after the Patrol's remark they threw their capes back to reveal their true form—troll and fae.

"Stop them!" yelled one of the Patrol and then the chase was on. Barnaby and Gwendolyn separated running off down the streets on the opposite side of the square. Nova was afraid the Patrol might catch them but he knew that they just had to get to the safe house in time. There were Informants waiting for them.

Nova's heart was racing. He looked and one Patrol remained in the square who was speaking angrily on his Communicator about what had just happened. Nova didn't have much time. He snuck quietly around the square to the opposite side of the Patrol. The Patrol was on high alert but was looking in the direction that Gwendolyn and Barnaby had headed. That was good. Nova hid for a short while then took cautious steps around the opposite side of the circular Chalice to the Patrol as quietly as he could. All he had to do was throw the vial.

Then, Nova heard the boots. They were walking heavily towards the square. There was no time. Nova threw the vial in to the Chalice and almost immediately a beam of bright light radiated its already flaming center and a crack that snapped through the air like a whip sounded. The Patrol that had just entered the square dropped to the ground. They had closed their eyes and covered their ears. As Nova was under the rim of the Chalice he was protected from the light. Seeing his opportunity, Nova ran back across the square as fast as he could to the drainhole he had come through.

Just as he rounded the corner to the side street he turned back and locked eyes with one of the Patrol.

"There!" screamed the Patrol who started running across the square.

Out of sight, Nova dropped down the hole and landed with a splash in the small stream in the bottom of the tunnel. Phoebe threw the lid over the opening just in time. They heard boots running their way but they ran past and up the street.

"What happened?" asked Callum.

"We need to go, quickly," replied Nova.

Nova, Phoebe, Cassia, Callum and Peter continued on for another ten minutes or so before they stopped again at another circular hole in the ceiling above. Phoebe did the same as before, lifting the hole up slightly and looking around. But this time she closed it quickly.

"Patrol, let's go on to the next one," she said, and rushed along down the arched pathway.

A shiver of cold went up Nova's body from his toes to

the tips of his fingers. He thought of the heavy boots that had just chased him. Those same boots were above him, walking on the streets. They were looking for him.

"You ok?" asked Peter, who was looking at Nova.

Surprised that it was Peter who had noticed his momentary fragility, he reacted at first with a wide-eyed expression but then smiled and responded, "Yes, something just came over me."

"Good," replied Peter, turning around to continue.

"Wait," said Nova, grabbing him by the arm like he had done in Aviary Tower, but this time it was welcomed. "Just be careful up there, is all."

Cassia was walking up in the front of the group, close to Phoebe. Nova had noticed that she had been staying farther from him today, but it was soon their turn to head up into Castlegar together, so she couldn't keep ignoring him. He needed her to be on his side, especially on a day like today.

Phoebe stopped again, and this time more carefully pushed up on the circle in the ceiling above them.

"This one is clear," she said as she popped up through the hole. Her hand shot down, and they heard her say, "Quickly."

One after another, they headed up above ground. Nova and Phoebe wore their hoods up, since they were the most recognizable from the group.

They were in the Dundrells. Nova could tell because of the dreary look to the buildings and the less-than-polished streets. It took a few minutes for them to get their bearings and for their eyes to adjust to the daylight. They were in a part of the town where there were very few people. It felt very different here than what it had felt like walking down the main streets and through the crowded plaza the other day.

"We need to split up now that are up here. We're too suspicious in our red capes all together. Nova and Cassia, you know what you need to do, right?" said Phoebe.

"Yes, we will see you later," said Nova.

Cassia nodded her head, looking away and up the street. "Come on, Nova, it's time."

"Good luck," said Callum, clapping Nova over the shoulder.

Nova let a wave of emotion rush over him. He felt a camaraderie between the group that rooted deep within him. He cared for them, and he wanted everything to work out. They were in this together, they would fight the Regime together. This was it, this was the moment. There was everything to be lost yet everything to gain. They were standing on the edge, and they had jumped.

"It's time that we show this Regime a thing or two."

Nova turned, seeking his destiny as he walked up the cobbled streets.

CHAPTER
18

The plan was simple, yet complicated.

Firstly, Nova, Gwendolyn and Barnaby would head to the Enchanted Chalice to squelch the eternal flame that prevented magic in Dacaan and caused magic to fade in Happenstance. Nova felt relief that this first task was complete. This point was essential if they were to fully action the rest of the plan.

Secondly, Phoebe would create some sort of scene on the far side of Castlegar to divert as much attention as possible.

Thirdly, Nova would return to Cassia and together they would break into the penitentiary using their magic and release the children. Although it was not in the plans, Nova was going to try to get into Big Penn to find his father. He had to at least try.

Fourthly, Callum and Peter would break into the building that was the headquarters of The Nexus Dacaan when there was no one around. They would turn on the transmission pathway and send personal messages to all the communicators and through all of The Nexus broadcasts channels so that when Nova returned the message could be made.

The final part of the plan was to get out of Castlegar

without being caught. This was the hard part. It was difficult to know how patrol would react and how Cravelda would respond once she realized what had happened.

"Cassia, hold on, you're going really fast," said Nova as he jogged to keep up with her.

"We don't have much time, and we need to be ready," she said without looking back at him.

Nova rushed up and grabbed her arm to slow her down. She jerked it away.

"We don't want to draw attention to ourselves, we need to be careful too," urged Nova.

She looked around and gave a meek smile. She must have been thinking about last night, but she was sure acting in a strange way about it.

"Ok, beansprout," she said. Her comment was meant to be a joke, but she hadn't delivered it in a funny way. It was the nickname she had called Nova when he went through a weird growth spurt when they were younger. He'd shot up and was awkwardly skinny before filling out again.

Nova smiled, looking back at Cassia, and felt that perhaps her joke had somewhat changed the tension between them, but he could tell she was still upset.

"Cassia, I'm really sorry about last night. I don't want to rush things," he said, stopping and starting over the words.

"Yah, I think we've just rushed things a little, Nova, like you said before. There's so much going on for us both right now, and I don't want either of us to get hurt," she replied, choking on the words like she was about to cry.

Just then two patrol walked up to them.

"You two okay? Why are you off work so early," one of

the patrol laughed, then more seriously continued with a snarl, "you do realize that it's past curfew?"

No one had told them there was a curfew in Castlegar. Perhaps this was something Cravelda had introduced since Nova's escape?

"We've been sent to see our grandmother, she isn't well," said Cassia quickly, like she'd rehearsed the answer in case she'd needed it. Nova was happy that he hadn't needed to provide a response, because he wasn't sure what he would have said.

"And where's that you're going to?" asked the other patrol.

"Just up the street and around the corner, we're almost there," replied Cassia.

"What's in the bags? Those don't look like standard issue," asked the patrol, tapping on Nova's with a baton. There was a loud clunk from where the baton hit the hard wood box.

"Let me inside there, please."

"We really can't be long, our grandmother is waiting on us. We are worried about her," pleaded Cassia.

"Then someone should call the infirmary. You know that's how it works," barked the patrol.

The patrol snatched at Nova's bag and started tucking his baton away. Just as he was about to open it up, the siren started. Phoebe must have been successful.

"Let's go, there's no time for this," said the one patrol to the other.

Looking Nova up and down, he threw the bag back into the mud in front of his feet. "Next time, boy."

The two patrol ran up the street, and Nova and Cassia picked up their pace, running through the alleyways that led to the stairs on Nova's map. The same stairs he'd taken with Phoebe.

Nova felt like his heart was dragging on the floor behind him after what had just happened with the patrol, but also from what Cassia had just told him. Surely she couldn't mean what she had said? But they had no time to discuss it now, and he had no time to focus on his emotions. They were in a high stakes game and there would only be one winner. Hopefully that winner was his band of Six.

They got to the stairs and sprinted up them. The urgency of the siren wailing behind them, and the yelling of the patrol along with crying on the streets, made Nova's adrenaline kick in. Compared to the other day when he could hardly manage walking these stairs, he was now flying up them, and in some sections took them two by two.

They were panting at the top, but there was no time to spare.

"Come on," said Cassia, looking back at Nova to make sure he was ok.

They continued with a brisk but steady walk up the road. Again, they didn't want to draw any attention. The penitentiary was just in front of them. Nova hadn't seen it before when he had been with Phoebe and they had entered the factory and the infirmary, because it was up the road and around a corner near the woods.

Once they arrived at the penitentiary, they hid behind a bush close to the cell window that had once belonged to Nova. He was sure this had been his cell because there was a slight opening on the top where the drip had come in from the outside. He had decided to come back to this room in particular because he could see in. He peeked through the shattered glass and could see that it hadn't been reoccupied since he'd left, which is what he had hoped for. Now all they had to do was wait.

Nova looked at his armband as they waited. They could see the main town below, and from where they were sitting they could see the Chalice. It was close to the castle at the top of the hill on the other side of the town, and the sun was setting behind it. Nova thought about his mother in the tower, the song that she had somberly played. She had promised they would meet one day, and he hung on to that hope.

"Look, the flame has turned from gold to blue," said Cassia.

Nova looked toward the Chalice, and, although it was subtle, it was true. His armband was now emitting some light to show that it was active. Cassia reached into her bag, grabbed her tiara, and put it on her head.

"Come on," she said again.

Awkwardly, they reached out and held each other's hand and then closed their eyes as they had practiced in Serendipity. In an instance they were in Nova's cell. They had both spent a lot of time learning how to travel short distances together using magic without making errors, but ultimately it was Nova's magic that got them through since Cassia could only do it with a spell.

They moved to the side of the cell where they could hide in the shadows. Nova could hear boots and the clanging of the keys farther down the hall, but it was slowly getting quieter, the patrol was moving away.

"We just need a set of keys," said Nova, "you wait here."

Nova closed his eyes again and was out in the hallway. He walked down it quietly and found what he had seen the last time he was here: the patrol's room. There was a patrol inside with his feet up on a desk and his arms crossed over his chest. He was looking up at a broadcast on The Nexus that was turned down low. But Nova knew that the patrol was sleeping from the gargled noise the man was making. He could see the keys on his belt. He could also see an obsidian sword.

Tiptoeing inside, he tried to be only as loud as the mice scurrying on the floors. The patrol was snoring pretty loudly, so it wasn't a problem getting there. Nova's fear was getting the keys off the belt without him noticing.

Suddenly, Nova heard another set of boots walking down the hallway. He had no choice but to hide under the desk where the patrol was asleep.

"Roy. Roy," said the voice as it entered the room, "you sleeping on the job again?"

"No, I'm watching the news, did you see the explosion?"

"I heard about it. Must be those wild men," said the man who'd entered the room, going to the refrigerator. He pulled out a handful of meat from a container and sloppily put it in his mouth, chewing loudly.

"Cravelda'll get 'em," said Roy, "she always does. They'll be here in Big Penn by sunrise."

"Latest," sputtered the guard through a full mouth.

"Leave me alone, I have another ten minutes," said Roy, shuffling himself slightly in his chair and moving his feet into a different position. Nova was so close that he could smell the mud on his boot.

"See yah later, man," said the other patrol as he left the room.

Nova waited, and it wasn't long before he heard loud snoring again. He wondered how someone could possibly have a full conversation and then fall into such a deep sleep so quickly, but he was thankful for it.

On tiptoes again, he went around the patrol and tried to loosen the grip that connected the keys to his belt. The keys jangled slightly, and the patrol moved slightly. Nova worried he would wake up, but the snoring began again. This time he was quieter, and he slid keys from the belt and walked backward toward the door. He was exposed in the blinking hallway lights, and was sure he would be found, so he rushed back as quickly but as quietly as he could.

"Cassia, quickly—let's go," he shouted into his old cell, trialing several keys until he got to 263 and moments later she was out.

Then the process began. The keys were heavy and made a loud clanging sound, alerting the young girl inside. At first she shot backward in her cell. This must have been how she usually reacted to the patrol.

"It's okay, we've come to save you. What's your inmate number?" whispered Nova.

"Five forty-seven," she gently replied. Nova found the key and unlocked the door.

It took her just a second to think before she snuck out of the cell and followed them.

Nova continued the pattern down the hall, and the children began to come to the front of their cells, noticing the change in the usual sounds of their captivity.

Toward the end of the hallway, Nova came to the cell holding Gabriel.

"Well, look who it is. You know, I thought I might see you again," he said with his confident air.

Nova smiled. "I couldn't leave you here, could I?"

Opening his cell, Gabriel instantly took the lead in telling the other children to be quiet and to stay low.

Patrol boots gave a warning signal; they were just around the corner. Lifting his hands, Nova used his magic to put the patrol to sleep. He picked up the keys from their belts and handed them to Gabriel.

"Go to the other floors. The inmate number matches the key to their cell. Meet us out the back," Nova instructed.

"Vance is in Cell Block Fourteen," said Gabriel.

"We will go and get him."

Nova and Cassia headed in the general direction toward the other part of the penitentiary.

"Nova, this wasn't in the plans," urged Cassia.

"We need to do this, and I need to go find my father. It won't take long. If you want to leave you can," responded Nova more gruffly to her than he usually would.

When they heard patrol boots they hid in the shadows or shifted so that they moved in another direction, invisibly and out of their reach. They got to the door that led to the second building where they would find Vance. Opening the door, Cassia walked down the three stairs into the space between the buildings. Nova was just behind her but had accidentally dropped the keys, so he ran back quickly to pick them up.

"Well, who have we got here."

Nova heard a familiar click of heels. Cravelda's heels.

"Cravelda!" gasped Cassia, who hadn't been expecting to see anyone there.

She looked around and noticed Nova was missing but didn't look toward the door. Nova knew that she was trying to control herself and not look his way. That way he wouldn't get found out also.

Fear ran through him. Should he run out and confront Cravelda too? It had been his fault that they had come this way. Cassia was right, it was not the plan, and it had been risky. Too risky. And she had now been found.

"I've been wondering when I'd see you again. Did you bring him?" asked Cravelda.

"No . . . I mean," stuttered Cassia.

"We knew it was only a matter of time before he'd come looking for his father. We knew that he would come here to find him, he saw us take him away," said Cravelda in a shrill tone, circling around Cassia.

Cassia looked up briefly as Cravelda was behind her and mouthed 'Run' to him with a pleading look on her face, but he stayed put.

"Now, he must have known his way around these parts, and I would imagine he has gone to the adults' penitentiary to look for him," said Cravelda snarkily. "Patrol, send three units to Big Penn, you are looking for a young boy who doesn't belong."

Cravelda smiled and got close to Cassia, close enough that she reached out and brushed the girl's hair behind one of her ears.

"Of course, he isn't in that part of the center where the explosion took place. That was a distraction. He is here with you now or in the Big Penn."

Nova stepped into the darkness inside the door as

Cravelda glanced up at it. She made another circle around Cassia.

"But what Nova doesn't know is that his father has been a *bad, bad* man," said Cravelda, her voice slowing over the words 'bad.' "We obviously couldn't put an ex-patrol in the Big Penn, now could we? He is just in this building over here."

Cravelda pointed to Cell Block 14, which was right next to them.

"What?" remarked Cassia, shocked, since Nova had told her upon his return what Cell Block 14 was. "Nova's father has been sick with amnesia for years. He was never in your patrol."

"Oh, yes he was. He worked for me for many years, sharing secrets, helping us in getting a better picture of who is good and who is bad in Creston. You see, no one suspects someone like Jacob Kerr, and they say all sorts of things to him. That's why we gave him the virus to begin with, to make sure he would do as he was told and get the information we needed him to get."

Cravelda laughed in a sickening way and then stopped in her tracks to look at Cassia. "That's how we found you. We knew you were weak. See, family, love, it makes us all weak."

"What have you done with my family?" cried Cassia, looking at her.

"You've been a good girl, Cassia. I will tell them to treat you family better—we struck a deal remember, you bring Nova to me and no one gets hurt."

Cassia looked up in the direction of Nova, throwing her hands over her face and sobbing loud, sloppy tears.

Nova's heart sank into a dark, black pool and then

shattered into a million jagged pieces. Confusion, anger, sadness, and every other dark emotion overwhelmed his mind and soul. His body felt weak, and he was doing all he could not to crumple over in pain. He felt like he wasn't there physically, but that he was an intruder on an awful nightmare.

Tears began streaming down his face too. His father, Cassia, all the people he cared about the most in this world had set him up! Feeling the anger reach boiling point inside of him, he stepped out from the shadows to face this dismal truth.

"Nova, no—I told you to run!" cried Cassia.

"Now why would you tell him that, remember our bargain?" said Cravelda, tugging on Cassia's hair so that her head held backward while Cravelda swung her head up to where Nova stood.

"You make me sick. You will not win this, Cravelda!" he screamed.

"Well, from where I stand now it looks like I have," she said in a jovial way.

A desperate malice rushed across his face as he looked Cassia in the eyes, and she winced as if it were more than a look, as if a dagger had struck straight through her heart.

"Ah, I see now, of course! Young love." Cravelda's face contorted into a twisted smile. "Well isn't this sad, Nova, so sad—you've been betrayed by both your father and your love."

"Nova, I'm sorry, I'm so sorry," cried Cassia through tears. "I didn't want to, she threatened to kill my family."

"Quiet, you," said Cravelda in a tempered voice that

didn't match the angry pull as she yanked Cassia's head back farther.

"This whole time . . . it meant nothing to you!" spat Nova.

"Please, Nova, please . . ." she sobbed again, and Cravelda pulled her hair back once more.

"Now if you come over here, Nova, no one will get hurt. You hear me?" said Cravelda. "Patrol, quickly he's here!" Her scream was louder than the siren going off in the town center below them.

"I will never be yours," shouted Nova back at Cravelda while looking with repulsion at Cassia.

And with that he was gone, leaving only Cravelda's reverberating scream echoing into the twilight as patrol including the one Nova had seen with the dark moustache at the Championships surrounded Cassia, whose sobs and betrayal he left behind him.

CHAPTER 19

Sometimes, time has the ability to move fast in slow motion. This is especially true at moments of chaos when everything speeds up. Things move so fast that it is hard to comprehend what is happening. Time, the almighty ruler of Action, steps in and offers a temporary sanctity to its participants. It knows that it must slow down so that the sounds of the moment can be heard above the beating of frenzied hearts and the pumping adrenaline coursing through engorged veins. It slows down to allow the fabric of every moment to become more detailed and more existent, like seeing the stitchwork across an elaborate tapestry.

Nova's mind was blank, and he felt disconnected from his limp body that lay weak on the penitentiary floor. Everything was blurry after he had opened his eyes back in Cell 263. All he had had to do was wish himself away from Cassia. He wanted to go far, far away from her and from his father. But, he had his duty, so he could not. Not yet.

The words of deception that Nova had just heard had been barbed, and his entire body felt like it had freshly cut lacerations. It was the stinging pain of emotional wounds and the salty tears that hadn't ceased in rolling from his eyes. He felt weak in mind, body, and soul.

He went through moments of hope, wishing that his eyes and ears had deceived him. It could have been a mistake. Cravelda might have just been playing some cruel trick. But then the thought of the guilty look on Cassia's face and her desperate pleas as she sobbed flooded back into his mind, and he cast aside all doubts.

The thought of her crying played tricks with his emotions. He wanted to save her and love her still. He wanted to do the same for his father. But he had no choice. His heart broke into a thousand little pieces at the thought that he had left the people he cared about the most in danger. But hadn't they already done the same to him?

Time was the only one there to help him now. It slowed, it provided clarity, even if it couldn't subdue his pain.

Nova had a duty to finish his quest. There was too much at stake for him to melt away into his emotions. He picked himself up from the floor and used these new feelings of betrayal, disappointment, and disgust pulsing inside of him as fuel to stoke his fire. The Regime must pay.

Running from his cell, he quickly found Gabriel out in the back of the Kids Penn.

"Well, I'm relieved to see you again. The patrol found us, but somehow the children used their magic. We managed to tie up about ten patrol and lock them in the cells." Gabriel was still calm, and pride washed over his face at their accomplishments.

"We shut down the Chalice," explained Nova.

"I guessed it, this is what we were told to prepare for," replied Gabriel with a wink of his eye.

Nova helped, using his magic to create a door through the fence in the yard, and the children began clambering through, offering their thanks as they passed him.

"You're the hero we have been waiting for," said the same girl with the two long braids that Nova had met when he'd been there before.

"I'm no hero, I'm just doing what has to be done," responded Nova despondently.

"Hey, hey, hey, what's gotten into you? What happened over there in Cell Bock Fourteen, and where is your friend?" asked Gabriel, picking up on Nova's emanating emotions.

"I tried to get Vance, but Cravelda was there. My friend was taken," Nova said sharply. "Cravelda knows what is going on, she knew I would come here. I need to get back to the others and make the broadcast as soon as I can before it is too late. Take the children to the Nomans up the river, you will be safe there."

"Nova"—Gabriel grabbed his hand—"may Lady Luck be with you."

The barking of dogs on the other side of the penitentiary gave the final alarm. The patrol were ready for a hunt.

"You too. Now run!" yelled Nova, pushing his friend toward the fence, and he watched for a minute as Gabriel and the children disappeared into the darkness.

❖

Nova rushed as fast as he could back down the stairs

and to the main square. There were patrol guarding the square, which wasn't part of the plan.

"Pssst, Nova—over here," came Phoebe, who was hiding in the shadows. It was dark now, but there were street lights and spotlights being shone around the town.

"Good to see you," she said. "Where's Cassia?"

Nova ignored the question. "We need to get to that speaker. We need to make the broadcast and get out of here."

"There is no speaker. We aren't going to be able to make the broadcast—look," she said in a hushed and agitated voice as she flung her arm out, pointing toward the patrol around the square.

"I'm not leaving here without making that broadcast," said Nova.

Phoebe grabbed him by both shoulders and gave him a hard shake. "There are patrol everywhere. They are on to us big time, Nova."

"I don't care. We came here for a reason, and this is the only way. We need to let people know what is happening here." He brushed her hands off him defiantly.

Nova needed to make sure that his plan worked or all of this would have been for nothing. Selfishly, he wanted to get this right to prove that he could do it. He wanted to prove that he was responsible enough, and that he was everything they all expected him to be. But, more importantly, he wanted to punish the Regime. The bitter taste of pride and revenge blended in his mouth.

"They have Callum and Peter," said Phoebe, knowing that this might cause a different reaction.

"What do you mean? Where are they?" he responded, moving back toward her.

"I don't know where they took them. I thought you might have seen them up on the hill going to the penitentiary already." Phoebe bowed her head. "I saw them wrestling with patrol, kicking and screaming as their hands were tied behind their backs."

Nova shook his head. "This is not how it was meant to happen, we are running out of time. If we can just use our magic to get past the patrol and onto that stage in the square, I can speak while you deal with the other patrol, and then we run. We can do this."

He turned to rush off again but stopped abruptly as Phoebe said, "Our magic alone is not enough to deal with that much patrol, Nova. Look at them all!"

Nova swung around. He was being reckless. "You're right. Where are Barnaby and Gwendolyn?"

"They are safe, they are waiting our instruction. But we just can't do it. Even with them, it is not enough," said Phoebe.

"There must be another way," said Nova.

Looking up on the hills in the far distance around him, Nova saw it first.

"The fires, the Nomans have started them early," said Phoebe.

"Perfect, this is our chance."

❖

"Fire, Fire, Fire!" yelled Barnaby in his baritone voice from across the square and up the street.

Nova could see the smoke coming from near the castle, but he couldn't see the blaze yet.

"Hurry, it's burning! Quickly!"

"There's fire on the hills too!"

Nova could hear the faux panic in Phoebe and Gwendolyn's voices. They had started the fire; more distractions and panic were what they needed. With fire near the castle, it was a danger that the patrol couldn't just ignore. They had a responsibility to their citizens to protect them, and while there were a huge number of patrol currently in the square, it couldn't be long until they would have to respond.

The first two patrol that were closest to the shouts went in pursuit of the calls for help. When the flames started to funnel upwards, several more of the patrol went running over to see what they could do.

Then suddenly, "Water, water! Bring water quickly!"

Not wanting to cause a real threat to the residents, Nova had instructed the others to start the blaze along the opulent row of shops that were currently uninhabited.

Lurking in the shadows, Nova was awaiting his chance. He looked up at the clock tower that chimed half past the hour; they needed things to move faster.

Then he heard it. *Click, click, click*. Heeled boots walking down the stairs. They were moving quickly. Nova's mind betrayed him, taking him back to the night of the feast when he was happy and dancing with Cassia in her heeled shoes. That feeling of happiness got flattened by a feeling of repulsion, and he shook the memory from his head.

Coming back to the moment, Nova realized that he was exposed as the sound of the clicking heels got closer. He was only slightly out of sight of the stairs, and he was worried that Cravelda must see him.

Luckily, when she got to the square, Cravelda rushed with full force forward, not seeing anything else but the smoke and the flame.

"Patrol, what are you doing just standing there? Get water—NOW!" she yelled.

"Yes, ma'am," replied the men closest to her, and they all ran toward the opposite side of the square.

"And send groups to the fires on the hills and to watch our perimeters. We are under attack!" she screamed manically.

Nova crouched in the shadows, watching. He was trying not to move. The square was now emptied of patrol like he had hoped for, but Cravelda was there instead. One challenge replacing itself with another. He watched as she paced back and forth. Her hands were out in front of her with her fingers pointed out, bashing at the air as if she were hitting something in anger. What was she doing?

"Get Queen Jocelyn out of that burning tower block immediately, and bring her here. Start the broadcaster," she yelled to a patrol who had just run down the stairs from the hill and was rushing across the square toward her.

"Yes, ma'am. Also, ma'am, the young girl is in her cell, and the two others that were found in The Nexus building have also been taken to the Penn. We are in pursuit of the escaped inmates who are heading through the forest toward the Rossland District," he replied before he went running in the direction of the castle.

"No, no, no, no," muttered Nova, and for a moment Cravelda looked his way before turning and walking up onto the stage.

On the opposite side of the square there was a flurry of motion. Patrol were running around frenzied. Families started piling out of houses onto streets, and babies were crying. Smoke made the air smell ashen and brought an air of destruction.

Phoebe, Barnaby, and Gwendolyn all hid behind a wall, and Nova could see their dark outlines. They were close, but not close enough for him to reach them. If he tried, Cravelda would surely see. The three of them were hunched and talking like they were making some sort of plan. They were pointing up to Cravelda.

Suddenly, it dawned on him what they were going to do, and a bead of sweat formed on the back of his neck. It was a bad plan. It would mean one of them would get caught.

Phoebe started to walk forward, but then Gwendolyn pulled her backward and rushed out into the center of the square. It was just her and Cravelda in the open space. At first Cravelda was too preoccupied in her own thoughts, but then she saw Gwendolyn, and a wicked smile engulfed her face.

"Well, well, well, who have we got here?" said Cravelda, moving forward.

Gwendolyn stopped; she looked poised and unafraid.

"We've been wondering where the rest of our new guests were. Perhaps the others are now here with you?" asked Cravelda, looking around and gesturing with her hands as if she were speaking to an audience.

Nova breathed in and pushed himself as close to the wall as possible to not be seen.

"It is just me," said Gwendolyn, taking a step forward.

"Well, we haven't been properly introduced, and, oh,

isn't it so rude to have guests around and not even know each other's names?" asked Cravelda menacingly.

"I'm Gwendolyn, Princess of the Fae. You destroyed our homes here on Earth, you killed many of our people, and then you made us a myth. You made us something imaginary and unreal to the people of Dacaan. You made us into your monsters when, look at you, you are the monster. Now you are stealing our magic," she spat at Cravelda.

Cravelda laughed and tutted, "Well, I'm shocked that you have been so rude to my warm welcoming. It seems to me like you are not a very good guest."

"No, I guess I am not," Gwendolyn replied, "but then again, it seems that you are a very bad host."

"Well, I'll have you know, Gwendolyn, Princess of the Fae, that you are wrong. It wasn't me who destroyed your homes and killed your people and made you into fae. No, it was my forefathers. And they did it because of your power, your danger, and your unwillingness to comply with the Regime. That is what happens to those who disobey. And, as for your magic, it is not me who is taking it from you. That is your own problem to be solved by those who live in Happenstance."

"Liar! You cannot hold us back any longer. It is time for the mighty Regime of Dacaan to fall. And we will gladly start by destroying you," Gwendolyn said with malice.

Nova knew that this was his cue. He could see from the side that Barnaby and Phoebe were waving him to go forward and to go up onto the stage. He was just about to make a run for it, but then she arrived. Even in the dark he could see her crimson hair and kind eyes in the moonlight.

"Oh fantastic, oh dear Jocelyn, I have someone for you to meet—in fact, she is royalty too, and I think she will make a fine addition to our collection. Wouldn't you say?" toyed Cravelda.

Queen Jocelyn looked up; she was already shocked by the fire and looked confused at what was going on.

"Patrol, don't you leave," screamed Cravelda. The fire was still blazing, but from the sound of it, things were easing down from the initial bonfire.

"Who is this, then?" muttered Queen Jocelyn.

"Well, go ahead, dear. It would be rude not to introduce yourself in front of a queen, wouldn't it?"

Nova looked around. Perhaps he could make it to the stage, but there were patrol and Cravelda now blocking his way. He would definitely get caught.

"I am Gwendolyn, Princess of the Fae, and I am here on a quest to overthrow this Regime!" she declared in the grand way that only someone of Gwendolyn's standing could.

"A quest," muttered the queen. "Nova's quest?"

"Yes?" said Gwendolyn with a question mark on her face.

Cravelda turned sharply and looked at Queen Jocelyn. "How did you know that?"

Just then, one of the patrol came rushing in. "Cravelda, ma'am, we are being attacked by the Nomans to the south of the city."

"Well send more patrol from the hill, and hurry!" she shouted, shaking her head with frustration.

Grabbing Nova's mother, Cravelda headed toward the

stage. "Bring her too!" she yelled at the patrol holding on to Gwendolyn, who was squirming in their arms like a slippery fish. But they were too strong, and she was outnumbered. Nova knew that she could easily shrink and take flight, but she was doing this for him.

Nova could see Barnaby, who was ready to rush the patrol, but he held his hand up indicating not to move.

Cravelda turned some switches on the side of the broadcaster to start a live feed to The Nexus. She stood behind a microphone and whispered in his mother's ear, telling the queen what she needed to say as she usually did at things like the Championships. Queen Jocelyn nodded obediently.

"People of Dacaan, we are under attack. The forces of evil are upon us. Magic has found its way back to our lands. We are doing everything that we can to put the attack at bay and will finally confront those who seek to hurt us."

At that, Cravelda grabbed the arm of Gwendolyn, pulling her scarf from her head and twisting it before wrapping it around her mouth so that she was muffled. Cravelda pushed her hair back so that her pointed ears were exposed and shoved her in front of the broadcaster.

Pushing the Queen to one side, she began, "This is one of them, this is an evil creature—a fae. If you see any more of them, notify a patrol so they can be restrained at once. We are offering a sizable reward for any brought to us dead or alive."

Cravelda pushed Queen Jocelyn back toward the microphone and smiled at her kindly.

"People of Dacaan. At times like these, we are afraid,

but at times like these we must stay strong and fight together against the forces of evil."

Nova could see his mother eyeing around. Was she looking for him? What would she say if she saw him? Cravelda stepped down from the stage and was speaking with a patrol, who was providing details of the fight on the south wall.

This was his chance. Nova stepped forward, just enough for the light to catch him and for his mother to catch a glimpse. She stopped squinting her eyes, and Nova could see her face change. It filled with something that looked like a blend of happiness and hope.

Cravelda turned around, looking back up as if to say 'continue' to the queen.

Queen Jocelyn hesitated, rocking back and forth slightly before starting again, "People of Dacaan, we are lucky..."

Cravelda looked again as if something were wrong, perhaps these words were unscripted, but she nodded her head and turned back to the patrol.

"We have spent our lives not having to worry, not feeling the pains of our forefathers because of the Regime. It protects us, it supports us, it provides for us. But have you ever thought of what the Regime really is?"

Cravelda cocked her head, and her eyes bulged in distress. She started running toward the stage again, but Gwendolyn stuck out her foot and tripped her. Barnaby and Phoebe ran over and began fighting patrol with their swords. Nova headed for the stage.

"Ignore everything that I said to you in all the years before. It was forced words given to me by the Regime, by Cravelda. I have been their puppet, and I am sorry for the lies I have told you to this day. The truth is that the Regime keeps us caged like animals to assert its own power. It lies to you, it betrays you. Those special children that you send here to Castlegar, they get treated like prisoners..."

Crying for help, Cravelda was writhing around on the ground, but over this sound came another. The people of the Dundrells were emerging from their houses. There were at first five, and then twenty of them, and then scores more. They came at the same time that the patrol were beginning to return from the fire and turn to the new challenge at hand in the square.

Then two familiar faces. It was Ariadne and Niall, nodding their heads at Nova in a sign of support and clasping each other's hands.

"Quickly, Nova, there isn't much time!" screamed Gwendolyn, who was attempting to hold Cravelda to the ground. The people had started fighting against the patrol, who were now making an attempt to save Cravelda.

Nova took a few strides and bound up the side of the stage. He looked around at the havoc and wondered if the broadcaster was still on or if there was still time.

"People of Dacaan, my mother speaks truth," he began. For a moment, the people below hesitated. They were looking up at him as he made this declaration.

"I am Nova. I have been sent from Happenstance, where magic was long ago banished by the Regime. Like you, I had lived my entire life in a district. I worried about invaders, about floods, about the virus. I worked hard at my talents and won this year's Championships in Creston. But . . ." Nova paused as a patrol had made it onto the stage. There was a short skirmish before Barnaby jumped on the patrol and pulled him away.

Picking up from where he left off, Nova started again, "But I realized that I had magic, and that magic isn't a bad thing. The Regime has used magic as a scapegoat to help lay blame on others and to deflect from its real motives. Everything it does is to manipulate and control you. Everything it does is a lie. Open your eyes, see the truth, stand up."

There was a cheer from the people of the Dundrells, who were fighting the patrol before him. Nova felt it signified the heart of the nation.

"Tonight, we have released your children, the ones that they put in cells in the penitentiary. They are free, we can all be free. All we ask is that you just believe!"

And with that, the patrol knocked over the broadcaster, and the signal to The Nexus cut off. The people of Dacaan had heard enough. They had witnessed enough for long enough. This was the cry to arms they had been waiting for.

CHAPTER 20

THE REAL FIGHT had now begun and the patrol, with their obsidian swords, were winning. That is until the Nomans came roaring in through the far side of the square, many of them popping up from the same gutters that Nova and The Six had come from earlier. They were passing out swords, pitchforks, hammers, and any sort of tool or weapon that they could find. It took just a few minutes before the people outnumbered the patrol.

In a cry of desperation, Cravelda screamed "Release the minotaurs!"

Cravelda had managed to squirm away from Gwendolyn and was standing on a wall out of reach from the rest.

Barnaby was close to Nova, and they fought back to back. "We need to leave, now!"

"What are the minotaurs?" asked Nova.

"You don't want to find out," said Barnaby in return.

They could hear it before they could see it. The pounding of hooves on cobblestone streets coming from the direction of the castle.

"Mother!" yelled Nova.

Queen Jocelyn was being restrained by more than one

patrol. They were taking her through a door in the side of the wall that guarded the square.

"Run, Nova, please. I promise we will meet again. I'm so proud of you, son," she shouted with tears streaming down her face.

"No, Mother!" Nova yelled, beginning to race toward her before feeling soft and steady arms wrapped around him. It was Phoebe.

"We must go, Nova, we must get to the moonbow. We've done all we can do here. We've done what we set out to do," she yelled at him.

He turned and looked in the direction his mother had been to see only her crimson hair flick around the corner, and she was gone.

"We can't leave, not now. We must fight with them and I must save . . . her," said Nova, thinking a confused thought of his mother, father and Cassia.

"We cannot stay, there is no time," Phoebe said, pointing to the clock that had now struck quarter to ten.

Suddenly, the air above them began to twist and turn. Nova's hair started moving in all directions, and dust stirred up a whirlwind around them.

"Hop on, quickly," shouted Osiris as he descended to the ground in front of them.

"We can't, not yet," cried Nova, turning to clash swords with a patrol.

Barnaby cut in and kicked the patrol away and threw Nova onto Osiris's back. He followed, with Phoebe and Gwendolyn jumping on too.

"Why? No, how could you?" screamed Nova through tears. He was leaving too much below, too much in Castlegar.

"You must go."

It was Ariadne and Niall. They had come to him.

"Nova, you must go quickly, we will all be fine," shouted Niall as he swung a hammer toward a patrol, who then lost balance and fell to the ground.

Nova realized that his friends were much stronger than he had ever imagined, and he felt a feeling of pride rush through him.

"We will be fine down here," Sedwin said, emerging from the fight. "Don't underestimate the strength of the Resistance! We have fire in our blood, and we have many on our side now that the Regime has been exposed. Nova, thank you."

Sedwin ran back into the fight. Osiris turned his head around, and his hard, yellow beak asked the question to which Nova didn't want to hear.

"Where are Cassia, Callum, and Peter?" asked Osiris.

"Gone," responded Phoebe, looking at Nova and putting her hand over his.

Nova looked down, and at the same time the minotaurs came running into the square. There were cries below as they stampeded around the people, and Nova realized that the Nomans and the people of the Dundrells who had been fighting were all being circled into the square, trapped. The minotaurs stood on all four feet; they were twice the size of the people with horns. They had bulging muscles and the ability to run quickly. They kicked up dust, and it was hard to see the destruction and carnage they left below them.

Nova was watching in despair. They were lifting higher off the ground but he could still hear the sounds of metal on metal, clashing bodies, boots, and hooves. A voice ran through his head, "Please, Lady Luck, let them get away."

They flew higher and higher into the sky, but Nova was close enough to see Cravelda on the wall as she screeched, "Minotaurs, fffllllllyyyy—don't let them get away!"

❖

Osiris was faster than the minotaurs, but not by much. He flew them to where Stannah was waiting in the skies, and Nova transferred onto her back. Amara, the unicorn that had chosen Phoebe, was also waiting, and Phoebe transferred onto her. The unicorns for Cassia, Callum, and Peter didn't join them. They must have known they wouldn't be needed.

It was a race to the moonbow; there was barely any time. Just minutes. Minutes that felt like hours. They charged forward, however, and they could see the grayscale in the skies before them.

"Faster, it's closing," yelled Phoebe. She was right, the moonbow was beginning to ascend into the sky.

Then they saw it, a cloud of black crows. It was swirling up into the sky, with a long skinny body that stood upright and a hooded head that looked like a serpent.

"The Dark Lord," muttered Nova, hardly loud enough for the others to hear. But they didn't need his warning.

The unicorns began to whinny. They weren't used to seeing such a foreboding spectacle in the sky. The murder of crows moved almost in unison like a wall of dark fury.

"Use your magic," yelled Barnaby.

"I'm trying," said Phoebe, looking frustrated.

"They've turned on the Chalice again. The unicorns are struggling to fly," said Osiris.

Nova noticed that Stannah had begun to slow as the minotaurs behind were encroaching. But surely their magic should wane too?

"It can't be the Chalice," Nova yelled. He was also trying to use magic to fix the situation, but nothing was happening.

"Look behind. It's not the Chalice, it's Cravelda," shouted Barnaby.

They all swung their heads around and saw Cravelda with a long, pointed wand directed at them. A red stream of light was coming from it, circling around them.

"Use Orion's sword," Phoebe said to Nova.

Nova spun around on Stannah and unsheathed the sword. He pointed it at Cravelda, and its blue stream of light caught against her red and began pushing her back. The minotaurs were now the ones that began struggling to fly while Osiris flew faster toward the moonbow with the others.

"It's working, Nova," shouted Phoebe back toward him. "Now you must catch up with us, quickly!"

"Aren't you the one who keeps magic from Dacaan with your Chalice, Cravelda? How is it that you have a wand and minotaurs, in that case?" questioned Nova angrily.

"Don't all good leaders have their forbidden secret weapons? Weren't you the one wielding your dark magic against that fae boy?" Cravelda laughed, and she forced a sudden burst of power that countered the power of Orion's sword.

Nova spun around, and Stannah galloped at full speed through the air toward the others. They were making much quicker progress now, but Cravelda and the minotaurs were closing the gap.

Then they came. More of the Nomans dotted along the rocky hills below them. They were yelling up into the sky and had bows and arrows in their hands, which they lit so that there were flames burning on the tips of the arrows. Half of them shot toward the serpent-shaped crows, and the other half shot toward the minotaurs.

The crows broke from their close, black cloud of anger that blocked the front of the moonbow. If only Nova and the others could break through, but the crows quickly banded together again.

Nova looked back, and a couple of minotaurs had been struck and were falling like great boulders toward the ground. Some had broken from the pack and joined a small group of crows before heading down toward the hills. The Nomans let loose another two rounds of fiery arrows in both directions before darting in all directions across the mountains below.

"Come on, Stannah, we can make this," cried Nova.

The group were at the tip of the moonbow, and it was fading fast. A few of the minotaurs were close on their tail and had also ascended the gray arches.

"We can't let them into Happenstance," yelled Phoebe.

The group spun around and began a counterattack against the minotaurs. The creatures were strong and fast, their horns were sharp, and their red eyes were rimmed with black.

Barnaby managed to cut his sword through two, who

went careening to the ground below them. Nova sliced the side of one, and it whimpered toward the treetops. There were now just three that were circling and swooping in at the group.

"There's more," yelled Nova as he looked out toward the horizon behind them and saw hundreds of minotaurs and a stream of helicopters now headed toward the moonbow.

Just then, the biggest of the three that were still fighting them got close to Nova and dug its horn into the upper right-hand side of his body. Searing pain rushed through him, and he could feel a cool liquid seeping down his vest.

"Novaaaaaaa!" cried Phoebe.

She quickly raced on Amara toward Nova and Stannah and propped him up so that they could move forward together.

"Bring him to me!" screamed Cravelda, who was just behind them.

Another pass, and the minotaur knocked Amara so that Phoebe almost fell off.

"Just hold on, Nova, we are almost there, just a few more steps," she pleaded.

Nova felt woozy, so he leaned forward and wrapped his arms around Stannah. He felt cold.

A final blow hit Stannah this time, and she whimpered with pain. Nova could see red glistening against her dazzling white coat. Was it his or was it hers? Perhaps both? It didn't matter because they were both falling now. They were victims of gravity. Everything was spinning, there were stars, and then there was a bright light. Nova couldn't tell if he was dreaming it or if it was real, but the shining comet, the Phoenix, was softening his fall. Perhaps it wasn't the comet at all, perhaps this is what happened when you die?

But Nova didn't want to die. He couldn't die. Or did he have a say? Breath suddenly rushed into him, and he lay on his back, winded. He didn't open his eyes, he didn't do anything. All the emotion that he had pent up came rushing back into him as his body lay numb. The betrayal, the lies, and deceit absorbed him.

Cries in the distance. Screeching. Howling. Hooved pulses hammering the ground, coming closer toward him. But he couldn't hang on anymore. And, although his eyes were closed and everything was already black, he seeped into the soil below him. He became one with the cold, earthen floor and trees that rustled around him. His spirit then pulled and ripped from his body. He began his ascent, up toward the twinkling stars in the sky. Maybe this was finally his time to learn them, to be with them.

And then he heard it, a celestial voice unlike anything he'd ever heard before coming not from a human mouth but from both the sky and the space around him. "This isn't the end of your quest, Nova, not yet. It has only just begun."

Nova's Quest doesn't end here...

Nova's Quest for the Spellbound Elixir

Coming June 2021

Go to www.mjirving.com to sign up for the latest news on the series, giveaways and the chance to win a signed copy of Nova's Quest for the Spellbound Elixir—coming June 2021!

You can follow M.J. Irving at @mjirving_official and see what other Questers have to say at #novasquest

The author kindly requests you to leave an honest review on Amazon, Goodreads and social media!

ACKNOWLEDGMENTS

So many people have supported me on my journey with this book, it is hard to know where to start, and I don't want to miss anyone out.

I would, first of all, like to thank all of the people who have inspired and supported me as I walked this road into authorhood. It is something that I have been building myself toward for years, and it is the people around me who have helped me grow as a person in both mind and spirit and to finally reach the finish line.

From my family, I would like to thank my mother, Susan Martin, for introducing me to the world of fantasy fiction and for teaching me that if you just believe then anything can become true. I appreciate everything that you have done and continue to do to push me further and to support me.

The deepest of love and respect to my grandmother Teresa Josephine Martin, sadly deceased, who taught me to laugh at all costs and who showed me that beauty only shines through if it comes from the inside too. I feel your light inside of me every day.

I appreciate the support provided to me by my father, Brian Irving, and for giving me so many pieces of himself regardless of time and distance between us. And to Lulu

ABOUT THE AUTHOR

M.J. Irving has always followed the advice that if you believe in something, it can come true. M.J. has spent her life following this philosophy, which has brought her to this point where she can share the magical worlds in her head with you.

M.J. is a Canadian of Jamaican, English, and Irish descent currently living in London, England with her significant other. She has a BA in English Literature from the University of British Columbia and has led a career in research, marketing, sales, and strategy management at one of the world's leading media companies in the events industry.

She has traveled to over fifty countries, and many of her experiences have helped in shaping her writing. When M.J. is not writing, she enjoys countryside walks, playing board games, and eating chocolate. She has a fascination with the unknowns of the world and the universe, and her mind is quite often in the clouds.

Printed in Great Britain
by Amazon